The charact
fictitious. Any simil   y
coincidental and not intended by the author.

I'M that rock which supports the foundation to a stable home. I'm the first line of defense that maintains a secure place to sleep. I'm the provider that keeps the family strong and well nourished. I'm the one that makes certain that everything's in working order. I'm that rod iron fist which supplies the family with love and substance. But, the truth is, underneath all this solid exterior is a man with a fragile heart.

Nicolas Coles

CHAPTER ONE

The County Correctional Facility

Surrounded by a huge wall made of brick and stone, it looked like an old European castle on a hill. The ancient foundation supported an unassailable wall that was thick and impenetrable. Staring up at the height of it would cause a neck ache. It towered above the surrounding buildings and the structure it protected, the sheer scale of the wall made it visible from miles away. A razor-sharp barbed wire fence ran through its perimeter with blades so keen that it could sever a man's fingers should he climb it in an attempt to escape. This was no fairytale castle, but rather a massive fortress built to imprison some of the countries most dangerous criminals. Highly-trained sentries whom were armed to the teeth guarded it. The fortress housed men like livestock. All either professed their innocence, snitched on fellow inmates, or wished and prayed to be released, even though some had no realistic hopes of ever walking the streets again as free men.

The County of Camden Correctional Facility consisted of twenty-four large main areas, each holding over one hundred inmates who shared two small televisions in each tier. Sixteen smaller tiers held less than fifty inmates who could not get along in the general population. The larger units held the majority of the inmates with misdemeanors and felony charges. This is where the men watched television, wrote letters, talked on pay-phones, worked out, gambled, and played cards and board games like dominoes or Scrabble. It seemed like a lot to do, but doing the same shit day in and day out caused it to dry out quickly. Metal payphones used by inmates to call their families, loved ones, or outside contacts lined the back wall. This was there only connection to the outside world. With more inmates than phones, long lines were not unusual. Some out-of-order phones caused conflicts between inmates over the few that did work.

Equipped with a threadbare white towel and a thin tan mattress rolled into a tube, the inmate was escorted by two guards through the housing unit full of inmates who were wearing orange jumpsuits. His orange jumpsuit sagged and smelled like the previous inmate's stench had been baked into the cheap polyester material. His outfit was completed by a pair of Bob Barker shoes that were a low-grade imitation of low-top Converse with no support.

His name was Nicolas Coles. Standing 5'10" and weighing 160 pounds with an average build, his light-skinned complexion exposed a cleanly shaven face with a small mustache and small beard. His wavy black hair was evenly cut. Even in the prisoner's jumpsuit, one could tell he did not belong there. His lost and terror-stricken visage made it quite plain he was out of his element.

The cells were simple concrete and iron bars from which the inmates had no possibility of escape...or comfort. The floors were painted gray, and the walls were poorly painted blue with splotches of white thrown in for decoration. The paint-splattered walls, uneven lines, and dried-up paint drippings only added to the building's depressing purpose. Graffiti created in ink or pencil of gang signs and street turfs covered much of the walls. Inmates had little use for canvas...or decorative skills.

With mute curiosity, inmates watched as the two guards escorted him into the area. Their expressions were cold as they calculated each step he took. What thoughts hid behind their cold faces? Could they be looking for an excuse to unleash their anger on the new prisoner? A reason to beat him to a pulp? Or maybe they were scheming to rob him of what little possessions he was allowed to bring with him—even his dignity. No doubt, some were craving to get him inside a cell and rape him. That was what he dreaded the most. Would they wait until he was asleep, sneak into his cell, and try to take his ass?

Nicolas was shocked by the minuscule size of the dreary jail cell, which was six feet wide by eight feet long with a metal bunk bed on one side and a sink attached to the toilet on the other. A metal table and stool were against the back corner of the wall, making it hard to move around in what little floor space was left. Polished metal on the wall above the sink was used as a mirror, but only gave off a clouded reflection. Hair follicles from the previous occupant clung to the sink and toilet. Pictures of naked women covered the walls, held in place by toothpaste.

He tossed his mattress on the bottom metal bunk and sat on the edge with his face buried in his hands, sobbing. It was quite evident that he didn't want to be here, but he had no choice. This was going to be his new home and the hardest part was trying to get use to it. Suddenly the room got dark, as if a black cloud unexpectedly appeared. Reluctantly, Nicolas looked up to see a dark-skinned, black male with cornrows stepped inside his cell.

"Nicolas Coles...is that you?" he bawled, excitement drenching his voice and face.

Nicolas gazed at him and then recognized who he was. It was Willy Mays, a young thug from Camden who wanted to buy a house in Merchantville, but was arrested the day Nicolas showed him the house.

Willy stood by the doorway, bobbing his head in and out of the cell, as if he was making sure no one approached him unexpectedly. Nicolas was not prepared to live his life in this fashion, not knowing who was out to get him.

"Yeah," Nicolas responded dishearteningly, returning his focus to the floor, not paying Willy any mind. *This isn't really happenin'. It has to be a wakin' nightmare,* he thought morosely.

It would take time before reality paid Nicolas a visit.

"Hey, man...I'm sorry 'bout what happened. Me and the guys jus' peeped it on the twelve o'clock news. I ain't know it was you who they were talkin' 'bout 'til you stepped on the block. But, now that ya here, you can't let these muhfuckas think ya soft. So, you gotta use a street name or nickname up in here. You don't want these muhfuckas knowin' your gov'ment. Ya feel me?"

Nicolas didn't know what he felt at that moment, and a nickname was the least of his concerns.

"So you got one?" Willy asked after a long pause. He was obviously waiting for Nicolas to answer.

"Yeah...Nick," he mumbled.

Willy folded in his lips and focused his eyes on the ceiling in deep thought. "Now, Nick does sound a lot better than Nicolas, but we'll work on gettin' you a nickname later."

"Yeah...right," Nicolas said with skepticism, his voice flat and emotionless.

A slanted grin and long gaze were sure signs that Willy was trying to choose his words wisely. The look of concentration was almost comical on his face. His grin was askew, and the vacant look in his eyes seemed to indicate some sort of retardation, but Willy wasn't slow. He had a street cunning that was deceptive, and he also called it like he saw it.

"Man, they gonna throw the chair at yo' ass for this shit." Willy chuckled.

It wasn't what Nicolas had expected to hear from his mouth, but Willy was just saying what he felt.

"It don't matter what the situation is. The fact that a nigga slept with a white bitch is like a smack in da face to them. So, you oughta tell me what happened, and maybe I can hook you up with some of my peoples I know on da bricks."

"The bricks?" Nicolas winced. "What's the bricks?"

"What's the bricks? Nigga, you dunno what the bricks is?"

Nicolas just kept his emotionless gaze on Willy.

Willy huffed before explaining. "You know...da bricks. Da outside. Da streets nigga."

"Oh...yeah." Nicolas nodded. "Nah, I'd rather speak to a paid lawyer instead."

"Well, good luck gettin' one, 'cause the media got'cha lookin' like a cold-hearted killa. Ya heard?"

Nicolas stared at him in disbelief. The way this guy was conducting a conversation with him was unlike anything he'd ever heard. Willy was rude, with nothing to fall back on but street knowledge.

"Well, I already have one on retainer."

"Good." Willy nodded. "What's his name?"

Nicolas paused with a long stare before responding.

"Charles Hunt," Nicolas muttered, not really up to talking to this ill-mannered individual.

Willy seemed to care a bit about Nicolas' predicament, but he was also distracting. There was probably not much Willy could do to help. In order to get himself out of this mess, Nicolas needed time to think things through, get his head right and then he could grieve later.

Now fully attentive, Willy stared at him. "Oh, Mr. Hunt? He's expensive, but he's good if you can afford him."

At first, Nicolas was hesitant to talk to Willy, an incomprehensible thug with no future. His life looked as if it consisted of getting high and a lot of jail time. However, as ignorant as Willy appeared to be, he was very informative, which was a major plus for Nicolas. Willy could be the ticket he needed to be one step ahead of the game, while pulling a few strings to get the fuck out of this shit. After a few minutes of conversation, Nicolas was glad to know there was someone in this place who he could talk to…or maybe he was starting to get a little too desperate. He figured Willy would be his ally. Besides, Willy was the only ear piece he had, and if he didn't get it off his chest, the pressure was going to cause him to explode.

"Okay, now listen up. I'm only gonna tell you this shit one time, and you can't go runnin' your fuckin' mouth about it," Nicolas whispered, trying to establish some ground rules.

"Look, man, I ain't no snitch!" Willy frowned at the thought. Just using the word *snitch* was more powerful than cursing out God himself.

Nicolas stared even harder at him. "Okay, then close the door."

He could see how eager Willy was to hear the story and wondered if he was making the right decision by talking to him...a total stranger. It didn't change the fact that he needed someone to use as a sounding board. Sometimes any opinion is better than none.

"Yeah, yeah," Willy murmured as he pulled the heavy steel door closed, rigging it so it wouldn't lock.

"First of all, I ain't sure if this is all a dream or not. I keep askin' myself how in the hell I got in this situation. Well, the truth is plain and simple. I fucked up. You see, Willy, I'm a businessman with a nice home, a damn good job as a realtor, and a cheatin'-ass wife."

Seeing the change in Nicolas' demeanor, Willy's eyes widened, but he remained silent with open ears.

"Yeah, I said it—a cheatin'-ass wife," Nicolas repeated, as Willy eagerly stood by the door. "I had my whole life ahead of me. I didn't expect it to turn out like this. I shoulda kept my sorry black ass in New York. Yeah, that's what I shoulda done. I blame love for this one, 'cause I was too blind to see the truth. And the truth is...I shoulda kept my sorry black ass in New York. I kept thinkin' that same shit over and over in my head like a tape recorder; until it became my personal mantra. Problem is, no matter how many times I repeat it time would not allow me to rewind it. So, now, I'm sittin' here wonderin' where the hell did I go wrong. Yeah, I've done my share of shady shit in the past, and maybe this is God's way of gettin' back at me. But, if so, I still want the world to know I had no part in what put me here.

"Now, I gots to rewind the clock for a minute and bring you along with me on this one. Havin' a hot gun in the crib was fucked up. I know that now. But, the shit that happened was an accident, and

I don't belong here. Maybe you'll help me find the answer and give me a better understandin', because this can't be happenin' to me. Maybe to someone else, but not to me. I've always played pretty much by the rules. So, pay close attention to what I gotta say.

"Things started to go downhill when my wife and I moved to New Jersey, also known as The Garden State, which I find funny since there's a lot more asphalt and strip malls than garden where I lived. It was Tuesday morning on the 25th of May..."

CHAPTER TWO

New York City

Beep! Beep! Beep!

The blaring sound from the Sony digital alarm clock announced the start of another day. Nicolas reached over and pushed the button to silence it.

"Aaaahhh!" Nicolas muttered, while stretching out his arms and yawning.

He stared at the blank ceiling that was painted antique white, then looked around the room at the empty walls while trying to shake off the sleep. Nicolas rubbed the morning dew from his eyes to clear the haze. It was only seven o'clock, and he still felt like he needed a few more hours of rest. It always took him a while to adjust to the brightness of the room. Even though the thin curtains were drawn, the light still bothered his eyes.

Nicolas turned toward the woman lying in bed next to him and stared admiringly at her, as she slept so peacefully without a care in the world. He reached over and gently brushed her long honey-blonde hair from her face to get a full view of her facial features. He admired her full, pink, Angelina Jolie lips, and her nice Brazilian tan added a little color to her pale skin, compliments of the tanning salon up the street. The Britney Spears look-alike was sculpted to perfection. Long, slender fingers with neat French-manicured nails and the rest of the ensemble followed suit.

Her name was Tammy, his cheating-ass, lovely, young wife, who had her claws completely sunk into the meat of Nicolas' heart. Like everyone else, Tammy and Nicolas had problems in their marriage that required a lot of time and attention. Still, he loved her with all his heart and wanted to work things out.

He couldn't help but gaze at her beauty under the light that spilled into the room from the window. They had a typical jock-cheerleader relationship in high school, and he was still hopelessly attracted to her.

After high school, they attended Temple University as business majors. Nicolas was on the basketball team, and Tammy was a cheerleader, who cheered for her man at every game. After receiving their degrees in business, Nicolas got a job as a realtor for Home Realty & Associates. His goal was to pay off all their bills, purchase a nice home as close to work as possible, and get married somewhere far away on a beautiful island with clear waterfalls and tall palm trees.

Tammy always dreamed of being a cheerleader for the New York Giants. Unfortunately, the competition was fierce for a spot on the squad, and she was cut after the first week of tryouts. The cheerleading coach told Tammy that she was a beautiful woman, but cheerleading wasn't for her. She wasn't athletic enough to keep up with the rest of the squad, and he added that she should try modeling. Then he handed her a business card for Studios, a modeling agency in Long Island.

Tammy felt bad for not making the team, but Nicolas told her that she only lived once and not to give up. He didn't want her to regret not pursuing her lifelong dream of becoming a cheerleader for a professional team. The professional basketball team cheerleading squad was more competitive and she was unable to keep up with the competition. So, Nicolas persuaded her to try out for the Jets cheerleading squad, but she was also cut from that squad. You see, Tammy had what some may call "the white girl syndrome." She had no rhythm and lacked soul.

Crushed, Tammy cried that whole night. Nicolas offered to take her to the Eagles tryout before the deadline, but she couldn't deal with another rejection. Nothing could affect her remorseful mood. He tried to make her feel better with a candlelight dinner and wine that night. Still, it had no effect on her at all. Her mind was on cheerleading. In the middle of dinner, Studios called and said they'd received her portfolio from the New York Giants' cheerleading coach. Surprised they had called and thrilled they were interested in her, Tammy decided to take the offer and try it.

She tried modeling for a few months, but she wasn't thin enough. They wanted her to lose so much weight that it became a health issue. Trying to reach the weight requirement, she would go for days without eating and pass out from lack of nourishment. The doctor told her if she continued to deprive her body of nutrients, she could permanently damage her organs or end up killing herself. So, she quit the modeling business. Her declining health was definitely a wake-up call for her. Plus, modeling was too boring for her. She wasn't at all the prissy model type and still had a little tomboy in her. Besides, Nicolas didn't want her to be all skin and bones. Her thickness is what turned him on.

Realizing she was chasing a dream that led nowhere, Tammy decided to settle down with Nicolas and live the American dream— getting married, buying a big house with a white picket fence, and having children. She found a good job working for Expansion, an investment corporation. Her job consisted of doing God knows what, but it came with a good salary plus benefits. Nicolas couldn't argue with that, or so he thought. However, an event occurred while she was at work that would change Nicolas' life forever.

CHAPTER THREE

The Start of a New Beginning

"Tammy, it's time to get up and start the day," Nicolas whispered, gently shaking her left shoulder.

"I'm up already," Tammy complained peevishly, burying her head under the soft tea-colored blanket with purple flowers that matched the pillowcases and curtains.

Nicolas gently pulled the blanket from her head and kissed her softly on the forehead, then got up and opened a window to let in a little fresh air. The splintered wood and fading paint of the old window made it hard to open. Positioning his body like a weightlifter curling heavy dumbbells, Nicolas used all the strength he could muster. With a silent heave, he prevailed. Sunlight bathed the room, and the air smelled sweet underneath the smoke, smog, and gas fumes. What did he expect living in New York?

Tammy quickly buried her head under the blankets again. The sunlight must have been too bright for her. Nicolas lay down beside her and reminisced about the day he and Tammy first moved into this house three years ago.

*****

Tammy and Nicolas lived on Bangor Street in Staten Island, north of the Staten Island Mall and south of its college central campus. It was their first house. Relieved not to be under her mother's thumb any longer, Tammy was excited and full of joy when she walked through the door. Her mother was overbearing and meddlesome to the point that it drove Tammy crazy, which actually drew her closer to him. After having her private dream wedding in Hawaii, Nicolas was confident Tammy would not go running back home to Mommy once he slid that three-carat ring on her finger. Both parents were upset that they weren't invited, but they had to deal with it. It was their wedding and what they wanted.

Nicolas loved New York, but he always had a hard time finding a parking spot, and parking rules were insane. The way the City of New York had everything set up, parking was only allowed on one side of the street for four hours, which meant he had to move his vehicle before they ticketed or towed it. He could've cared less about a parking ticket, but his concerns were being towed or having his car booted. The way he saw it, the people who setup those parking arrangements only did it for personal gain or for a revenue enhancer for the city—a scam, no matter how they tried to justify it.

After Tammy and Nicolas moved into their new home, they never had a chance to meet the neighbors, because they were always on the go, to and from work. Oh, they gave the neighbors a quick hello and a smile when they passed them, but that was all because everyone kept to themselves.

It was hard to get a good night's sleep with the noisy vehicles, sirens wailing, and people on the street talking loudly all hours of the night. Once, it had gotten so loud that Nicolas yelled out the window, "Keep it down!"

"Fuck up!" they yelled back like typical New Yorkers.

Mad as hell, he ran outside with his Louisville Slugger that he kept under the bed for protection and chased them down the street.

He wasn't going to do any thing. He just wanted to scare them off. They must've thought it was a gun or else Nicolas would have gotten his ass kicked. This was the price one paid for living in the city that never sleeps. He was determined to move to a quieter, more peaceful place and say goodbye to old memories.

*****

Nicolas stood by the window and watched an elderly woman walking her little gray poodle. The strange, gray-haired woman was bundled up in a gray wool hat and matching coat. She wore black shoes, thick white stockings, and a tattered black skirt on the hottest day of May. She was bent over, with a slight hump in her back like a camel. Nicolas recognized the dog, because it yelped all night long.

"There's that nosey-ass neighbor, Mrs. Wanna Be, walking that loud-ass dog," Nicolas said.

He never got a chance to catch her real name, but who cares. He couldn't wait to move as far away from her as possible. Every time he went outside to work or dump the trash, the old bag would be standing in her window peeking through the curtains. She never said much. She just stared out the window all day and night. He couldn't stand the ol' hag. The woman had no life whatsoever. It's bad enough she had no sense of fashion, but she would look at other people strangely as if they were out of style. And her loud dog drove them crazy, barking all hours of the night nonstop. He wanted to kick her front door in, but she was an elderly woman and he didn't want to be held responsible for her having a massive heart attack. Besides, he wasn't built like that.

After taking a quick shower and brushing the nasty coating off his teeth, Nicolas put on a navy blue sweat suit and white Nikes. Then he turned his attention toward Tammy, who was lying in the bed staring at him with her beautiful green eyes.

"You want some breakfast?" he asked.

Tammy stretched out her arms and released a low grunt. "That would be nice."

CHAPTER FOUR

The Pink Diary

Rolling over, Tammy reached for a cigarette and her pink lighter. As the smoke formed a white cloud above her head, she pulled out her pink diary like she always did when she felt the urge to put her thoughts in writing. Tammy loved the color pink. If she had it her way, every room in the house would be painted pink.

She rested the cigarette in the ashtray on the bed and began writing.

Dear Diary:

Today is the day Nicolas and I move out of this NOISY neighborhood and into a quieter one. I never thought I would get tired of living under these noisy conditions, but after we went to closing yesterday, I couldn't wait to move...now more than ever. I grew up in this neighborhood. All my family and friends live here. But now, it's time for a change. You know what I'm saying? The crowd and the noise don't excite me anymore. Plus, Nick is REALLY GETTING ON MY NERVES. I'm getting tired of his insecurities. He thinks every time I go out or don't answer my cell phone, I'm out cheating. I admit I made a mistake in the past, but I'm human, and he refuses to let that shit go. It's the past. GET OVER IT!

But, this is going to be a good day, and I am not letting that get me down. So, hopefully, this move to New Jersey will help our marriage. Nick really needs to work out his insecurities. I'm moving quite a distance away from my family, so that's got me a little nervous. The school system is much better than here, though. Moving away from my loved ones is hard, but it's a good move for the family that we plan to have someday soon.

I'm glad we finally sold our house! I thought we were never going to sell this place with the way the economy is going. Nicolas had to sell it at twenty-five percent lower than the market value, thinking there could be a good chance for us to have a bidding war to get closer to our ideal price. But, out of all the people that did a walk-through of the place, only one investor was interested. We took a heavy loss on the house and ended up getting twenty thousand dollars instead of sixty thousand dollars extra. We ended up using majority of the money as a down payment on our new home. With Nicolas being a realtor, I expected more money out of the deal. But, Nicolas stated the economy had a horrific effect on the real estate market. So, we took that offer and ran with it.

However, he strongly believes everything is going to pick back up with Barack Obama winning his second term in office. I was hoping for Hilary Clinton to be the first female president in the first election. I think a woman in power would do us a lot of good. There won't be a lot of bickering with these other countries. She's straight to the point and all about business.

As for Nicolas, he believes President Obama is going to put this economy back on its feet. I admit he's been making a lot of powerful moves. I'm impressed with all the work he's putting in to create new jobs. I wonder if he's getting any sleep.

I'm just getting tired of these lying-ass men running this country. They fill you up with so much hope, just to let you down once they're in office. It's no different from men trying to get laid.

They promise you the world to get into your panties. Once that happens, they suddenly end up with selective memory and you're treated like a second-class citizen. A woman running this country would be a major plus. Hey, we run our own households, so why can't we run our own country? Whatever obstacles we face, we prove ourselves over and over again, and the men can't stand it.

SO, I DO BELIEVE WE DESERVE THAT CHANCE!

Feeling appeased after jotting down her thoughts, Tammy closed her diary and tucked the little pink book in a box that contained her undergarments and unmentionables. She then selected a matching purple thong and bra and headed for the shower to start a monumental day...hopefully.

CHAPTER FIVE

I Know How to Cook Breakfast

Nicolas fancied himself as a chef when it came to making a healthy breakfast for his wife. Humming Lou Rawls' hit song "You'll Never Find," he put bacon on to fry, cracked a bowl of eggs to scramble, and laid out two slices of whole wheat bread to toast. He had left out a frying pan, the toaster, coffeemaker, and a few bowls and plates when he packed up everything from the kitchen the night before. When he was done, he put their plates of food on the kitchen counter and called Tammy down for breakfast.

*****

After throwing the butt of her cigarette in the toilet, Tammy turned on the shower to let the water warm up. She wiped the steam off the mirror, brushed her teeth, and then got in the shower. She closed her eyes as the hot water cascaded down her entire body, massaging her shapely physique. Suddenly, a hand slowly reached in and caressed her round, plump ass. Jumping from the sudden contact, Tammy inhaled a mouthful of water.

"AAAAHHH!" she screamed.

Shaking with fear, her body tensed up, and her hands balled into two tiny fists.

"I knew you were going to do that!" She squeezed out a giggle with a frustrated look on her drenched face. "Get out of here or I'm going to scream even louder," she announced with her body leaning against the wall, using the shower curtain as a shield.

Her smile was a strong reminder of her beauty. Nicolas had an incandescent love for Tammy. One that couldn't be broken.

She smacked at Nicolas' exploring hands whenever they got near, until he was able to grab a hold of her wrist.

"Yo food is ready, baby. So, you better come outta that shower or I'm comin' in," Nicolas said, releasing his grip.

He then laughed uncontrollably while still caressing her wet ass that had a shine to it. He loved to find ways to sneak up on Tammy and get a good scream out of her. It turned him on.

"Okay! Okay! Give me a second," she howled, laughing hysterically while still clutching the shower curtain.

"I'm gonna finish packin' everythin' up. I hope you're ready by the time I finish. It's a long drive from here to Merchantville," Nicolas told her, trying to catch his breath from laughing so hard.

"It's only an hour and a half away. Stop exaggerating." She splashed warm water on his face.

Nicolas leaned back, wiping the water from his eyes with his hands. "Well, it's long since I'm doin' all the drivin'," he stated in his defense.

"Boy, I can't wait to get out of here," she said with enthusiasm. "I'm so tired of the noise here. I need some peace and quiet."

"So what do you think about livin' in Merchantville?" Nicolas asked, as Tammy wrapped her body in a pink towel.

Her cleavage protruded out from the top of the towel like two ripe melons. Nicolas could feel the blood flowing through his manhood.

"Well, I think it'd be a perfect place for me to raise some kids —"

Nicolas abruptly jumped in mid-sentence. "Hold on. Hold on a minute there, little girl." He frowned jokingly. "That *me* became *we* the day we got married in Hawaii. So, change that sound and flip that '*M*' upside down," he sang in his Drake voice.

Tammy laughed inwardly at his weak rap before correcting herself. "My bad, Mr. MC Rap and Scratch. It's a perfect spot for *we* to have kids and raise our children." This time, she laughed out loud, while tucking the towel a little tighter by her left breast.

Nicolas tried to correct her again, but she cut him off with the rise of her finger. Her body was a work of art, and Nicolas began to lose all interest in the conversation as his loins started to build.

"And don't interrupt me. I hope to have two to three children," she shared, as she smoothed lotion on her legs. "I dreamed about being a stay-at-home wife and mother, packing your lunch for work, and having your dinner hot on the table when you come home in the evening," Tammy said wistfully, dropping the towel and exposing her nakedness.

She slowly teased the purple thong over her little firm legs, pulling them tight against her body, revealing the shape of her tasty love box. She was good at what she did, turning Nicolas on and out in short order. She loved to seduce Nicolas, and he was a willing victim.

Nicolas gazed at her smooth skin and derriere, which was as round and firm as a nectarine. His rod grew with excitement.

"And me," she continued, "shopping all day, buying shoes, clothes, and purses at the mall while you're at work and the kids are in school. Oh, but I'll pick something up from the store for you and get home in time to fix something good to eat for you and the kids," she said, but Nicolas wasn't listening.

He was in a deep gaze, enjoying the visual delight Tammy had to offer. Nicolas thought back to the time when Tammy first exposed herself to him. Her body looked the same as it did nearly ten years ago.

Aroused by her nudity, Nicolas quietly snuck up on Tammy just as she was placing a Virginia Slims cigarette between her lips. Inebriated with lust, he pushed her down on the bed, and the unlit cigarette fell from her lips. Nicolas pinned her to the bed face down and gently climbed on top of her, his shaft poking her backside. He nibbled on the back of her neck while she softly moaned and giggled.

"You think we can get one in as a farewell to our memories here?" he whispered in her ear.

Tammy gracefully tilted her head back and looked at him. "What about breakfast?" she asked, trying to break free of his grasp.

It was a poor attempt on her part. She wanted it and Nicolas knew she was enjoying every minute of it. Tammy loved when Nicolas wrapped her in his strong arms. She felt so safe there.

"Don't worry, we'll work up an appetite. Then you can get your eat on later."

As he undressed himself, Nicolas kissed her backside while breathing in the sweet fragrance of her skin. He gently sucked her neck so her sensitive skin didn't bruise. Moving slowly to her ear, his warm tongue danced around it, causing Tammy to giggle. Turning her over, Nicolas kissed her deeply. He moved lower to her breasts and suckled her hard, ripened nipples. Feeling her arousal intensify, he continued down her stomach, past her navel, and then moved between her legs. Tammy shivered from the feeling of Nicolas' tongue slowly flicking her clitoris, arching her back as he inserted his tongue deep inside of her entry and covered the entire pussy with his full lips. His fingers gently spread apart both sides of her outer labia, and he kissed her nipple-sized clitoris, sucking on it like it was a Blow Pop. Tammy jerked a little from her sensitivity and moaned with pleasure. Feeling a bliss that set her entire being free, her eyes rolled back into her head. Nicolas' approach was smooth and well rehearsed. No matter how many times they did this, it always felt like their first encounter, and Nicolas was loving it.

He French-kissed her pussy like it was his first and last meal, taking pleasure in the sensual flavor of her juices, causing her legs to shake as she released a stuttered moan. Her hot liquids flowed, lubricating her entry. Needing more of her, Nicolas reached underneath Tammy, cupping her ass cheeks while continuing to eat her snatch like a fresh watermelon.

Tammy grabbed the back of Nicolas' head, held it tightly between her legs, and began panting harder…and harder. Moaning louder…and louder. Trying to push his entire head deep inside of her. Her eyes closed tighter as she reached the peak of ecstasy.

Her orgasm was short, but intense, and it left her insides aching to be filled with Nicolas' thick love muscle. When Nicolas finished her off, he sat up to catch his breath. They looked deep into each other's eyes and felt a mutual love. A strong love that seemed unbreakable. Nicolas knew this look all too well. This was the same look she had given him at the altar before she said *yes*…or maybe it was the same look she gave him when she wanted more. It didn't matter; he knew he had to answer her silent call.

Not wanting to spoil the mood, Nicolas gently kissed her stomach and suckled her hard nipples again. Mounting himself on top of her, he sucked her neck and slowly inserted his rock-hard dick deep inside her vaginal walls. Tammy's body was fully receptive to his penetration, meeting his thrusts and receiving multiple orgasms as her pussy walls wrapped around his magic stick, massaging it.

Nicolas moaned in pleasure with each stroke, locking her body in place with his massive arms, breathing heavily in her ear while passionately kissing her soft lips. Sweat glistened and dripped off his smooth golden skin as he pumped harder...and harder. Stroking her faster...and faster. Savoring each stroke. Her lubricated walls massaged his rock-hard shaft. He raised his ass in the air, rotating his hips in a circular motion, giving her every last bit of him. She held his penis inside her, passionately kissing his full lips, causing both of them to moan harmoniously in one accord.

The intensity in Nicolas' loins started to build. His ass muscles tightened, and his dick hardened like stone while inside her. Her excitement heightened his senses, causing his heart to beat faster and harder like an adrenaline rush. Nicolas was on the verge of exploding from hearing Tammy's moans turning into screams. But, he stopped abruptly, grabbing Tammy in a bear hug. His body trembled and the room started spinning.

"AAAAHH!" he cried out, erupting inside her like a volcano, his hot juices pumping inside her like hot lava.

Nicolas rolled off her, gasping for air. Totally satisfied, he immediately fell into a deep coma-like sleep as if he'd been knocked out by a Mike Tyson power punch.

CHAPTER SIX

That Afternoon

Nicolas awoke five hours later and looked at the blue digital numbers of the alarm clock on the nightstand. It read 1:15 p.m.

"Tammy, wake up! We overslept," he announced, shaking her.

Tammy bolted upright. "Damn, that was good!" she said, placing her right hand across her forehead. "What time is it?"

She stretched her arms forward like a cat. She looked for the wall clock, but it was packed, leaving the outline of an empty round circle on the wall.

"It's one-fifteen, Tammy! Time to go. There's no need to reheat the breakfast I made earlier. We'll have to stop and get somethin' at a drive-thru. We gotta get goin', or we'll get stuck in rush hour traffic," Nicolas told her, sounding flustered.

They quickly dressed in their sweat suits and tossed scattered items in one of the empty boxes that were piled up in the corner of the room. Nicolas rushed downstairs with a few boxes in hand. As he reached for the doorknob, there was a sudden knock at the door. Never stopping his flow of motion, Nicolas opened the door and saw Mark and Dave, his two buddies since preschool, standing there with favorable smiles.

Mark, who stood six-feet, five-inches tall and was two hundred and eighty pounds of pure muscle, had dark brown skin with a chin full of hair and a bald head, looking like a Muslim. But, it was more of a fashion statement. He wore khaki shorts with additional pockets on the sides, a green tank top, and white Reebok sneakers.

Dave was six-foot-one, two hundred pounds, light skinned with a stocky build, and kept his goatee and hair neatly trimmed. He wore blue jeans, a black t-shirt, and black Nike sneakers with blue trim.

Mark was the shy one and too afraid of commitment. He thought every woman was only interested in him for his money. However, he didn't have enough money to take a woman out on a good date even if he wanted to, because he was addicted to the stock market. Mark would put his entire paycheck into the stock market, only leaving himself with enough money to make it through the rest of the week. Nicolas admired his determination, but he couldn't gamble with money like that, especially with the way the economy had fallen apart with unemployment on the rise. The women he dated thought he didn't have a job, because he was too cheap to take them out. Mark would always cry broke. He worked as a supervisor for Bolt Lock Security, a big security company in New York, making good money. Mark had all kinds of tricks up his sleeve. Women he dated thought he was a security guard making minimum wage, and he always found a way to get rid of them before the holidays to avoid spending extra cash on them. Mark was a dog and a miser, but Nicolas liked the guy even though he mistreated women.

Dave, on the other hand, was a clown. He would poke fun at every situation. The women he dated never took him seriously. It would get to the point where they would leave him for playing entirely too much. Dave had a good job working as a store manager for Home Depot, but he wasn't ready to commit himself to one woman. His entire world revolved around sex. His day was never complete without him getting some ass. He didn't care how they looked, as long as they were dropping their drawers.

Mark and Dave were both single. Their lives consisted of chasing women and partying all night, and Tammy didn't feel comfortable with Nicolas hanging with them. Because Nicolas had married and made a commitment before God, his time spent hanging with Mark and Dave was slowly diminishing.

"Wassup, partna?" Mark said in a loud voice.

Both Mark and Dave stood in the doorway giving Nicolas a firm handshake and a half hug.

"Yo, wassup, son? Mark and I came to help you pack up the rest of your belongings and to see if you have any more *porn flicks*," Dave said, flaring up his chest and getting all up in Nicolas' face as if trying to intimidate him.

All Nicolas could do was laugh, thinking back to how much fun they use to have together collecting phone numbers from different females during the warm weather months. They were like three squirrels storing away numbers so they'd have nuts to bust later. When the winter months arrived, they would have enough phone numbers to last them through the cold nights. That was during their younger years. Now Nicolas was moving out of town with his wife Tammy to start a new life.

"Well, I needed your help about six hours ago. We're in a rush right now, so y'all can help us finish loadin' the rest of these boxes in the back of the truck. I doubt if I have any more *porn flicks* left since you guys stole all my movies the last time you helped us move."

Out front, the big U-Haul truck sat with Nicolas' rust-colored Cadillac SRX with tan leather interior and long, extended glass convertible top hooked up to the back.

Dave advanced forward, forcing his way into the house. He then stopped and stepped back, sniffing the air. "What the fuck is that smell?"

Dave placed his hand over his mouth and nose, exaggerating the extent of the smell while staring at Nicolas.

"I dunno what the hell you're talkin' about," Nicolas said, hoping he didn't notice Tammy's scent.

Dave leaned toward Nicolas. "It smells like," he rolled his eyes, "pussy." He sniffed the air long and hard. "It is! It is!" Dave squawked like Tweety Bird. "Yo, I know pussy when I smell it, and you're wearin' that shit like cologne, son," he said, fanning away the smell.

Nicolas was embarrassed with Mark staring at him like an orphan. He wanted to tell them both to get the fuck out of his house and to never call or come around again, but he didn't. He just waited for Mark to add his two cents, which he did.

"Yo, dawg, please don't tell me that you're headin' outta the spot smellin' like pussy?" Mark pinched his nose and leaned up against the doorway, shaking his head.

Overwhelmed with shame, Nicolas had to use a good lie to get out of being the butt of their jokes. "Nah, dawg, I just had some *tuna fish* with *onions* for breakfast," he said, sniffing his shirt for added effect.

Dave and Mark looked at each other, then back at Nicolas.

"Yo, son, I ain't convinced. But, if you're tellin' the truth, nigga, you need to stop eatin' that nasty-ass shit before it ends up killin' ya. But who am I to tell you what you can and can't eat, though? I'm just your boy tryna watch yo' back, but you're too hardheaded to see that shit," Dave said, burying his face in his hand in a mock cry.

Nicolas pushed him toward Mark, and all three broke out in laughter. It felt gratifying to Nicolas to finally let out a hearty laugh.

"But, anyway, you don't need those movies now that you have a very attractive wife. We're still single, and we need somethin' to help our day go by, retired playa," Dave said, playfully punching Nicolas on the arm.

Nicolas returned the punch, as they laughed some more while playfully wrestling around and air boxing like little boys.

Stopping to look at the time on his watch, Nicolas said, "Yo, my nigga, I'm runnin' behind schedule, and we have to go. Besides, why are y'all so late? I told y'all to be here before ten o'clock."

Dave and Mark always arrived late whenever there was work to be done, which meant the job was already completed or at least halfway done, making less work for them.

"We overslept," Dave chuckled.

"Overslept? Nigga, please. You could have come up with somethin' better than that. I ain't even gonna get into it with you two muhfuckas 'cause I'm already behind. Here, grab the rest of this shit." Nicolas motioned to the boxes piled up by the door.

"Damn, Nick, y'all taped the shit out these boxes," Dave said, looking at the boxes that were covered with so much tape that they appeared to be sealed for freshness like perishables in a supermarket.

"That's because we didn't want you two goin' through all our shit again lookin' to steal some more of our porn flicks," Nicolas explained, carrying a couple of boxes to the truck.

Dave and Mark looked at each other and laughed it off as if that was their game plan from the start.

While heading back into the house for more boxes, Mark called out, "Yo, Nick, where's Tammy?"

"She's upstairs packin' up the remainin' boxes."

"Naw, son, I think she's upstairs washin' your scent off her," Dave cracked.

"Like they say, you are what you eat. So, I got to be a *pussy*," Nicolas shot back. "And that must make you a *dick*."

"Ooh!" Mark burst out laughing, pointing at Dave. Dave's face frowned up and his focus was now on Mark.

"So you must be an *ass* then," Dave cracked back at Mark.

"It's better than bein' a dick, muhfucka," Mark retorted before turning his gaze to Nicolas. "Is Tammy's mean-ass mom stoppin' by before you leave, so she can stab you in the heart with her wooden broomstick?" Mark jokingly asked, knowing how Nicolas couldn't stand her.

Nicolas thought to himself that these guys didn't know the half of it! As much as he despised that old bitch, he had to admit she was one of the biggest reasons why Tammy loved him. He wasn't stuffy and prejudiced like her mom, and she liked the freedom afforded by Nicolas' hard work.

Nicolas checked his watch one more time.

"Hell naw, and that's another plus to movin' to Merchantville. I'm gettin' really tired of puttin' up with her bullshit," Nicolas responded, thinking about how Tammy's mother never liked him and was always giving him a hard time whenever she came around.

"Yo, son, if you got drama with Tammy's momma, you shoulda called me. I have no problem with gettin' her ass whacked," Dave said, entering the house like he was some big mafia don.

"Only thing you're whacking is that pitiful thing between your legs, and you can't even whack that right. Now, how 'bout that!" Tammy said, coming down the stairs. "Aw, let me guess...you need some more of Nick's porno flicks to help you out."

"Ooh...that hurt," Mark added, struggling hard not to laugh.

"Yo, Nick, I'll throw your wife in for free," Dave said, jerking a closed hand with his thumb pointed toward her like a hitchhiker.

"Then you'll have to deal with my brothers," she threatened, knowing they were joking, but that she could always depend on her brothers whenever she needed them.

"Oh no! Not the big guys," Mark bellowed.

"What? Those big, dumb jocks? All I got to do is give them meat sticks some colorin' books and magic markers," Dave cracked with a weak Italian accent.

"Nooo! Please tell me they're not that fuckin' stupid," Mark yelled, still laughing.

"Nick, you better get him," Tammy said, giving Dave a cold stare. Then she turned her focus toward Mark, the instigator. "I assume Mark's the *cheerleader*. All he has to do now is play with his pompoms and shake his ass a little. But not too much, 'cause I see how Dave looks at him every time he bends over to pick up a box."

Mark quickly stopped laughing and frowned at Tammy before bending over to pick up a box. Then he turned his gaze at Dave who countered with an even harder gaze back at him for letting that bullshit even cross his mind. Mark then covered his ass with both hands and walked to the other side of the room with his back against the wall.

"You tryna to be funny muhfucka!" Dave barked at Mark for trying to play him out. The excitement on Tammy's face revealed that she was enjoying it.

Nicolas had to put an end to this before it got out of hand. "Okay now. I've heard enough. Since you two are here, could y'all kindly help me put the bed in the back of the truck?"

"No problem, dawg, as long as it doesn't smell like tuna," Dave muttered sarcastically, then stuck his tongue out at Tammy.

Tammy returned the juvenile gesture before leaning over to sniff Nicolas' face.

"Aaahh, Nick, that tuna does smell. Go wash it off," she said, holding a finger to her nose.

She must have overheard their conversation from upstairs.

"Okay," Nicolas said, running up the stairs.

That was definitely a good save on her part! Nicolas had to confess that Tammy could think quick on her feet and had a devious streak a mile long and thicker than a football field. Sometimes that gave him reason to worry, especially with indiscretions from their past. To him, though, it felt like she truly loved him, and before she ever crossed the line again, she would know that line needed to stay uncrossed. In short, he did trust in her love for him.

CHAPTER SEVEN

You Should Be Watching the News

With everything packed in the U-Haul, Nicolas started the truck. Its roaring motor vibrated his entire body. After Tammy locked the front door for the final time and headed to the truck, she stopped and turned to look at the house.

"Goodbye, old memories," she said, as if the house heard and understood her every word.

"Tammy, let it go. It's only a house," Dave yelled, while standing on the driver's side of the truck with Mark.

"Oh, shut the hell up!" She waved her hand at him.

"Tammy, let's go, girl. We ain't got all day," Nicolas called out.

"Okay, okay." She walked slowly to the truck.

"I know the feelin'. I felt the same way when they closed the club last night, and Mark and I had to go home alone," Dave said, sniffling like he was crying.

"You keep it up with those corny-ass jokes, and you'll alway go home alone like Macaulay Culkin. Now, how 'bout that!" Tammy smirked.

"Aaaahh, good one." Dave put his hands on the side door of the truck, as if he was about to respond to Tammy's remark, but he bit his tongue instead and exhaled loudly. "I'm gonna leave that one alone," he said, reaching through the window to shake Nicolas' hand. "Now you make sure you give us a call so we can hang out over there at your new place, 'cause I need me a Jersey girl."

Nicolas sat there not responding to Dave's extended hand. "I thought you guys were gonna follow us out there and help unpack," Nicolas said, shaking his head.

He knew Dave and Mark would come up with an excuse to avoid doing any more work. They would rather spend their time at a club or sports bar, exercising their testosterone levels.

"Naw, y'all be a'ight," Dave replied. "Plus, we're on our way to Myrtle Beach for the Memorial Day weekend."

Dave always tried to get in veiled insults, flaunting his carefree alpha male lifestyle. The fact of the matter was that Nicolas didn't miss that life at all. Of course, sleeping with different women on a weekly basis is appealing to any man, but he felt he had met the best girl out there. So, why keep looking?

"Yeah, we still have to finish packin' our things and clean our bikes before we leave," Mark added.

Nicolas frowned in disbelief. "But it's only Tuesday. The bike rally is three days away. You have plenty of time to get ready."

"Not this time. We're leavin' early so we can get better rooms and get ourselves situated. The ride alone is over ten hours. So, it's gonna take me a few days to recover from that long-ass trip," Mark said, justifying their refusal to help unpack.

Nicolas rubbed his chin, remembering the fun he used to have at the bike rally. Every Memorial Day weekend, he and his friends headed to South Carolina for the Myrtle Beach Bike Rally—one big parade of motorcycles and one of the largest gatherings of Black folk in one area, showing off their motorcycles and sport bikes. Oh, and the women! They walked around in their sexy outfits looking for a joyride.

Maaan, the females down south are some of the finest women in the world...like a new breed of women with beautiful, flawless, dark skin that's smooth as silk, Nicolas thought to himself. *Thick as hell, but well proportioned like their mommas were feedin' them good quality biscuits, grits, and ham.*

But, Nicolas had given all of that up to be with Tammy. Even sold his bike to help with the down payment for their new home.

"You guys are full of shit," he said, knowing they'd be home or at the bar sitting around doing nothing until it was time to head out on Friday morning.

"It ain't your fault, son. You're married now and not allowed to have fun anymore. That's part of the deal when you say 'I do' at the altar," Dave said, standing upright, feet together, and head in the air, mimicking a priest holding a Bible in his hand. "Do you, Nicolas Coles, take Tammy and her mean-ass motha and dumb-ass brothas for better or worse, good or bad, pain and sufferin', losin' your friends and not being able to have fun ever again as long as you both shall live?"

"Whatever. You're just jealous," Tammy chimed in.

"Don't kid yourself, girlfriend." Dave rolled his eyes at her.

Nicolas needed to cut this conversation short before they got started with the wisecracks. "So how long y'all gonna be out there?" he asked Dave.

"The whole week, jinks!" Dave and Mark replied in unison, giving each other high-fives.

"And before you two say anythin' 'bout us being too cheap to stay the whole week, I already booked us a room. It's on the end facin' the main road. So, we don't even have to leave the room. We can stick our hands out the window and still smack a few asses walkin' by," Mark said with great exaggeration.

"Or stick a tin can out for loose change since you spent your whole paycheck. Now, how 'bout that," Tammy threw in for good measure.

"Oh shit, Tammy's on a roll now!" Dave mocked, with his hand covering his open mouth.

"Well, anyway, give me a call once y'all get settled in," Nicolas said, half wishing he was going with them.

"A'ight, my nigga. Y'all drive safe now, ya heard?" Dave sung. "And try to stay away from that mob boss," he added and then extended his hand again, but Nicolas left him hanging again.

"Mob boss? What mob boss?" Nicolas asked, clueless.

"You know, that guy Frank DeBartello," Mark explained. "He's been all over the news this whole week for all kinds of shit. They say he got this *hit-man* with enough bodies on his jacket to populate a small village in Africa. Now they got this mob boss on trial, but all the witnesses are too afraid to testify."

"Nope. Haven't heard about it," Nicolas mumbled, twisting up his lip.

"That's 'cause you work too much. You need to watch the news instead of those porn flicks and know what's goin' on in the world," Mark said, smacking the side of the truck. "Yo, get your asses outta here before y'all get stuck in traffic."

Nicolas looked at his watch, realizing he was on a time schedule and running late.

"Hey, don't forget to call me if you're lookin' to buy or sale any homes. I'm still licensed in New York as a realtor," Nicolas reminded them, while pointing a finger at Mark and Dave.

"Don't worry, fam. We'll definitely give you a call if we decide to do one or the other, 'cause you'll beat our ears in 'til they bleed if we don't," Mark said, knowing how Nicolas could complain for days about them not doing what he asked them to do, especially when it came to making money.

Nicolas finally shook Dave and Mark's hands before putting the truck in gear. "A'ight, we'll see y'all later," he said, then slowly pulled away from the curb.

Driving away from the house, Nicolas looked in his rearview mirror and watched Dave and Mark head in separate directions. The reflection of the house got smaller until the surrounding buildings swallowed it whole, as it became a part of their past.

CHAPTER EIGHT

Destination: New Jersey

By the time they got on the freeway, it was quarter after two in the afternoon. The drive to Jersey was quiet and serene. The road was a painted canvas...picture perfect. The clouds were no more than big fluffy cotton balls floating in the sky. The highway was framed with lush greenery and cultivated fields. Nicolas and Tammy enjoyed the view while listening to Miguel "Adorn" pumping through the poor-quality U-Haul stereo, which added a feeling of good things to come. The sunlight favored Tammy's flawless complexion, as it poured in through the truck's windshield.

While they reminisced about their past together, the New York radio station started to fade and got distorted. So, Nicolas changed the channel to a Philly station and heard a song by DJ Cooley being played. The song was hot, and they listened to it while bobbing their heads. Nicolas looked at his wife enjoying the music and smiled. He loved her more than he loved himself. If he could, he would give her the world and everything in it.

Who woulda thought I would marry my high school sweetheart, Tammy Spenser? She was the youngest, with two older brothers. Those big-ass muhfuckas hated my guts for marryin' their little sister and wanted to bash my face in. Tammy had to tell them to respect her wishes and to leave me alone, which they ended up doin' after makin' a few verbal threats, just like a typical big brother would do.

They let me know if I lay my hands on their little sister that they will come after me in the worse way...go figure!

Nicolas chuckled to himself and shook his head. He looked at Tammy, who was paying him no mind. She was in her own world, staring at the greenery that lined the highway and the large businesses that were a distance away.

It was hard for them to watch their little sister gettin' involved with a young, successful black man. They would've rather seen her with a lowlife bum as long as he was white instead of a black man like myself. They claimed they didn't want her kids to come out with an identity crisis. Being involved with me is what Tammy wanted, so they had to accept it.

John and Adam Spenser's mother must have gotten their names from the Bible since she was a religious person. However, that became more of a smack in the face to her since all they did was get in legal trouble. Nothing major, just traffic violations or child support issues that caused them to spend the majority of their free time in court paying fines and fighting tickets. Instead of sending them to jail, the judge would place them on the Sheriff's Labor Assistance Program, better known as *S.L.A.P.*, which was nothing more than performing community service of cleaning up parks and government buildings for a certain number of hours that would equal time served in jail.

Both brothers played football in high school and college. Everyone knew they were abusing steroids from the way they packed on so much muscle, at least twenty pounds a year. The coaches didn't care as long as the team was winning games. However, when they tried going pro after college, they couldn't pass the piss test. Their high school and college coaches were so busy worrying about winning games, they never stopped to tell them that the NFL took the use of steroids very seriously. It's considered cheating, and both John and Adam were completely banned from the NFL.

They ended up with good jobs, though. John started as a construction worker and then got promoted to supervisor. Now he wore suits to work and didn't get his hands dirty. Adam coached high school varsity football. Good pay, but it required a lot of hours, which wasn't good for his wife and kids.

With their size, they could have easily ripped Nicolas in half if they wanted to, but Tammy did a good job at keeping them at bay. Her brothers were more of a father figure to her, keeping her out of trouble and making sure Nicolas took good care of her.

Now, her father on the other hand, George Spenser, retired as a soldier in the army. He died from a massive heart attack at the age of forty-six. It was later learned they have a family history of bad hearts. Tammy and Nicolas went for routine checkups, and so far, Tammy showed no signs of having heart disease. But, they could never be too sure, so she got an electrocardiogram at least once a year.

Tammy's mother, Martha Spenser, hated Nicolas' guts. She never liked him from the time Tammy introduced him to the family. She claimed she liked him until he put his hands on her daughter, but Nicolas thought otherwise.

Before Nicolas and Tammy met, Tammy, who was a freshman at the time, was dating Pete, a junior attending another school. He was a football jock who had the entire female population going crazy over him. Nicolas, on the other hand, was a freshman playing on the varsity basketball team. He wasn't a star player, but he was a starter and able to put a few points on the board. One game, he claimed to have dunked on a seven-foot–two player from the opposing team, and the crowd went wild. Nicolas was guilty of embellishing that fateful day, and every time he told the story, the opposing player he dunked on was a few inches taller before the previous story. In other words, it was a typical fish tale story that grew with each retelling.

Nicolas could have gone pro if he wanted...well, not really. He tried playing for the Philadelphia 76ers, which was the worse NBA team at the time, and still didn't make the team. The coach told him, along with the rest of the players that got cut from the squad, that they weren't good enough for the team and better luck next year. That hurt Nicolas to the core, but thank God he had his degree to fall back on. Pete and Tammy were dating for a while before Nicolas met her. However, things weren't working out, because Pete gave all the other girls in school his attention and treated Tammy as if she wasn't even there.

Nicolas never had a chance to meet this football jock nor was he interested in doing so. Tammy stated she'd gotten tired of being with him, so they broke up. Then Nicolas showed up, a new kid transferred from another school. Tammy fell in love the first time she laid eyes on Nicolas. He was young, light brown skin, and very handsome. It seemed like fate when they met, or at the least infatuation. They hooked up, but Pete hated on Nicolas hard. Nicolas knew he had to hold his ground if Pete ever thought about stepping to him the wrong way. Pete couldn't face the fact that Tammy was happier being with Nicolas, the new black kid on the basketball team.

It was during lunchtime that they would meet under the big oak tree in front of the school building. They even carved their names on it—*Nicolas and Tammy*—with an arrow piercing through the heart. However, one day, Tammy wasn't there, which seemed sort of odd. She was never late. Whenever Nicolas got there, Tammy was always waiting for him. Something was wrong, and Nicolas felt it. A few minutes later, she showed up with an uncomfortable look on her face, which increased Nicolas' suspicion.

"Are you okay?" Nicolas asked weary eyed.

"Pete came up to the school to talk to me. He wants to be with me, and he promises he'll do better—"

Nicolas wanted to find this guy for coming to his school and disrespecting him, but for some unexplained reason, a calm came over him.

Nicolas finally gathered enough strength to ask, "Do you still love him?"

He didn't have time to hear all the in-between bullshit she was feeding him. All he wanted was the truth, so he would know where he stood in this relationship. At first, she was hesitant. Maybe he appeared too aggressive in his posture with his hands balled up in a fist, or maybe it was the fury in his eyes and the hard tone of his voice. It didn't matter; all he wanted was answers.

"Do you love this fuckin' guy or what?" he roared impatiently.

"Yes," she squealed, with the audacity to say it right in his face while still having her arms wrapped around him.

Fucks wrong wit'cha!

Nicolas saw red. He didn't hear anything else she said, because the fact that she still loved the fucking guy cancelled everything else out. Nicolas pushed her down to the ground and walked away, leaving her in tears.

One of the security guards, who had been patrolling the perimeter, saw Nicolas push her down. So, he snatched Nicolas up and took him to the principal's office. Nicolas received a suspension and had a lot of explaining to do to his mother, Laura. After hearing what happened with Tammy, she wasn't too thrilled about him dating her.

"These young girls are no good for you," she would say. "All they'll end up doin' is gettin' you in trouble." But, Nicolas didn't pay that any mind, because she had said the same shit when he brought Mark and Dave over to visit her. "Those guys are no good for you. All they'll end up doin' is gettin' you in trouble."

'Nuff said.

Later that night, Tammy called Nicolas. "We were just talking," she tried to explain.

"I don't want you seein' him anymore!" Nicolas demanded.

"Okay, I won't. I promise," she replied in her softest voice.

It didn't take much effort on her part for them to be together once again. Admittedly, Nicolas was crazy about her. However, when Tammy's mother found out Nicolas laid his hands on her sweet little angel, she wanted him arrested. Oh yeah, she was hot as hell and wanted to burn him good. Nicolas could actually see the flames of hate smoldering behind her eyes, and he knew she would do anything to pull her daughter from him, even if it left some nasty scars in the process. He would have to watch this one. However, Nicolas was still a minor, so the judge thought his suspension was good enough punishment. God had a watchful eye over him that day.

CHAPTER NINE

Breaking Bad Habits

Before they left the street of their old home, Nicolas noticed Tammy had become very emotional. He had not said anything then, but decided to breach the subject now.

"So what was up with the emotional breakdown back there? I thought you wanted to move outta that old house?" Nicolas asked, while admiring an all-black Ram truck that had customized 26-inch chrome rims and limo tint on the windows as it passed by. The stereo system in that thing was so loud he could hear the bass pumping.

It reminded him of his Ford F-150 that he had customized the same way. It was definitely a female magnet, but Nicolas wanted to be with Tammy, and therefore, he decided to get rid of his childish things. He ended up selling it to pay for their wedding and purchase Tammy an eighteen-carat platinum diamond engagement ring. Now Nicolas regretted getting rid of it, because it was his favorite truck.

It doesn't matter, he thought to himself. *There are plenty more trucks where that one came from.*

Tammy pulled out a Virginia Slim cigarette and lit it. "It's not the home that I'll miss, but the memories it holds."

Nicolas' head shifted from the road to Tammy and back to the road again. "Girl, put that thing out. You know it's bad for you. Plus, I thought you said once we left New York, you were gonna quit?"

Tammy held the cigarette between her fingers, fighting the temptation. "I know, but I'm so nervous about moving to another state."

"We'll be fine. There's no need for you to worry," Nicolas assured her.

"You're right. I'm going to work on it today. We did say we were turning over a new leaf." Tammy put the cigarette out before flicking it out the window. "So that means no drinking for you either, mister."

How'd she know I was drinkin'? Nicolas had to be smooth as glass about it.

"I did stop drinkin'," he lied.

Tammy pointed her index finger toward him. "Wow!" She then rubbed her chin. "Now we're lying?"

Nicolas knew she was on to him and was waiting for him to slip up.

"I dunno what you're talkin' 'bout," he said, preserving his calm.

Nicolas had started drinking once he found Tammy in the restaurant with her so-called co-worker. But, then, his heavy drinking got out of hand when it started affecting his job as well as his marriage.

"Well, last night, while I was packing the rest of my things, I found a few empty bottles of Henny stuffed in the trash can, and I smelled it seeping through your pores last night while you were sleeping."

Nicolas never left a bottle in the house. He always threw the empties in the old lady's trashcan and then snuck back home before that loud-ass dog detected him. He had to have been drunk as hell to throw the empty bottles in his own trashcan at home.

Tammy crossed her arms, waiting for him to try to dig his way out of this one.

"I dunno. Maybe the stress of movin' to another state affected my judgment, but I promise that I'll stop drinkin' startin' today," he said, before quickly changing the subject. "Girl, I'm sure gonna miss that rundown piece of crib back there. Do you remember when we first moved in and you saw a mouse scurryin' across the kitchen floor?"

Tammy rolled her eyes. "Don't remind me. And anyway, that was a damn rat."

Nicolas giggled. "No, that was a mouse. A little baby mouse at that!"

Tammy threw her hands in the air, bobbing her head left to right with an attitude.

"Nicolas, if that was a mouse, it was on steroids! Okay? Don't make me pull out my pink diary, because I wrote it all down that same night just in case you decided to exaggerate the whole story like you usually do."

"I don't exaggerate stories. You do," Nicolas responded, cringing.

"I don't think so, Mr. Exaggerate Every Story," she said, adding a new title to his name. "Plus, you can't talk anyway, because you were too afraid to come in the kitchen! Now, how 'bout that!"

Nicolas tried to think of a good cover story. "Wait a minute now. I thought the mouse might be carryin' rabies or the plague or maybe somethin' even worse. So, I had to play it safe."

"You couldn't even kill it, Mr. I Had To Play It Safe. It got away, and who knows where it went."

"Yeah, it probably had a few dozen baby mice runnin' all through that house." Nicolas added.

Tammy covered her face, as if it was making her skin crawl. "I couldn't take it anymore, not knowing if one of those nasty little critters might jump out from behind the counter while I was cooking. If you hadn't hired an exterminator, we would have gotten a cat to take care of it, because I wasn't staying in that house with critters run around."

"We wouldn't have gotten a cat, that's for sure." Nicolas shook his head to show his total disagreement with having a cat in his house. Mice, rats or bats wouldn't have convinced him.

Tammy looked at Nicolas, bewildered. "I love cats. Why couldn't we have one?" she whined.

"You know I'm allergic to cats," Nicolas squawked, mad that Tammy was pretending not to know about his allergies.

"Oh, Nicolas, you're allergic to everything. We'll just have to take you to one of those allergy specialist, so they can take care of that or place you in one of those big-ass bubbles," she huffed, changing the radio station.

Nicolas reached over and softly put his hand on her knee. "I'm not allergic to you, though, baby."

A smile grew across her face. "Awww, that's so sweet." She smiled, gazing into his eyes. "I'm so glad we're moving to a better neighborhood. Just think, Nick. No more nosey neighbors. No more noisy cars and loud music. No more having to move your car every four hours to avoid getting a ticket."

"That's right, and no heavy traffic to and from work. I'm glad they transferred me to the Cherry Hill office in Jersey. Now it'll only take me five minutes to travel from Merchantville to work instead of forty minutes to a job that's only fifteen minutes away. That New York City traffic is crazy."

Nicolas tried taking the subway to work, but that was an even bigger pain in the ass. The train was so crowded, he'd have to stand up against a bunch of strangers with them breathing on his neck, their breaths smelling like stale coffee and cigarettes. He never felt safe. He'd even had his pockets picked twice in one day. So, he would catch a cab an hour early just to make it to work on time.

Tammy found a smooth radio station on 105.3 FM.

"Those extra minutes saved on commute time will give us more time together," she said, enjoying the relaxing sound of Avant's "Long As I Live". It was one of her favorite R&B tracks. Nicolas loved how it always put a smile on her face, so it ended up being their wedding song.

"Well, Merchantville is an older community, and I heard the cops out there don't play around. One of my co-workers told me that the cops pulled him over and gave him a ticket for speeding when he was only going five miles over the speed limit."

Tammy leaned forward, dangling her finger at him, and scowled. "Ya see, that's your problem." Her smile was gone, and her tone was a higher pitch.

"Whaaaa...?"

She continued, preventing him from getting a word in. "You're quick to listen to those knuckleheads at work, like their word is the gospel. Why do you believe everything they tell you?"

"Because they..."

"But when I tell you something, oh no," she said, cutting him off again, "it goes in one ear and out the other. Stop believing everything you hear. Knowing the cops are on top of things makes for a better neighborhood. I just hope they don't give us a hard way to go. Too many people still don't approve of a black man marrying a white woman, you know."

"Yeah, you're right, but not everyone's as negative about it as our parents," Nicolas said, thinking about how Tammy's mother gave him a hard time every time she came around. No matter how hard she tried to upset him, he would always showed her respect.

"You're absolutely right about that. Our parents still don't accept us being together. That's why we had to move so far away in the first place. Life would be so much better if everyone was the same color or if they didn't stereotype interracial relationships."

"Or color blind," Nicolas added, as the sight of the home that marked their new beginning interrupted his thoughts. "Look, baby! There it is." He pointed to the house.

The view was spectacular.

"Lovely, ain't it?"

"It's beautiful." Tammy's eyes lit up like a little girl seeing lit candles on her birthday cake.

They had been through the house several times before purchasing it. However, now, they could call it their own, and that made the sight of the house even more astonishing.

CHAPTER TEN

A Place Called Home

They finally arrived at 809 Maple Avenue. After slowly driving up the concrete driveway, they sat in the truck absorbing the experience. The feeling was unexplainable; hitting the lottery could best describe it. After a few minutes, they got out of the truck and walked around the perimeter of the house in amazement. Inspecting the home and admiring the home were two totally different feelings.

The large single-family home was over thirty years old, but to them, it was new. The red brick house with white shutters had been well kept. Its dark brown roof with matching trim gave it a stately look. It had a solid oak door with a huge brass door-knocker. The two-story, four-bedroom, two-and-a-half bath house had large formal dining and living rooms with solid oak floors. The kitchen was a cook's delight, with its white cabinets, stainless steel appliances, and sand-colored granite countertops. The basement was unfinished, but the house had a two-car garage.

Now this is what dreams are made of, Nicolas thought.

What took a lot of hard work and effort had finally paid off. He'd purchased Tammy's dream home. Now he could hold his head high when he visited his hometown, letting everyone know he'd done it. However, his only wish was that his grandmother, Emma, could've been there to see it all.

Emma practically raised him. He was the only child, and his mother worked many hours taking care of his grandmother and him.

Nicolas took care of Emma after school when his mother wasn't home. Old and very fragile, she spent the majority of her time laying on the couch in the living room, watching television all day and night.

One night while Nicolas lay asleep in his bed, a burglar tried to break into the house. He came in through the living room window and ended up stepping on Nicolas' grandmother, as she slept on the couch. When the burglar applied pressure to her with his heavy foot, Emma let out a scream, so loud it woke up the entire neighborhood and scared the burglar half to death. He didn't know what was going on. All he knew was he had to get out of there quick. So, he dove out of the window and broke his arm in the process, hitting his face on the hard concrete. Not long afterwards he ran to the cops who were patrolling the area, seeking medical attention. The burglar told the cops that a car had hit him and kept going, but the cops were already looking for him, because of Emma's perfect description of the burglar, which led to his arrest.

Emma ended up dying from natural causes shortly after that. After her funeral, Nicolas' mother found it hard to live in the house with so many memories. So, she moved them to the other side of town, and Nicolas ended up at a school that led him to a beautiful woman who he now called his wife. Even though she fucked up a few times, he believed this time was going to work out for the better.

"Now all I need is a second vehicle to fill this empty space," Tammy hinted, while looking around the garage and exposing all thirty-two of her teeth.

Her grin was infectious, and within seconds, Nicolas had a big, dumb smile on his face, also. Her always insinuating for him to buy her high-priced items could get annoying, but not today while his spirits were soaring.

"I know where this conversation is goin'. Anyway, let's get our things outta the U-Haul and start unpackin' while it's still daylight," Nicolas said, grabbing boxes out of the truck.

With a cleaning rag in hand, Tammy entered the kitchen through the garage. "Yeah, since we do have a lot to unpack."

Sitting one of the boxes on the living room floor, Nicolas said, "It's gonna take us weeks to unpack and get everythin' in its rightful place."

He was breathing hard from carrying the heavy boxes, while wishing Dave and Mark were there to help him.

"It doesn't matter. Anything's better than living in that small-ass house we had. Plus, your mom kept popping in unannounced all the time," she replied, relishing the thought.

Nicolas nodded. "Yeah, it was beginnin' to drive me crazy, too. I'm her only child. Guess she just wanted to make sure her son was okay."

"She was just being nosey," Tammy blurted out, as she started to scrub the oven with a hand brush that had been dipped in a bucket full of water and Clorox bleach.

"Yeah, you're right. But, she's still my mother, and I love her," Nicolas responded, hoping Tammy realized how her last statement had stung.

Tammy was free-spirited and rarely kept her thoughts to herself. She would say what was on her mind without taking time to think about how it affected others. Her bluntness caused plenty of arguments between them, but Nicolas accepted that about her and loved her dearly anyway.

"You're right," Tammy said, realizing she was being a little too harsh. "You do have a good mother," she added, wrapping her arms around him and pressing her face against his shoulder. It didn't take much to calm him down.

"So how does it feel being in a new home and away from everyone you've grown to love?"

Tammy smiled and threw both arms in the air. "It feels so good. For the first time in my life, I feel free," she replied in an outburst of joy.

Nicolas laughed. "You said that same crap when we moved in the last house."

"Yeah, but I started to feel trapped in that small-ass house. This house is three times the size of the old one. I finally have room for my clothes." She smiled, dancing around the room like a ballerina.

"So it's your clothes that finally feel free," Nicolas said jokingly.

"Whatever, smarty pants." Tammy waved him off, laughing as she continued to clean.

"Well, I like knowin' I can go into another room to get away and be at peace if I need some space." Nicolas thought of the times they'd argued and how they'd had no place to go let off steam away from each other.

Tammy stopped cleaning and turned around. "Get away? From what?"

"You know how you get when you're mad at me," Nicolas said, expressing it in a non-confrontational way, as he thought about how she nagged and pouted all around the house like a spoiled brat when she didn't get her way.

"You can't talk, momma's boy. When you get upset, you stomp around the house like a little boy with your bottom lip hanging." She paraded around the house mocking him.

"That was just the New York air gettin' to me," was the excuse he used.

"You see?" She waved her finger at him. "There you go again, Mr. Exaggerator." She mocked him in a low, deep tone. "It was the New York air gettin' to me."

"Whatever," Nicolas said, stung by her mockery.

Walking away to avoid any more of Tammy's verbal lashing he glanced out the living room window to get a look at the neighbors, but no one was outside. It was only ten minutes to four in the afternoon, so he figured everyone was still at work. Hopefully, the neighborhood would liven up in the next hour or so when people returned home and began their evening run or walking their dogs.

"I still love you anyway," Tammy said, breaking the silence. She joined Nicolas at the window. "I hope the neighbors are okay."

"Me, too. This neighborhood seems so peaceful, but then you never know. It looks quiet, almost abandoned. Actually, right now, it reminds me of a ghost town."

Tammy put her arms around him. "Think we'll get used to this quietness?"

Her soft voice had a hint of nervousness. So, Nicolas, whom wanted to play the role of protector and confidant, felt he needed to offer her some reassurance, even if they were only words.

"Sure. It'll just take some time. We've spent all our lives surrounded by the noise of New York City, so this quiet neighborhood is a big contrast. But, it won't take long before we get used to it."

CHAPTER ELEVEN

Our New Neighbor

Nicolas and Tammy wasted no time unpacking boxes that same day. When someone knocked on the door, interrupting them, they were a bit surprised.

"Who could that be?" Nicolas asked.

They tried looking out of the window, but ended up bumping into each other. They both moaned in frustration. It was hard to see anything while peering through the glass, because of a big evergreen bush that was in front of the house. It must have been planted there when the house was built over thirty years ago. Now it had grown to an overwhelming size that nearly blocked the entire front window. All they were able to see was the street and part of the driveway. There were no cars parked out front, except for their rented U-Haul truck.

"I wonder who it could be. Your mother perhaps?" Tammy said with a little sarcasm and a smile.

"Nah, not this soon, but don't worry. I got this." Nicolas carefully approached the door with caution. "Who is it?" he yelled out.

"It's me...John Newman. I live next door," responded the strange but nervous voice from the other side of the door.

Nicolas opened the door to a tall, middle-aged man who wore glasses and had a receding hairline. His skin was darkly tanned, and he was smiling like a used car salesman.

"Hi. I'm John Newman, your next-door neighbor," he greeted with a welcoming smile.

Nicolas opened the door wider and extended his hand.

"Hi, John. I'm Nicolas Coles. Glad to meet you." They shook hands.

"Hello, John. I'm Nick's wife, Tammy. Pleased to meet you," Tammy yelled out as she forced herself into the doorway, excited to meet her new neighbor.

"Yes, the little loudmouth woman is my lovely wife, Tammy," Nicolas stated with criticism.

Tammy reached out to shake John's hand, but he hesitated, looking at Nicolas as if he needed his approval. Then he looked at Tammy and slowly extended his hand to give her a soft handshake.

"It's okay; her bark is bigger than her bite," Nicolas jokingly said, as the laughter seemed to break the tension.

"I just wanted to stop by and welcome you to the neighborhood. I was wondering who bought this house," John said, looking beyond them into the front room, only to see a pile of cardboard boxes stacked everywhere. "It's been on the market for a while now, and it made the neighborhood seem...you know...empty."

Nicolas tried to offer a little hospitality. "You care to come in for somethin' to drink?"

John held his hand up, revealing his palm. "No, thanks. I don't want to be a bother. I know you guys have a lot of unpacking to do. Plus, I'm on my way to work in a few minutes. I usually grab something from the Dunkin' Donuts up the road. The manager there usually hooks me up for being a regular customer."

Looking at John dressed in his blue polo shirt with white stripes, blue khaki pants, and black Hush Puppies, Nicolas' curiosity took over. "What do you do, if you don't mind me askin'?"

"Not at all. I'm a cab driver for Blue Bird Taxi."

"A cab driver." Nicolas nodded his head. "That will definitely come in handy since we only have one vehicle."

"No problem. Just call me when you need me. I'm not too proud to drive my neighbors where they need to go." John handed Nicolas a business card. "I've been a cabbie for five years now. So, I know the area pretty well. I really don't need the job; it's just something for me to do. I have no bills, and my house is paid off from my lawsuit settlement."

"Lawsuit settlement!" Nicolas repeated, fully attentive as if he received a burst of adrenaline.

"Yes, sir. I got hit by a bread truck while working at my old job, and got paid well for the two broken legs and three cracked ribs. The driver was drinking while on the clock, which worked in my favor."

"What type of job did you do?" Nicolas inquired.

"I worked for a construction company," John cheerfully mentioned.

"I bet that job paid well," Nicolas uttered.

"It did, and it had great benefits."

"I hope you were compensated enough for all that suffering," Tammy commented with concern.

John stood proudly. "Oh, I was. I'm living off a monthly disability check. Plus, I still get a pension since I had time in on the job. So, I really don't need to work, but I need something to keep me occupied." He hesitated for a moment and then asked, "So, Nicolas, what do you do?"

"I'm a realtor. My wife and I moved here from New York to start a family. I work for Home Realty and Associates. It was too busy for me in New York. I was workin' late hours and not spendin' enough time with my wife. When I found out there was a spot open out in Cherry Hill, I put in for a transfer, and it was accepted. Thanks to my wife. If it weren't for her, I woulda never found out about this area. So, if you're lookin' to buy or sell, here's my card." Nicolas reached in his pants pocket and pulled out a business card. He always made sure to keep one handy at all times.

"Thanks." John glanced at it before placing it into his pocket and turning to Tammy. "Have you all been watching the news lately?"

"No. Why?" Nicolas asked, eagerly listening.

"Well, in the past few weeks, there's been a rapist on the loose around these parts."

"No kiddin'!" Nicolas said, astonished.

"Oh yes and the police wanted to keep a lid on it, but the media got a whiff of it. Now it's all over the news."

Tammy and Nicolas gave each other a frightful stare, then looked back toward John.

"Thanks for lettin' us know. I'll make sure all the windows and doors are locked tight," Nicolas affirmed, turning his attention back to Tammy. "Baby, make sure you call and get a home alarm company out here tomorrow."

"I'm two steps ahead of you," Tammy said, using her pink cell phone to call directory assistance. She then turned and walked into the house for some privacy.

"I also heard about some mob boss out here on trial," Nicolas said, hoping John might fill him in on that.

"Yeah, Frank DeBartello. He's like the John Gotti of the millennium, with his own Gambino crime family. He's a feared man and well respected. He even has a hit-man that's untouchable. He's been accused of a bunch of murders, but avoided being charged for lack of evidence. Everyone out here knows he has the police department and the courthouse judges on his payroll. But, this time, they got an undercover federal agent who's going to testify in court this week, and they say he has enough evidence to put him away for good."

Nicolas nodded, realizing he'd better start watching the news on a regular basis. For some reason, though, he couldn't stop thinking about John's settlement money.

"Have you ever thought about investin' some of that lawsuit money?"

John rubbed his chin while in deep thought. "It did cross my mind a few times, but I don't know a thing about investing."

Thinking about the commission he would receive, dollar signs danced in Nicolas' head.

"Well, if you have any questions, call me. I'll be glad to give you some input."

"Thanks. I may just do that." John added with a geeky smile.

Tammy rejoined them with a troubled look on her face. "I called several different alarm companies, and the earliest time we can get the alarm installed is three days from now. That's through Watch Guard. The other home alarm companies said we would have to wait a week."

62

"That's too long!" Nicolas announced, exasperated they would have to wait so long to have an alarm system installed while this so-called rapist was all over the news.

Just then, a mysterious car drove slowly down the street. Being spooked by a rapist on the loose, Nicolas and Tammy stared at it, trying to see who was behind the wheel. Was it the rapist stalking their home, or was the hit-man on another assignment? Nicolas didn't know what to think with this car cruising up at a walking pace. He could hear his heart pounding as the vehicle approached. Nicolas and Tammy were so focused on seeing who was driving the car that they totally ignored John, who stood there still having a conversation with them. His words were nothing more than mumbles to their ears. The anticipation was starting to drive Nicolas insane, but it ended up only being an elderly couple driving like they were part of a Thanksgiving Day parade. Seeing the couple posed no threat, Nicolas and Tammy finally let their guards down, and that's when they noticed John standing there as if he were waiting for a response.

Tammy then jumped in with the information she had. "Well, the customer service lady said they were backed up from all the orders in this area," she said, shrugging her shoulders. "What else can we do but wait it out?"

"This thing is really serious," Nicolas commented, suddenly having second thoughts about living in Merchantville. Just the mere thought of a rapist shot fear through him.

What could Tammy do if the rapist tried to snatch her little ass up? Nicolas thought. *She doesn't know any form of self-defense, but what they taught her at her last job as a requirement in verbal command. Her only weapon would be her big mouth, but it wouldn't be loud enough to scare off her attacker.*

The mafia situation was now the least of Nicolas' concerns. He grew up in New York, which was full of mob bosses and mob wars, and he never had a problem with them. They were real good at keeping a low profile.

"Well, it was good meeting you and your lovely wife. Hope you all like your new home," John said, interrupting their moment of silence.

"All right. Good meetin' you too, John. Take it easy now," Nicolas replied, then closed the door.

Now that should have been a sign for Nicolas right there. He should have gotten all their things and headed right back to New York. A mob boss, a hit-man, a rapist on the loose, and home alarm companies backed up with installation orders. He should have researched the area before moving there. However, he didn't take it seriously, which was a big mistake on his part. Now the shit was going to weigh heavily on his mind. Some realtor he turned out to be —lazy, always taking the easy route. Not having the foresight to set up a home alarm prior to them moving in or at least grab a sign to post in the window or on the lawn as a deterrent was just another small mistake adding its weight to the considerable mound of mistakes Nicolas had been making. Soon...no, sooner than anyone would think...those mistakes were going to bury Nicolas in a bad-choice avalanche!

CHAPTER TWELVE

It Must Be Playtime

Taking a break from unpacking, Tammy and Nicolas were eating some potato chips she found in one of the boxes. Nicolas couldn't stop thinking about the rapist. The more he thought about it, the more constricted his throat felt. He took a long swig of Pepsi, but the soothing feel of the ice-cold soda was not enough to clear his head. His mounting anxiety over these new developments was almost too much to take. The whole point of moving to the sticks was to avoid this type of shit! He was getting mad and had to speak on it.

"Now I'm gonna worry all day while I'm at work. Maybe I should call in sick until they install the alarm system," he announced, knowing it may crush his credibility with his new job.

Tammy rubbed the side of Nicolas' head and softly tugged at his ear, her hands soft against his skin like a baby's touch. "Don't do that. I'll be okay. I'm a big girl. Besides, tomorrow's your first day at work, and you need to make a good impression with your boss and new co-workers. Go to work and make my money, bitch!" she joked, slapping Nicolas' ass.

Nicolas jumped from the sudden sting. "Ouch! You're not supposed to do that. It's my job to do the smackin'," he said, rubbing the pain away.

He loved to smack Tammy's plump ass every time he had the opportunity, and she returned the favor whenever she had the chance. The day they met in high school, Nicolas told her that he knew she had to be mixed with Italian and Irish even though her last name was Spenser, because she was built like a black girl, with nice tits that stood on their own with no support and a perfectly round ass designed to absorb forceful impact.

"Whatever! That works both ways." Tammy walked away with an attitude, her full hips swaying.

Nicolas abandoned the sneak approach and gave chase. Laughing, Tammy ran up the stairs.

"No! Stop it!" she yelled, running in the bathroom and locking the door.

Nicolas tried opening it, but it wouldn't budge. "You're gonna have to come out of there sooner or later, and I can wait."

As he continued manipulating the doorknob, he could hear her jumping up and down like a little girl in her safe haven, tickled that he hadn't been able to catch her.

"No, I don't. I'll wait it out in here 'til you leave for work tomorrow!" she yelled out in laughter.

Defeated and outsmarted, Nicolas rested his head against the door. "Okay, you win. I surrender. Come on out. I ain't gonna do anythin' to ya," he said in a soft voice, trying to con her into opening the door.

There was a brief moment of silence.

"You promise?" Her voice was timid.

"I promise," Nicolas repeated in a soft tone.

She hesitated before responding. "Okay...here I come."

Tammy slowly opened the bathroom door an inch.

"See, I told you that I wasn't gonna do anythin'," Nicolas said, using his mushy voice, as Tammy reluctantly exited the bathroom.

However, when she opened the door wide enough for him to enter, he unexpectedly grabbed her and held her tightly.

"Aha, I lied!" he sang out joyfully.

"No fair! You cheated!" With her bottom lip hanging, Tammy pouted like a small kid, while struggling to break free of his hold.

There was no use. She couldn't get away. He would have his way with her, christening every room...and he did!

CHAPTER THIRTEEN

Laura Got Jokes

While fixing hoagies for dinner, after working up an appetite, Tammy heard the door-knocker banging against the solid oak door.

"Nicolas, can you get the door?" she yelled out, hoping her words would reach him.

Nicolas looked out the living room window and saw a familiar car in the driveway.

"It's my mom," he said, his voice filled with excitement. Nicolas couldn't believe she had driven all the way out there.

He opened the front door, greeted her with a big hug, and kissed her plump cheek.

"Hi, Mom."

Laura Coles was a five-foot-two, heavyset, medium brown-skinned woman who wore a black wig. Outdated prescription glasses dangled from a silver chain around her neck like a prized piece of jewelry. She preferred dark-colored skirts that hung below her knees. The flat, black leather shoes looked like they hurt her feet, and her long, white knee-high socks drove Nicolas crazy. He'd taken her shopping several times, hoping she would change her style, but she always reverted to her preferred wardrobe.

"Hey, baby. Where's Tammy?" she asked, looking past him, trying to get a look at the new house.

"Tammy, my mom's here," he called out, making his mother believe Tammy was unaware of her arrival.

Nicolas' momma was such a handful, walking around with that Michael Jackson look. *I'm just waitin' for her to do the moonwalk across the livin' room floor*, Nicolas thought. He tried once to get rid of all her white socks, but she knew he had hid them, and she tried to beat the devil out of him. Nicolas had never seen her so mad before. Maybe it had something to do with it being a Sunday morning and him causing her to leave late for church and "lose all of her blessings," as she would put it.

Whatever it was she gave him a good ass whoopin' that day with an extension cord, which is why he now knew what she meant when she would wave her long finger at him and say, "Child, don't let me get dat cord. 'Cause I'll put somethin' on ya, booooy, that God can't get rid of!"

Nicolas' friends laughed at him whenever she was around, but that didn't bother him because their mothers wore the same shit. Maybe it was the fashion statement of older Christian ladies. Laura was a wholehearted woman, and Nicolas loved her to death. However, along with her lack of fashion came her commitment to speak. Laura loved to talk. She could pick a topic and talk about it for hours.

Nicolas loved her for being the woman who raised him into the man that he was, though he wasn't quite sure if she really liked Tammy or not. She hid her feelings through conversation and a pleasant smile, because it wasn't good for her to judge people and still call herself a *born-again Christian*. Laura was a very religious woman. She went to church every Sunday to hear *The Word*. Tuesday was bible study and Thursday was prayer meeting. She watched the gospel channel and kept her radio on the gospel station every day of the week. Nicolas also believed in the Lord, but there was a difference between being religious and being a fanatic.

Nicolas believed you only lived once, that we're just visitors here on Earth. God put us on this earth to praise *Him* and die. And once you stand in front of *Him* on Judgment Day, you are held accountable for all the works you've done on Earth. So, no matter how you look at it, you're going to die anyway. Therefore, the way Nicolas saw it, he was going to work toward being rich first so he could enjoy all the pleasures God blessed him with right here on Earth. However, he would try not to overindulge in it, because the Bible says, *Greed is a sin.*

Nicolas was hoping he could find a good church in Merchantville, because with all the things he'd done wrong, he needed to get his life right with God. Admittedly, he was no saint. He loved to hang out at nightclubs and get his drink on occasionally. He even ventured into a few strip joints and got a few lap dances, but that's as far as it went. He never cheated on Tammy, even though he was tempted a few times.

Yet, he couldn't say the same for Tammy. He caught her a few times smiling in different men's faces like a Cheshire cat, but he wasn't sure if she fucked them or not. For all he knew, she could have gotten it in while he was at work. The more he thought about it, the more it pissed him off.

With so many opportunities to get it in with other chicks, his mother raised him right, and he just couldn't do it, not even with Bubbles, the stripper. She was five-foot-eight and 160 pounds of all legs and ass. Her upper body was thin with small breasts, but her bottom half was thick as hell. He forgot what her face and hair looked like, because that was irrelevant to him. He had turned her down, though. Maybe it was the fact that he was married and didn't want to cheat on Tammy...or maybe it was because she charged too much. Either way, he turned her down, and that's all that mattered.

Attending church was very important in order for them to strengthen their marriage. They had a church home in New York, but they'd started missing a few Sundays here and there until they stopped attending all together. It'd been a year since they went to church, so finding a church home was their first priority once they were settled into their new environment.

"Hey, this is a surprise," Tammy said, entering the room. "I didn't expect you'd be here so soon."

"Oh, stop lyin'. You know you didn't miss me, child," Laura said, giving Tammy a big smile and a loose hug.

Nicolas could see the fake placating nature of the embrace and wished the two most important women in his life had a better rapport.

"Mom, you never give us a chance to miss you," Nicolas blurted out.

"If I did, you'd think I didn't love you anymore," she said, placing her hand on Nicolas' face. The look in her eyes showed how much she adored her only son. "I was in the neighborhood and thought I'd come by to see if y'all needed a helpin' hand."

"Why were you way out here?" Nicolas asked, knowing she would make up a story.

After taking a seat in a chair, Laura started going through her pocketbook and pulled out some bills. "Well, I heard Jersey is known for their high taxes. So, I figured I'd head down here and give them some of mine." She laughed, while Nicolas and Tammy cracked a smile. "I knew you had a lot of unpackin' to do. So, I thought I could help you out, plus be nosey at the same time."

"We figured that," Tammy mumbled.

"What was that, dear?" Laura asked, leaning forward with a slight turn of her head for better listening.

This was exactly the type of bullshit Nicolas had enough of between these two. Tammy didn't help with her thoughtless sarcasms, but his mother needed to be more mature about Tammy.

"Oh nothing," Tammy responded, then quickly changed the topic. "Well, what do you think about our neighborhood, Mrs. Laura?"

"I think it's beautiful. Now when are y'all gonna give me some grand-babies?"

Put on the spot, Tammy's face turned a hot pink.

"Mom!"

Nicolas was surprised at his mother's inquiry.

"I ain't gettin' no younger, you know, and I know you're gonna need a live-in babysitter."

"We have to make sure our finances are straight first," Nicolas explained. "We're not ready for that just yet. We're tryna be smart about it."

"Wise decision! But, Nicolas, all you have to do is have sex. What do you need—a sex education course?"

"Mom!" Nicolas yelled. "You're actin' up again."

She threw her hands in the air. "Hush yo' mouth, boy, and stop makin' so many excuses. You'll be all right. Besides, you have a very good job."

"What's wrong, baby?" he finally asked, concern flowing through his lungs.

"I think the bed would have been better in that other corner," she said, pointing.

"I thought about that, too, but it wouldn't fit. I even had the movers measure it to make sure, and they both agreed the space was too small." Nicolas looked at the king-sized bed that dominated what little space the room had to offer. They definitely needed a bigger room.

"It's okay. I can work with it," Tammy mumbled, trying to figure out how to maximize the remaining floor space.

"Well, let's see how much unpackin' we can get done before it gets dark. I don't wanna be in the way when y'all decide to break the bed in," Laura said, laughing.

"Mom, you're embarrassin' me again." Nicolas pouted like a big kid. Laura always made him the butt of her jokes, and he didn't like it.

"Oh, stop bein' a big crybaby. You're a grown-ass man now. How the hell you think you got here in the first place, Nicolas?" Laura said, raising her voice. "Lord Jesus, please forgive me," she prayed aloud, realizing she used the wrong choice of words to get her point across.

At the same time, Nicolas prayed to himself silently. *Oh Lord, please don't let my momma start actin' up again.*

Sometimes, there was no stopping her once she started up, and that was not the housewarming he wanted at all.

"Good. You can bring it on in." Nicolas said flexing his alpha male status with his head up and chest out, the typical ego thing.

Nicolas opened the door wider, pretty sure that neither of the guys were the Merchantville rapist, unless one of them was using their delivery job to case the place. Nicolas couldn't let his persecution complex disrupt his logic.

"We'll have it set up in no time," the tattooed man said before turning to go help his partner unload the furniture.

Nicolas propped the front door open so they could get the big pieces through.

"Okay, ladies, they're here to deliver the bedroom furniture. Why don't you show Mom the basement and garage area?" he told Tammy, not wanting the guys to see her just in case.

Tammy caught on when she heard the urgency in his voice. "Okay. Mrs. Laura, follow me," she said as the two women headed down the basement stairs.

After the delivery guys got the furniture set up, Nicolas gave them twenty dollars each. "Thank you, sir," both movers said, glad to get the generous tip on their way out.

Nicolas waited for the delivery truck to pull off before he closed the front door behind him and called out, "Mom! Tammy! Come see the bedroom set!"

Within minutes, Laura and Tammy were entering the bedroom, where Nicolas stood admiring the bed.

"This is really pretty," Laura commented, looking at the mahogany sleigh bed, dresser, and nightstands.

Tammy didn't say a word. She just stared at the bedroom furniture with a blank expression, which Nicolas noticed. *I hope she likes it. She picked it out, so what's the problem?*

CHAPTER FOURTEEN

Someone's at the Door

As they unpacked a few boxes, Laura made jokes, recalling every embarrassing moment Nicolas went through while growing up.

Bang! Bang! Bang! The heavy brass door-knocker sounded loudly as it hit the oak door. "Geesh, who could that be?" Tammy asked.

"Probably the delivery company," Nicolas said, while on his way to the front door.

"So now that you're here, Mrs. Laura, would you like to have a tour of the place?" Tammy announced, taking over the floor.

"I would love to," Laura cackled.

"Yeah, it's the delivery guys," Nicolas called out, opening the door.

"Hi. We have a delivery for Mr. and Mrs. Coles?" said the man covered in tattoos.

"I'm Mr. Coles," Nicolas told him.

Nicolas looked past the man standing in front of him and saw the other delivery guy opening the double doors to the moving truck. They looked strong enough to lift a car. Both black men looked as though they had spent a majority of their time behind bars.

"We got the bedroom set you ordered, sir." The deliveryman's voice broke Nicolas' inner thoughts.

"Well, when we do decide to have a child, we'll surprise you with the good news." He smiled, hoping it would give her some reassurance of future grand-babies.

Laura jerked her head back. "Surprise me? You know my heart can't take surprises." She grabbed her chest. Tammy now knew where Nicolas got his dramatics.

"Good try, Mom, but you're not supposed to know until we tell you."

"Well, don't take too long to tell me." She shook her head with an attitude.

Nicolas threw his hands in the air like a referee signaling a successful touchdown.

"Mom, I promise you'll be the first person to know after the stick turns blue. Stop tryna stress us out about it."

"Okay. I guess that's the best I'm gonna get from ya. Let's start unpackin'," Laura said, ending the discussion on her terms, which was no surprise to Nicolas since his mother had an uncanny ability to get in the last word.

CHAPTER FIFTEEN

Too Much Information

Laura was off the hook, but she only embarrassed Nicolas when people were around. Although she was a Christian woman, get her mad enough and her walk of faith went right out the window. She could curse like a sailor when provoked, and don't get too close to her when she reached that boiling point, because she may haul off and hit you. Laura had a mean right cross that could knock out Floyd Mayweather, but then she'd beg for forgiveness once she realized what she had done. Her number one weakness was her temper, which she'd been trying to work on for years, but even to this day, there hadn't been much of an improvement.

"Okay, Mom, I get the picture. You didn't have to cuss and get yourself all upset about it," Nicolas said, trying to calm her down.

"What picture? I thought your daddy got rid of all our nude photos," she cracked, trying to save face after losing her cool for a moment.

Nicolas' mouth dropped, looking like a baby bird during feeding time, while Tammy broke into laughter. Maybe she was laughing at Laura's joke or the expression on Nicolas' face. Either way, she was enjoying every minute of it.

"You're just kiddin', right, Mom?" Nicolas asked, not wanting to hear anything about his parents' bedroom secrets.

"You know I am, baby. I'm just pulling your leg."

Nicolas sighed loudly. The mere thought of it almost caused him to have permanent psychological damage.

"And speakin' of pullin' legs, I loved when your daddy would pull my leg." Laura moaned and pulled her skirt up to her knees, revealing the black and purple varicose veins that ran up her legs. "He would take that—"

"Mom!" Nicolas interrupted her. "Stop it right now! I don't wanna hear this!" he said, placing his hands over his ears.

He knew his mother was once a young, vibrant woman with an active sex life, but that was long ago and he wished his mother would act her age.

"Hear what?" she barked with a demanding attitude.

"About you and Dad's sexual encounters!" he exclaimed, turning up the corners of his mouth.

"You sure have a dirty mind, son. I was talkin' about my leg gettin' stiff. Now that your dad's gone, I don't have anyone to pull my leg, and it's been botherin' me all week," Laura said, but Nicolas knew she was playing mind games with him...or was she? Nicolas didn't know what to believe.

Tammy continued to laugh in the background. "Speaking of getting a stiff leg," she added jokingly, while Nicolas gave her a sharp look, "let's stretch our legs and head downstairs for some homemade tea."

Now she got jokes!

*****

Laura sat on the love-seat enjoying the sweet, cold iced tea. "I was watching the news this mornin', and I heard somethin' about a rapist on trial for workin' for a big mob boss out here," she said, getting the two news stories confused.

"Yeah, we heard about it, too. But, it's a rapist on the loose and a mob boss on trial. It's two separate stories, Mom." Nicolas then explained what little information he knew about the mob boss and the Merchantville rapist.

"I'm worried about Tammy bein' home alone while this maniac is on the loose," Laura expressed, her eyes reflecting sincere fear and concern for her daughter-in-law.

However, Laura was really more concerned about keeping an eye on Tammy while she was living with her only son. It was okay for her to visit and make a few jokes about Nicolas here and there, but to live under his roof and have the privilege to embarrass him every day, all day would be a little too much for him to handle. So, he had to make light of the situation.

"Mom, don't worry about us. We'll be okay. Tammy called a home security company, and they're gonna install an alarm system."

"Good, 'cause I was gonna stay here to make sure that rapist don't step foot in dis house." Laura grabbed her pocketbook from off the top of a box and stuck her hand inside as if she was about to reveal a concealed weapon.

"So you're a thug now?" Nicolas asked, fully expecting to see a .38 Smith & Wesson.

"Child, please, get over it. This is the millennium, and Momma needs protection, too, from all these killers and psychopaths runnin' the streets." She fumbled her hand inside her pocketbook before pulling out a can of mace. "This hot juice right here has brought a lot of grown men to their knees. I've carried this since you were a boy, when I had to work late hours at the diner. I've actually had to use it a few times."

"Mom, that was years ago. That stuff doesn't work on this new breed of psychos terrorizin' folks nowadays," Nicolas said, now worrying about his mother as well as Tammy.

Laura looked at the canister for a moment, gave it a good quick shake, raised it in the air, and aimed it at Nicolas' face. "Here, let's see if it's effective."

"Good Lord!" Nicolas quickly ducked, using his hands as a shield. "Momma, don't aim that at me!" he yelled, running toward the kitchen.

"Well, I should test it on somebody to make sure it still works." She dissolved into laughter, while placing it back into her purse.

"Not on me!" Nicolas whined.

"I thought you said the stuff doesn't work anymore?" Tammy chimed in. Tickled, she couldn't stop laughing.

"I know what I said," he wailed.

"Then why are you duckin' and runnin' around the room like a headless chicken?" Tammy asked, still giggling.

"Well, it might still work, and I ain't willin' to be her guinea pig. Plus, I got to go to work tomorrow, and I don't wanna go in with my eyes swollen half shut," was the excuse he gave them.

Laura checked her watch. "Kids, it's startin' to get late. I better leave before I get too tired to drive back home. But, I wanna have prayer before I go," she said, breathing heavily.

Laura, Nicolas, and Tammy formed a small prayer circle, but Nicolas found it hard to focus on his mother's words. His concentration was interrupted with thoughts about his first day at work and what he needed to do to make a good impression, and the neighborhood rapist on the loose was a whole problem within itself. Nicolas had to protect Tammy and keep her safe. He imagined the worst—coming home from work to find Tammy raped and murdered, and him hating himself for not being there to protect her.

"In God's name we pray, Amen."

Those were the only words of his mother's prayer he distinctly heard.

"We'll walk you to your car, Mrs. Laura," Tammy announced. She was starting to become fond of her mother-in-law. Maybe she started to realize that Laura was really a sweet person or Maybe it had something to do with her embarrassing Nicolas every time she came around.

Yeah that was it.

Once inside her car, Nicolas' mother buckled her seatbelt and settled in behind the steering wheel of her big ole four-door Mercury Grand Marquis that seemed to be the preferred mode of transportation for anyone over fifty years old. Nicolas made a promise to himself that he'd rather walk before he drove an ugly relic like his mom's car.

"You drive safe now, okay?" Tammy said in a childlike voice.

"Call us when you get home, Mom, so we'll know you got there safely." Nicolas leaned inside the car window and gave her a kiss on the cheek.

"I will, baby. Y'all get some rest, and don't kill yourselves unpackin'. And make sure y'all find a church home out here so you don't lose out on your blessings," she demanded, while waving her index finger in a stern manner.

"We will, Mom," Nicolas promised.

"Maybe God will bless me with some grand-babies," she blurted out, starting up the car with a strange look on her face.

"Mom, don't start that again," Nicolas whined, hoping she didn't reload and unleash some more embarrassing moments.

"Oh, hush yo' mouth," Laura uttered with a wave of her hand. "It don't hurt to try." She placed the car in drive and began to slowly pull away. "Bye, baby. You and Tammy enjoy your beautiful new home. I love it," she added, then blew a kiss with admiration.

Tammy turned toward Nicolas, her eyes lit up and her teeth exposed as if she was at the dentist. "Your mom is off the hook," she said as Nicolas watched the taillights until his mother turned onto the main road. "Does she know her way home?"

"She should since she use to live down the street."

"Down the street? I knew your mom was from Jersey, but I didn't know she lived in Merchantville." Tammy was surprised. "How come I never knew this?"

"She lived out here when she was younger with some guy named Eric. She almost married the guy."

"Wow!" Tammy howled in disbelief. "What happened with that relationship?"

Walking back to the house, Nicolas told her what little information he knew about it.

"The guy was abusive towards her. So, after puttin' up with that for four years, she moved to New York to get away from him. That's when she met my dad. They got married and had me."

"The evening is so beautiful. Let's walk around the neighborhood," Tammy said, feeling adventurous. Or maybe she could see the hurt in his eyes and thought a nice walk would ease his mind.

"That sounds good, but I don't think you oughta be paradin' around the neighborhood with a rapist on the loose. Who knows? He may live on this street," Nicolas murmured, his eyes scanning the neighborhood.

"Does that mean I can't leave the house? What about shopping or going out to eat?"

Her tone was hard and defensive. Sensing her disapproval, Nicolas held her hand like a father would do his own daughter to calm her down.

"I think the less you're outside the better, at least until they catch this lunatic."

"It's just wrong for me to be locked up in my own house like a criminal. Why don't I just go home and live with my mother 'til they catch him?" she vocalized, angry at Nicolas' suggestion to be homebound.

"You don't really mean that." Nicolas winced, displeased with the mere thought of it.

"Yes, I do." She rolled her eyes. "I refuse to be a prisoner in my own home," She added, crossing her arms.

"Well, give it a few days. I'd rather us be safe than sorry. If they don't catch him soon, we'll both stay at your mother's house 'til they do catch him."

The thought of Tammy being home alone was disturbing, but moving in with her mother was straight demented.

"Okay. I can work with that—for a few days," Tammy agreed, unfolding her arms.

They re-entered the house, and Tammy headed upstairs. "I'm going to finish unpacking the rest of the boxes in the bedroom," she told him.

Just then, her cell phone rang. The caller ID identified the call was from her mother. She answered her pink phone.

"Hi, Mom... I love it... It's beautiful... Okay, we'll see you tomorrow."

Nicolas remained downstairs, unpacking more boxes as dusk replaced daylight. His cell phone vibrated in the hip pocket of his khaki shorts. It was his mother calling to let him know she'd made it home safely.

After their brief conversation, he stepped out on the deck to get some fresh air. Nicolas took a deep breath; no smoke, gas fumes, or smog. The still night seemed restrained. Nicolas was amazed at the number of lightning bugs flashing their pale, yellow lights in the evening air. New York had few of them, and therefore, he thought they were close to extinction. He had forgotten just how beautiful they were twinkling in the night like Christmas lights.

CHAPTER SIXTEEN

Silent Screams

Steam surrounded the Irish, pale-skinned, brunette woman who had just finished taking a shower. Young and vulnerable, she had to be in her mid twenties. She must have weighed at least 115 pounds soaking wet. She was well proportioned for her small frame.

The woman stepped out of the shower and slipped on a short, white terrycloth robe. Leaving her glasses laying on the sink, she stepped into her bedroom.

While looking through her lingerie drawer, she heard a slight noise to her left. Turning to see if it was her cat, Muffin, she was stunned to see a man standing in the doorway of her bedroom. A horrific chill raced up her spine with enough force to cause her body to shiver uncontrollably. Fear shot through her body, as a soft cry emanated from deep within her. Without her glasses, the details of the man were blurred. His frame looked tall and husky, dressed in a dark blue sweatshirt and pants. The intruder had large hands built for manual labor; his ice-blue eyes were filled with hatred. Even though the woman could see none of these scary details, she felt them.

"Who's there...?" she asked, terrified. "What are you doing here...? What do you want...?"

"You," he answered, his voice resonating with evil and lust.

The deep tone of his voice caused her to shiver more as if a cold draft had entered the room. She suddenly dashed toward the bathroom, slamming the door behind her and locking it.

Her heart thumping wildly in her chest, she picked up her glasses from the sink and put them on. Now she was able to see clearer. How did this man get inside her house? She never left her doors or windows unlocked, especially with the knowledge of a rapist on the loose. Horrified, she remembered the news reports of all his victims turning up dead, and she didn't want to end up like them. Therefore, she had to think fast.

"What do you want?" she screamed. "If it's money, you'll find some in the blue shoebox in the closet! Take it and go!"

Frantically, she glanced around the bathroom for something to break the thick, decorative, double-glass bathroom window, but the hardest object was a can of hairspray. She began screaming and banging on the hard glass in hopes that someone might hear her, but the glass was too thick. She was trapped like a rabbit in a cage.

She got quiet for a moment, listening intently. She heard nothing. Maybe he had taken the money from the shoebox and left. She placed her head against the door, trying to detect sound or movement. Total silence is all that lingered.

Is he gone? she silently asked herself, uncertain and fearful.

Suddenly, the door was kicked open, knocking the woman backward into the tub, cracking her head on the faucet. Her glasses flew off her face. As she tried to sit up, blood flowed from the top of her head, running down her face and into her eyes, blurring her vision even more.

The big, blue, hulking stranger stood over her with the bedroom light shining behind him, looking like a huge shadow.

"Please don't hurt me," she begged.

Outside, the misty morning air clung to the well-groomed lawn, lazily absorbing the faint noises escaping from the well-insulated walls of the house. A bird chirped.

Aggressively, he grabbed her slender ankles, pulling her up and out of the tub. Her body slammed against the floor, almost knocking the wind out of her lungs, dazing her momentarily.

Blood streaming from her head, she grabbed both sides of the bathroom doorway in desperation, but the petite woman was no match for the merciless hulk, who held her by the ankles with enough force to crush bones. With one hard yank, he pulled her free from the doorway, breaking her recently manicured nails. The woman shrieked in agony, releasing her grasp.

She swung at him with both hands, while crying out, "HELP ME! NO!"

The man threw her on the bed and held her down with one arm, as he pushed his sweatpants down. Wearing no underwear and with his breath smelling of alcohol, he climbed on top of the woman and wrapped his hands around her. His 250-pound body pinned her to the bed. One hand covered her screaming mouth, while the other forced apart her legs. Her cries were muffled, leaving a faint sound that hummed through her nose. He penetrated the woman, causing her eyes to widen from the damage he was making by forcing himself inside of her dry walls. The pain was more than flesh and blood could stand. Digging her raggedy nails into his skin to make him stop seemed to be to no avail. It only exhilarated him even more. This was what he wanted, and he loved every minute of it.

Bleeding, hurting, and worn out from the struggle, she stopped fighting and endured the sweating pig on top of her. The man wore no condom or gloves. With her not putting up a fight, it caused his arousal to slowly diminish. He then placed both hands around the exhausted woman's throat and squeezed, causing the woman to make every effort to get some air. The struggle intensified the man's sensation, resulting in him cumming with excitement. The woman tried to put up a fight, but was weakened by the lack of oxygen. Her breath slowly dissipated until there was no more fight left in her.

*****

When he was certain she was dead, he got off of the woman and released his hot urine all over her corpse before pulling his pants up. It was his sick way of marking his prey like a wild animal.

Wrapping his hands tightly around her ankles, he dragged the corpse off the bed, down the stairs, and out the front door. The night was still dark and quiet, and the residents were sleeping peacefully. No one was aware of the torture that had taken place...not a one. This became another one of the killer's best-kept secrets.

He moved towards his car in the shadows cast by the streetlights. The car was a black Ford Crown Victoria with dark gray cloth interior and a dent on the rear bumper. He opened the trunk and placed her body on the clear plastic he'd carefully placed there earlier. To avoid blood spill, he gently lowered it and applied pressure until he heard the latch click. Then he hopped in the driver's seat.

With the headlights off and his car door still open, he put the gear in neutral and gave the car a push with his left foot. The car rolled silently down the slanted driveway. At the end of the driveway, he gave the wheel a sharp turn to the left; the momentum of the car made the turn. Then he started the car and drove down the street, not turning on the headlights until he came to the nearest intersection. The whole time, he was careful to maintain the speed limit to avoid any added suspicion. He did not want to be questioned why he was out and about so early in the morning. The police wanted him bad, but as long as he kept being careful, the cops couldn't even come close to his description, let alone his name or arrest record.

He pulled into a park next to a bike trail and got out the car. The night air was brisk and moist with dew. He visually inspected the area to make sure no one was nearby, but there was total silence. It was 3:47 a.m. and too dark for anyone to be out there. He saw no one, and all that could be heard were the sounds of the night.

Perfect.

He popped the trunk, hoisted her body, and carried her up the bike trail to a group of pine trees. The cracking of dead leaves and branches beneath his feet seemed amplified in the noiseless air. He tossed her body in the wooded area of the park. The hard impact against the unforgiving ground caused the woman to gasp for air.

She was still alive, but barely.

He couldn't let her live. She had seen his face and could identify him. The man grabbed the plastic that he used to line the trunk of his car and wrapped it around the woman's head, suffocating her. The woman was too weak to put up a tussle. The hotness of her breath fogged up the plastic. Her mouth opened, straining for air as she sucked the plastic hard enough for it to smother her face like plaster. The burning feeling in her lungs intensified until they collapsed. Once dead, he looked around again. The coast was still clear.

Wonderful.

The death stare reflected the horror she had endured. Even though it was evident she was dead by the way her eyes were open and dilated, he still had to make certain. So, he placed her on her stomach and twisted her head to the left until he heard the vertebrae in her neck crack like a brittle branch of a tree in a ceaseless cold winter wind. With the deed done, her head bobbled like a ball and string. Thick skin was the only thing that connected her head to her body.

Fully satisfied with his evildoing, he rolled her small, lifeless body beneath the pines and returned to his car, driving off into the still night.

CHAPTER SEVENTEEN

This is a Kodak Moment

The alarm clock buzzing felt like a knife penetrating through Nicolas' ears and into the center of his brain. He reached over and slapped the alarm off. It was six o'clock Wednesday morning. He had been up half the night worrying about this day. He was too excited about getting the day going to notice if he had gotten enough sleep or not. Tammy rolled over toward him. "Good morning, handsome. It's time to prepare for your first day at work."

"Good morning to you, my beautiful princess. Ah, this is a Kodak moment," Nicolas said, laughing at Tammy's wild morning hair, her face without make-up, and the moisturizer clumped beneath her right eye.

He didn't care; the love he had for her was blind. What would have been a roughed-up, unattractive female to some was more of an adorable-looking woman to him...his sweetheart.

Knowing he was laughing at her, Tammy mugged him, pushing his head back, and turned her back toward him. Nicolas got out of bed and headed for the bathroom to shower.

Once dressed for the day, he went downstairs and started breakfast. They hadn't unpacked all the kitchen items, so after getting eggs and butter out of the fridge, Nicolas started looking through boxes for a frying pan. After a couple minutes of searching, he was unsuccessful with finding a pan, but came across his thin baseball bat that he used to chase the loudmouth individuals away from his old house.

"There you are, buddy!"

He placed it in the living room closet for safekeeping. Then he called up the stairs to Tammy, hoping she may know where the rest of the kitchen utensils were, but got no response. So, Nicolas returned to the kitchen to retrieve a bowl from one of the boxes, and after putting the butter and eggs back in the refrigerator, he grabbed the milk. He found a box of Cheerios in another box and filled up a big bowl with the cereal. Sitting at the kitchen table, Nicolas decided to take Dave's advice and used his cell phone to watch the news off the Internet. It was time that he kept up with what was going on in the world.

A young, black male reporter appeared on the small screen reporting the story.

"Mob boss, Frank DeBartello, is still under investigation for allegedly contracting a hit-man to kill Thomas McCarty, an off-duty federal agent who was to testify against him today. Agent McCarty was involved in an undercover sting operation, which led authorities to this Cherry Hill warehouse behind me."

The camera switched to a wide-angle shot of federal agents and local police officers behind yellow "Do Not Cross" crime scene tape that surrounded the building.

The reporter continued. "Over five hundred loaded handguns and AK-47s and six million dollars' worth of drugs and money were found in this warehouse. The sting took place when the undercover agent tipped off authorities of his finding. Before authorities were able to place the agent under protective custody, the hit-man got to him and the two officers who were standing guard at the Hilton

Hotel building two blocks away from the Police Administration Building. How he was able to get inside of a secured room is questionable.

"Police believe the murder was planned to look like an accident. But, when officers, who were posted just outside the door, heard a commotion inside and attempted to intervene, Officer Jim Kline and Sergeant Anthony DeRocca were shot with a Glock 23, ironically the same type of weapon federal agents are issued upon graduation from Quantico, Virginia. The perpetrators escaped, leaving the murder weapon by McCarty's bedside. Residents in the hotel said they heard gunshots, but none actually saw anyone fleeing the building. Police believe it was an inside job, because it would take someone who knew the security system to be able to disconnect the cameras from the outside. Officials believe the mob boss has connections within the police department. The questions investigators are seeking to answer are, who is the hit-man, and is he connected to the Merchantville killings? Live from Cherry Hill, New Jersey, I'm Randy Ingram. Back to you, Steve."

Nicolas closed the scene out and placed it in his pants pocket. Then he headed upstairs to kiss Tammy goodbye. When he entered the bedroom, she was sound asleep. He stood quietly, watching her sleep. She looked like an angel, and her beauty stirred his senses and warmed his heart. He didn't want to leave her at home alone with a serial rapist/killer stalking the neighborhood, but this was his first day at work and he needed to make a good first impression. So, he had to shake off his paralyzing feeling of dread and get on with the necessities of life. When he bent down and kissed her forehead, her eyes opened slowly, and they wordlessly said goodbye.

Nicolas looked sharp dressed in a dark blue Giorgio Armani suit, white Jos. A Banks dress shirt, light gray Paul Malone tie, and black patent leather Prada shoes that looked like they'd been licked clean to a shine that sparkled from a shaft of morning sunlight coming through the bedroom window. Nicolas had big money written all over him.

"Damn, boy, you look good!" she said with fire in her eyes. "You should give me some before you go, because you got me all worked up." She grabbed at Nicolas. "Those women at work are going to be all over you. Just don't let them destroy our marriage."

Tammy sprung from the bed to pull Nicolas back in with her.

Chuckling, he jumped back, trying to dodge her grasp. "I won't, baby. You're the love of my life. I gotta go before I end up bein' late my first day. I'll call you later. So, answer the phone this time."

"I will! I will! I don't want to go over that again." She fell back into bed, rolling her eyes. Nicolas would get upset with Tammy for not answering her cell phone when he tried to call her from work. The arguments they had over it would last all day and sometimes all night.

Before leaving the house, Nicolas double-checked the back door and windows to make sure they were secured. While locking the front door, he found a note taped to it from the U-Haul company stating they had come by earlier that morning and got the rental truck parked in front of the house. Nicolas did as he was instructed and left the keys in the glove compartment, so there was no need for them to disturb their rest. Nicolas walked to his whip, eager to start the day at his new job. As he pulled his car keys out of his pants pocket to unlock the doors to his vehicle, he dropped them on the ground.

"Woe there, buddy, can't afford to lose those bad babies."

He leaned down to pick them up, and before he stood up completely, he noticed John standing in his front yard watering his lawn.

So, Nicolas did the neighborly thing and said, "Hey, John! What's going on neighbor?"

"Oh, nothing. Just making sure the grass is green," John replied, standing in one spot.

"Don't stand there too long or you'll start to grow your own roots," Nicolas cracked.

They both laughed it off. Even though the joke was corny as hell.

"Yeah, well, that might be an improvement," John added, still laughing.

Nicolas waved goodbye, jumped into his Cadillac SRX, and drove off while playing smooth R&B music by Ronald Isley.

*****

It was Nicolas' first day at work, and he was going to be the best thing that ever walked through those doors. His hands were sweaty, his heart was racing, and butterflies were break dancing in his stomach. His main objective was to learn the ropes. He had his game face on and was determined to learn the ins and outs. He had experience working in The Big Apple, so how hard could it be in Jersey? Just point him in the right direction, and he'll take care of the rest. As long as he kept his head on straight, he was sure to gain cool points like he did in New York once they saw him coming. You couldn't tell him shit; his confidence was overwhelming.

CHAPTER EIGHTEEN

Torn Feelings

Tammy got out of bed a little after seven in the morning, freshened up, and then headed for the spare room, where she began looking through the boxes for her diary.

"Where is it? Where did I put it?" She went through several boxes before she found it. "Here it is!" she called out, pulling out her pink, cloth-covered diary with its attached matching pink pen.

She sat down on the floor Indian style and opened the book. She then took the slender pen and began to write.

Dear Diary:

Yesterday was a very interesting day. We finally moved into our new home. Nicolas' mom couldn't wait to see where we live, so she paid us a visit. She sure is nosey—but funny as hell. I think she gets a kick out of embarrassing Nick. He doesn't like it one bit, but I find it hilarious. She's somewhat okay. But, our relationship would be a lot better if she weren't so nosey and if she didn't run her mouth as much.

No matter what we do or say around her, she calls all her nosey friends from church and tells them everything. So, when Nick and I were going to church, they would whisper and give us funny looks. That's why we haven't been to church in almost a year now. Hopefully, we'll find a church here where the people mind their own business.

Now, as for the house—I love it! The biggest problem is all the unpacking we still have to do and the fact we need a bigger bedroom. One of the neighbors—John—stopped by and introduced himself. He's not at all attractive, but he seems like a nice man who deserves a good woman. He told us that there's a rapist on the loose in the neighborhood. I guess I should lock myself in the house all day while Nick's at work.

NOT!

I'm sorry. I just can't sit around the house all day and do nothing. I want to go out and explore my new surroundings. If I imprison myself in this new house, I'll stress out. I have to go out and get some air before I lose my mind. I'll do some shopping! That always relaxes me. Nick wants me to be a prisoner in my own home, but what's stopping this rapist from coming in here? It ain't like we got an alarm system.

YEAH...LIKE THAT WOULD PROTECT ME!

I just can't let some sick-minded psycho trap me in my own home. So...

I'M OUTTA HERE!

Sighing, Tammy closed the diary and placed it back in the box. Next, she put on a white Ralph Lauren sundress and matching Ralph Lauren four-inch, open-toe sandals, nothing fancy. Even though she refused to stay locked inside her house, she didn't want to draw any added attention to herself, especially with a rapist on the loose. After grabbing her purse and house keys, she headed out the front door. In her haste, she forgot her cell phone on the bedroom dresser.

"Hey, Mrs. Coles," a gravelly voice yelled from behind her, as she was locking the front door.   Startled by the deepness of the timbre, she spun around quickly to see John standing in his yard watering his bushes.

"Oh, hi, John." Tammy smiled, relieved to see it was her neighbor. "I see that you're watering your grass."

"Yep. Trying to maintain this property," John replied, turning off the water and throwing the green garden hose on the ground. "Where ya headed?" he asked, while drying his hands on the side of his pants.

Dear God, what does this perverted-looking man want from me? His smile gives me the creeps. I hope he's not trying to be that extra friendly neighbor when Nick's not around. This guy is geeky weird.

Nervous, Tammy rubbed the back of her neck. "I'm heading to the store to do some grocery shopping," she said with a tremor in her tone.

John's head jerked back as if she were speaking a foreign language. "Food shopping?" he uttered with a stunned look. "Do you realize how far it is to the nearest grocery store?"

"I saw one not too far from here when we bought the furniture." She looked up and down the street as if she expected the store to rise up in plan view.

John laughed and shook his head, his hair looking like it could benefit from a shampoo. Taking it as a sign of disrespect, Tammy asked in an unpleasant tone, "What's so funny?"

"That wasn't a grocery store you passed. That was one of those dollar stores," John informed her, chuckling.

"A dollar store?" she barked. Her face was flushed with embarrassment.

John sucked his gut in and adjusted his belt. "Yep, and even if you wanted something from that place, the dollar store is quite a long way from here. You'd have to take that into consideration and figure out how you'd carry your shopping bags back by yourself in those heels." He pointed down at her four-inch sandals as her eyes followed.

"I'll be alright," she responded, her eyes now focusing on the clovers growing among the blades of grass.

John put his hands on his hips like a comic book superhero and took a deep breath, expanding his scrawny chest. "Why don't you take a cab?" He pointed to the taxi parked in his driveway. "My cab."

Since Tammy had no transportation, this was the opportunity John needed to make some extra money.

She shook her head, and while holding on to what little pride she still had left, she replied, "That's okay. I'll walk."

"It's on me. Plus, I'll take you to a nice grocery store that's only five minutes away. It's new, and you'll like it," he said, trying to convince her that he meant no harm.

Tammy paused, thinking about it for a moment. She could find no wrong in getting a ride to the store. "Well, okay, but as long as you bring me right back."

"No problem. I'm tryin' to get as many customers as possible, but this one here is on the house. I'm just hoping you'll enjoy my services and become one of my regulars," John told her, while walking toward his taxi. After opening the rear passenger door for Tammy, he said, "Now let's go shopping!"

Dear God, please don't let him put those terrifying hands on me, Tammy prayed as she got into the cab. "Thank you," she said, looking up at him before he closed the door.

To her surprise, John's taxi was so clean that it looked like it had just returned from a detail shop, and it smelled like fresh vanilla inside. The seats were covered in light grey cloth, and a silver cross on a chain hung from the rearview mirror. To Tammy, the cross was a clear sign that John was a God-fearing man, so with a sense of security, she settled deep into the seat and put on her seatbelt.

"You're welcome," John said, closing his door.

Once behind the steering wheel, he pulled his keychain from the pocket of his faded jeans. The keychain had at least thirty keys on it.

"Geez, you'd think I was a school janitor with all these keys! Aha, there you are." He placed the key in the ignition and started the car. "And away we go," he said, while slowly pulling out of the driveway. "So, Tammy, what type of music do you listen to?" he asked, reaching for the knob of the radio as they cruised down the road.

"It doesn't matter. I'm flexible," she replied, while enjoying the ride and getting a good view of the neighborhood.

The temperature was a perfect eighty-four degrees, so Tammy decided to let her window down to enjoy the cool breeze. She loved how the big oak trees lined the roads with silver antique streetlights alongside them. This was a historical neighborhood with lots of stories to tell. John turned the radio station to some opera music. It didn't matter, because her hearing suppressed it.

"So how long have you and Nicolas been married?"

"About five years now." Tammy began to feel a little uncomfortable sitting in John's cab.

Yeah, I see where you're going with this. Not in this lifetime boss playa. She thought to herself.

"How's the married life?"

"It's wonderful. Why do you ask?" She sounded defensive, and her face began to form an unmistakable scowl.

"Well, you know—he's black and you're white." John shrugged his shoulders. "I'm just curious to know how you two were strong enough to last this long."

Seeing that he meant no harm, she smiled with her eyes closed, remembering their wedding. Her alabaster cheeks flushed with warmth. "Well, during the first two years, I wasn't sure if we would make it this long, and it's still very hard at times. But, with a warm smile and a soft kiss, Nick always reassures me that against all odds, everything is going to be just fine."

"That's good to hear," John said, watching her through the rearview mirror. "A lot of marriages don't last very long in today's society. I love to see a couple staying together no matter what life throws at them. You make sure the whole world knows that love will prevail, and God will find a way to balance everything else out."

Tammy leaned back in her seat, relieved that the tension of the biracial questions had passed. Now it was her turn to pick his brain and learn a little more about her new neighbor.

"So what about you, John? Is there a woman in your life?"

John quickly glanced up at her through the rearview mirror. Her innocent eyes were enough to tame a beast.

"Not anymore." He shook his head, lips folded outward.

Tammy detected a note of sadness in his voice. "What do you mean?" Her soft green eyes displayed mournfulness.

"I caught my wife, Maryann, in bed with another man." His expression became hard and cold.

Tammy felt an instant sympathy for this funny-looking man she hardly knew. "Oh my, I'm so sorry. No one should have to go through something like that."

"Well, it was really hard." His voice was low and filled with pain.

"So what did you do?" she pressed on, eager to hear more.

"Nothing," he blurted out so easily, like that was the end of the story, but Tammy wasn't going to let that happen.

"What do you mean nothing? You had to have done something. How long were you with her?" she asked, digging for more details. The anxiousness in her voice was starting to show on her face.

"Thirteen years." He chuckled as if he couldn't believe it himself.

"Thirteen years!" she shouted. "That's a long time. What happened?"

"Well, one day, I came home from work. I was working construction before my accident," he said, forgetting he had already told her and Nicolas that bit of information when he came to welcome them to the neighborhood. "I went home early that day, because it was raining. You can't work construction when it rains, so we got the day off. As soon as I walked into the house, I knew something wasn't quite right. You know that feeling you get when something is wrong with the picture? Like something in the room is misplaced or moved to where it doesn't belong?"

Tammy nodded her head in agreement, not saying a word. She sat there like an adolescent being read an amazing story.

"Well, my wife was usually up cooking or cleaning while I was at work. However, the house was quiet that day. The TV wasn't even on. It wasn't like her to be in bed around that time of day. I say it had to be close to lunchtime...eleven or twelvish. So, I went upstairs to the bedroom to make sure she was okay." John paused for a moment, as if he were holding back some angry or hurtful tears. "When I went in the bedroom, there she was sleeping in our bed with another man. I couldn't believe they were all hugged up in my bed like I didn't exist. It was bad enough they had sex in my house, but to actually fall asleep after sex in our bed was a sure sign of disrespect. So, I just grabbed some clothes and left everything else behind."

Tammy leaned forward in her seat, intrigued and bright-eyed. "What happened to the guy she was with?"

"Aw, he was some young guy who spent his life in and out of jail. It didn't last long at all."

"So she lost a good man with a good job...and for what? A few minutes of pleasure that led to nothing but heartache and pain," Tammy said softly, feeling even sorrier for John.

"Yep, that's what she did alright," he announced in agreement.

"Did you ever hear from her again?"

He laughed, a half smile gracing his face. He looked as though he was struggling with his emotions.

"Once. Right after we got divorced, she begged me to take her back, and I really thought about it, but I couldn't get the picture of her and that guy together in our bed out of my head, though. So, I told her no, and when I said that, she thought she was going to keep everything and take half my pension, too. But, the judge ruled in my favor. She was left with nothing."

"You seem to be a good man. The right woman will come along and sweep you off your feet," Tammy reassured him, placing her left hand on his shoulder.

"Why, thank you, Tammy, but I'm too big and old now to be swept off my feet. Anyway, I'm content with my life, and at my age, I can't have a woman changing up my lifestyle."

"Change up your lifestyle? It doesn't seem like there's a lot to change. You seem like a decent man with your head on your shoulders. Don't you ever get lonely?"

His head rose, looking vacantly through the rearview mirror until their eyes met.

"I'm just used to the peace and quiet I have now. Plus, I couldn't deal with the nagging and bickering like my ex-wife put me through."

"Well, peace and quiet sounds okay and all, as long as you're not the Merchantville rapist or the mob's hit-man," Tammy said jokingly, with a natural humor and beautiful smile that put people at ease.

"Awww…that's cold." John laughed it off. "Why would you say something like that?"

"I watch a lot of detective shows, and it always ends up being someone that's been hurt in the past or someone you least suspect. You have a few signs of being one of the two."

"And what are the signs, Detective Tammy?"

"That's *Mrs. Detective Tammy* to you, mister." She giggled, alleviating all tension that lingered.

After talking to John for a few minutes, she realized he wasn't so bad after all. Just misunderstood by his unusual appearance.

"You've been heartbroken, and it caused you to isolate yourself from everyone."

"Hold up. Let me stop you there a moment, *Mrs. Detective Tammy*. I never said I was an innocent hermit. You know, when I hit the clubs at night, the ladies call me Poppa Disco," he said confidently, rubbing his hand across his chin.

"Poppa Disco?" She imagined him in a white Elvis Presley suit dancing like John Travolta under disco lights.

"Ya darn skippy! As soon as I enter the clubs, I hit that dance floor, partying 'til closing time, surrounded by all kinds of lovely ladies. I'm a female magnet. Don't let my quietness fool you. I have all types of honeys sneaking in and out of my house all hours of the night."

"Stop playin'! They only come around because your cab is out front and they need a ride home. Now, how 'bout that," Tammy said, and they both guffawed.

"Now that was a good one. I can't top that."

Laughing, he snorted through his nose. Tammy found it hilarious and couldn't stop laughing. After pulling into a parking lot, he turned around in his seat to face Tammy, giving her his full attention. They both exhaled.

"Alright, here's the supermarket, *Mrs. Detective Tammy*. Girl, you're funny as hell." He took a deep breath and gave her a warm smile. The kind of smile a proud father gives his daughter. "You do your shopping, and I'll wait for you right here. Take as long as you want. I've got all day."

"Thank you, John. I promise not to be too long, because I'm not finished interrogating you yet," she said, waving her finger at him.

Tammy got out of the car, while John bellowed in his seat.

CHAPTER NINETEEN

Doing a Little Shopping

While approaching Wegman's Market, Tammy noticed an elderly white woman in a long white apron and a tall chef's hat standing at a table outside of the store. The aroma of vegetable soup wafted through the air.

As she approached the table, the woman spoke to her. "Hello, ma'am. Care to taste some homemade soup?"

The delicious smell coming from the pot made Tammy's empty stomach growl. "Yes, I would love to." Her eyes lit up with anticipation.

The woman submerged a small ladle into the pot, stirred the hot soup, then brought the ladle up filled with vegetables and broth and poured it into a small cup.

"Here you go. Be careful. It's hot." She carefully handed the cup to Tammy, who immediately tasted it.

"Mmmmm...this is delicious." Tammy's smile widened in satisfaction. "It's been a long time since I've had homemade soup. I usually get the Campbell's brand."

Back in New York, the street vendors served a variety of foods, but she couldn't remember ever buying soup that tasted this good.

"Where can I get this?" she asked the woman with true interest.

"Honey, jus' go to the deli in the back of the store. You can't miss it. You can buy an individual serving or enough to feed yo' family," the woman replied, laughing as she eyed the next potential customers walking toward her.

"Okay, thank you very much." Tammy tossed the small sample cup into a trash container nearby and kept it moving.

Entering the store, she noticed how clean it was and how fresh the food looked. Everything was neat and stacked correctly for convenience. The store was very bright and had aisles wide enough for a car to pass through. Scanning the store, Tammy failed to notice the police officer standing in front of her and accidentally bumped him with her shopping cart.

"Oh, excuse me, sir," she muttered indistinctly, too embarrassed to look up.

"You're excused, pretty lady," he said, smiling.

Startled by his comment, she gave him a puzzled look, her green eyes sparkling with curiosity and flirtation.

"Peter! Peter Wright! Is that you?" She said, over whelmed with excitement.

"Tammy! Tammy Spenser! Is that you?" he responded, mocking her every word. He smiled with recognition, while reaching over to touch her arm.

Tammy pulled away before he made contact. "That's Mrs. Tammy Coles to you, Mister Officer."

Peter looked as if he stuck his finger in an electrical outlet. Something he did when he took a person lightly. "Well, excuse me, *Mrs. Tammy Coles*. So how have you been?"

Back in high school, Tammy loved to role-play and change her name up whenever she saw Pete. So he took her new name lightly.

"I've been okay." A smile formed on her face.

"What are you doing way out here?" He playfully pushed her backwards.

Tammy threw both hands in the air, imitating a suspect at gunpoint. "Watch it, Mister Officer. That's an assault charge."

"Not if I get you for resisting arrest," he joked.

"Ay, good one!" She waved her finger as they both shared a laugh. "So what's going on with you?"

Tammy bounced up and down on her toes like a three-year-old child that couldn't keep still. "Well, my husband and I decided to move out here and start a family."

The look on his face portrayed his disappointment.

"Husband?" Peter choked. "I didn't know you got married. I thought you were kidding when you said Coles was your last name. So where did you move to, Mrs. Coles?" He cleared his throat.

"Merchantville, Officer Peter Wright."

His eyes flashed with this new knowledge "I live in Merchantville myself," he told her, revealing his teeth over his bottom lip.

Excited now, she gave him an even bigger smile. "You do?"

"Yeah." He nodded, his face looking like he was meditating on a distant memory.

Tammy and Peter had gone to high school together, and she immediately recognized it was the same flirtatious look he used to give her whenever he wanted more than just dinner and a movie. Along with him being in uniform made it almost irresistible! She had to keep in mind that she was a married woman.

"That's good to hear. I see you're part of Merchantville's finest." She checked him out, thinking he must have been lifting weights to have a set of shoulders filling out his uniform like a UFC fighter.

Peter shrugged his manly shoulders, not realizing the effect he had on the woman, or did he. He continued talking like he wasn't melting her insides just with his presence.

"It's a living, and I enjoy what I do."

"That's good. I like to hear that. So is there a special someone in your life?" She playfully poked her index finger in his chest.

"No." He lowered his eyes and shook his head. "I still haven't gotten over you yet." He slowly raised his eyes, looking deep into her soft eyes for the reaction he knew he could rouse in her.

Tammy paused, caught by his blue eyes and confident manner, and for a moment, the words lodged in her throat. "That…that was… seven years ago."

"Yeah, I know, but I can't help the way I still feel about you. You left me for some black guy on the basketball team. Whatever happened to him?"

She smiled, thinking about how her man wooed her and got her to wear his ring. "I married him."

Peter winced. "Are you kidding me?"

"No, really, I did." She held up her left hand to show the beautiful three-carat diamond set in an eighteen-carat white gold band.

"Who would have thought that?" He chuckled nervously, apprehensive about his lost love.

"Hey, even I didn't expect it to last this long." She rolled her eyes, grinning like a Cheshire cat, showing her willingness to her former classmate and lover.

They sighed, then stood silently gazing into each other's faces, losing all sense of time and space, desensitizing themselves of their surroundings. Thoughts of "what if" filled her mind. What if she had stayed with Peter and married him instead of Nicolas? What would their future be like? What if they had children? Would he be a good father? Would he treat her better than Nicolas? Could he still satisfy her like the way he did in high school?

Two small boys running up the aisle finally broke their gaze.

Directing his attention back to Tammy, Peter said, "After all this time, you're still looking good. Any children?" He grinned devilishly.

"No, not yet. I'm still trying to maintain this Barbie doll body!"

She sucked in her stomach while standing on her toes, accentuating her already scrumptious figure. Her hands traced her silhouette down the contour of her body.

"You're not looking bad yourself, Officer Wright. You must be eating your spinach and visiting the gym a lot."

She placed her hand on his rock-hard shoulder and gave him a gentle shove.

"Well, thank you very much. I still do a little something at the gym to stay in shape. I'm just not motivated like I used to be when it comes to working out," he said, attempting to portray a fake modesty that wasn't convincing.

"I know what you mean," she agreed, as if she had a membership at a gym.

The only cardio workout Tammy did was at the mall, while shopping and in bed with her husband getting it in, but he was the furthest thing from her mind at that particular moment.

"It's great seeing you again." Peter paused, still checking her out.

The look in his eyes revealed that he was very pleased with what he was seeing. His eyes were filled with lust, and Tammy was loving every minute of it. She had full custody of his attentiveness and was keeping it captive. It had been a long time since they met, and it felt good to know he still wanted her in the worst way, even after all these years.

"Well, I guess I better get back to my grocery shopping."

As she uttered this sentence, she could feel her body having a power struggle with her mind. She wanted the unsolicited and illicit attention, but she knew it was wrong! She was married for God's sake!

Her heart was telling her to stay. *He's a better man now and needs you in his life. He's been waiting for you all these years, and you know you still love him.*

But, her mind was telling her to go. *He's no good for you. You're better off with Nicolas. He will only bring you heartache and pain.*

"Yeah, I have to head on to work," he said breaking her trance.

His eyes could not lie as well as his mouth, and she knew he was thinking the same thing as her. However, her loyalty to Nicolas was the only thing standing in her way...or was it?

There was something in his big, blue eyes that felt like they were pulling her closer. She lowered her eyes to protect herself from giving in so easily. The attraction between them was palpable.

"We sure had great times together." Peter grabbed Tammy's hand. "I just want you to know that not a day has passed that I haven't thought about you."

She quickly tried to turn away, but he locked his eyes on her like a huge tractor beam, refusing to let go. That left her frozen in time, seizing the moment. He leaned over and softly kissed her hand. Tammy's mouth dropped open; she was speechless and felt herself slowly melting in his hands.

Before heading out of the grocery store, Peter gave her a grin that said, *I got you now!* Tammy watched Peter as he walked through the automatic doors and out of sight. Feelings of the distant love they had shared stirred in her heart. She stood there hoping he would come running back into the store and sweep her off her feet, but he didn't. It was only an illusion. Confused by her feelings, she stood there temporarily frozen in time, remembering how much fun they had shared and how he always made her smile. She remained transfixed until an elderly woman bumped into her. The old woman nearly knocked Tammy off balance with her being so preoccupied with Peter walking away.

"Excuse me, young lady. I don't have insurance for this here cart," she cackled in that raspy old person's voice that grates your last nerve.

"Oh, that's okay. I don't have a policy for shopping cart crashes either."

They both shared a laugh.

Realizing she had left John patiently waiting in the parking lot, Tammy grabbed her shopping cart, pulled out her grocery list, and began shopping.

CHAPTER TWENTY

Nicolas' First Day at Work

Nicolas pulled into an available parking spot at his new real estate office, located inside a building on Kings Highway in the uppity part of Cherry Hill. The early morning flow of traffic was heavy, but it still had nothing on the congested streets of New York that constantly stayed at a crawl. It was 7:35 a.m., and Nicolas wasn't due to clock-in until 8:00. So, he sat in his ride thinking, trying to focus on what he needed to do.

This was it, a new beginning. The plan was to get started right away. Once he got his feet wet, he'd be okay. He would later work on getting rich, but first things first. Today he needed to make a good first impression, because that first impression—*good or bad*—would be branded on the memory section of their brains like a tattoo.

He wanted to call Tammy and tell her how much he missed her, even though they had only been separated for ten minutes. To Nicolas, every minute felt like a day. When they were apart, it made it hard for him to breath. It was like having an asthma attack. It was like someone snatched the oxygen from the air. Nicolas needed Tammy. She was his inhaler. He adored her so much, his delicate flower, so soft and fragile. Every time he laid eyes on her, it brought joy to his heart and a smile on his face.

He pulled the sun visor down and stared at his reflection in the mirror to make sure his collar was sharp and the knot in his tie was perfect.

So this is where my life really begins, he thought. *Right here in this big-ass building. One could get lost in a place like this. But, a company this big does generate a huge cash flow. The one back home was pretty big, but not as big as this one.*

The building was massive and looked more like a museum than a business. Its main entrance consisted of two huge double-glass doors with large brass handles. The walls and flooring in the foyer were covered in white obsidian marble tiles, with specks of dark brown, green, white, and black spindled in it like pepper. Expensive paintings and artwork hung from the walls. Thirty feet above him was a massive crystal chandelier, its prisms sparkling like Leo diamonds. It glittered with brilliant colors as if a rainbow had exploded, and the shattered colors filled the room. A huge vase sat on a large pedestal in the middle of the main foyer. There were many different companies that shared this building, including State Farm Insurance, Brinks Home Security, and Bolwicz Law Firm. Everything needed to sell or purchase a home was located inside the twelve-story high-rise.

"Good morning, Mr. Coles!" a loud voice called behind him.

Nicolas turned around to see Bill Satario, the CEO.

"Good morning, Mr. Satario," he responded, his voice timid, muted by his footsteps across the marble floor.

Bill adjusted his pants before shaking Nicolas' hand. Nicolas remembered seeing Bill's picture hanging above the time clock in the New York branch. He had memorized that face before he transferred from the old office, because it was the one face he would see whenever coming to or leaving from work.

"Please, call me Bill. I like that better." Bill Satario's smile was reassuring. "Plus, Mr. Satario makes me feel old." Yeah, he was living in denial.

Standing six-foot, two inches, Bill was a lot taller than Nicolas and overweight with a big potbelly that could compete with Kris Kringle. He was dressed well in a Stuart Hughes tailor-made suit and wore expensive black handmade leather shoes by Giorgio Brutini. On the other hand, his toupee looked like a cutout piece of rug sitting on the top of his head. His clothes told of a man who spared no expenses, but the toupee showed he was still dealing with a lot of insecurities that the expensive gear could not conceal.

Nicolas paused for a moment, choosing his words carefully. "Okay, sir...I mean, Bill."

"You have your Jersey realtor's license handy?" Bill asked, with his hand held out.

"Yes, right here." Nicolas reached in the inner pocket of his suit jacket, pulled out his New Jersey real estate license, and handed it to Bill.

He looked it over, handed it back to Nicolas, and placed his right arm around his shoulders like a proud father would do his son.

"Well, Nicolas, here we are...one big family!" Bill said as co-workers passed by in a rush. "Everyone here gets along, and that makes the job a whole lot easier and less stressful. You do understand this?" He squeezed Nicolas' shoulders tighter.

"Yes, sir...I mean, Bill," Nicolas stuttered, feeling uncomfortable calling his new boss by his first name. He had seen Satario's name and photo on walls, computers, and television, but actually seeing the boss in person and calling him by his first name made him feel awkward. Bill Satario was a very respectable man, like a celebrity, and Nicolas' mother always told him that calling your boss or an adult by their first name was a sign of disrespect.

"Don't worry about it," he said with an Italian accent. "A better work environment makes a stronger foundation. So, whenever there's a problem, come see me, and we'll find a way to work it out."

Bill and Nicolas walked down the brightly lit hallway toward a huge, solid oak door.

"Well, Nicolas, here we are. Make yourself at home, but first take care of all the paperwork. Then hit the streets and move those properties," Bill said, opening the massive door. He hiked up his pants and jerked his head for Nicolas to enter.

As they entered Nicolas' new office, Nicolas tried to hold back the excitement mounting in his chest, but his external appearance sold him out.

"If you need anything, feel free to call me," Bill said before closing the door behind him, leaving Nicolas alone to take it all in.

Nicolas stood there with his mouth open, but no words came out. It was as if someone had hit the mute button.

Aw, man, Nicolas thought. *I can't believe it. I've never had my own office, just a small cubical shared with other realtors, which made it hard to use the phone with all the noise and telephones ringin'. I would spend my time out in the field buyin' or sellin' homes, because I was able to get more work done and it helped me keep my sanity.*

With Nicolas now having his own office, he felt important and had more privacy to do his job more effectively. He was sold already and needed to get himself together. Normally, he never had a problem talking to people, but Bill had caught him off guard.

I can't believe that guy had me stutterin' like Porky Pig. But, it's all good, though. All I gotta do is stay focused.

CHAPTER TWENTY-ONE

Making a First Impression

Nicolas, who was really feeling himself, took the time to take in his surroundings. He marveled at his new office, which included charcoal gray carpeting and a solid oak desk complete with a black Herman Miller chair. The walls were devoid of art, but he had a few things in mind that he wanted to hang on them to give the office that finishing touch. It would most likely be something connected to his beloved New York Giants football team. Even though he moved to New Jersey, he was still a die hard Giants fan.

Nicolas made a mental note to fill the oak bookshelf that stood along one wall with as many books as possible. He believed it would give him a more professional appearance for his clients. *Appearance is everythin'*, he thought. Behind his desk was a tinted glass window that provided a nice view from his second-floor office down to where the employees rushed back and forth to work. The object of the game was to look busy. Well, they wouldn't have to worry about that. Nicolas was a team player and good at looking busy.

"If you want a better view, you'll have to work your way up to the top floor," said a young man of Italian descent, while entering Nicolas' office. "Depends on how many homes you sell with this company."

The man wore a hot pink shirt with the top three buttons open, revealing a thin, gold chain. His dark blue suit was custom made, maybe Alexander Amosu or Ermenegildo Zegna. His hair was thick and curly.

"Hello there! You must be Nicolas Coles," he said, his broad, friendly smile revealing flawlessly white teeth.

As smooth as Nicolas was, he could clearly see this guy was smooth, as well. Maybe even smoother than him. He had a GQ pretty-boy look with a rough edge. His open shirt and gold chain gave more cockiness to his style. His attire screamed fashion, not business. Laid back with a carefree attitude, the man had a hint of soul, and the tone of his voice denoted he had been raised around black folks. Yeah, the guy was too cool for this job.

"My name's Antonio Satario, but you can call me Tony. Oh by the way, if they haven't told you yet, Bill is my uncle. So, I do get away with a lot of shit around here, but I still get the job done."

The two men shared a knowing grin.

"Gary Hanson was scheduled to train you today, but he came down with a cold and called out sick. As usual! So, that leaves you stuck with me as your trainer...the one guy my uncle Bill is afraid of, because he thinks I'm goin' to corrupt you and have you thinkin' you can do what ever you want and get away with it. So, for the record, that is not true, and it will not happen. Understand?" His deep tone carried weight.

"Loud and clear!" Nicolas howled with a mock salute, feeling like he was answering a drill sergeant on his first day of boot camp.

"Now that we cleared that up, let's get somethin' to eat." Tony rubbed his stomach.

Nicolas looked up at the hand carved wooden clock hanging above the door. "But I just walked in here thirty minutes ago."

"Ah, you need to get some breakfast up in you before you hit the field."

Feeling uncomfortable about the situation and fearing the impact it might have on his job, Nicolas replied, "I'm good. I had breakfast already."

"Well, I didn't. And I can't train you right without a good breakfast." Tony held open the office door. "So, let's go. We ain't got all day, you know," he demanded.

Nicolas threw up his hands to calm Tony down. "Yo, fall back, playa. This is my first day," he said, standing ground like a fire hydrant, refusing to move.

Tony flashed a devilish grin. "Be easy, dawg. You have nothin' to worry about. You're bein' trained by the best. So relax! Have fun! I got this." He pounded his chest.

Nicolas was hesitant to go, fearing the consequences he'd face if he got on the boss's wrong side. However, Tony, arrogant and cocky, seemed unfazed about leaving the workplace during working hours for personal gain.

Maybe this guy really does have a juice card and his uncle allows him to do whatever he wants.

"A'ight, let's do this." Nicolas was easily persuaded.

"That's what I'm talkin' bout. Follow me. I'll lead the way," Tony said, his head bobbing in time with his natural swagger.

This muhfucka got swag, thought Nicolas.

The two men headed down the hallway and stopped by the break room filled with female co-workers getting their morning cup of coffee. Everyone was already staring at them. The room had over a dozen long tables in rows of two, with soda and snack machines lined up against the walls. Tony introduced Nicolas to the women.

"Hello, everyone! This here is our new co-worker Nicolas. He transferred from the New York office," he shouted, before turning to Nicolas. The excitement in his voice displayed his joy with having a new co-worker. "Nicolas, this is everyone."

The women greeted him simultaneously. Smiles and whispers lit up the room as he introduced himself with handshakes and head nods.

Nicolas' face was flushed, and his palms were getting sweaty from nervousness, feeling like he was on a rerun of *Cheers*. However, he remained cool on the outside, and that's all that mattered for now.

Tony grabbed Nicolas by the shoulders and turned him around. "Hey, wha—"

Tony interrupted him before he could form a sentence.

"Shut up and take a look at that."

Nicolas was instantly filled with elation. His eyes widened as he feasted on a visual treat. Standing on the other side of the room was a tall, sexy woman with smooth, chocolate-covered skin and light brown shoulder-length hair. Her eyes were golden brown like a tigress. Her eyebrows were superbly trimmed and even on both sides as if sculpted by a professional artist. She was built like Serena Williams, evenly toned with no fat. Her hips flared from a waist that looked small enough for a man to completely wrap both hands around and still be able to touch all fingertips. This woman was blessed with a gorgeous ass that pushed out the back of her dress, stretching the material taut. The fabric gave that alluring sense of hollowness between her cheeks as if she were not wearing panties.

Nicolas had never been interested in tennis until Serena Williams showed up on the court. After that, he never missed a match, watching her run up and down the court with her fine ass. However, this woman standing in front of him was the next best thing to Serena. She was definitely God's greatest creation. He was certain that no matter what she did in the past, all her sins had been automatically forgiven, and her beauty alone was a free pass into the pearly gates of heaven.

The woman was professionally dressed in a black V-neck sleeveless blouse, showcasing full breasts that needed no support. Her nipples pointed straight out like rocket launchers aimed and locked on their targets, indicating she wore no bra. Her arms were nicely toned, the product of a health and fitness club, and her black skirt stopped a few inches above her knees, displaying her well-toned legs and silky skin. This woman's seductive look and killer body was unquestionably voluptuous. Her mesmerizing hazel eyes pulled Nicolas in like a powerful magnet. She looked like she had stepped off the front cover of *King Magazine*. She attracted attention like water attracted ducks. Over all, she was sexy and her body flawless—a perfect ten. To call her a model was an understatement. She was a Nubian goddess.

Nicolas fell in love the moment he laid eyes on her. *Now...would you look at that fine piece of ass standing before me,* he thought to himself, lost momentarily in a fantasy. Her oily skin glistened under the bright lights. He could feel the blood rushing to his love muscle, engorging it. Nicolas badly wanted to get to know her, to hold her close to him, to feel himself deep inside of her. Just to smell and taste her lovely fragrance. He wanted to pick her brain to see how her mind worked. He wanted all these things and more.

Through her peripheral vision, she noticed the twosome staring and began to saunter toward them in her six-inch stilettos that made her look like she was six feet tall. The tapping sound of her heels on the marble floor was rhythmic. It was like music to Nicolas' ears.

Uh oh, she's comin' this way. Time to put on my game face, he thought.

"Hi, my name is Kimberly Davis. I'm pleased to meet you," she said casually, giving off a sweet scent of strawberries.

Her voice was soft over the loud chatter that filled the room. Her approach was strong and direct as she extended her right hand, displaying perfectly French-manicured nails.

Slowly melting in front of her, Nicolas gave her a soft handshake. "The pleasure is all mine," he responded flirtatiously, hoping to capture her attention.

"She works out!" Tony blurted, destroying the mood.

Nicolas, still maintaining his cool, giving her a half-smirk.

"Don't pay him any mind," Kimberly said, her eyes still locked on Nicolas' like a pit bull refusing to let go. "He just wants a little attention. And just so you know, this is all natural," she added, while seductively rubbing her hands over her shapely hips.

"I love when she does that!" Tony said, fidgeting with excitement like a kid in a candy store.

Nicolas smirked at Tony, while mentally taking back any idea that Tony was smoother than him. At that moment, Tony had lost all cool points in Nicolas' book, but working with Kim could do that to any man.

"You look so young. How old are you?" she asked.

Nicolas was still taking in her beauty before her words registered.

"Twenty-six," he blurted out.

"Twenty-six! You look more like nineteen, twenty." She looked him over with skepticism.

Nicolas responded with a light chuckle. She had him feeling very uncomfortable.

"So how old are you?" he asked to break the tension.

Kim gave him a deep gaze that made Nicolas' knees buckle. "If I tell ya, then I'll have to kill ya. You'll have to use your own imagination."

Great choice of words, thought Nicolas. He knew he would be using his imagination in overtime with that fine piece strutting around the office. He knew asking her age was not the right thing to do, but the pressure was too much to bear. He needed some kind of scapegoat before she ended up making him cum in his pants.

"Don't let Tony get you in trouble. I would hate to see you go because of him," Kimberly warned Nicolas, with a smile that displayed utterly white, straight teeth.

Everyone here must have a great dental plan, Nicolas thought.

She slowly spun around and walked away with an extra sway in her hips, like a pendulum in a grandfather clock. Each cheek swelled with every step she took, causing the lower back end of her skirt to whip side to side with force. Like a lion tamer at the UniverSoul Circus, she had all the guys in the office ready and willing to leap through a ring of fire on command. If she was looking for attention, she surely got it with that walk. The men gazed in her direction, hypnotized by her walk, each lost in his own lustful thoughts.

Tony turned toward Nicolas. "Did you see how she looked at you, man?"

He spoke in an undertone, hitting Nicolas on the shoulder, but Nicolas played dumb.

"No! How did she look at me?" He gave Tony a sarcastically serious look.

Nicolas knew what Tony was trying to insinuate, but this was his first day on the job, and he didn't know Tony well enough to express his feelings about Kimberly. For all Nicolas knew, it could have been a setup to send him back to the New York office—or worse—have him terminated for sexual harassment.

Tony looked around to see if anyone was close enough to hear their conversation. Then, while leaning up against Nicolas' side, he said in a loud whisper, "Man, I've never seen her show anyone that much attention. I think she wants to give you some play, and I'm jealous as hell, because she wouldn't give me the time of day. Maybe I need to darken my skin up some," inspecting his skin tone by raising each arm close to his face.

Tony laughed, but Nicolas didn't respond or show emotion. Tony must've noticed the seriousness in Nicolas' face, because he quickly gathered himself, substituting his cheerful look to a muted expression.

"Nicolas, are you married or somethin'?" he asked in a reedy voice. "You seem awfully uptight."

"Yes, I'm a happily married man," Nicolas responded, as the other voices in the room seemed to blend together.

Tony punched Nicolas lightly on the arm. "Ha! That's what you're supposed to tell them to make them want you even more. But, you still mess around a little, right?"

Nicolas' head jerked back and his eyebrows furrowed. "No, I don't."

"Well, *Mr. Good Guy*, workin' with Kim will help you change that attitude real quick. Come on, let's go eat."

CHAPTER TWENTY-TWO

Mind Blower

"Nick, let's take my cah," Tony said with an accent, as he and Nicolas walked through the parking lot.

"Cool, fine with me." Nicolas uttered, knowing he didn't know the areas that well. Tony drove a jet-black whip of an unknown make and model. The exterior had a shine that looked like black glass. It was a beauty—nice chrome rims, tinted windows, and chrome grill with a spider web design. Definitely a car kit, but an expensive one. Equipped with custom wing, integrated air intakes on the side, and an outsized sunroof, it was a sweet ride and judging from the body, it could have been a Mercedes CL550 or BMW 740. The personalized license plate read: BLK-OUT. He definitely rode in style.

"Oh man, what is this?" Nicolas asked.

"I would tell ya, but then I'd have to kill ya before Kim does for askin' her age," Tony said, dodging the question with a cocky smirk. "This bad baby right here is my Black Widow. I customized it myself. Get in. The door is unlocked."

The interior was soft black leather. The stereo system was a Pioneer touch screen monitor with DVD, CD, MP3 player, SD/USB input, navigation, and Bluetooth, with Memphis speakers. When it came to auto entertainment, it did it all except drive the car. This was the top-of-the-line stereo system with additional speakers in the doors and panels.

"So, Nicolas, what do you think?" Tony crowed with pride.

"This thing is hot!" Nicolas sung.

"This right here is my female magnet. There's times when I would find ladies panties on my windshield under the wiper blade like a traffic ticket," Tony joked, relishing his moment with pride.

And Tammy thinks I'm big at exaggeratin' things, Nicolas thought.

When Tony started the engine, it roared like a prehistoric dinosaur. Nicolas could feel it vibrating through the seat.

"Oh, that engine sounds like a beast. It must be a powerful V-8," he yelled over the loud hum.

Tony leaned over toward Nicolas and gave him a hard smile. "V-10, and it's turbo charged with six hundred horse powers under the hood."

He shifted into drive and peeled out of the parking lot, leaving a cloud of smoke. The sudden thrust caused their heads to snap back like they were taking off in an F-4E Phantom II fighter jet.

"I put a lot of money in this bad baby. She's the fastest ride around. You wouldn't believe how many women I've pulled in this. But, as long as I stay focus, I'll always stay on top. My father would always tell me that you lose money chasin' bitches, but you could never lose bitches chasin' money."

The sun was at its brightest. Not a cloud in the sky and the temperature at a nice eighty-six degrees was good enough reason for Tony to cruise with the windows down so everyone outside could get to hear his boomin' system.

"I strongly agree with that, even though I'm happily married." Nicolas checked out the console. "I've never seen so many lights and gadgets. It looks like the Starship Enterprise. Let me guess, you've been racin' against other drivers at the Atco Raceway to see who has the fastest ride, right?"

Tony scowled. "What would you know about the Atco Raceway?"

Nicolas had never been to the racetrack, but he had heard something about it years ago on some television program or commercial. He made up a good story just to see what Tony had to say, just to see where his head was before he opened up to him.

"A buddy of mine loves to race his car out there on the weekends. He would come back and talk about this black whip that he couldn't beat," Nicolas said, baiting him in.

Tony stuck his chest out, with his face contoured and filled with confidence. "Yeah, I've been out there a few times, and so far, I haven't been beaten yet," he said, taking the bait.

These Jersey muhfuckaz is easy, Nicolas thought to himself, working his magic on Tony. Before the week ended, Nicolas would have Tony eating out the palm of his hand.

The interior was clean enough to eat off the floor. "So you were able to get a ride like this workin' as a realtor?"

"Well, I make pretty good money, but I did need a little help from my dad."

"What does he do?" Nicolas asked, imagining what his father's bank account looked like.

"He owns his own collection agency."

Visions of dollar signs flashed before Nicolas' eyes. "Does it pay well?"

"Uh, he lives in a mansion. Need I say more?" Tony said, glancing at Nicolas with shifty eyes.

Nicolas got the message. That look let him know there was a lot of crooked activity going on in his father's business, and Nicolas didn't want any parts of it. The less he knew, the better.

So, he backed away from the subject by saying, "I definitely get the picture."

"Now check out this system," Tony said, breaking the uncomfortable tension. He turned on the stereo for Nicolas to hear the quality of his sound system, but caught the first part of a breaking news report.

When Tony reached out to change the channel, Nicolas caught his arm.

"Hold on. Let me hear this first."

In today's news, a few children playing at The Cooper River Park found another body in Pennsauken, which is right outside of Merchantville. It was the body of an unidentified white woman. It appears to be the work of the Merchantville rapist. Police were also able to collect a few DNA samples from the victim's body. We are unable to get the victim's name or information at this time. The Pennsauken Police Department has a witness who claims to have seen a black Mercury Grand Marquis with a dent in the rear bumper cruising around the area. Make and model are unknown at this time. Police want this person to turn themselves in for questioning. This person is not a suspect. However, investigators believe this person may have vital information that could lead to an arrest. A full investigation is underway, and the rapist's DNA should bring investigators closer to finding out who's behind these brutal murders.

When Nicolas heard the news, his body went cold all over. Could that be Tammy? Nicolas didn't know what to think. His fragile moment of happiness evaporated. If that were Tammy, he wouldn't be able to live with himself. He pulled out his cell phone and pushed the speed dial number to call Tammy.

Tony looked over at him and asked, "Who you callin'?"

"I'm tryin' to call my wife," Nicolas said, starting to lose his patience.

"What for, man? You just got to work!" He made a face that Nicolas had the urge to flatten.

"We live in Merchantville, and she's home by herself."

Tony could hear the panic in Nicolas' voice.

"But the reporter said it was a white woman," Tony said, assuming Nicolas' wife was black.

"My wife is white," Nicolas responded. Tony pulled his whip over to the side of the road and waited while Nicolas dialed Tammy's number again.

"Tony, I ain't gettin' an answer. You've got to take me home right now!" Nicolas demanded, as he listened to the ringing on the other end. "Take me home now!" he repeated desperately.

The seriousness of his tone caught Tony's attention. "No problem. Where you live?"

"My address is 809 Maple Avenue in Merchantville."

"I'll get you there in less than ten minutes," Tony told him, then made a quick U-turn, burning rubber and leaving a trail of smoke behind them.

CHAPTER TWENTY-THREE

Where's My Wife?

After they pulled into the driveway, Nicolas jumped out of the ride and ran inside the house. Tony followed behind him for back up.

"Tammy! Tammy!" Nicolas called out, while frantically running from room to room.

As he called her cell phone again, he heard ringing coming from the bedroom. Nicolas entered the bedroom to find her cell phone on the dresser, but no Tammy.

"She's not here!" Nicolas yelled, dropping to his knees in front of the walk-in closet with its doors open.

"Do you have any idea where she might be?" Tony asked, eager to help as he entered the room.

"No," Nicolas muttered. He dropped his cell phone on the floor and covered his face with his hands, with clothes hanging above his head on hangers.

Tammy was his everything. He needed to find her more than he needed the air in his lungs. His hands started shaking and he felt himself ready to breakdown, but now wouldn't be a good time. So, with his legs trembling, he got up, picked his cell phone up from where he had dropped it on the floor, and headed downstairs.

"I'm calling the police," he said dialing 911.

"Nine-one-one. What's your emergency?" a woman answered flatly.

Adrenaline pumped through Nicolas' body as his heart raced, and he was breathing hard like he had just ran four or five laps around the block.

"My name is Nicolas Coles, and I wanna report my wife missin'."

"When was the last time you saw her?" asked the operator in an uninterested tone.

"This mornin' before I went to work," he stated as he walked over to the front room window and stared out of it.

Just then, John's taxi pulled into the driveway behind Tony's ride and Tammy got out, her arms full of grocery bags. She walked into the house to see Tony standing in the living room with Nicolas.

"Hello, sir. Are you still there?" the operator kept repeating, breaking Nicolas' long gaze.

"Never mind, operator. She just walked into the house," he replied, never taking his eyes off her. "Where have you been?" he demanded in a loud, deep tone while disconnecting the call with the 911 operator.

Tammy placed the bags on the floor. "I was at the grocery store. Can't you tell?" She gestured to the bags with sarcasm, then turned her gaze to Tony. "And how are you doing? My name is Tammy. I'm Nick's wife," she said lightly, giving Tony a smile.

"Glad to meet you. I'm Tony Satario," he responded hesitantly, looking as if he was wondering what would happen next.

"Yeah, sorry about that. Tony, this is my wife Tammy. Tammy, this is Tony." Nicolas' breathing was still rapid and his voice quavered.

Copping an attitude, Tammy placed her hands on her hips, and with her lips tightened, she asked, "Why are you here instead of working?"

Breathing hard now from frustration, Nicolas said, "I *was* at work until I heard that the Merchantville rapist struck again. I was afraid it was your body they found. So, I rushed home to make sure you were okay. But, you weren't here."

Tammy's hard expression softened. "I'm so sorry, honey. I needed a few things from the store and a little fresh air." She spoke in a calm, gentle voice, as if making light of the situation.

Nicolas pointed his finger in her face. "Don't you ever do that again without callin' me first. You had me worried sick," he squealed in a fit of anger.

Tammy smacked his hand away. "First of all, you're going to put that finger down and show me a little more respect, especially in front of a total stranger. What's wrong with you?" she barked.

Nicolas turned to Tony. "Give us a moment here. I'll be out in a few minutes."

Tony nodded his head. "No problem, man. It was nice meetin' you, Mrs. Coles." He waved goodbye, eager to get away from this indoor hurricane.

"Nice meeting you, too, Mr. Satario," Tammy smiled before Tony closed the door behind him, her voice still pleasant.

"How come you didn't take your cell phone with you? I could have had a heart attack worryin' about you," Nicolas announced once Tony left the house.

"Um, for one thing, I forgot to put it in my purse before I left. And you can stop over exaggerating about having a heart attack, Mr. Exaggerator. You're too young for one."

Nicolas wasn't buying the story that she forgot her phone. Not the way she loved to call her mother all through the day and night. The only reason she would leave her cell phone in the house would be to go out and do something she had no business doing.

"Tammy, the alarm won't be installed for another two days. You have to keep your cell phone with you at all times."

"I'm sorry. It was an accident; I forgot. And you didn't have to raise your voice to get your point across, especially in front of someone I hadn't even met."

Thinking it was Tony trying to rush him, the hard knock on the front door angered Nicolas, and he was ready to curse his ass out... maybe even hook off.

"Who the fuck is it?" Nicolas yelled, balling his hands into fists, ready to teach Tony a thing or two about disrespecting a man's home. Even if it cost him his job, it would be worth it.

"Merchantville Police Department! Open up!" a voice boomed from the other side of the door.

Nicolas' anger quickly changed from rage to fear. He gave Tammy a quick glance before opening the door. Two white cops stood their ground in their dress blues. Both stood well over six feet tall and were eager to bust some heads. Not the conformation Nicolas was looking for on a workday morning.

"We received a 9-1-1 emergency phone call about a missing wife. Are you the person who made the call?" the taller officer asked. He appeared to be 240 pounds of sheer muscle and had intimidating tattoos that lined both arms. His eyes looked over Nicolas' head, scanning the foyer.

"I made the call, but I told the operator to cancel it when my wife walked in the door," Nicolas replied with a thin smile, hoping

135

to minimize the hostility that lingered. This was not the attention he was looking for.

"That's understandable, but each time a 9-1-1 call is made, the operator dispatches a unit to the location to make sure everything is okay. So is your wife home?"

"She's here," Nicolas answered, followed by a long pause.

"So where is she?" the officer inquired, peering over Nicolas' head again.

His partner stood just to his right with his feet spread apart and his hand gripping his weapon, looking ready to put a few rounds in Nicolas if provoked.

"She's in the family room. Hold on." Nicolas turned his head and called out, "Tammy! Come let the officers know you're here and everything's okay!"

As Tammy emerged from the other room and started walking toward the front door, she gave the officers a big smile. Both officers' eyes lit up as if overcome by her beauty...or shocked to see Nicolas was married to a white woman. Probably a combination of the two since this was Redneckville!

"Hi, I'm Tammy Coles, the lost wife of Nicolas Coles. Pleased to meet you."

"Nice meeting you, ma'am. Is everything okay?" the officer said, eying her from head to toe.

"Yes, sir. There's no problem here," she said, still smiling at the officers.

The officers exchanged a quick glance at each other, nodded, and then focused their attention back to Tammy. The look they gave Tammy said they meant business.

Not a good sign. Nicolas inwardly cringed.

"When we approached the door, we heard yelling," the officer continued, still stiff as a board.

They gave Nicolas and Tammy the impression that they had drank a gallon of cement and were refusing to move until they got to the bottom of this situation.

Now they were diggin', thought Nicolas apprehensively.

"That was nothing. We were jus' havin' a little disagreement," Nicolas said, beginning to get aggravated with the officers giving Tammy a little too much crude attention.

"I wasn't talking to you, *boy*. I was talking to the young lady here," the taller one barked, giving Nicolas a look hard enough to burn a hole through him.

Nicolas could see the veins protruding out of his tattooed covered neck as if he wanted to pistol-whip the shit out of him! This was more than Nicolas could stand.

"*Boy?* Who the hell are you callin' boy?" he responded in defense. *I know this muthafucka ain't tryna degrade me in front of my wife.*

The officer stepped closer, getting right in Nicolas' face. "I'm talkin' to you, *boy*, so you better know your place. Unless you want some problems."

Nicolas felt helpless and stood there frozen in fear. He knew the officer was looking for a reason to stomp his face in or arrest him on some trumped-up charge. So, Nicolas remained silent, but he didn't break eye contact with the officer. The second officer never said a word; he just stood behind the taller officer with his hand resting on his weapon.

As if Nicolas weren't standing right in front of him, the officer redirected his focus back to Tammy. "Now what was that, ma'am?"

The officer's cockiness was unbearable. Tammy exploded with anger. "You better get the hell off my property before I report you to your supervisor!" she screamed, her blood boiling and her face turning beet red.

"Hey, no problem. Y'all have a pleasant day," the taller officer said, giving a quick nod as he and his partner stepped off the small porch and headed for their patrol car. Tammy slammed the door shut with enough force to shake the house. "They can't talk to you like that and get away with it!" Tammy wailed, shaking in vexation from the officer's comment.

"Or what?" The words ejaculated from his mouth like hot steam. "This is their town, and there's nothing we can do about it."

"We can report them to their supervisor," she roared, hands in a fist so tight that her knuckles were white from lack of blood flow.

"Look, it's our word against theirs. If we go above their heads on this, they'll win and harass me every time I walk out the door. Those muthafuckz can't stand to see a black man with a white woman."

Nicolas had seen this play out too many times. No matter where he and Tammy went, people had a problem with them being together...to the point that it started to affect their marriage. Once, it got so bad that they went to marriage counseling to save their relationship.

With her body fully erect, head in the air, and her hands still balled up in fists, Tammy tried to calm herself down with deep breathing. "I know, and you don't want any problems. But, one day, you're going to get tired of people walking all over you like a doormat." Tension reflected in her gestures. "Nick, I still love you.

So, go to work and make my money, bitch!" Tammy said, while smacking him on the ass.

Remembering that Tony was waiting in his ride and that nothing could be settled now, Nicolas gave Tammy a quick kiss and headed for the door.

"I love you, and I'll see you later. If you leave the house again today, don't forget to take your cell phone," Nicolas told her in his demanding voice.

"I know...I know. I love you, too. You be careful and make it back home safely."

Nicolas looked out front to see that John and his cab were nowhere to be seen, but Tony was still in the driveway patiently waiting. He jumped in the whip with Tony and waved to Tammy as they drove away.

CHAPTER TWENTY-FOUR

Get Down On the Ground

"What was that all about?" Tony questioned after they had cleared the driveway.

"Two redneck cops givin' me a hard way to go." Nicolas was still angry and frustrated.

"Why? Because you're with a white woman?" Tony asked, contouring his face as if he were truly insulted by what had transpired.

Nicolas felt his body tense up again. "Yeah, and we get the same treatment no matter where we go."

"Even in New York?" Tony questioned like a curious schoolboy.

"Hell yeah!" he howled. "That's the main reason why we moved out here. We'll hear it no matter where we go. Even our parents still have a problem with us bein' together."

"Man, that's gotta be rough. Listen, you're gonna have to be careful out here. This is a predominantly white neighborhood, and the cops have a reputation for bein' racist. Now me, I like to mix it up a bit to add a little flavor," Tony joked to soften up the situation. "But, I ain't ready to commit because of those reasons. The day that this..."

Tony's words trailed off as he spotted a patrol car behind them in his rearview mirror, its blue and red lights flashing.

"Now what?" Tony murmured, pulling over to the side of the road. "I was doing the speed limit."

"Just play it cool," Nicolas suggested, as if experienced in this type of situation.

Nicolas flipped the visor down to watch the cops in the mirror. The officer on the passenger side of the patrol car stepped out with his gun drawn and aimed in Nicolas and Tony's direction.

Not a good sign at all.

Nicolas felt his blood run hot and cold at the same damn time.

Then the officer on the driver's side exited the car and used his loudspeaker.

"Driver of the car, turn off the engine," the officer demanded.

Tony obeyed and waited for the officer's next order. The temperature in the vehicle seemed to rise an extra twenty degrees.

"Damn, here we go again!" Nicolas barked in frustration, as if this was a routine ritual.

"Driver of the vehicle, take your right hand and drop the keys on the ground."

Trying to remain calm, Tony began to laugh. "He must be fuckin' wit' us because he's bored to death," he said, pushing the button to allow the window to roll down and dropping the keys to the ground.

Nicolas pushed the button rolling the passenger window down, as well, to let some cool air in, but that didn't help at all.

"Driver of the vehicle, take your right hand and open the car door from the outside of the vehicle. Then step out of the vehicle and walk backward towards us."

"Nicolas, if anything happens to me, let all the sexy women at work know that I loved them, even though they didn't wanna have my baby."

Nicolas didn't know if Tony was serious or trying to make light of the situation.

Too nervous to smile, Nicolas smirked and said, "I'll make sure they get the message."

With a raise of his finger, Tony replied, "Not all of them, just the sexy ones."

"Driver of the vehicle, step out of the vehicle now!" The officer's demanding voice elevated to a more aggressive level.

"Okay, here I go." Tony slowly opened the car door, and while keeping his hands in the air, he stepped out of the vehicle. He stood straight facing away from the officers and started walking backwards toward them.

The officer on the driver's side of the patrol car stepped away from his vehicle with his weapon now drawn. "Stop right there," he ordered.

Estimating he was near the patrol car, Tony stopped and asked, "Now what, Mr. Officer?"

"Get on the ground. Face down with your arms and legs spread open and the palms of your hands facin' upward," ordered the officer with authority lacing his tone.

Complying, Tony laid on the ground as the officer instructed, while he patted him down and cuffed his hands behind his back.

"Why did you pull me over, Mr. Officer?" Tony asked, while still laying on the hot asphalt.

"I have reason to believe there are drugs in your vehicle. Do you mind if I search the vehicle?" the officer asked, removing Tony's wallet from his back pants pocket.

"Yes, I do mind, because I know there's no drugs in my cah, and for all I know, you could be tryin' to plant some on me. I wanna call my lawyer," Tony demanded.

"Well, that's on you then. I'll just call it in and have them fax over a warrant, and we'll see what you're tryin' to hide in there."

"Go right ahead. Knock yourself out. But, I still have a right to call my lawyer, because I know there's nuffin' in there except my registration and insurance cards. Do you know who my lawyer is?" Tony said angrily.

"Frankly, I could give two shits about you and your goddamn lawyer," the officer replied, then walked back to his patrol car and reached for the microphone used to talk through the loudspeaker. He leaned his elbows on the top of the patrol unit's door while using its open door as a shield.

"Passenger of the vehicle, take your left hand and open the car door from the outside of the vehicle. Step out of the car and walk towards me backward."

Nicolas took a deep breath. With his stomach souring, he slowly opened the car door. He got out and began walking backward toward the officer, thinking and hoping maybe this was just a case of mistaken identity. Maybe after seeing they had the wrong people, they'd apologize and let them go. However, no matter how this situation was resolved, Nicolas was determined to report them. The only thing running through Nicolas' head at that moment was to not let this turn into another Rodney King beat down, but if it did, hopefully someone would have enough sense to record it.

"Stop right there." There was a long pause before the officer spoke again. "Are you feeling froggy today, son?"

The nervousness showed in Nicolas' voice. "N...N...No, sir!" he stuttered, trying hard to swallow the tennis ball that magically appeared in his throat.

Were these the same two cops who were just at his house looking for a reason to beat him down? But for what? Why, because they couldn't stand to see him with a white woman, someone who had no interest in them? Nor would it disrupt their choice of living. Memories popped into his head of him and Tammy standing at the alter renewing their vows, with him placing on her finger. The sparkling, expensive ring that took him three years to pay off.

Suddenly, Nicolas snapped back to reality when the officer said, "Get on your knees and place your hands on top of your head."

The officer's familiar tone sent a cold chill up Nicolas' spine.

Nicolas lowered himself to the ground, getting on his knees. His face became drenched with sweat as the officer approached and handcuffed him from behind.

Then while leaning over and patting him down, he whispered in Nicolas' ear, "You didn't think I was goin' to let you go that easy."

The tone of his voice raced through Nicolas' entire skeletal system like a surge of lighting escaping through his fingers and toes. The threat his words carried were unmistakable.

"Especially after you tried to get tough with me earlier in front of your wannabe black bitch. What do you have to say now, *boy*?"

Nicolas' blood turned to ice water when he realized it was the same cops who had been standing at his front door not thirty minutes ago.

When a backup patrol car pulled up, the officer backed off. Nicolas saw three yellow stripes on the officer's sleeve, indicating he was a sergeant from the same precinct, and thought it might be a good thing since he was probably their supervisor.

"What seems to be the problem here, officers?" he said, approaching from his vehicle.

"Well, sir, as they drove past us on Main Street, I smelled what seemed to be marijuana smoke comin' from their vehicle. Permission to search the vehicle, sir?" asked the officer with heavy contempt in his voice.

"Pot smoke! Man, you know there's no drugs in my cah, and I'll gladly take a piss test!" Tony yelled.

"Did they give you the okay to search their vehicle?" the sergeant asked, visually inspecting the area.

"No. I'm waiting on a search warrant as we speak. I was hoping you had it on you."

The sergeant responded with a negative shake of his head. Just then, a K-9 unit pulled up in a Ford Expedition with a drug sniffing canine in the back. The officer got out his patrol unit and handed the sergeant a piece of paper, which Nicolas figured was the search warrant.

The sergeant read the document, looked at the officer, and said, "Permission granted."

The K-9 officer gave Officer Rodeski a quick glance and a half nod before allowing his canine to enter Tony's vehicle. He then looked over at Tony and gave him a smirk as if he was getting pleasure out of all this.

"Sir, I wanna report that officer," Tony said.

"For what?" asked the sergeant in a militant tone.

145

"For harassment and not allowing me to contact my lawyer. The officer knows there's nuffin' in my vehicle. He's bored and doesn't have anything better to do."

"If I were you, I'd let him do his job. Put a lock on that pie hole of yours, if you know what's best for yah," the sergeant said, giving Tony a hard stare.

The K-9 unit officer put his canine on a leash and had the dog sniff the outside of Tony's vehicle before letting the dog climb inside.

"Pets are not allowed in my ride. Now I gots to get it detailed all over again," Tony voiced, disgusted.

The sergeant gave Tony a piercing stare that was sharp enough to bore a hole through him. "You need to watch your mouth. That dog is also an officer. So, I'd think twice about my next choice of words if I were you, or you'll be facin' additional charges," he warned.

Once the officer and dog completed their vehicle search, they approached the sergeant.

"Did you find anything?" Asked the sergeant with expectancy.

"No, sir. They must have gotten rid of it when they saw us coming," Rodeski stated, seeming frustrated that he didn't find anything to pin on them.

"Then send them on their merry way. But, I want a report on my desk before you clock out," the sergeant ordered, then got in his patrol car and drove off with the K-9 unit following close behind.

"Yes, sir," mumbled the tall officer, loud enough for only Nicolas to hear.

The tall officer removed the cuffs from Tony and Nicolas' wrists and handed Tony his wallet. "Now you two fellas head out of here and mind your damn business, unless you're lookin' for more trouble." He gave them a hard grin.

After Nicolas and Tony brushed dirt and gravel off the front of their pants and dress shirts, they headed to the black whip, eager to put some distance between them and this scene of humiliation. Driving off, they could still see the two officers standing by their patrol car, watching observantly, waiting for another opportunity to catch them slipping.

"Damn, what the fuck was that all about?" Tony asked.

Nicolas was still dusting the rest of the dirt off his pants. "Hell if I fuckin' know! Crooked-ass cops."

"Yo, Nick, stop dustin' that shit off in here. Wait 'til you get the fuck out first. That nasty-ass dog did enough damage already!" Tony said, still aggravated.

Nicolas stopped brushing off his pants and put both hands in the air. "Oh, sorry about that, officer," he said mockingly.

"Oh, we got jokes now? You ain't feel like playin' when they pulled us over, though. But, anyway, who the fuck were they?"

Nicolas looked at Tony in dismay. "Those were the same two cops who were at my house earlier."

Tony's jaw dropped, leaving his mouth wide open. "Oh man, now you're on their shit list. You've got to file a report on those two cops so they can have it on record when you cross paths with them again. I got the names of the loud-mouthed cop and the sergeant. Both name tags said M. Rodeski." There was a long pause. "Not good, Nick. Not good at all," Tony whispered, shaking his head.

"So they must be related," Nicolas claimed, checking around for any more bored cops lurking around.

"I couldn't get the name of the officer who was waving his gun around like Jesse James. He kept himself hidden behind the passenger door," Tony said, while making sure to maintain the speed limit.

"Don't worry. I got the license plate number. Take me to the Merchantville Police Station. I'm going to report them to the Department of Internal Affairs," Nicolas said, believing he had enough evidence to press charges on the two officers.

CHAPTER TWENTY-FIVE

Seeking Justice

The Merchantville Police Station was a red brick building with a light brown stucco facade. Its glass door entrance displayed a bronze plaque on the wall to the side that read *Merchantville Police Department* in big, bold letters.

An older, out-of-shape white sergeant with bushy hair sat at the front desk doing a crossword puzzle. His uniform was wrinkled and faded, and he looked as if he had been assigned to permanent desk duty for many years.

Seeing Nicolas and Tony enter, the sergeant pushed the crossword puzzle aside. "May I help you, gentlemen?"

"We wanna speak with someone in Internal Affairs," Nicolas announced, his face and voice reflecting the aggravation and anger he felt.

"Go straight down the hall," the sergeant said, pointing them in the right direction. "You'll find the Internal Affairs office at the end of the hall to your left."

"Thank you," Tony said, showing a little courtesy since Nicolas refused to do so.

As they headed down the hallway, Nicolas glanced back and saw the sergeant talking on the phone. He guessed the sergeant was giving someone in Internal Affairs a heads-up.

A six-foot-six thin black man, with short, clean-cut hair, a goatee, and dressed in a nice two-piece suit, stood in the middle of the hallway. He was drinking a cup of coffee. First impression revealed that he took pride in his appearance. As inexpensive as it was, he made sure his suit was neat and his shoes were shined. He had a lean build and projected a laid-back attitude.

"Hello, gentlemen. I'm Detective Andy Morris. How can I help you?" he said with a firm handshake.

"Ah, first of all, could we speak to you in private?" Nicolas asked in a respectful tone.

"Certainly. Head right through these doors." Detective Morris pushed open a door, which had brown-stained glass that took up forty percent of the door. The words *Detective Andy Morris* were written in blue letters on the glass. The detective closed the door behind them once they entered the room. Metal file cabinets lined two of the walls. A computer sat on a long, black, metal desk, and a black leather armless chair also occupied the room. Nicolas figured this was where the detective spent a majority of his time working.

"Have a seat, gentlemen." Detective Morris motioned toward two wooden chairs in front of his desk. "Now what seems to be the problem?"

He placed his coffee cup on his desk. Then he quickly raised the cup to place a napkin underneath. The aroma of the Starbucks' vanilla latte filled the room.

Nicolas could feel the nervousness building in his stomach. He hated police stations. His only thought was to get this over with so he could continue with his normal life.

"I'm Nicolas Coles, and I'm being harassed by two of your officers."

"Do you know the officers' names?" The detective pulled a notepad from the drawer of his impressive desk. Then he leaned back in his black leather chair and took a pen from his shirt pocket.

"Yes, the one officer's name is M. Rodeski, and his license plate number is MPD-U16, but we didn't get his partner's name." Nicolas said, giving him the proper spelling of the name.

"And I'm a witness to the whole incident," Tony spoke out.

Officer Morris paused for a moment, laced his fingers together, and glared at Tony.

"What's your name and how are you involved?"

"Tony Satario, and I was with Mr. Coles when we were pulled over today."

Detective Morris wrote their names on his legal pad, laid his pen on the desk, and leisurely took a sip of latte. He moved like he had all the time in the world.

Nicolas' eyes scanned the room before landing on the detective's hollow photos of nothingness. The pictures illustrated unimportant images of one's memories. However, to Detective Morris, these were priceless moments of him receiving awards and commendations from his superiors. Additional plaques hung on the walls as mere bragging rights for all his achievements.

"Okay, start from the beginning and tell me why you think my officers are harassing you." Detective Morris picked up his pen and prepared to take notes.

"Well, it all started when I made a 9-1-1 call looking for my wife."

"What? Your wife is a 9-1-1 emergency dispatcher?" Morris asked.

"No." Nicolas shook his head, blowing out hot air.

Nicolas' blood was simmering. He wanted to search through the police station for those two guys who called themselves cops and beat the living shit out of them. But, that wasn't realistic at all, just a violent fantasy for the moment, which could only get him nothing but prison time.

"Let me start further back so you can understand a little better."

"Please do," Morris said, patiently waiting.

"I heard on the radio that the rapist had struck again in our neighborhood, and I panicked when I couldn't reach my wife by phone. So, I had Tony drive me to my house," Nicolas explained, gesturing toward Tony.

"What happened when you got home?" Detective Morris asked, absorbing it like rain to dirt.

"Well, she wasn't there, so I called 9-1-1. But, in the middle of my report to the operator, my wife walked in the house carryin' grocery bags. So, I told the operator to cancel the call, but a few minutes later, two cops showed up at my front door. I explained to them that everythin' was okay, but they didn't wanna accept my word. So, my wife came to the door and told them that everythin' was okay. But, even that wasn't good enough for them. That's when Rodeski thought he was Clint Eastwood and started playin' the Dirty Harry role by threatenin' me for being married to a white woman. His partner even kept his hand on his weapon like he was ready to blow my head off!" Nicolas explained, embellishing the story a little bit.

Detective Morris made notations on his notepad, then looked up at Nicolas. "And what makes you think being married to a white woman has anything to do with the officers' behavior?"

"Well, everything was okay before my wife came to the door. Then when I tried to explain myself, he told me to shut the hell up and called me 'boy' all in the same breath. Now get this. When I left to head back to work with Tony here," Nicolas pointed at Tony again, "they pulled us over with their weapons drawn. They put both of us in handcuffs in the middle of the street. Officer Rodeski said I was showin' off in front of my 'wannabe black bitch'. Then when his sergeant M. Rodeski pulled up, he told him there were drugs in the car," Nicolas said, struggling to remain calm.

Detective Morris frowned and shook his head in disbelief. "Drugs in the car! How would he know that?"

"He told his sergeant that he smelled it comin' from the car when we drove past him and his partner, but the thing is, we never drove past him and his partner. They were followin' us after we left the house."

"Well, my officers been stressin' over the mob boss situation and the Merchantville rapist for the last few days now," Detective Morris said, trying to excuse the officers' behavior.

Nicolas leaned forward in his chair and slammed his fist on the detective's desk. His anger cancelled out all his senses, including pain.

"It wasn't stress that had them drag me from my boy's ride at gunpoint. It was their racist views!"

Detective Morris raised his hand in submission. "Put a leash on that aggression. So you're tellin' me that racism is the reason why my officers are givin' you a hard way to go?"

Nicolas squinted at him hard. "Yes, and my wife was a witness to it."

Detective Morris placed his pen down and gave Nicolas a long, hard gaze. "So where is your wife?"

"She's at home!" A confused expression replaced the anger.

The detective leaned forward in his chair. "She's at home? And why is that?"

Nicolas felt disgusted. He started to feel like he was wasting his time being there, because the detective was acting like he didn't believe a word of his story. And even if he did, would he do anything about it? Everybody knows the police stick up for each other no matter what state or city. It's a brotherhood with a code of honor. Even this black brother appeared to be a part of it.

At that moment, Nicolas became irate. "Well, if you let me finish, then you'll understand why she's not here." He tried to control the rage and fear forming in his gut, a bad combination. His voice was rife with annoyance, as his tone rose with anger.

"Okay, please proceed." The detective leaned back in his chair.

Nicolas swallowed hard and lowered his voice a few decibels. "Well, after standin' in my face makin' verbal threats, my wife jumped in and told him that she was gonna report them. So, they headed for their patrol car and drove off with an attitude radiatin' from them toward me. After they left, my wife and I talked about it for a few minutes, and she suggested I come here and file a report."

"And where was Tony while these officers were harassing you?" Morris asked, appearing to take the report more seriously.

"I was in my cah waitin' to head back to work with Nicolas," Tony blurted out, eager to add his two cents.

"And what type of work do you do?" Detective Morris asked, ignoring Nicolas' theatrics.

"Both Nicolas and I are realtors." Tony smirked, while still maintaining his cool.

"So were you able to hear the officers threatening Mr. Coles from your position in the car?"

Tony threw his hands up, shrugging his shoulders. "I'm afraid not," he admitted, dropping his arms down and smacking his hands against his thighs.

Detective Morris turned his attention back to Nicolas. "Alright, please continue."

"As I was sayin'," Nicolas said sarcastically. "While Tony and I were cruisin' down the road, these same two officers rolled up behind us with their lights flashin'. When we pulled over, they drew their guns and made us get out of the car and lay on the ground."

"So you're tellin' me that they had their weapons *drawn and aimed* at you?" the detective asked, seeming unmoved by the whole situation.

"Yes, they did," Nicolas said, seeing that the detective wasn't convinced.

Turning his attention toward Tony, Detective Morris asked, "Did Mr. Coles give an accurate and truthful account of the events?"

"Yes, sir, he did," Tony affirmed, nodding his head.

"And how do you pronounce your last name again?" Morris asked, holding his pen to his notepad.

"*Sa-ta-ri o*." Tony pronounced his name slowly.

"Spell it for me."

Articulating slowly and savoring each syllable, Tony complied. "*S-A-T-A-R-I-O.*"

"O.I. right?" asked Morris trying to spell it correctly.

"No, I.O."

"And Tony is short for Anthony, right?" Morris asked as if it really mattered.

"Correct."

"Anthony," Detective Morris mumbled, while writing the name on his legal pad. When he finished, he looked up at Nicolas and said, "Okay, Mr. Coles, continue."

"While I was on my knees in handcuffs, Sergeant Rodeski pulled up and Officer Rodeski told him that he smelled drugs in the car. So, the sergeant gave him the okay to search his ride."

The detective pointed to Tony. "Were you there to witness this incident?"

"Oh, I was there alright...in handcuffs. And I didn't appreciate them messin' up my cah after I've put so much money into it. They brought a dog and had the dog sniffin' and lickin' all in my cah. I work hard for my money. There's no need for me to sell or buy drugs! Plus, they refused to let me call my lawyer when I asked them if I could!"

"Did you give them permission to search your vehicle?"

"Hell no, I did not. So they had some K-9 unit officer get a search warrant. For all I know, it could have just been a blank sheet of paper. They never gave me a chance to read it nor did they give me a copy to—"

"What realtor do you guys work for?" the detective threw out before Tony had a chance to finish.

"Aahhh, Home Realty Association," Tony stuttered, after being thrown off by the detective's question.

Nicolas had about all he could take of questions that seemed to have nothing to do with the illegal procedures he had suffered.

"That's beside the point. Your officers threatened us, and I want somethin' done about it. Or I'll take this matter to a civil rights activist! I will take this to the federal oversight committee and the media. I will sue this city, you, and the entire department." Nicolas glared at him. "Before this thing is over, I'll have yours and those officers' pensions. Those officers better not continue to harass my wife or me. I'll have you know that I know people in high places, and if you don't believe me, then try me," he stated with conviction.

Detective Morris calmly put his hands up, palms facing outward. "Calm down big guy. There's no need to take this matter to that extreme."

"So, Detective Morris, start *detectin'* those crooked-ass cops that you call officers." Nicolas barked.

Detective Morris shook his head in disbelief. "Don't worry. I'm going to get to the bottom of this, and there will be a whole lot of heads rollin'. Please tell your wife not to worry. I will personally take care of those officers, and you will not be hearing from them again."

"Thank you, Detective Morris. We appreciate that very much," Tony said, relieved that he wasn't going to have to check his rearview mirror for red and blue flashing lights.

"I'm gonna hold you to your word on this," Nicolas said, waving a finger at him.

"Don't worry about it. I'm a man of my word," Morris promised.

Handshakes were exchanged before Tony and Nicolas exited the station. They were glad to get the hell out of dodge and continue with their daily activities.

CHAPTER TWENTY-SIX

Pissing off the Boss

While cruising down the road, Tony said, "Did you see the look on that detective's face when you said that?"

They laughed to release some tension.

"Yeah," Nicolas chuckled, thinking it was funny. "But, I'm still upset about how he was tryna play us out, like we were nobodies just wastin' his time."

Tony then mimicked Nicolas. "If I can't get any justice, I'm gonna sue this whole department and go straight to the civil rights activist and President Obama and blow this whole thing outta the water like an atomic bomb, with you along with it."

Tony's horrible impersonation of Nicolas made both of them laugh for the next three miles.

"Well, I didn't say it quite like that, but I hope it brings an end to the harassment."

Nicolas thought about the way he barked at Detective Morris. He didn't know why he said what he said, but he knew half of it was what Tammy had said earlier about him being a doormat. He was tired of being treated like such. The rest of his motivation was unknown, but it felt so good to release that rage at a worthy target.

"Well, only time will tell. Right now, I gotta get Black Beauty detailed and have them get rid of that dog smell." Tony pulled into the office parking lot.

After returning from their disastrous excursion about 12:25 p.m., they stepped through the double-door entrance of Home Realty Associates, eager to finally get the workday started.

"TONY! NICK!" a voice boomed.

"Great!" Nicolas said. His first day at his new job, and he goes and pisses off the man who signs his paycheck. *Now that's gonna leave an everlastin' memory as my first impression. What progress was I makin'. Not!* he thought bitterly.

He would be lucky if Bill didn't fire him and send him on his merry way. How would he explain that to Tammy? He didn't think she'd take it lightly, so he quickly decided to play it cool and try to ride it out.

Bill walked toward them. He was steaming mad, biting his lower lip. His face contorted in a look of pure aggravation with his toupee looking like a wild animal on the top of his head. "Just stay cool and follow my lead. I got this," Tony whispered before turning toward Bill. Under lighter circumstances, they would have gotten a good laugh from his mean look. Bill was looking like a white version of Homie D. Clown in an expensive suit with no make-up, but this was too serious to even think about cracking a smile, let alone laughing in his face.

"Before you blow a head gasket, we had a problem with some Merchantville police officers harassin' us. So we went down to the police station and filed a report. I'm sorry I didn't call to inform you of the situation."

Bill stood fuming for a moment and turned to Nicolas.

"Nicolas, what's goin' on?" he growled at him. His words tried to bend Nicolas' spine until it broke, but Nicolas maintained his composure.

"There were two officers who had a problem with the color of my skin and thought they were above the law. They decided to point their guns at us with the entire city watchin'. After they handcuffed us and made us lay on the hot asphalt, they searched Tony's vehicle for no apparent reason at all. So, we decided to go and report them for harassment."

Bill looked at Tony with a deadpan stare. "Is what he's sayin' true?"

Tony sucked in some air and loudly exhaled it through his mouth before speaking.

"I know I did some bad things in the past, but I did nothin' to deserve any of this. Neither did Nick. We have no reason to lie to you. You can call the Merchantville police department and ask for Detective Andy Morris. That's who we spoke to about the situation. I'm sure he'll gladly fill you in."

"Oh, I'll do just that. And I want you two eggplants to get a copy of that police report. Get it on my desk ASAP!" Bill yelled, with spit flying in their direction.

He gave them a hard look and then bulldozed his way between them with enough force to knock them off balance. He continued down the hallway, mumbling to himself in Italian, "Ay ya ya. Mi sono perso...!"

Tony sighed, "That was close. I've never seen him that angry before."

"I can't afford to get fired on my first day at work, Tony. My wife would kill me." Nicolas cringed at the thought of it.

"Don't worry about it. I'll take the blame. Believe me, I have a way of gettin' over on Big Bill." Tony's words were semi-convincing.

As they neared Nicolas' office, Kim came out of her office and headed their way.

Tony put on his game face, adjusting his suit. "Hey, here comes lil' Kim. Why don't you ask her out for lunch?"

"No! After all I've been through this mornin', I lost my appetite."

Even though Nicolas was straight lying, deep down he wanted her bad, but his pride and marriage were the only two things that protected him from making idiotic decisions.

Kim stopped right in front of them, as if demanding to be admired. Nicolas had to admit she looked splendid with her thin platinum necklace around her neck. It draped comfortably across her collarbone, with a two-carat solitaire diamond that matched her earrings. Her beauty had Nicolas' heart pounding like it was trying to escape his body. He could even hear his heartbeat pulsating through his eardrums. He hoped she couldn't hear it.

How embarrassin' would that be?

"Hey, fellas, I see you found your way back to work," she said, with the alluring fragrance of an edible fruit.

How erotic, Nicolas could not help thinking. "Hey, Kim," he said, while trying to keep it together.

"That's *Ms. Kim* to you," she said playfully. The smile on her pouty lips was seductive, and her milky white teeth perfect. "But *you* can call me Kim."

Her eyes were so provocative that it rendered his soul captive. To make any attempts of escape was impossible. It felt like they were the only two individuals in the hallway. This time, he was all hers and she was all his. Nicolas was filled with desire and wanted her so bad that he could feel it in his groin. Thoughts of losing Tammy or his job never even crossed his mind.

Vying for Kim's attention, Tony leaned over Nicolas, bringing him back to the real world. "Hey, Nick wants to holla at'cha, but he's married."

Nicolas' mouth dropped open as if his jaw muscles had decided to stop working. *How the fuck this joker gonna play me out like that? He doesn't even know me well enough to try to insult my intelligence like that!* Nicolas was furious.

Kim moved closer to Nicolas, rubbing up against his chest with her soft breasts. Her silky smooth, flawless dark skin, hair and make-up were immaculate. He could feel his third leg about to poke her in her stomach.

"That's okay," she replied. "I like married men."

Nicolas froze as if he had stage fright, even while his loins stirred. He felt like a virgin. If he had been trying to paint a picture of himself, it would have been hard for him to stay in between the lines with her standing there. His facial expression could easily be mistaken as a look of fear or distress; she had him dumbfounded. Kim's looks were far from your average soccer mom.

"They all get tongue tied when I flirt with them," Kim said, winking at Tony with a look of satisfaction right before turning to head down the hallway.

Her dress and heels complemented her frame. Nicolas and Tony stood there mesmerized by her well-toned frame.

Damn! Look at the fine ass on her. She's built badder then a muhfucka, Nicolas thought. *I can't risk my marriage, though. It's just one of those 'the grass ain't always greener on the other side' situations. But, from where I'm standin', it looked like that well-*

manicured grass was gettin' plenty of sunlight and water. Damn, how I would love to trim those hedges with my weed whacker and fertilize that lawn. Oh, the things I would do to her would definitely keep her grass green all year round.

"AAAAHHH! She got you!" Tony yelled, guffawing and breaking Nicolas' reverie. "You shoulda seen the look on your face."

"Yeah, she had me all choked up," Nicolas confessed, trying to laugh it off. *That was a good one. I need to be on my toes more. Who knows what other jokes they got saved up for the new guy.*

Nicolas felt powerless over his body in her presence, and he was pretty sure his co-worker knew it.

"She gets them all with that move...even me. She does it to see where you stand and where your head is, and from the look of things, it ain't on your shoulders," Tony said, gesturing toward Nicolas' groin.

Nicolas quickly looked down to check himself and noticed the big bulge in the front of his pants.

"Damn!" he cursed under his breath, adjusting himself. "That's a cruel way of doin' it," he murmured, knowing she had him in her seductive stronghold.

"Cruel, yes. But effective!" Tony raised an eyebrow. "She swears she's proven a point when she does that, because she believes all men do nothin' but think about sex. And with her lookin' that good, she can get away with murder."

"Or sexual harassment," Nicolas blurted out.

Tony waved him off. "Nah, Kim ain't like that at all. She's cool peoples. If she wanted to do that, she woulda got that off three years ago when she first started," he exclaimed, opening the door to Nicolas' office.

"Okay, let's get started. It's time for a little trainin'. I'll try to bring you up to speed. Now, the object of the game is makin' money through buyin' or sellin'. It really doesn't matter 'cause you get six percent out of either deal. Now, I'm goin' to show you how it's done here in Jersey. The rules here are slightly different from the New York branch. And since you already know how it's done in New York, it shouldn't take you long at all to catch up," Tony said with a wink, as he closed the office door.

CHAPTER TWENTY-SEVEN

The Long Day

Later that evening, Nicolas looked and felt like a train wreck. As he headed to punch out, a loud voice called his name before he could pull out his timecard from the slot that held it.

"NICOLAS COLES!" Bill roared.

Still shaking in his shoes from nervousness, Nicolas responded, "Ah, yes, sir." He was too exhausted to display a fake smile.

"I didn't appreciate that stunt you and Tony pulled earlier today, leavin' to go eat while on the clock. That's not goin' to look good on your evaluation. So what do you have to say about yourself, young man?"

Nicolas looked pensively at him. "Sir, I apologize and promise to never do it again. I'm a grown man, and I take full responsibility for my actions."

Placing his hand on Nicolas' shoulder, Bill patted him appreciatively. "It's okay. I know Tony put you up to it. He just called and apologized. That spoiled-ass brat took it upon himself to train you when Gary Hanson couldn't make it. He knows I don't want him to do any trainin', but he felt as though he needed to impress me. Well, it didn't work. So, first thing tomorrow, I'll have Gary show you the right way we run things around here. I appreciate you standin' up like a man, though. I just don't want to see you get in trouble or lose your job."

"Thank you. I'm grateful for that, sir." Nicolas nodded meekly.

Bill squeezed Nicolas' shoulder, his face filled with anticipation. "So how was your first day here?"

Nicolas blew out air like a deflating balloon, as if all his remaining strength evaporated through his lungs into thin air. "It was okay. I just need a little time to understand all the paperwork."

"Don't worry; you'll have this whole thing down pat in no time at all. You'll see that things here are a little different, but not that much different. The only major change is the rules. Go on home and get some rest so tomorrow we can do this thing right. Also, be prepared to work late since you wasted your day at the police station."

"Believe me, I'm lookin' forward to it. Have a nice day, sir," Nicolas overstated with a wave of his hand before walking out the door and heading to his whip.

The ride home was anything but pleasant. Nicolas half expected trouble again from the same two officers he and Tony had encountered. So, he watched the speedometer to make sure he didn't go over the speed limit. Apprehensive and needing to calm his nerves, he turned on the radio and tried to relax, but still couldn't help checking the rearview mirror as he drove. The news reporter talked about investigators finding more evidence on Frank DeBartello and his connection with the hit-man, but they were unable to make it stick. The Merchantville rapist kept them at a standstill, as they continued to collect more clues and DNA from the victims.

When Nicolas stopped at an intersection, a police car pulled out from off a side street. Nicolas looked, but couldn't tell if it was the two racist cops. When the light changed and he stepped on the gas, the patrol car pulled behind him and followed very close.

"Oh shit," he whimpered.

Growing edgy, Nicolas tightened his grip on the steering wheel. He thought about making a quick getaway, but knew he wouldn't get far. He wanted to call Tammy on his cell phone, but he remembered it was against the law to use your cell phone while driving in the state of New Jersey. That would only give them the reason they needed to act stupid. Instead, he kept his cell phone on the seat beside him just in case they started any trouble and he needed to call Tammy. That's if she answers the phone this time, because she could be a witness for him in a court of law if it came down to that. Hopefully, it wouldn't.

He had broken no laws and was doing the speed limit, but Nicolas believed these cops were waiting for him to slip up. From what he had experienced earlier, he feared they wanted to get him in an isolated area so they could pin some shit on him or beat the brakes off his ass. So, Nicolas made sure he stayed on the main road, while the patrol car stayed glued to his tail turn for turn.

Nicolas' heart raced and the road seemed very narrow...too thin for him to stay between the lines. Nicolas thought for sure they would pull him over to see if he had any alcohol in his system. He couldn't keep his eyes out of the rearview mirror, anticipating that the cops would activate their flashing lights.

Then, suddenly, the patrol car turned off onto a nearby street. Nicolas exhaled in relief. When he saw it hadn't been Rodeski and his partner behind him, Nicolas began to think maybe he was exaggerating his predicament and just maybe Detective Morris had already taken care of the situation like he promised.

*****

Upon entering the house, Nicolas smelled something good cooking.

"Honey, I'm home!" he called out.

Tammy ran out of the kitchen with her arms wide open. Like butter on toast, she would melt in Nicolas' arms whenever he held her close. He loved her more than life itself.

Nicolas gave her a big hug and a kiss on the lips. "Sorry it took me so long to get home from work."

"How was work?" she asked. Her warm smile could melt the coldest heart.

Nicolas plopped down into the nearest chair and kicked off his shoes. "There was so much to learn, but dealin' with those cops prevented me from gettin' as much accomplished as I could have. I ended up gettin' in trouble on my first day. I definitely made a first impression. Sad to say, it wasn't a good one. But, the boss was cool about it once Tony called and told him the whole story."

"Story? What whole story?" Tammy flinched, not knowing about the incident with the two officers who had followed Nicolas and Tony after they left the house.

Nicolas filled her in on the racist cops and how they ended up going to the station to report them to the Internal Affairs Department.

"Why didn't you call and tell me?" she argued.

Nicolas tried to make light of the situation. "Honey, it's okay now. We've got it all taken care of. Plus, I didn't want you to worry."

"You didn't want me to worry! You're my husband. I'm supposed to worry about you. If you had called earlier, maybe I could've helped."

"It's cool now. Tony and I spoke to a Detective Morris, and he's gonna take care of everything," he assured her.

"I don't trust any of them!" She pouted while sniveling. "For all you know, they could be drinking buddies looking out for each other."

Nicolas nodded in agreement. "You may be right, but as long as they're not harassin' us, I'm cool wit' it."

"Yeah, they may stop harassing us, but what about the other interracial couples out there. That's not fair to them either. Something should be done about it."

One thing about Tammy, her heart was always in the right place.

"I know, but I ain't ready to call Al Sharpton and start a Million Man March out here."

"But, this isn't right. It's the twenty-first century, and we live in a free country. People have rights." She spoke with vehemence.

Nicolas reached out to comfort her. "I totally agree with you. This whole ordeal got me spooked. On my way home, I saw a cop car and got jumpy. I just wanna go to bed and sleep until tomorrow. Puttin' some distance between me and this awful day sounds real good right about now."

Wide-eyed, she broke free of his grasp. "Well, you can't. You need to mow the lawn."

Nicolas stretched his neck and looked out of the window. The grass was pretty high, but he was beat-down tired and not up to mowing nearly an acre of grass.

"Can't that wait 'til tomorrow?" He glowered at her suspiciously.

"No, *Mr. Working Man*. The Township is going to fine us a thousand dollars if it's not cut by tomorrow morning. They sent a warning letter, and *I'm* not going out there to mow it with a rapist on the loose."

She was clever using the rapist as an excuse while waving the letter from the Township. Nicolas quickly scanned the letter. "Okay, I'll do it, but I'm ready to move up outta here. Mob bosses with hit-men, a rapist on the loose, cops harassin' us, and now the Township threatenin' to fine us a thousand dollars for not cuttin' the grass. Ain't that special?"

"Hey, these rules keep the property value up," Tammy said, raising the lid and stirring whatever she was cooking. Steam wafted out, creating a mist-like cloud.

"By the way, did you hear anythin' from the home security company today?" Nicolas asked admiring her booty from afar.

"They called and said they would be here tomorrow morning to install the alarm," she told him, placing the lid back on the pot.

"Good." Nicolas got up to go change into a pair of sweats, t-shirt, and Nike tennis shoes. "I'll eat after I cut the grass."

"I'll have everything ready by the time you finish." Tammy lifted the lid again and sprinkled a little salt in the pot. "Before you get started, I want you to try this."

Nicolas walked over and tasted a spoonful of the food, which caused his eyes to light up. "Mmmm, this is really good. What is it?"

"Homemade soup," she replied, her tone filled with pride.

"You made this?" he asked.

"Yes. I bought the veggies and beef at the market up the road," she lied, trying to take all the credit for someone else's hard work.

"This soup is bangin'!" he exclaimed, then listened as Tammy told him all about her adventure at the supermarket. However, she left out the part about her encounter with Peter Wright.

Now why would she do that?

CHAPTER TWENTY-EIGHT

Getting Spooked

Nicolas walked through the high Bermuda grass toward the shed. A flock of pigeons hidden in the tall grass twittered away. The vast number of birds caused Nicolas to crunch over, shielding himself with his arms.

Dumb animals.

He pulled out the lawnmower left by the previous owners and tried to start it. It was old, rusty, and one of the wheels was wobbly.

"Are you all right there, neighbor?" John's familiar voice yelled across the four-foot-high fence.

This guy is a fuckin' busybody, Nicolas thought. "I'm tryna get this damn thing to work," he said, unable to get it started.

He never had to worry about mowing grass in New York, where a majority of the property is concrete.

"Let me see what I can do."

John came through the gate and checked the gas and oil levels. He then gripped the handle, squeezed the clutch, and pulled the string. The motor struggled and sputtered with a loud bang like a shotgun. It died, emitting a cloud of dark acrid smoke. Both men coughed while fanning the black cloud.

"Well, it looks like I need a new lawnmower." Nicolas wondered how in the hell would he be able to get a lawnmower and mow the lawn before it got dark.

"You could borrow mine until you get a new one," John offered.

Nicolas wanted to accept his offer, but the alpha male inside him stood its ground.

"Naw, that's okay. I'll go to the nearest hardware store and get one."

Nicolas didn't need his help. To him, John was no more than a total stranger. He could do this on his own without his help.

Damn, I don't even know where the nearest hardware store is located. On second thought, maybe a little helpin' hand won't hurt. Tammy did say we would be fined if it's not cut by tomorrow, and after workin' all day, I wanna relax and unwind.

With a look of regret about declining John's offer, he asked, "By the way, where is the nearest hardware store?"

Seeing how Nicolas was trying to save face, John chuckled softly. "Don't worry about it. You're just as stubborn as your wife. I have a brand-new lawnmower sitting in my shed and have no problem with letting my new neighbors use it."

His smile was genuine, and Nicolas didn't see anything wrong with his generosity. So, he decided to give in.

"You sure? I don't wanna be that annoying neighbor that keeps knockin' at your door with his hand out."

He laughed and waved Nicolas off. "I'm positive. I'll bring it right over."

John returned riding a new Craftsman lawnmower, its *Home Depot* tag still hanging from it. He handed Nicolas the instruction manual and showed him how to start it. Then he left to watch his favorite television series, *Dexter*.

Nicolas sat on the mower and scanned the user's manual. He chuckled to himself thinking about New York City and how it had a strong reputation for being known as the concrete jungle, because of its lack of grass. Feeling confident, he turned the key and the lawnmower hummed. As he put it in gear and started mowing the back lawn, Nicolas felt like a little kid at the carnival. Tammy, who watched from the cedar deck, given him a big smile.

Finishing up the backyard, Nicolas drove the mower to the front of the house, where he saw a patrol car moving by very slowly. His focus shifted from the grass to the car. The patrol car stopped abruptly, causing it to jerk. Nicolas turned the mower off and sat waiting for the cops to make a move.

No one exited the patrol car. They just sat there in the middle of the street with the car idling. Unable to see the person driving the vehicle, Nicolas got off the mower, and using a hedge for cover, he moved closer to get a better view. If it were those crooked-ass cops trying to pump fear in him, he would see to it personally that charges were made against them. His stomach started to churn and the acid burned his stomach lining. Then, just as suddenly as it had stopped in the middle of the street, the patrol car peeled off, its tires screeching louder than a canine caught in a bear trap and leaving two black tire marks behind.

Able to read the license plate, Nicolas whispered, "MPD-U16."

His whole world was standing still. Would Officer Rodeski and his partner harass him every time he stepped out of his house? From the look of things, Detective Morris hadn't kept his promise. Nicolas started to feel like he had just wasted his time going to the police station with Tony.

Nicolas walked to the middle of the street and looked up the road, but saw no sign of the patrol car. However, an old man with white hair, thick prescription glasses, and who was driving a gray Buick Skylark slowly drove toward him.

"Hey! Get the hell outta the street before you get run over!" the elderly man said, sticking his arm out of the window, waving a fist.

Nicolas laughed inwardly, admiring the old man for flexing what little machismo he still had.

"Sorry, sir." He stepped to the side to let the old man pass.

The elderly man drove past him very slowly, still yelling and cursing with his fist in the air.

And just think...that could be me forty to fifty years from now. Nicolas thought while shaking his head. Then he headed back to the mower to finish cutting the grass.

CHAPTER TWENTY-NINE

Stepmama Drama

Nicolas sat silently at the kitchen table with Tammy as they ate her so-called homemade soup. The soup that had tasted so good only a couple minutes ago now tasted like cattle feed. He was too nervous to even enjoy it.

Tammy, who sat across from Nicolas with a small plate of food, noticed he was lost in a daze. "You look like an orphan who's just lost his best friend. What's the matter, baby?"

Nicolas looked into her eyes. "While I was cuttin' the grass, a patrol car drove up and stopped in the middle of the street. But, when I got closer to the car, the driver sped off, flyin' down the road with no lights or sirens."

"You think it was the same two officers from earlier?"

"I believe so. Tomorrow mornin' after the security alarm system is installed, I'm goin' back to the police station and givin' that whole department a piece of my mind. Nobody should have to live like this."

Tammy could hear the aggravation in his voice. "Nicolas, maybe you should leave it alone. Whoever was driving that patrol car was just trying to scare you."

Nicolas picked up a spoon full of food and held it in mid air before putting it in his mouth. "Well, if that's their intention, it ain't workin'. I'm afraid it might be more than just a scare tactic, though.

I got the license plate number, and it matches the plates on the patrol car those two racist cops were drivin'."

"Ah, I don't think you should be stirring up any more trouble with those guys."

Nicolas laid his spoon down and gave her a hard look. "What's the problem, Tammy?"

"Nothing," she said, then took a drink from her cup as if to hid her expression.

"You were all for it in the beginnin', so what changed your mind all of a sudden? Did those guys come back here while I was at work and threaten you?"

"Nooo, they didn't come back here," she shrieked nervously. "I just don't want anything to happen to you. And if you cause trouble for those cops, who knows what they might do."

Nicolas sat for a moment fuming. His grip on the fork was so tight his hands started to lose its pigmentation.

"You're right. I'm gonna let this one slide for now, but the next time those cops do anythin' to me or you, I'm gonna raise all hell up in that department, and that's my word."

I should've listened to Mark and Dave when they told me not to move out here in the first place, Nicolas thought as he tried to stomach the now cold homemade soup. *I thought they were just tryna deter me from movin'. What I need to do is find me a good lawyer before those crooked-ass cops find a way to put me behind bars for good.*

Nicolas knew it was going to be a problem living in Merchantville. It went from bad to worse. Instead of the crooked-ass, racists cops wasting the citizen's tax dollars harassing him, they should have been out looking for that hit-man and rapist who were reducing the town's population.

As Nicolas continued to eat, Tammy cleared the table of her dishes and placed them in the dishwasher.

"You go on upstairs and take a shower after you finish your food, because you're sweaty and stinky." She pinched her nose with one hand, while fanning the air with the other. "I'll be up as soon as I finish cleaning up this kitchen."

"Okay, baby."

Nicolas tried to enjoy his meal, but a knock at the front door interrupted him.

"Finish your food. I'll get it." Tammy dashed to the door before Nicolas could respond.

Upon opening the door, Tammy was both shocked and happy to see her mother, Martha Spenser, standing before her with a big smile.

"Hi, Mommy." Tammy gave her a big hug.

"Hey, Tammy. How are you doing, girl?" Her mother gave her a big kiss on her cheek, then wiped off the blood-red lipstick.

"I'm doing fine. Come on in, Mom." She pulled her mother by the arm, rushing her inside.

Martha stopped in the middle of the living room and scanned the area as if looking for booby-traps. "Where is he?" she asked with a stone face like Nicolas was an infectious disease.

"Nick's in the kitchen. We just finished having dinner. Would you like something to eat, Mom?" Tammy offered.

"No, I'm okay," Martha said, taking a seat on the couch and watched her daughter adoringly, as she disappeared into the kitchen.

"Who was it, baby?" Nicolas asked, finishing his glass of iced tea as Tammy entered. "I heard laughter, so I assume it wasn't the hit-man," he clowned.

Tammy smiled and rolled her eyes. "It's my mother."

"Oh shit, that's even worse!" Nicolas blurted out before he could catch himself.

He couldn't stand being in the same room with that nagging ass bitch. Martha bad-mouthed him every chance she got.

"Watch your mouth," Tammy said, while staring at him and pointing her finger. "Please be nice this time."

"Okay, I will, but your mother has a way of ruinin' the day." Nicolas frowned like a little boy who had just dropped his double-scooped ice cream cone.

"Yeah, but she's still my mother," she threw in as a reminder.

"You're right, and if it wasn't for her, you wouldn't be here." For that reason alone, Nicolas felt the need to respect her mother.

Nicolas wiped his face with a paper towel and headed toward the living room to greet Martha. He told himself to play it cool and put his game face on.

"Hey, Mrs. Spenser. How are you doin'?" Nicolas met her with a meaningless smile devoid of any warmth, with his own shallow grimace.

"Fine," she simply replied while staring at the television, refusing to make eye contact with him.

"What a surprise to see you here. Tammy told me that you were comin' by, but we didn't know when. Did you have any trouble findin' your way out here?" Nicolas pretended to be interested in having a conversation with her, but really, he didn't give a fuck about her or the conversation.

With her eyes still fixated on the television and sarcasm flooding her voice, Martha said, "No trouble at all. I used my On-Star."

"Oh, I didn't know you had one. That's great." Nicolas tried to butter her up a little. "So what you got, a Cadillac?"

Trying to engage her in conversation was becoming difficult.

"Yeah," she responded.

Nicolas looked over at the television to see that she was watching *Judge Mathis*. Even though that was his and Tammy's favorite program, he wanted to jerk the plug out of the socket and tell her to take her mean ass home. That wasn't in his character, though. Nevertheless, the thought put a bigger smile on his face.

There was a long pause before Tammy jumped in. "So what's up, Mom?"

Martha finally broke her focus on the TV and turned toward Tammy, giving her a big smile. "I just wanted to come see your new house and make sure you were okay."

"Mom, I'm fine. What were you worried about? Nicolas takes good care of me." Tammy frowned, her demeanor giving her away. Martha's words were making her very uncomfortable.

Martha scowled. "I don't want to hear about him laying his hands on you."

Leaning against the wall, Nicolas tried to stay calm, but oh, the things he wanted to tell that old she-devil.

"Mom, that was years ago. We were newly weds, and I was to blame for that," she said, pointing her index finger between her breasts.

Martha's eyebrows folded inwards with anger. "What do you mean you were the one to blame? There's not an excuse in the world sufficient enough to excuse a man from beating a woman. Good grief, Tammy. He threatened to kill you." She got up from the sofa, ready to take Nicolas on right then and there.

"Mom, I was with another man at the time!" Tammy cried out, swinging both hands down to her sides in a chopping motion.

"WHAT?" Martha hollered, her head jerking back like some unseen force had punched her. "What are you talking about, girl?"

"I was with another man at the time," Tammy repeated in a lower tone.

"What do you mean by that?" Martha stood there dazed and confused.

Tammy finally opened up. "Nick found out that I was meeting someone…a co-worker…at a restaurant up the street from my job for lunch. He was very upset with me. It wasn't anything serious and nothing happened between us. But, I was upset that Nick yelled at me and said he was going to kill me. So, when I called you, I only told you half the story."

Martha looked at Tammy for a moment and then shifted her hard stare at Nicolas. "Was that the reason he made you quit your job?"

Tammy looked down at the floor, overwhelmed with guilt.

"Well, is it?" she snapped, impatiently waiting for an answer.

Tammy looked over at Nicolas as if waiting for his approval, but Nicolas continued to lean against the wall and stare up at the ceiling. He didn't want any parts of this conversation. Ready to explode with anger, Nicolas knew if he opened his mouth, he would lose it, and that was a risk he couldn't afford to make. Tammy was on her own with this one.

"You answer me, young lady, when I'm talking to you!" Martha ordered.

"Yes! I had to quit to save our relationship," Tammy finally responded, running both hands through her hair and gripping it tight in frustration as if ready to pull it out by the roots.

"Tammy, if you're not happy with the man, then come home with me."

Nicolas knew that was coming. Martha always found a way to throw those words into the equation to get Tammy to go to that miserable place she called home. That's when she would attempt to fill her head up with more garbage. Nicolas fought hard to maintain his self-control, but felt himself slowly losing the fight.

Tammy approached her mother and held her by the hand. "Mom, I'm very happy. What I did then was very stupid. Nicolas is a good man."

*****

During the beginning of their marriage, Nicolas found Tammy giving another man all her attention. He wasn't sure if she cheated on him with the guy or not, but he did know she was spending time with him. When she started distancing herself from him, he felt something wasn't right. So, one day, he decided to pay her a little visit at work to make sure she wasn't spreading any of her *special sauce* around.

When he walked through the doors of her job, everyone looked at him as if he was wearing a ski mask and holding an M16 semi-automatic rifle. Her co-workers told him she had stepped out for lunch and would be back shortly. When he asked where she'd gone, no one knew anything. They just sat there cock-eyed.

Something was up and he could feel it. So, instead of waiting for an hour or so for Tammy to return, he told them, " Let her know I stopped by to say hi." Then he left to go searching for her.

Given the time the workers got for a lunch break and her not having a vehicle, it would mean, wherever she went it wouldn't be far from work.

Nicolas canvassed the area looking through the windows of all the pizzerias, fast food, and Chinese joints within an eight-block radius, but came up with nothing. Just as he started to head home, he came across another restaurant four blocks away from her job. He thought Tammy wouldn't be caught dead in a place like that, especially since every time he offered to take her there, she would turn it down, saying it was too expensive and overrated. In spite of all that, Nicolas decided to say fuck it, and ran over to look inside. When he peered through the glass, there she was sitting at the table with some guy dressed in a business suit. He was a distinguished looking Hispanic male with curly salt and pepper hair. He had strong features and looked as though he worked out. He seemed tall, but Nicolas couldn't tell his height from a seated position.

The lights inside the restaurant were dimmed, giving it a romantic atmosphere. This was the type of place you took someone who you were trying to impress. The tables were covered with white tablecloths and had a burning candle with roses surrounding it. Nicolas had wanted to take Tammy there to show her how much she meant to him, but instead, she chose to substitute him for this Antonio Banderas lookalike.

While smiling and showing this character all thirty-two of her teeth, she quickly turned her head in Nicolas' direction. Their eyes met.

...Busted!

Nicolas thought with both triumph and sadness.

She was caught with her hand in the cookie jar. She gave Nicolas a blank stare. As if all the blood had drained from her face, Tammy sat there looking pale as hell. If only Nicolas could read her mind, but her facial expression was good enough. Tammy's mouth fell open and her eyes increased to the size of a 50-cent piece.

When Nicolas entered the restaurant, the guy sat there speechless, his eyes focused on Tammy like he couldn't function without her approval. Tammy was caught and had nothing to say. Guilt was written all over her face.

"What's going on, Tammy?" Nicolas said. The cool, relaxed tone he used was filled with confidence and tinged with subtle righteous violence.

"He's just a friend I'm having lunch with."

Nicolas witnessed the look in her eyes as they sat at the table, the way she gazed into his eyes and smiled. It was the same look and smile she'd given him when they started dating. She was lying straight through her teeth and he knew it. Unable to look him straight in the eyes, she kept her gaze directed toward the floor.

Anger and hurt consumed Nicolas that day. He cursed Tammy's ass out, then made her leave the restaurant. When she returned home, she told her mother a fictitious story about him threatening to kill her. This was her way of getting her mom to take her side.

Later that night, after she got her lies straight, Tammy called Nicolas and told him nothing was going on with her and the guy. He was too old for her. She explained she was just lonely, and he gave her the attention she needed. Like a dummy, Nicolas fell for the story and took her back, but only under one condition: she would have to leave her job. To his surprise, she ended up doing just that. Still, his image had been tainted with her mother, and it was all because of Tammy's lies.

*****

Martha gave Nicolas a stern look. "Did he put his hands on you?"

"Mom, he would never put his hands on me. Nick wouldn't hurt a fly!" Tammy pleaded to her.

"I don't give a damn about him hurting *flies*. My main concern is you." Martha's eyes widened as she continued to give Nicolas the evil eye.

"Mom, he wouldn't hurt me. He's not a violent person. He's gentle and caring towards me."

Tammy's eyes smiled at him. Even though he displayed a stone-faced expression, his contained emotion was revealed through his glassy eyes.

"Just because he's not physically violent doesn't mean he's not verbally violent."

Now she's diggin'. I just wish the wicked witch would leave. I'll even buy her a new broomstick, he thought to himself.

"Well, he's neither," Tammy protested.

Nicolas was impressed at how Tammy held her ground. *That's right, baby! Tell her!*

"Well, I still don't trust him." Martha held Nicolas in her cold stare.

Thank God she doesn't have heat vision. I can only imagine the size hole she's dyin' to burn through me. Nicolas could feel the hate coming off her in waves.

"Mrs. Martha, I may say a lot of things when I'm angry, but I would never lay a hand on her. I love Tammy too much to hurt her," Nicolas murmured once he gained his composure.

Tammy walked over to him, giving him a warm hug with an added smile. However, Nicolas was too upset to notice. Barely responding to her gesture, he walked into the kitchen to cool off. It was the best thing for him to do before he ended up saying something he might regret later.

"Is he cheating on you?" Martha asked, not satisfied to have peace.

"No, not that I know of. Are you, Nick?" Tammy yelled out, while giving her mother a speculative glance.

Nicolas re-entered the living room, pissed off that she would even think to ask him an injudicious question like that. Tammy knew him better than that, or at least he thought she did. However, now wouldn't be a good time to unleash his emotions. That would only justify Martha's speculation of him.

"Baby, I would never cheat on you and you know that." As hard as it was, Nicolas smiled to reassure her. "It's gettin' too hot in here. I'm gonna take a shower."

"Sounds good," Tammy said, pinching his cheek. Then she smiled and turned to her mother. "Mom, let's go to the Cherry Hill Mall. We haven't been to the mall together in a long time."

Martha looked at her with uncertainty. "Cherry Hill Mall? For what?"

"I want to check out Nordstrom and see what's the latest fashion in Jersey, and since you have On-Star, we should be able to get there and back with no problem," Tammy exclaimed, excitement spreading across her face.

"Okay. Well, let's get going so we can get back here before dark."

"Yaaaay!" Tammy started jumping up and down like a little kid, but then halted unceremoniously. Turning her attention towards Nicolas, she said, "You don't mind, do you, honey?"

"Naw, go ahead. Knock yourself out," he responded sarcastically. The rhetorical statement was directed towards Martha, though.

Nicolas watched Tammy as she gracefully danced out the door with her mother in tow. Although worried about Tammy going out with a rapist on the loose, he held his tongue, not wanting Martha to find out. Since she hadn't mentioned it, he assumed she knew nothing of it.

CHAPTER THIRTY

Stepmom Has Gotta Go

After Tammy and her mother left for the mall, Nicolas finished unpacking before taking his shower. He grabbed a steak knife from the kitchen to cut open the taped up boxes in the bedroom. As he sawed through the tape of one of the boxes, his cell phone rang. He checked the caller I.D. to see Mark's name across the screen. Nicolas touched the screen to answer it.

"Wassup, playa!" Nicolas said, slipping into his street dialogue.

"Nuffin' much, my nigga. Just to let you know, we made it to the bike rally safe and sound." Mark giggled as if he was tickled.

"What time did y'all get there?" Nicolas placed the knife on the nightstand and collapsed on the bed.

"Around twelve-thirty. So how's the new home?"

"It's good. We still have a lot of unpackin' to do. Naw Mean?"

"Yeah, I feel yah."

Hearing Dave in the background, Nicolas asked, "What's that fool yellin' about?"

"Nuffin', man. Don't pay that nigga no mind. He's just doin' a lot of talkin' 'bout nuffin'."

"Let me talk to him," Nicolas said.

A rustling sound could be heard as the phone was passed over.

"Yo, wassup, son," Dave yelled into the phone.

"Ain't nuffin'. Wassup wit'cha?" Nicolas responded.

"I'm coolin'. How's the house comin' along?"

"It's gettin' there. Now what you yellin' at Mark for?" Nicolas asked, cutting to the chase.

"This nigga right here is stupid as hell. Ya see, we just got the fuck out here, and this place was dead as a doorknob. It's just startin' to pick up a little. But, this muhfucka is tryna hook-up wit' this light-skinned, crazy-ass bitch. And you know how I feel about those light-skinned chicks. No offense to you, my nigga, but somewhere durin' slavery, the white man impregnated our black women, mixin' their DNA with our DNA, causin' us to become unstable. But, those light-skinned chicks got a little too much of their DNA, which made them all crazy."

Nicolas laughed at Dave's philosophy. "So what does she look like?"

"Don't get it twisted my nigga. She's bad as hell, wit' big titties, a flat stomach with a small waist, a fat ass and all, like Pam from *Martin*. Shit, given the chance, I'd probably fuck that bitch myself, if her breath didn't stink."

"Aw, her breath was stinkin'?" Nicolas frowned at the thought of it.

"Yeah, dawg. This chick had morning breath all day long. She needs to see a dentist or a mouth specialist."

Nicolas couldn't stop laughing. "So what makes you think she's crazy?"

"Yo, check this out. We were chillin' outside waitin' for them to straighten out our room before we went in to unpack our shit. This light-skinned bitch walked past with her ass bouncin'.

So, Mark yelled out this ol' ass corny line, talkin' 'bout, 'Hey, you got some fries to go wit' that shake'?" Dave said, mocking Mark.

"No, he didn't." Nicolas chuckled.

"Yeah, he did, and what's even sadder is that bitch was hooked. She turned around all slow, smilin' hard as hell like she was *Alice in Wonderland*. She stood there waitin' for this nigga to step to her, but the handle to her cheap-ass pocketbook snapped, causin' all her shit to fall all over the pavement."

"No, it didn't!" Nicolas yelled out, laughing.

"Yes, it did. Shit cracked me up, too. But, *Super Save-A-Ho* here flew over to her like he was wearin' a muthafuckin' cape and helped pick her shit up."

"There's nothin' wrong wit' that," Nicolas said, struggling to catch his breath from laughing so hard.

"Yes the fuck it is. That bitch lost cool points for wearin' that cheap-ass bag durin' this joyous occasion!" Dave replied.

For the women, it was bike week, but for Dave and Mark, it was an *ass* parade, because of the variety of women strolling up and down the sidewalk in skimpy outfits, bikinis, and bathing suits, revealing as much flesh as possible.

"And Mark lost all cool points for using that corny-ass line. So, anyway, this bitch was talkin' 'bout how he was such a gentleman, unlike her baby daddy."

"Baby daddy!" Nicolas blurted out.

"Yeah, dawg. This bitch got three kids and two baby daddies. Both baby daddies are locked up doin' time."

"That right there is a no-no. He shoulda bounced right then and there," Nicolas commented.

"Yeah, but Mark was hooked on gettin' that ass. She said her last baby daddy, the one she got two kids with, was messin' with some other chick in her apartment complex. I asked her if she caught him cheatin' on her with this other girl, and she said no. So I asked her how did she know he was cheatin' on her. She said she could tell by the way he smiled and looked at her every time they spoke. So this crazy-ass bitch said she slashed three of his car tires and three of the girl's tires. When I jokingly asked her why she didn't slash all four tires, this bitch had the audacity to tell us that she woulda, but the insurance company woulda covered it and got them all new tires."

Dave paused so Nicolas could catch his breath from laughing.

"Yeah, bruh, that shit does sound crazy."

"So I asked her what happened with the first baby daddy, and she said she caught that nigga cheatin' and paid a crackhead to put sugar in his gas tank while she was at work. That way, when the cops questioned her, she could use her job as an alibi."

"So how did both her baby daddies get locked up?"

"I dunno, but Mark is gonna try to get her drunk tonight to find that out before they smash."

"He's still gonna hit that after hearin' her crazy-ass confessions?" Nicolas squawked with skepticism.

"You already know."

"What about her friends? Does she have any?"

"Yeah. She went back to her hotel to get them."

"How many friends does she have with her?"

"Two. That's why we need yo ass here. See, if you were here, that woulda been a major plus."

"Naw, I'm good. They might all end up bein' light-skinned and crazy!" Nicolas cracked.

"I don't give a fuck, as long as I get some ass."

"Yeah, until you find out they're all stalkers." Nicolas grinned.

"We're two steps ahead of you, nigga. We didn't give them our real names."

"Now that's good thinkin' on y'all's part. What's Mark doin' now?"

"He's still tryna holla at a few more bitches while we're out here," Dave said, then yelled out to Mark, "Yo, Mike, come get the phone!"

"Mike? That sounds too close to Mark."

"Yeah, I know. I told this dumb muhfucka to come up wit' somethin' better than that. Here he is, Nick."

Nicolas heard the phone being passed to Mark.

"Yo, what up, my nigga?"

"Mike! You couldn't come up with somethin' better than that?"

"Well, you know how Dave be gettin' shit fucked up. So, in case he slips up and says Mark, it won't be so obvious."

"So what name did Dave come up with?"

"Muhammad," Mark grunted.

"Muhammad!" Nicolas repeated. "Let me guess. He told her that he was Muslim?"

"You already know. But, when someone asked him about Islam and the Prophet Muhammad, he quickly finds a way to change the subject."

"I told him about actin' like he's Muslim. What's the name of the chick you're tryna get wit'?"

"Rolisha Johnson." Nicolas could hear Mark grinning through the phone.

"Rolisha!" Nicolas roared in disbelief. "That sounds like somethin' you put on a hotdog," Nicolas guffawed, hitting the side of the bed with his fist.

"It doesn't matter, as long as she's droppin' drawers. Ya feel me?" Mark sung, sounding like The Notorious B.I.G.

"I feel ya. Hey, look, y'all two lovebirds enjoy yourselves and call me later. Tammy's mom came down to visit, and I gots to prepare myself mentally for her."

"Damn nigga, you need any help with that?" Mark asked, sounding sympathetic. "Naw, I'm good. Plus, y'all too far away to do anythin'."

"Hold on. Dave wants to holla at'cha before you bounce."

"Yo, Nick?" Dave yelled through the phone. "We'll be back on Monday. If you need us to take care of that old hag, just give me that hit-man's phone number out there and I'll hire him to do her dirty. As a matter of fact, give me the rapist's phone number and I'll pay him extra to give her what she really needs. Ya feel me?

"I'll make sure to keep that in mind." Nicolas laughed from his belly. "I'll check y'all out later...one." Nicolas disconnected the phone call and looked around at the boxes.

Time to get started.

CHAPTER THIRTY-ONE

Time to Make-up

Tammy and her mother carried in multiple bags.

"Mom, just put them right over there." Tammy pointed to the corner of the living room near the television set. "I'll take care of it later. Nick, we're back!" she yelled up the stairs.

Worn out, the last thing Nicolas wanted to do was talk to that old, hateful bitch again tonight. However, he put on some clean sweats and headed downstairs to show some hospitality.

"Hey, baby." He gave Tammy a hug and kiss. "Hey, Mrs. Martha."

He damn sure didn't want any hugs or kisses from her. So, he gave her a fake smile instead.

"You better go over there and give my mother a hug," Tammy pushed him toward Martha, rolling her eyes.

Nicolas reluctantly gave his mother-in-law a loose hug and felt her stiffen. She didn't even attempt to raise her arms to hug him back.

"Now that's more like it. We can be one big happy family." Tammy's naivety had her believing a hug was enough to smooth things out. "Nicolas, wait 'til I show you what I got at the mall." She was excited.

"Oh yeah? What is it?" Nicolas uttered, pretending to be interested.

"I'll show you later when my mom leaves."

"Well, that must be my cue. I need to leave anyway 'cause it's getting late." Martha reached in her pocketbook and pulled out her car keys. "But, I'm keepin' an eye on you, Mister." Emphasizing the word *Mister* with a hard look and pointed finger like a loaded gun.

"Oh, Mom! Let's not start that again."

She and Nicolas walked Martha to her car before she got started on Nicolas again.

"Have a nice evenin', Mrs. Martha." Nicolas waved, relieved to see her go.

Martha did not wave back, but she did give him a look that would freeze pineapples in Hawaii. Nicolas held his peace and headed back into the house. As Tammy and her mother talked for a few more minutes, Nicolas assumed it was about him.

What else is new? That woman only has vile words for me.

Nicolas went into the kitchen and poured a glass of orange juice.

"Pour me a glass, hun," Tammy said, smiling as she entered the kitchen.

"Think she'll find her way back to the Interstate?" Nicolas asked, getting another glass out of the cabinet.

"Yeah. She has On-Star, remember?"

"Oh, yeah, I forgot." Nicolas flashed a devilish grin, while secretly hoping she got lost on her way home. Tammy playfully pushed him. Their eyes connected, and at that point, it seemed all the anger and bitterness he had toward Tammy's mother dissipated.

"Nicolas, I'm sorry about my mother's behavior. She's getting old," she whispered, giving him a hug.

"It's okay. She never did like me. She uses that incident as an excuse to stay mad at me. But, why would you tell her about me threatenin' to kill you and not about you bein' with that guy?" he uttered with anger.

Tammy waved her arms around as if directing traffic. "I was upset at the time, and I knew she wouldn't listen to my side of the story if I told her the truth."

"See, fillin' your mom's head with all that nonsense made her hate me even more."

Nicolas felt a fresh anger toward Tammy for having cheated on him. Even though, according to her, it wasn't physical, just the mere thought of it was considered cheating.

Tammy pleaded for mercy. "I'm sorry, Nicolas. I was confused at the time. Now she's upset with me for not telling her the whole story."

"And she oughta be. I know I am. I'm so upset right now that I gotta go upstairs before I say or do somethin' I might regret."

Nicolas just wanted this day to finally be over. So, he headed upstairs to cool off. Sleep would definitely do him some good.

"Nicolas, I'm sorry. Please don't go to bed mad at me," she cried out.

"It's too late now. You better straighten this shit out with yo' momma. I dunno how much longer I can deal with her comin' up in my spot with that attitude like I"ma fuckin' kid. I'm a grown-ass man," he yelled back.

Nicolas headed straight to the bathroom and took a long shower to relax. After that verbal beat down he received from Tammy's mother, it made him feel like a dirty whore. He closed his eyes, letting the warm, soothing water cascade over his body.

"Aaaahhh, got you!" Tammy yelled out, grabbing Nicolas' private parts.

Startled, Nicolas quickly grabbed the shower curtain, using it as a shield to protect his vital organ.

"Knock it off!" he yelled, still angered by Tammy's mother.

"Why, so you can stay mad at me? I don't think so, buddy," she said, still grabbing at him.

"Okay, okay, I ain't mad at'cha." Nicolas broke down laughing as Tammy started tickling him, water spraying on her and the floor. She looked so good wet.

Tammy stopped and looked at him with a beautiful smile that seemed to melt his heart. "Good, I'll be waiting for you in the bedroom, and if you don't hurry up and join me, I'm coming back in here after you," she said, her hard nipples pushing against her wet t-shirt.

"Oh, I'll be in there alright. Just give me two minutes and I'll be out," he said effervescently.

"Don't take too long." She gave him a sneaky grin, as if she had some naughty thoughts running through her pretty little head.

"I won't," he sung, as she walked out of the bathroom.

Nicolas slowly released his grip of the shower curtain and peeked his head out of the shower to see if Tammy was still around. He knew how she loved to play games as much as he did. With the coast clear, Nicolas felt relieved she honored his privacy.

Suddenly, Tammy swung the bathroom door open.

"Aaaahhh!" she yelled again, causing Nicolas to jump back and pull the shower curtain with so much force that the railing fell down, exposing his nudeness.

"Now look what you made me do," he whined, trying to fix the rail.

Tammy's mouth dropped. Overwhelmed with laughter, she ran out of the bathroom.

*****

Nicolas got out of the shower, dried off, and climbed in the bed with Tammy. It was hard for him to stay mad at her for her playfulness. She had a beauty that seemed to extinguish the anger burning inside him.

"Tammy, I love you, but I'm still upset with you." Nicolas looked at the sheet and gave it a sniff. "What, you changed the sheets?"

"Yeah," she replied, shrugging her shoulders.

"You never washed the sheets without at least gettin' a weeks in." Nicolas said.

"I felt like doing some early spring cleaning." Tammy responded.

Keith Sweet's "How Deep is Your Love" was playing softly in the background. The small clock radio did no justice for the song, but it sounded so sweet to him.

Nicolas smiled. "You must really love your new home to start your weekend laundry this early."

Tammy rubbed her index finger down Nicolas' nose. "Did you mean what you said?" she asked, quickly changing the subject.

"Said about what?" Nicolas asked, bewildered.

She stared at his chiseled chest while rubbing her fingers down the middle. "That you would kill me if you found me in bed with another man."

"When did I say a thing like that?" he muttered.

"That night in bed when you said I had to quit my job."

"I didn't say that," Nicolas sang.

"Yes, you did. You were like, '*If I catch you cheatin' on me, I'ma kill ya'*,'" she said mocking his tone.

Nicolas thought back to that night and remembered he had indeed said that to her.

"I did, didn't I?" he confessed, feeling the intensity of the pain again. He wanted to slap her hateful mother for dragging that awful night from years ago into the present.

"You are so adorable when you're mad." Tammy tried to make light of the subject.

His love for her overrode his pain and anger, and he gave her a warm smile. He began to reminisce about the past—the happy times of their past.

"Remember how I tried to get with you, but you kept brushing me off."

She giggled. "I only did that because I thought you were just a playa tryin' to get some ass."

Nicolas nuzzled his face in her hair and inhaled the sweet scent of her shampoo. "Well, it's true I was tryna get some ass, but I wasn't a playa."

Tammy pushed his head back. "Make sure you remind me to call your mother tomorrow and tell her what you just said."

"My mother is a grown woman; she'll understand. Then again, you better rethink callin' her. Knowin' my mother, once she finds out how peaceful it is here, she might try to move in just to get away from all that noise out there in New York, and we don't want that."

"You're absolutely right. Not until we have kids. Then she'll be our live-in nanny."

"Well, I ain't ready for her, but I'm definitely ready for you. So, let's get ready to rumble," Nicolas howled like the boxing ring announcer Michael Buffer as he tossed the sheet over their heads, initiating the first round of foreplay.

Tammy removed the sheet. "Hey, I thought you said you were mad at me."

"I was, but it's time to make-up." Nicolas threw the sheet back over their heads.

Tammy looked down, watching him slowly work his way towards her. She loved his smile with his nice white teeth. As he kissed her gently, he probed his rock-hard dick around her pussy, massaging her vaginal walls. Tammy closed her eyes, licking her lips and shivering from his warm touch.

Nicolas pulled back and then inserted a finger inside her, lubricating it first for a wetter entry. Tammy moaned while raising her hips, her body craving more than his tender touch. Nicolas inserted another finger as she spread her legs wider. He suckled her hard, ripened nipples while inserting a third finger. With three fingers inside her, Nicolas mildly stroked her in a circular motion, bringing his head down between her legs to softly blow and kiss her clitoris. He heard Tammy's quick intake of breath, savoring the moment.

He licked her clitoris like a strawberry ice cream cone. Moving her hips in rhythm with his fingers caused them to go deeper inside her. Nicolas felt her love juices flowing, and he could taste her excitement.

"Mmmmm…"

When he wrapped his lips around her clitoris and began sucking on it like a lollipop, she couldn't take any more.

"AAAHHH...AAAHHH...I'M CUMMING!" she cried, her body trembling.

Nicolas locked his lips and sucked harder, causing Tammy to shiver. She arched her body forward, and scream, "AAAAHHH... SHIT!"

Her legs locked up, squeezing Nicolas' head tight like a vice grip. She had reached her climax. Nicolas could hear her muffled cry as her legs pressed tightly against his ears. Just as the climax began to recede, she lessened the pressure of her legs and collapsed.

Nicolas leaned back for a moment, catching his breath, and then slowly worked his way upwards to insert his throbbing, hard penis inside her. Tammy held him in place, her hands around his waist, stopping his flow of motion.

"Baby, wassup?" he whispered.

"I want you to lay down," Tammy said, directing him onto his back.

It was Nicolas' turn now. She wanted him to experience the same feeling she had just gone through. He watched as Tammy softly kissed him, working her way downward. She kissed his smooth chest and sucked on his nipples. She worked down to his flat stomach, and grabbing his big black dick, she began kissing the head of it softly. He watched as it disappeared between her big, pink, Angelina Jolie lips. Quivering, he grabbed both sides of the mattress and held on for the ride.

Tammy took more of his hard shaft in her mouth and sucked it with a rhythm-like flow. Nicolas' eyes rolled back in his head. She sucked harder and harder, his dick going deep in her throat. Nicolas' rod got harder, and his passion built to the point of no return.

"AAAHHH!"

Nicolas cried, pumping his seed between her swollen pink lips. "AAAHHH!"

He continued to yell while cumming inside her mouth, his body jerking with each ejaculation. She kept sucking until she sucked him dry. Her lips made a popping sound each time she pulled her head away. She continued to do so while eating the rest of his semen from his genital tract. Tammy smiled at the way his body kept jerking from the sensation. Then she began to kiss on his balls and stroke his penis as it slowly went limp. Nicolas collapsed from exhaustion, every muscle in his body relaxing.

Just as he started to fall asleep, Tammy began sucking him again. Smiling, he looked at her, his dick still in her mouth, orally fixated on it. As she sucked, it slowly grew in her mouth. She closed her eyes enjoying every moment. Nicolas felt his passion building as she alternated between pulling on his caramel dick and licking his balls.

"OH SHIT, BABY! YOU'S A FREAK!" Nicolas screamed in pleasure, while running his fingers through her honey blonde hair.

Tammy's head bobbed up and down with aggression, causing him to yell louder.

"DAMN, GIRL, THAT SHIT FEELS GOOOOD!" Her face relaxed as she sucked him like a porn star. This was a side of Tammy that he had never seen before, but he loved it.

"DAMN!" Nicolas grunted, while she sucked his stone-hard dick. His body stiffened as he watched her deep throat his shit without the gag reflex.

"I'M CUMMIN'…AAAHHHH!" He screamed, fireworks shooting off in his body as he exploded in her mouth again. She swallowed all his juices like a creamy milkshake.

"Mmmm, that was good," she said, while looking up at Nicolas and rubbing her stomach with deep satisfaction.

Nicolas gasped for air, as if he were asthmatic. "You…got…my…knees…shaking," he stuttered, trying to collect himself.

Tammy giggled. "You bring out the freak in me when you eat this pussy like you hungry and shit."

"I was filled with a lot of frustration," he said, curling up in a fetal position.

She smiled. "Well I'ma start pissing you off more, because the make-up sex is all that and some."

"As long as you do what you just did to me, I'll find a way to break-up just to make-up," Nicolas whispered, drained and fatigued.

Tammy playfully pushed him. "You're so bad."

She moved into his arms before falling into an exhausted, satisfied sleep.

CHAPTER THIRTY-TWO

Mirror Mirror on the Wall

The buzzing of the alarm clock felt like a hammer in Nicolas' head. He reached over and turned it off. It was six o'clock Friday morning. No matter how many times it's been done over the years, Nicolas could never get use to waking-up so early in the morning. He had to sit on the edge of the bed and gather himself before heading towards the shower.

"Good morning, baby." He leaned over, kissing the top of Tammy's forehead. "I love you."

Tammy looked at him through sleepy eyes and said, "Love you, too," and then turned around and fell off to sleep. Tammy rested so peacefully. Nicolas always wondered what's going on in that pretty little head of hers. Maybe she was dreaming about her new home and how she loved everything about it except for the size of the master bedroom. Tammy always wanted a bedroom that came with a sitting room. *Maybe I'll convert one of the rooms into a dressing room for her.* He thought to himself.

The uninterrupted flow of traffic and continuous movement of people helped her feel safe in New York. Nicolas hoped that the quietness wouldn't end up driving her crazy down the line. Tammy being the interior decorator was good for her nerves. Nicolas never bother to interfere with it, because it would help her appreciate her new home more. Nicolas was a workaholic, married to his job. His only concern was making money and watching it grow.

Nicolas slowly made his way to the bathroom, brushed his teeth and shaved. Looking at himself in the mirror, he pretended he was arguing with Officer Rodeski. A therapeutic way of venting out his anger and frustration before heading to work. "What! Who you callin' a nigger, fool? I'll fuck you up if you mess wit' me." He flexed and admired his strength. "I'm from *New York*, where pigs get a beat down daily. Huh, what?"

Tammy yelled out. "Nick! Stop playing around, smelling like tuna fish and onions, and get yo stinkin' ass in the shower before you wind up bein' late for work stinky!" she cracked, using Dave's line.

"Okay, ma." He flexed a little more before getting into the shower.

*****

Nicolas finally dressed and primped before he looked down at a sleeping Tammy. She seemed so angelic, making it hard for him to leave her home by herself. But, they had bills to pay, and his main goal was taking care of his wife.

"I'm off to work. I'll call you later." He kissed her gently on the cheek.

"Okay. I love you," mumbled Tammy, more asleep than awake.

"By the way, I'll be working late, so I'm not sure what time I'll be home. Listen now, keep your cell phone on so I can reach you." His words were direct and unswerving.

"Okay, okay, I will." She pulled the sheet over her head, ending that conversation.

*****

Nicolas checked the windows and the doors to make sure the house was secure before he walked to his ride.

John was watering his front yard. "Hey, Nick!" he called out and waved.

"Good morning, John. I see you're still workin' on that yard."

"Yeah, I have to." John smiled with that used car dealer look. Sorta slimy and friendly at the same time. What a fucked-up combination.

"Keep an eye on the house 'til I get back," Nicolas said with a wink, before getting into his vehicle.

"No problem. It's in good hands." John chuckled.

"Yeah, well as long as it's in good hands, I shouldn't have to worry," Nicolas yelled out the car window as he backed out of the driveway.

CHAPTER THIRTY-THREE

Saved By the Bell

Nicolas greeted everyone at work with a friendly smile and headed toward his office. While he was pulling files, someone knocked on his door.

"Mind if I come in?" Kim was already halfway through the doorway.

"No, I don't mind at all. Come on in," Nicolas said, sitting up straight in his chair with his chest out.

Kim walked over and sat on the edge of Nicolas' desk. "I thought this would be a good time to talk since your friend Tony isn't here yet. I don't usually do this with all employees, but there's somethin' I've been wanting to tell you ever since I first laid eyes on you."

Her eyes were sultry, making Nicolas very uneasy. Intimidated, he pushed himself back against his chair. When she scooted across the desk to be nearer to him, he could feel his breath being snatched from his lungs. The room's temperature rose ten degrees, and beads of perspiration appeared on his forehead. She leaned in so close that Nicolas could feel the warmth of her breath blowing gently against his skin. She smelled of sweet passion fruit, which made her irresistible. Nicolas couldn't keep his eyes off her.

Is this woman crazy? Nicolas thought.

His brain went into warp mode, working at a faster speed.

He'd just started working there yesterday and this woman was trying to throw herself at him already. Might it be because he was fresh meat and she wanted to be the first woman in the office to break him in properly. Either that or she was playing another Jedi mind trick with him, and he didn't know the rules. He wanted to tell her to get the hell out of his office, but the words refused to make the short trip from his brain to his mouth. He simply sat there speechless, half hoping Tony would walk through the door and save him from whatever the hell was going on.

Suddenly, the fire alarm sounded, and the fragile moment of expectancy evaporated.

"Oh..." She paused for a moment, inches away from him. Her eyes danced around the room. "Saved by the bell," she finally said, then laughed.

Nicolas couldn't move. Stuck on stupid, he blurted out, "What do we do now?"

From where he was sitting, he was almost sure Kim was coming on to him. She seemed very aggressive. However, he couldn't be one hundred percent certain since nothing had actually happened. Thank God for the fire alarm.

Kim slid off the desk and adjusted her clothes. "The smart thing to do is to get the hell out of here and head for the nearest exit. They have regular fire drills here, but you never know if it's just a drill or if the other half of the building is already a blazing inferno."

Nicolas got up, grabbed her arm, and followed her to the nearest emergency exit. Since he didn't smell smoke, he figured it was probably a fire drill.

Once outside, they crossed the street with the other employees and waited for sirens or an *'all clear'* announcement. While waiting, he used the opportunity to pull out his cell phone and call Tammy, but he got her voicemail. He checked his answering machine; there was one new message.

"Hi, baby. It's Tammy. I got a call from the alarm company saying they were tied up on another job and wouldn't be able to get here until late this afternoon around five o'clock. So, I'm going to take a little nap and wait for the alarm guy. Hope you're not too late, but I'll be here waiting to give you a big hug when you get in. Love ya."

"Hey, are you okay?" Kim asked, her pretty brown eyes sparkling under the sunlight.

Nicolas powered his phone off and put it back in his pocket. "Yeah, I'm just waiting patiently to hear what you were tryna tell me," he responded, quite eager.

Kim took a quick breath and opened her mouth to speak, but nothing came out. Noticing her eyes were focused on something at a distance, Nicolas turned around and spotted Tony heading in their direction.

"Oh no, here comes trouble. We'll put this one on hold for later." Kim quickly headed over towards a group of female co-workers and joined in their conversation. Nicolas could tell she didn't want Tony in her business.

I wonder why, Nicolas thought.

There seemed to be something more to this story, but Nicolas wanted to know if Kim was trying to push up on him or not. He was trying not to get ahead of himself now that the alarm broke the spell she had on him. Nicolas wondered if maybe Tony might have set him up as a joke or just wanted to see where his head really was. Yeah, she looked good and all, and Nicolas wanted to test the waters. What man wouldn't? But, truth be told, he was a happily married man with a new job and mortgage payments. No way would he let any woman cause him to lose his job, his house, or his marriage. Well, maybe if it was Serena Williams, but the fucked up part about it is that she looks just like her.

Not good—not good at all. His infatuation with this woman was becoming critical.

"Hey there, buddy. What's goin' on?" Tony said, rubbing his hands together, acting happy like he had just won the Nobel Peace Prize.

"The fire alarm sounded, so we're waitin' for the hook-and-ladder to pull up."

Tony started pouting. "Damn, that's goin' to put us behind on our work. We've got contracts to fill out and deeds to research."

Nicolas looked over at Kim who was still holding a conversation with the small group of women. Kim looked over and their eyes met for a brief second. Kim then turned her attention back to the women.

"I thought Gary Hanson was gonna train me today?" Nicolas questioned, trying to keep his focus on work, but couldn't keep his eyes off Kim.

"He called out sick again, and Bill had no one else available. So, I volunteered." Tony stood next to him and wrapped his arm around Nicolas' shoulders like Bill did in the hallway when he first started. "Isn't this great?"

Nicolas cursed under his breath.

"And Bill okayed it after all that nonsense we got into yesterday?" Nicolas asked, wondering if Tony was up to no good.

Tony frowned. "Well, not really. I just took it upon myself to sign you up as my trainee."

"You're gonna get both of us in big trouble with your uncle. I don't want any part of it!" Nicolas barked, shaking his head in uncertainty. Mr. Satario had given him a second chance, and he wasn't about to blow it on a wild scheme of Tony's.

"Don't worry about it, Nicolas. I got everything under control." Tony grinned.

It wasn't the grin that bothered Nicolas; it was the way he grinned in a dark, sinister way. What evil thoughts lurked beneath that thick, black, curly hair?

Nicolas waved his hand. "Listen, Tony, I'd like to believe you, but my gut is givin' me a weird feelin'. I feel if we hang out together, we're gonna somehow end up in trouble with the old man again."

Tony rolled his eyes. "Nicolas, stop sayin' that shit. I'm already feelin' bad about gettin' you in trouble yesterday."

"If you were tryin' to make up for gettin' me in trouble yesterday, then why the hell are you comin' in twenty minutes late?" Nicolas' tone started to attract attention from the surrounding employees.

"I had some business to take care of. Plus, I had to check on this property for half-a-mill. Don't worry, Nicolas. I'll have you caught up to speed by the end of the week. As long as you come to work on time, you have nothing to worry about. I got you covered on everything else."

Sirens interrupted their conversation.

"Here come the fire trucks. Guess it wasn't a false alarm," Nicolas said, while watching the big hook and ladder truck pull up in front of the building.

*****

With it being close to noon, Nicolas' stomach started to growl. A few moments later, a fireman exited the building and used a bullhorn to make his announcement.

"Attention, everyone," the fireman said, addressing the crowd and causing the loud mixture of chatter to come to a complete silence. "There appears to be a gas leak. The building will be closed until the leak can be located."

A few moments later, Nicolas saw Bill talking to the fireman who made the announcement.

"Knowin' him, he'll have us workin' out here on the curb." Tony chuckled, but Nicolas could hear truth in his words.

Bill motioned for all the co-workers to gather around him.

"As much as I hate to do it, I'm going to close the office for the rest of the day. You can go home and do some marketing research. I don't want anyone draggin' in here late tomorrow. In fact, I want you all here two hour early for a meeting."

A low grumble could be heard amongst the employees.

"I knew this was too good to be true." Tony shook his fist in resentment.

"Yo, Nick, I'm out. Care to hang with me and a few fellas for a couple drinks?"

"Nah, I'm good. I need to take care of somethin' at home. They're gonna install the home security system this afternoon, and I'd like to be there with Tammy when they do."

Nicolas was still worried about Tammy being home alone. For all he knew, the alarm guy could be the Merchantville rapist, but he didn't want Tony to know he was stressing over it. Dude might think he was soft and try to play him out in front of the other co-workers. He definitely couldn't let that happen.

"Well, if you do decide to change your mind and wanna get into a little somethin', somethin', I'll be glad to tell the wife that you're still at work. Just buzz me on my cell phone. I got your back."

Tony handed Nicolas one of his business cards. Nicolas accepted the card, but was baffled by the guy's arrogance. He came off like a heavyweight champion. No matter who you put in the ring with him, he always ended the fight with the belt still in hand.

"Thanks for the offer. I'll catch up with you later." Nicolas said, placing Tony's business card in his inner suit pocket.

They exchanged handshakes and headed in separate directions toward their vehicles.

Kim beeped her horn and waved as she pulled out of the parking lot.

What was she tryna tell me? The thought percolated in Nicolas' brain.

Nicolas aggressively pulled out behind her. He would wait until they were far enough from the job and then try to pull her over to see what she was trying to tell him. Dying to know what was on her mind, his curiosity was definitely getting the best of him.

Kim flew up the main streets like a bat out of hell, but Nicolas kept up with her strive for strive. After a quick moment of hesitation, Nicolas had to come to a full stop. Kim was able to make it through the traffic light, but Nicolas didn't want to risk getting a ticket.

Before turning off and heading back home, he laughed at himself for looking like a crazed stalker. Still, thoughts of what she was up to and thinking continued to haunt him during his return trip.

CHAPTER THIRTY-FOUR

Someone's Been Sleeping in My Bed

It was 12:17 p.m. when Nicolas walked in the door, hoping to take Tammy out for lunch if the security installation had already been completed. He felt it would be good for her to unwind and share her day with him, and he would do the same. Discussing the close encounter he had with Kim would be left out, though. While it was good to be honest, telling her would only cause problems. The way he looked at it, not telling her everything was not considered lying...or was it?

"Tammy, I'm home!" he yelled.

Noticing the house was a mess caused him to pause and visually inspect everything. Spotting a broken wine glass on the dining room floor and a chair knocked over sent a chill up his back.

"Tammy!" he yelled, turning 360 degrees.

Dishes were piled in the sink and pillows from the couch lay on the floor. A couple of boxes of clothes were strewn about.

"Shit! Someone broke in! Where the fuck is Tammy?"

He grabbed the thin baseball bat out of the living room closet and started on the first floor. He searched the downstairs bathroom, pulling the shower curtain back, searched closets, and even looked out the back door to check the backyard. There was no sign of Tammy or anyone else. Next, he checked in the basement, but still no sign of Tammy. Then he heard noises coming from upstairs when he got halfway up the steps. There was definitely a stranger in his house.

He hurried upstairs in the direction he thought the sound had come from. With his pulse racing, he noticed the master bedroom door was ajar. His stomach churned the closer he got. He was too nervous to notice the sharp pains shooting up his arm from gripping the bat so hard. Slowly, he opened the bedroom door, trying to be as silent as possible, but the door hinge squeaked like an alley cat begging for food. He stopped to listen and heard a voice he didn't recognize. Fear ran through his veins, and his chest tightened so much he felt like he was being asphyxiated. Swallowing seemed like an impossible task as the saliva in his mouth dried up completely.

He peered through the crack of the door and saw a naked stranger in his bed on top of his wife.

What the fuck! Nicolas thought, his mind trying to make sense of what his eyes were seeing.

Tammy was naked, as well, but he couldn't see her face. All he could see of the stranger was his naked back. Hoping it was all a dream, Nicolas blinked hard to clear his vision, but it felt too real for him to be having a nightmare. The man had her arms pinned to the bed, his naked ass thrusting madly in the air as Tammy whimpered continuously like a badly hurt puppy. Nicolas stood there in a faraway stare. The television was on channel zero, leaving him staring at a continuous blizzard of static on the screen.

With his blood boiling and his vision blurred, all he could see was the man's bare ass thrusting up and down with aggression. Seeing another man on top of his wife, penetrating her, overrode his fear. Something inside him snapped. Without delay, he raced into the room, screaming with rage. His senses heightened; everything appeared to move in slow motion. He swung the bat at the back of the man's head with lightening speed, knocking him unconscious. He then grabbed the man by his hair, pulled him off the bed face up with the bat still in hand, he began bashing the man's upper body and head. Nicolas heard guttural sounds coming from the man's throat as he continued to beat the man repeatedly. Blood flew everywhere. Unaware of the number of blows the strange man suffered from his own hands, he finally stopped his attack. His adrenalin left his body as fast as the momentum was built.

Struggling to catch his breath, Nicolas gazed at the bizarre scene. There was blood splattered all over the room, and the stranger lay motionless with his face disfigured beyond recognition.

He turned to check on Tammy, who was curled up in the corner of the bed sobbing hysterically. His emotions getting the best of him, Nicolas began to cry uncontrollably, too, after throwing the bloody bat to the far corner of the room. He climbed on the bed to comfort her and let her know everything was going to be all right. Then he heard the stranger coughing up blood and teeth.

Oh shit! He's still alive...but barely.

Looking into the stranger's swollen eyes refueled his anger and dismissed his every thought. Nicolas spotted the steak knife he had used the night before to open a few boxes on the nightstand. He grabbed the knife, and holding it with both hands, he jumped on top of the stranger.

"Die, muthafucka!" Nicolas growled through clenched teeth that exposed the hate and outrage displayed on his face. His eyes were blazing with fire.

Remarkably, the man had enough strength to grab Nicolas' hands, preventing the knife from penetrating his skin. Tears blurred

Nicolas' vision as he used all the strength in his body to try to kill this muthafucka, who struggled to hold on. His bloody face showed the titanic effort he was using to save his life. His eyes bulged out of his face. He was fighting for dear life—his own. A life he didn't deserve to have. Nicolas leaned forward applying all his weight, causing the knife to descend closer. His arms quivered with tension until the sharp blade broke through the man's rib cage. A crackling sound could be heard as it punctured his heart.

Nicolas gazed into the stranger's eyes as they widened with agony. The man then grabbed for Nicolas' face and neck, trying to hold on to what little strength he had left. But, it slowly withered away and his breath hissed from his body like a punctured tire. His hands dropped to the floor. Blood flowed from his mouth to the floor, while his eyes remained fixed on Nicolas. With the knife still in the man's chest, Nicolas jumped up and watched the man's pupils dilate, a sign that the man was dead...gone...deceased. To make sure, Nicolas kicked the man. There was no movement, and his eyes stayed focused on the ceiling, staring into a space of nothingness.

He's dead alright.

With that thought, everything started to come into focus. Nicolas had killed a man! It was surreal. The room looked like a movie scene from *Halloween* or *Friday the 13th*. He gazed at the lifeless body for a moment; his breath was short and shallow, his head pounding with adrenaline.

After viewing the scene, reality set in. *Did I do this?* he thought to himself, unaware of being capable of committing such a horrendous crime.

Nicolas turned his attention back to Tammy, who was still in the upper corner of the bed curled in a fetal position and hugging herself.

"Tammy, I'm here," he said as he sat down beside her and tried to calm her. "It's okay now."

*****

"Nine-one-one emergency. How may I assist you?"

Nicolas fought hard to catch his breath as the hot air burned his lungs.

"My wife…was just raped…and I killed the man." Nicolas told the operator.

He tried to control his breathing and spoke in a calm voice, while Tammy was in the background weeping.

"What is your name, sir?"

"Nicolas Coles. My wife's name…is Tammy Coles. Send the police...and an ambulance. We live at…809 Maple Avenue in Merchantville."

"Did you say your wife was raped and the man that raped her is still there?"

Nicolas tried swallowing to get some moisture into his throat before it closed completely. It felt like a balled-up sock going down and the shit hurt.

"Yes…but I think he's dead. There's blood everywhere."

"Okay, sir. A patrol unit and an emergency dispatch unit are in route. Just don't hang up, sir. Stay on the line until help arrives. Is there anyone else there besides your wife and the intruder?"

"No…not that I know of," Nicolas answered, a fresh chill had grabbed the back of his neck.

"Are you or your wife injured?"

"I'm okay, but I ain't sure about my wife. There's blood everywhere," Nicolas stated, scanning Tammy's body.

"Are you able to communicate with your wife?"

"Tammy! Tammy! Are you okay?" he yelled out.

"Is she responding to you, sir?"

"No. She won't stop cryin', but I don't think she's hurt."

Suddenly, the sound of loud banging came from downstairs, as if someone was trying to knock the front door off its hinges.

"Mr. Coles, the police have arrived. Stay on the phone with me and let them in."

Nicolas got up and started down the stairs just as the police banged harder. Nicolas could see an explosive blue and red lights flashing through the living room curtains.

"They're here, knocking on the door."

"Good. You are now free to disconnect this phone call. Good luck, Mr. Coles."

Nicolas glanced out the window at the patrol cars and the EMT vehicles. He threw the phone on the couch and opened the door.

The officers' eyes widened when they saw Nicolas standing there covered in blood.

"What's goin' on here?" asked the bald-headed white cop, with his hand resting on his sidepiece. He had a thick mustache that covered his upper lip. He stood at least 6'3" tall, and weighed well over three hundred pounds. Three yellow strips were on the arms of his shirt, and his name tag read Sgt. Carter. The other officers behind him had their guns drawn, while additional officers surrounded the home.

"My wife is upstairs. I'll take you to her," Nicolas responded with weary eyes and a troubled tone.

"Hold on a minute there, spunky. Does anyone have any weapons we need to be concerned about?" the hesitant sergeant asked, scanning the home's interior through what little opening Nicolas provided.

"No," Nicolas answered.

"Who are you?" questioned the sergeant.

More officers arrived on the scene with itchy fingers.

"I'm Nicolas Coles. I live here."

"The dispatcher said someone had been raped and another person injured. Is that correct?"

"My wife was raped. I beat the man with a baseball bat and stabbed him. He was raping her. They're upstairs. Follow me."

Nicolas turned, leading them upstairs.

"Whoa there, big fella. You're goin' to wait right here with this officer."

Three more police officers entered the house with their guns drawn. From the look of things, it appeared that the entire police department had responded to his call.

"Turn around. O' Riley's goin' to cuff you for your own safety."

"Cuff me?" Nicolas said, more confused than angered. "But my wife is upstairs with a dead body next to her."

"Look, sir, you're covered in blood and talking about you stabbed someone. Now turn around," Sergeant Carter ordered. "We can do this the hard way or the easy way. It doesn't matter to me."

The EMTs were standing in the front yard with their gurney ready and waiting for the "all clear" from the officers.

Nicolas, traumatized and nearly numb, turned and leaned against the wall, submitting to the cuffs without argument. Blood from his clothes smudged the wall.

Two more officers arrived and drew their weapons.

"Bennington," the sergeant murmured, "you and Tyler check downstairs. Connell and I will check out the upstairs."

Officer Connell and Sergeant Carter worked their way down the upstairs hallway, checking rooms as they went. Before entering the master bedroom, there was a brief moment of silence. All that could be heard were voices and chirping sounds over the officers' radios. More officers ran upstairs to assist.

Nicolas heard one of the officers gagging.

"Good grief! It looks like a pig's been slaughtered in here. You think he's still alive," one officer asked his superior.

"What the fuck is this? How the hell could anyone with his face smashed in like that be alive?" the sergeant answered. "Look here, the handle of the blade looks like some kind of steak knife. Radio Tyler and tell him to send the EMTs up here ASAP!" Sergeant Carter yelled, but his voice was loud enough for everyone downstairs to hear.

While Nicolas watched helplessly, the EMTs raced upstairs before the officer had a chance to follow through with the sergeant's orders.

"This one's gone," a voice said.

"What about the woman?" yelled another voice.

"Woman?" Nicolas barked. "She was okay when I left her. Did that muthafucka come back to life and lay his hands on her again while I was standing here. No, let me out of these cuffs! TAMMY!" he cried out.

With the help of another officer, the officer standing nearby pinned him against the wall, smearing more blood.

"What have I done? I've done nothin' wrong!" Nicolas shouted.

Then he heard the officer's voice say, "She's good. She's still alive!"

Nicolas nearly collapsed from the relief of hearing that news.

"Miss, are you cut anywhere? Are you hurt?"

Nicolas held his breath as he waited for her to respond. *Baby, please say somethin'*, he prayed out loud.

Tammy moaned. Nicolas exhaled after holding his breath for what seemed like hours.

"I'm going to get you on a gurney and take you to the ER. You have to get checked out."

"AAAAAAAAGH!" Tammy screamed.

"I need help over here!" yelled the EMT.

Nicolas could hear the commotion. "Tammy, it's okay, baby. I'm right here," he yelled out to her, hoping the sound of his voice would calm her down.

The EMTs finally carried Tammy downstairs strapped to the gurney and placed her in the back of the ambulance as she continued to scream.

"It's okay, baby. I'll be there shortly," Nicolas whispered while still in handcuffs.

"This is him, boys...the Merchantville rapist," Sergeant Carter said, heading down the stairs. "We can't get an ID on him until forensics and the detectives get here to go through his clothes for his driver's license. His face is so disfigured that even his momma wouldn't be able to identify him. So, don't touch anythin'," he explained to the officers present.

Nicolas could still hear Tammy's screams.

"I need to be with my wife! Please let me go!" he squawked, trying to break free of their grasp before the officer slammed him to the floor.

Two other officers who had just arrived offered back up, but Nicolas was too focused on Tammy's wellbeing to worry about the bumps and bruises he would suffer the following morning. If necessary, he would give up his life to save hers. He was her husband—her protector—but now, he couldn't do anything, which left him feeling helpless.

"You're not going anywhere!" one of the officers said, pulling his nightstick out of its holder.

As Detective Andy Morris entered the room, he slipped on a pair of blue medical gloves and now stands over him. "So, Mr. Coles, we meet again. Now what happened here?" he asked, looking around to inspect the area.

The officers raised Nicolas to his feet, only to watch him slide down the wall to the floor, tears running down his face.

"Uncuff him," Morris ordered. After one of the officers complied, he said, "Tell me what happened here today, Mr. Coles."

Detective Morris pressed record on a small recorder he pulled out his suit jacket and placed it on the coffee table. Then he reached for his pen and notepad.

Nicolas stared at the floor as he spoke. "When I left for work his morning, the home alarm guys were scheduled to be here to 'all our security system."

"What's the name of the home alarm company?"

"Watch Guard Home Security. They were sending people to install a home alarm system this afternoon. Tammy was home alone. There was a gas leak at my office today, so we were let go early. I thought since I had the opportunity, I'd come straight home and be here with Tammy when they came." Nicolas paused in deep thought.

"Okay. What time did you get home?"

Nicolas' eyes diverted to the floor. "A little past noon."

"Okay, and what happened when you got home?"

Nicolas looked up at the ceiling as the tears continued to flow. "When I walked into the house...it looked like...like someone had broken in and ransacked the place. There was glass on the floor."

"Glass from what? What was broken?"

"I think it was a wine glass. For all I know, Tammy could have been drinkin', but if she broke a glass, she woulda cleaned it up right away. She can't stand a dirty house."

"Was anything else out of place?" the detective asked, leaning back in the folding chair he got from the front porch.

"We had a box of clothes that we hadn't unpacked yet, and they were strewn all over the floor. Oh yeah, and that chair was turned over." Nicolas gestured toward a chair lying on its side in the dining room.

"Okay," the detective replied, while writing in his notepad.

"I grabbed my baseball bat from the living room closet and searched the house. Then I heard noises comin' from upstairs, so I started up the steps."

Nicolas paused, trying to contain himself.

"What kind of noises?" the detective questioned, holding his gaze.

Nicolas' hands began to shake. "It sounded like…like…I dunno...deep moans and grunts."

"And what did you see when you got to the room?" Morris asked, skipping to the meaty part of the story.

The words spared no effort in departing from his lips. "When I got to our bedroom, I found that muthafucka on my wife, fuckin' her!" Nicolas said, slamming his fist on the hard metal table.

"Okay. I know you're upset, but try to calm down," Morris said in a neutral tone.

"I ain't sure what happened after that. I must've blacked out. Savin' my wife was the only thing on my mind." Nicolas looked at the detective with a hard stare.

Morris could see the thirst for revenge still lingering in his burning eyes.

"Do you happen to know the man you found in bed with your wife?"

"No," Nicolas responded in a raspy voice.

"Nick, did you stab the man that was in bed with your wife?"

"Yes," Nicolas replied, his stomach churning, the scene of the man on top of his wife still vivid in his mind.

"How many times did you hit him with the baseball bat?"

"I dunno." Nicolas rubbed the side of his head hard, as if he had a migraine.

"When you stopped the beating, what did you do?"

"I grabbed the knife off the nightstand and stabbed him with it."

Morris paused, as if he wasn't prepared for Nicolas' answer. "So, after you stabbed him, what did you do next?"

"I called you guys."

The small room started to close in on Nicolas.

"Mr. Coles, that man you killed today may or may not be the Merchantville rapist."

"Can I have some water?" Nicolas asked, feeling himself getting sick. "Are you chargin' me with a crime?"

"You better hope he's the rapist and not your wife's secret lover; because if he was your wife's lover, I'll be arresting you for murder. Now, if you knew that man and your wife were having an affair, it would be to your advantage to give me a full confession right now."

"My wife wasn't havin' an affair with him or anyone else." Nicolas felt rage welling up inside his gut.

"Listen, a man is dead. Let me say this again. We don't know right now if he's the rapist or your wife's lover. If he was your wife's lover and you knew it when you killed him, you'll be charged with murder," Morris reiterated. "You're not under arrest for his murder as of now. I could hold you for twenty-four hours while we investigate this, but I think your wife needs you more than I do at this time. So, I'm going to release you. But, you are not to leave town. Do I make myself clear?"

"Yes," Nicolas replied with a sniffle.

"Since you're not in your right state of mind frame to drive, I'll have an officer escort you to the hospital to check on your wife. Do you need any medical assistance, Mr. Coles?"

Nicolas started checking his arms and rubbing his hands up and down his body feeling for cuts and bruises. "No...not that I know of."

"Great. Hold on for a second." Detective Morris walked over to one of the officers and spoke to him quietly. The officer looked over the detective's shoulder at Nicolas, who was leaning against the wall staring at the floor with tears in his eyes. The officer gave the detective a head nod and escorted Nicolas to Cooper Medical Center.

CHAPTER THIRTY-FIVE

The Longest Ride Ever

On the ride to the hospital, Nicolas couldn't get the visions of Tammy being raped out of his mind. He kept rewinding the video in his head, filling in the gaps with his own imagination.

The rapist used tools to unlock the back door and then creeped through the back of the house. Tammy was drinkin' a glass of wine in the dining room, turned and saw him, and dropped the wine glass. She knocked over the chair and boxes of clothes tryna get away; the rapist chased her up the stairs. Tammy tried to close the bedroom door, but the man was too fast and shouldered his way through, knockin' her to the floor. The rapist stood over her, grinnin' as she crawled backwards tryna escape. He then grabbed her, liftin' her in the air by her hair until her feet were danglin' off the floor. Tammy must have screamed for help, but the rapist hit the side of her head, knockin' her unconscious. Then he threw her on the bed. That's when the beast tore her clothes off, got on top of her, and penetrated her with no condom, like he had done with his other victims.

Nicolas was overloaded with vexation, even as his heart broke from thinking about Tammy regaining consciousness, terrified and crying in fear while the rapist had her pinned to the bed—helpless. He pulled out his cell phone and powered it on to call his mother, but realizing she would tell the whole church about it, he decided against it.

"Here we are, Mr. Coles," the officer said, as they pulled into the Cooper Medical Center Emergency entrance right off Benson Street in Camden.

Nicolas squeezed his eyes shut, trying to block out the thought of it all.

"Thanks a lot, officer," he said, getting out of the patrol car.

A security guard seated at the entrance seemed to be more interested in writing in his oversized logbook than acknowledging Nicolas at the door.

The ER waiting room was filled with patients waiting to be seen. A young, black nurse with a short Afro and nose ring sat behind the glass typing on the computer. Nicolas walked past the security guard and approached the nurse.

"Excuse me. My wife, Tammy Coles, was just brought in about a half-hour ago. Could you please tell me where she is?"

The nurse finally looked up at him with an uninterested gaze. "What's her name, sir?" she retorted in a bored tone.

"Tammy Coles, and I'm her husband," he said, breathing heavily from anxiety.

The nurse began typing on the computer again. "May I see some I.D., please?"

Nicolas reached into his back pocket and pulled out his wallet. He took out his drivers's license and handed it to her.

The nurse wrote his information down on the sign-in sheet. "She's in room 903. Here's your visitor's pass." She handed him a big orange pass with a metal clip to hang from his shirt. "Go through those double doors. I'll open it for you. Take the elevator to the ninth floor. Once you get off, make a right. It's about halfway down the hall on your left."

"Thank you," Nicolas said, as the doors automatically swung open.

On the nineth floor sat a pretty black nurse with red hair.

"May I help you, sir?" she asked with a Jamaican accent.

Nicolas pointed to his visitor's pass. "I'm here to see my wife Tammy Coles."

"She's in 903," she said softly, pointing Nicolas in the right direction.

"Thank you," he muttered, then quickly headed towards the room at a fast pace.

*****

It was close to 2:30 p.m. when Nicolas entered Tammy's room. She was lying in the hospital bed staring up at the ceiling.

With a big smile, Nicolas leaned over her, blocking her view to get her attention. "I'm here, baby. You okay?"

Tammy didn't respond. She didn't acknowledge him or give him any eye contact. She just looked away.

"Sorry it took me so long to get here," he told her, feeling guilty for his tardiness. "Detective Morris kept askin' me a bunch of questions and wouldn't let me leave. After he finished questionin' me, he had a patrol officer drive me here."

Tammy just laid in silence.

Nicolas reached over and gently took her hand.

"Don't worry, baby. He'll never bother you again," he said, trying to comfort her, but it only seemed to upset her more.

It tore him up inside to see the woman who he loved so much hurting and all his efforts to make her feel better having no effect.

CHAPTER THIRTY-SIX

The Examination

Nicolas sat by Tammy's bedside until she cried herself to sleep. It was two hours later, and Nicolas' legs were starting to fall asleep. So, he tiptoed out of the room and headed for the gift shop. He got her some pink roses and was looking at boxes of candy, trying to decide which one she would like best, when his cell phone vibrated. He quickly answered it.

"Hello?"

"Yo, son, wassup? I got Mark on the line with me."

Nicolas was glad to hear the familiar tone of his friend's voice, but wasn't ready to talk about what happened yet.

"Yo, what up?" Nicolas said as the cashier rung up his items.

"Are you at the store or somethin'?" Mark asked. "I hear a cash register."

"Yeah. I'm jus' gettin' Tammy some flowers and candy." Nicolas paid the cashier and then looked for a more private place to talk.

"Flowers and candy! What you do wrong now, playa?" Dave yelled through the phone.

"There y'all go assumin' the worst. I like to go out and get my woman some flowers and candy—*just because*," he lied.

"Just because, huh?" Mark added.

Eager to talk, Dave jumped in. "Yeah, *just because* he did somethin' wrong. Well, anyway, I don't wanna hear that lovey-dovey bullshit. Man, I called to tell you that this fool got this crazy-ass light-skinned bitch movin' into our hotel suite."

"Just because Rolisha cooked us breakfast and fell back to sleep in my bed after we ate don't mean shit!" Mark said in her defense.

"Made y'all breakfast?" Nicolas blurted.

"Yeah, and the shit was good, even though Dave refuses to admit it."

"I never said her cookin' was bad. I have no problem with her cookin'. I got a problem with her refusin' to leave. I wanna feel free and let my nuts hang, but I'm limited 'cause this guy threw a monkey wrench in the game."

"Where's the girl at now?" Nicolas asked, although he really didn't care.

"She still at the hotel, eatin' up all our damn food!" Dave protested.

"And where are y'all?"

"We're up the street watchin' the ass parade," Mark stated.

"Yeah, Mark said it right. We're watchin', 'cause we can't do nuffin' wit' that bitch in the room. I told you she was crazy!" Dave said, aggravated with the whole deal.

"So why don't y'all just ask her to leave?" Nicolas suggested.

"We can't. No one has the heart to say shit, because she might decide to retaliate!" Dave announced.

"Retaliate? For what?" Nicolas asked.

"'Cause this dumb-ass fool fucked her last night instead of her friend!" Dave said.

"Yo, Nick my dude, her friend is five-foot even and weighs four hundred fuckin' pounds. No lie," Mark said, laughing.

"So, Dave, where were you when Mark was gettin' it in?" Nicolas asked, his head beginning to ache from the conversation that was starting to make less and less sense.

"I was busy takin' care of her other girlfriend. Yo, you had to see this bitch. She had beautiful dark skin and a body like Trina, the rapper. And you know how I love me a dark-skinned woman. Yeah, dawg, she was the baddest bitch," Dave sang, using Trina's line.

"Did she seem as crazy as the one Mark smashed?"

"I dunno, and I didn't let her stick around long enough to find out, with her fat-ass girlfriend all in our fridge eatin' up our damn food. I told her that I was a fugitive on the run, lookin' to face a possible ten to fifteen year sentence behind bars. The shit must've worked, 'cause she never looked back when she left the room. I ain't care, 'cause I got mine."

"So what y'all gonna do about the one that's there now?"

"Who? Rolisha?" Dave questioned.

"Yeah, whatever her name is."

"I dunno, but I know one thing. If she's there when we get back, I'ma sleep in the car, 'cause I can't take that stinkin' ass breath of hers. You know how these country girls do," Dave said, starting with one of his off-the-wall philosophies.

"Naw, what they do?" Nicolas asked, rubbing the back of his head, eager to hear it.

"They like to hang around the barns lickin' the assholes of a baby calf. That's how these country muhfuckaz get high."

"Say what?" Nicolas asked, wondering if he really heard what came out of Dave's mouth.

"You know how they get mushrooms from cow shit and get high from eatin' it?"

"Yeah."

"Well, my theory is that it's the new shit they got goin' on out here. Get it? The new shit?" Dave cracked, hoping everyone caught on to the joke, but Nicolas and Mark were too committed to hearing the entire story to start laughing now.

"You know, like huff-in aerosol cans?" Dave continued. "They get high off the methane gas the cows produce when they fart. So, they lick calf ass! That's why her breath be smellin' like goat shit."

Everyone laughed, including Nicolas. The laughter relieved some of the pent-up emotions of the most terrible day of Nicolas' life.

"Yo, I gotta go now. Holla at me later and let me know how it turns out."

Dave had a few more jokes before ending the phone conversation, but Nicolas wanted him to save them for later when he knew he would need them most.

Nicolas rode the elevator up to the ninth floor and returned to Tammy's room. He put the roses and candy on a small table by her window, pulled a chair next to her bed, and sat down. All he could do at the time was simply be there for moral support.

CHAPTER THIRTY-SEVEN

The Heavens Cried That Night

"Has she been awake?" a young, black, cheerful-looking nurse in yellow scrubs and a Winnie the Pooh top asked. The combination looked cute together.

"Not yet," Nicolas whispered.

"Are you her husband?"

"Yes. I'm Nicolas Coles."

"She's doing good. The doctors completed a few test on her and everything appears to be normal. So, he's going to let you take her home. She was heavily sedated so we could run the tests. Therefore, she's going to be pretty groggy. You need to try to start waking her up. I stopped the sedation about an hour ago, so she should be waking up soon."

"You guys did all this while I was gone?" Nicolas asked in disbelief. He looked at his watch, which read 9:48 p.m.

"Yes. We tried waiting for you, but couldn't find you. So, we proceeded without you."

Nicolas had been roaming the halls a little to gather himself and must have lost track of time before heading back to the room.

"Okay," he said, wondering how he was going to take Tammy back to the house where she had been raped...the house of horrors and nightmares.

"The doctor prescribed some medication to help her sleep. She's to take one pill at bedtime with food or milk and she's not to drink any alcohol while taking this medicine. She will have to have a pregnancy test. The soonest she can take the test is five days before her next period. She'll need an AIDS test in six months. She can have that done by her primary care physician or at the health department. The doctor recommends post-rape counseling. The contact number is on the top of the page." The nurse handed Nicolas the paperwork and medicine bottle.

Nicolas couldn't take his eyes off Tammy; he felt himself slowly starting to fade, embarrassed and ashamed that he wasn't there to protect Tammy from the rapist. If he hadn't moved them there in the first place, none of this would have happened.

"Thank you for takin' good care of her," he said submissively, but what else was there to say. *I was too engulfed in my work to worry about my own wife and makin' a good impression was more important than protectin' her.*

Nicolas knew he was going to spend the rest of his life anguishing about whether or not he made the right decision to move there.

"You're welcome, Mr. Coles. When you get her up and dressed, buzz me and I'll take you all down. She also needs lots of support from her family and friends to help her through this traumatic experience. The doctor wanted to keep her here under his care for a few days, but your wife was very persistent in going home. I have her release papers for her to sign when your ready to leave."

The nurse started readjusting Tammy's IV bag, but stopped and glanced over at Nicolas. His facial expression was covered in shame.

"Mr. Coles, I know this is hard for you, but it's even harder for her. My sister was raped, so I know how you feel. But, you both will get over this in time. Just be patient with her," she said, compassion showing in her large brown eyes.

"Thank you." Nicolas swallowed hard, the saliva feeling like shards of glass going down his throat.

"Here, let's see if we can get her to wake-up." The nurse moved to Tammy's bedside. "Mrs. Coles, can you wake up for me?" She rubbed her arm. "Would you like a drink of water?"

Tammy moaned softly and nodded. When the nurse left the room, Nicolas pulled out his cell phone and called for a taxi to take them home.

*****

When the Blue Bird taxi pulled up to the hospital's entrance, Nicolas was relieved it wasn't his nosey neighbor John behind the wheel. Nicolas helped Tammy into the taxi and got in beside her. The driver was a young, light-skinned Hispanic male with braids and tattoos on his neck with the faces of friends and loved ones. He had a hooped nose ring and a short chin beard.

"Where you headed?" the cabbie asked with a heavy Hispanic accent.

"Merchantville, 809 Maple Avenue."

During the ride, Nicolas sat holding Tammy's hand and staring out the window. Tammy hugged his arm with her head resting on his shoulder. His mind and body felt like they were running on autopilot. He didn't know what to think or how to feel. Maybe the past forty-eight hours was only a bad dream from which he would awaken.

Rain started to fall. The windshield wipers squeaked on the glass as the raindrops beat on the roof like the floodgates of heaven had opened, unleashing tears of sorrow and pain that added to their misery. The rain made it hard to see. Only the streetlights could be identified in the darkened blur. Visions of Tammy being raped kept flashing in his head over and over again like a broken video recorder stuck on automatic replay.

After what felt like the longest ride home he had ever taken, Nicolas helped Tammy out of the cab and paid the driver. Tammy got out of the car slowly. She was almost catatonic. She stared at the house as if having second thoughts about entering their home. As the rain continued coming down hard, the only thing Tammy had to shield her was the big box of chocolates Nicolas bought at the hospital. At least they were good for something. When they approached the house, they noticed a note taped to the door. Nicolas read the note, which said a clean-up crew had been able to clean up the master bedroom and that they were free to use it once the rug dried.

Nicolas tore the note off and unlocked the front door. After guiding Tammy to the guest bedroom, he ran a bath and gently washed her with Dove soap while she whimpered softly. It was killing him inside to see her this way. He felt so helpless and unable to ease her pain. He dried her off with a soft towel, put one of his t-shirts on her, and carried her to the guest bedroom. He carefully laid Tammy on the bed and gave her a kiss on the forehead.

Tammy lied there in bed, staring into space while tears ran down her cheeks and dropped onto the pillow. It was no longer the comfy material used for a good night's rest. It became an oversized sponge used to soak up her pain.

"It's okay, Tammy. You'll be okay. We can get past this." He pushed her hair away from her eyes. "I'm gonna fix you a cup of tea. Would you like a bite to eat? Maybe some crackers and cheese?"

Tammy shook her head, indicating she wanted nothing and reached for a Kleenex from the nightstand.

"Maybe later then."

Nicolas had no clue what to do. He couldn't even get her to talk to him.

"I'm gonna go take a shower and a couple of aspirins, okay? I'll go ahead and fix some tea in case you change your mind," he told her, while rubbing the tips of his fingers across her cheek. Tammy turned her head away from his touch and closed her eyes.

On his way to the kitchen, Nicolas cracked the master bedroom door and looked in. The room reeked with the coppery smell of blood. Images of the man on top of Tammy flashed through his mind, causing him to gag. The cleaning crew tried covering it up with pine-scented products, but it didn't work. He closed the door and headed for the shower, knowing there wasn't enough water in the world to wash the memory from his mind or even calm his nerves. Nicolas took a cup of tea sweetened with orange blossom honey in the room to Tammy, sat it on the nightstand, and laid down beside her. When he tried to hold her, she pulled away, moving to the other side of the bed.

He knew the last thing she wanted was to be touched by a man...any man. So, he turned over with his back toward her so she couldn't see the hurt in his eyes.

CHAPTER THIRTY-EIGHT

Taking the Day Off

It was May 28th on a Saturday morning. The early morning sun poured through the slats in the Venetian blinds. The alarm clock was painfully loud before Nicolas cut it off. He got out of bed, threw on some sweat pants, and went to make Tammy and him breakfast. On his way to the kitchen, he picked up the clothes strewn about the living room and straightened up the house. He then put on a pot of coffee and ran upstairs to check on Tammy, finding her still asleep. While sitting at the small desk, Nicolas took out his cell phone and called work to let them know he wouldn't be in.

"Home Reality and Association," a cheerful voice answered.

"Bill Satario, please."

"May I ask who's calling?"

"Nicolas Coles."

"One moment, please."

Nicolas listened to the Bee Gees' "If I Can't Have You" while he waited.

"Hey, Nick, what's goin' on?" Bill answered, his tone unsettled.

"Hey, sir, how are you doin'?"

"I'm fine, and call me Bill. What can I do for you?"

"I have a family emergency, sir...I mean, Bill," Nicolas stuttered. "I'm not gonna be in the office today. It's a serious family matter or else I would be there," Nicolas added, not wanting to get on Bill's bad side.

"Family emergency? Well, I hate to see you miss work. You know you haven't put in a full day since you started. But, if you have a serious problem to tend to, then by all means do that," Bill replied with a measure of understanding. "I believe family comes first. Just get in here tomorrow, if possible. If you can't be here in the morning, I'll need to hear from you."

"But tomorrow's Saturday," Nicolas said, not sure if he should leave Tammy alone that soon.

"What about it? Do you have to go to church or somethin'?"

"No...not really," Nicolas said, although he knew he needed to find a good church nearby. "I didn't know the office was open on Saturdays."

"Well, technically, it's not. Since you're on salary pay, I can't pay you overtime. But, most of the agents come in for a few hours on Sundays to catch up and have a game plan for the week."

"Okay. No problem, sir. I'll be there first thing in the mornin'." Tammy needed him more then the job did and taking that risk to save his career was a bad move on his part.

"Okay, I'm goin' to hold you to your word. So, don't disappoint me." Bill said, sounding more like a pissed-off boss.

"I won't, sir," Nicolas reassured him, sounding more confident than he felt. Leaving Tammy all alone while at work wouldn't be safe after the trauma she went through, but Nicolas was walking on eggshells with Bill keeping a close watch over him.

"See you tomorrow then, and stop calling me sir," he complained.

"Got'cha. Thanks, Bill. I appreciate it."

Nicolas ended the call and turned on the TV in the bedroom. He lowered the volume so he could watch the local morning news without waking Tammy. *God knows she doesn't need to wake up to that,* Nicolas thought. He knew the story would make the media, but hoped they didn't reveal their names. It would have been wiser to watch television in another room, but Nicolas didn't want to leave her side. If his and Tammy's mothers saw it on TV, they would be at his house yelling and screaming at each other, trying to place the blame. They could not be under the same roof together without getting into an argument. Once, Nicolas had to physically pull his mother away from Martha.

"In today's top story, the Merchantville rapist struck again, or did he? Police are not giving out that information right now or the family's identity. But, what we do know is that a man broke into this house behind me here in Merchantville and attacked a woman who was home alone," the male reporter said, standing in front of Nicolas' and Tammy's house.

Visions flashed in Nicolas' head as his body went cold all over.

"The rapist was beaten and stabbed to death by the husband, who happened to come home early from work." The reporter paused and pressed his earpiece closer against his ear.

"I am being told that the man stabbed to death was Officer Peter Wright, a local police officer who has been on the force here in Merchantville for six years. The Chief of Police is calling for a full investigation. Residents in this neighborhood are hoping this is the end to the reign of terror that has struck this quiet neighborhood. I interviewed a concerned resident, John Newman, earlier this morning and this is what he had to say."

The video showed John standing in his front yard.

"The young couple just moved in a few days ago. Uh...I've met them, and they're a wonderful couple. But, for the husband to come home and see his wife being attacked by that sick maniac had to be very traumatic. I just hope they can get over this horrifying situation and continue their lives, because they're so young and have their whole life ahead of them."

The reporter reappeared on the screen.

"It's not known at this time if the couple are in their home this morning. I did check with the hospital, and the wife was discharged late last night. We're hoping to interview them later this afternoon. I'm Ron Little. Back to you, Bob."

Bob, the morning news anchor, appeared on the screen.

"Thank you, Ron. Now, in other news, mob boss Frank DeBartello is under investigation for another alleged hit yesterday on Supreme Court Judge Edward Powell. The judge was scheduled to make a final ruling in this case later this week, when a suspicious fire took his life as well as his wife's. Their charred bodies were found on their bedroom floor, evidently trying to escape the flames and smoke. The police chief said the department is waiting for the coroner's report to establish the cause of death. It may be that they were killed and the fire was an attempt to cover up the cause of death. An unconfirmed tip said the coroner found signs of smoke in Judge Powell's lungs, which would clearly indicate it could be accidental, but we have not been able to confirm the report. According to his son, Eric Powell, his mother and father didn't smoke. His father also had asthma. It looks like the hit-man may have struck again. Police are diligently working to find out if mob boss Frank DeBartello was behind the Powell's death."

Nicolas cut the television off and glanced over at Tammy. Seeing that she was still sleeping, he went downstairs to fix breakfast.

CHAPTER THIRTY-NINE

I'm On To You

Nicolas fixed Tammy a tray with scrambled eggs, sausage, buttered toast, orange juice and milk. She really needed to eat something, even if she had to force it down. He noticed the bruises on his body by the excessively aggressive officers last night, but it was nothing serious. Nicolas was no stranger to lumps and bumps from years of experience in sports.

"I made you some breakfast, baby," Nicolas said, placing the tray of food on the nightstand.

Tammy sat on the side of the bed rubbing her head.

"Do you need some aspirin?" he asked, before going downstairs to get his plate of food.

"No," she mumbled, then headed to the bathroom.

She had spoken, and that was progress.

Just as Nicolas hit the bottom stair, someone knocked at the front door. He looked out the window and saw Detective Andy Morris standing on the doorstep and a Channel 6 mobile news van parked near the curb. None of what he saw could possibly be a good sign. Panic raced through Nicolas.

He's gonna arrest me for murder, and he's brought the media to get video footage! Nicolas thought.

Taking a deep breath, he opened the door and prepared for the worse.

"Good morning, Mr. Coles. We need to talk," Detective Morris said, holding a manila folder in his hand.

Need to talk? So that must mean he's not gonna arrest me then. Good.

Nicolas opened the door wider. "Come in."

Nicolas glanced at the stairs to see if Tammy had heard the chatter. As he led Detective Morris to the dining room, he hoped Tammy wouldn't hear them.

"I saw the news this mornin'. Sorry about your fellow officer. Care for somethin' to eat?" Nicolas said, offering hospitality.

"No, thank you. I had breakfast on the way here," Morris answered.

Nicolas motioned for him to have a seat.

"I'll just stand," Morris said, which meant he wasn't staying long.

"I thought you were in Internal Affairs investigatin' those officers who harassed me the other day?" Nicolas sat down at the table, grabbing a piece of toast. Unable to remember when he last ate, his body was screaming for sustenance.

"Yeah," Morris said, shaking his head while biting on his bottom lip. "Due to uncontrollable circumstances, I had to put in for a transfer. So, here I am back on the streets as a detective working this case. I must've pissed someone off, because they put a bug in the chief's ear, which led me to investigating crime scenes instead of bad cops."

As if reading his facial expression, Morris narrowed his eyes at Nicolas. "You don't happen to know who could have gotten into the chief's ear, do you?" He gazed at Nicolas like a boxer facing his opponent before the fight.

"No, I'm afraid not, detective," Nicolas responded, wondering where this conversation was going and if Morris was trying to place the blame on him for his abrupt transfer.

Morris relaxed his face. "I wanted the hit-man case, but they gave me this one instead, which is the third biggest case next to the hit-man and Merchantville rapist."

"Is that good or bad?" Nicolas asked, practically inhaling the toast.

"Good for me, but bad for you," Morris stated, raising an eyebrow.

Nicolas swallowed and looked up at him.

Detective Morris's body language and attitude changed suddenly. "Okay, Nick, let's cut to the chase here. Did you know Officer Peter Wright?" he asked with an expressionless stare.

"No," Nicolas replied, confused. "I dunno anyone from Jersey, why?" Despite being scared and high strung, he made eye contact with the detective.

Detective Morris pulled some photos out of the folder and threw them on the table.

Nicolas looked at the pictures. "Oh yeah, that's Rodeski's partner...the quiet one."

Detective Morris gave Nicolas a stone-cold gaze and leaned toward him. "I had a speedy preliminary DNA test on him, and the results came back negative this morning. Peter Wright was not the Merchantville rapist. His DNA doesn't match the DNA of the other rape victims."

"What in the hell are you tryna say, detective?" Nicolas boomed loud enough for Tammy to hear.

"Did you file that harassment report on Wright because he was having an affair with your wife?" Morris asked with a firmness that was utterly convincing.

Nicolas bristled with anger. "Do you have any proof that my wife was havin' an affair with that muthafucka? If so, I suggest you arrest me now, 'cause I'ma kill her fuckin' ass if it's true."

Nicolas laughed, which wasn't in good taste, but it was either laugh or cry.

"Not yet, but I expect to. Oh...and I do have a witness who has already given a statement under oath that on the same day you filed the harassment report, he saw a patrol car outside of your house twice that day—once that morning and again that afternoon after you left for work," the detective stated icily.

That wasn't the answer Nicolas was expecting or the one he wanted to hear.

"Am I under arrest, detective?" Nicolas asked, dropping his fork on the floor.

"Not until I can get the okay from the investigating squad."

"Do you have a search warrant?" Nicolas roared, his anger growing.

"No, but I'm working on that, too," Morris said, flashing a sarcastic grin.

"Then, as of this moment, I refuse to answer any more of these off-the-wall questions. I want my attorney present." Nicolas stomped to the front door and swung it open with so much energy that a blast of wind blew in, knocking Tammy's paperwork from the hospital all over the floor. "Get the hell out my house, detective!" he bellowed.

Nicolas was so angry that he wanted to peel the skin off Morris's face with his fingernails, just to watch him suffer. Detective

Morris started for the front door, leaving the photos behind. "Oh, you'll hear from me again. And you can keep those photos. There's plenty more where those came from."

After Morris left, Nicolas threw the manila envelope containing the photos in the trash and stood in the kitchen angry and confused, trying to put the pieces of the puzzle together. He realized the license plate number on the patrol car he saw cruising his street and the plate he saw on the patrol car of the cops who'd had him face down tasting asphalt were the same—MPD-U16—Rodeski's.

Naw, this shit is crazy.

Nicolas ignored the thought and decided to keep his mind focused on work. He had a very big day coming up the next day, and the last thing he wanted to do was slack off.

CHAPTER FORTY

The Sacred Book

Needing to prepare himself and catch up on the job, Nicolas was on his knees in the spare room rummaging through unpacked boxes of books in search of his book on New Jersey real estate tax laws. His past due cell phone bill was in the box so he folded it up and placed it in the back pocket. That's when he stumbled across Tammy's diary. *What is her diary doin' stuffed in this box and not under the mattress where she usually keeps it?* he wondered. While looking at the pink book in his hand, his mind began to wonder. *Maybe the truth about Tammy and Wright is in this diary? Was she really havin' an affair with him?*

His curiosity overpowered his judgment, making it hard for him to resist the temptation. "Fuck it!" He uttered without a second thought for Tammy's privacy. With his powerful hands, he tore the small, insubstantial lock off her diary and began reading.

Dear Diary:

This is day two of us moving into this neighborhood and I thought it would be boring, until I bumped into an old friend at the grocery store. I was madly in love with him over eight years ago. He was my first true love. I lost my virginity to him, and after all these years, I still haven't gotten over him. I feel bad that I've kept this secret from Nick, but I know he wouldn't understand that Peter will always have a special place in my heart. If he ever found out, I would just die.

Nicolas realized Peter was the reason Tammy didn't answer the phone that day when he called her from work. She was at the grocery store smiling all in Peter's face. Then Nicolas realized that she didn't have her phone that day. She claims that she accidentally left it at home, Yeah right.

He said he can't stop thinking about me and still loved me...in so many words. I've been thinking about him a lot, too, but I didn't tell him that. His timing was on point. Nick got a new job, which requires a lot of hours. I know it's for the family, but I have needs, too. So, I took his number. It was smooth how he placed it in my hand before he left the grocery store, leaving me in a daze.

Nicolas was stunned to find out that Peter Wright was Tammy's ex-boyfriend Pete from high school. *It must be the same Peter, because she never mentioned anyone else,* he thought. He visualized Peter smiling at Tammy as he handed her a piece of paper with his number on it, his hand caressing hers. He could see Tammy watching him walk away, then opening the piece of paper before placing it between her breasts, close to her heart.

When I got home, Nick was worried sick about me. It was eating me up what I did, and I couldn't look him straight in the eyes.

Nicolas clenched his fist and punched a stationary box out of frustration. It bothered him knowing how Tammy loved that added attention from other men.

It's quiet as hell in this boring-ass neighborhood and the only friendly neighbor is John Newman. He looks like a stalker, but he's still a nice guy, who needs a good woman to treat him right. I admit that I'm flattered he flirts with me in a nice way, but I know he means no harm. If I weren't married, I'd probably give him some. Who am I kidding? I'd definitely give him some. He has a nice physique for a man his age. He must work out, because you don't get a body like that from watering grass.

Shaking his head in disbelief, Nicolas thought about John smiling and saying he'd watch the house while Nicolas was at work and how it was in good hands, like he was talking in riddles about trying to push up on her.

But, as for now, I'm weak. I admit that my flesh got the best of me. Even John would do right about now, but now I feel guilty. I did something very bad. I cheated on Nick.

Nicolas' head jerked back hard enough to cause whiplash. *Am I readin' this shit right?* Nicolas' mind started to unravel. He couldn't understand what he was reading, but as hard as it was, he continued on.

I don't know how it happened. Pete and his partner were giving Nick a hard way to go. I didn't like the way they treated him like a criminal on our front step. Nick never met Pete, so I know he didn't recognize him. This evening, while Nick was at work, Pete came back alone to see if everything was okay. Before I knew it, I was in bed with him. The same bed Nick and I sleep in.

Nicolas was devastated. His eyes started to water with bitterness. Holding back the hot tears, he forced himself to continue reading.

It was like a breath of fresh air. I forgot how great this man was in bed, and now I feel like a crackhead on dope. I just had to have more, and he gave it to me again and again. I loved the way he man handled me. His aggression turned me on. I didn't want him to stop.

Then the phone rang. Was it Nick or what? Pete put his clothes on as I straightened up the room.

It looked as if a hurricane ripped through here. Pete rushed out the front door, promising to see me tomorrow. Man, I just got to have it. Pete promised to come by early tomorrow morning while Nick is at work. And since he's working late, I'll let Pete do what he wants to me all day long.

Now I got the munchies, as if I just smoked a joint. Got to make some dinner before Nick gets home. Thank God I got that soup from the market. But, before doing that, I better straighten up and change these dirty sheet so Nick doesn't get suspicious.

Nicolas thought about how Tammy sucked his dick so good that night, causing him to cum twice. She never allowed him to penetrate her. Maybe she thought he would be able to tell the difference, but she still allowed him to eat her nasty ass pussy after that muhfucka stuck his dirty dick all in that raw dog. Then he thought about how she cleaned the sheets and lied about that soup.

"Fuckin' bitch," he cursed under his breath, only to look up and see Tammy standing in the doorway, her mouth agape.

"How could you?" Nicolas said, overcome with sorrow.

If Nicolas were to kill Tammy where she stood, it would have been fully justifiable. He wanted to beat the living shit out her, but something held him back. Maybe it was his conscious letting him know that if he reacted on emotion, he would destroy everything he worked hard for. But, it was more powerful than that. Everything was happening too fast for his conscious to intervene and if it did,

Nicolas wouldn't listen. So, it had to be God. Only God would have the power to stop his fury from taking over.

"What are you doing? You know you're not supposed to read that."

Tammy ran back to the bedroom, jumped in the bed and started crying under the sheets.

Nicolas followed her.

"Is that all you can say?" he roared, pulling the sheet from her face and waving the diary in front of her, wanting to wrap his hands around her fucking neck and choke the breath out of her fucking ass. "Did our marriage mean anythin' to you?"

Nicolas' anger turned into a hurt he could never believe possible. He was heartbroken and felt like crying.

"Do you know I'll probably spend the rest of my life in prison for murder? Do you want that? Was this pencil-dick cop worth destroyin' our marriage—our lives?"

Nicolas cried, shaking. His voice cracked. The anger inside him was going to drive him to unleash his wrath in an act of physical violence. He knew if he didn't get out of the house he might end up killing her with his own two hands. He started to throw the diary at her, but stormed out of the house taking the diary with him.

"You'll never see this pink piece of shit again!" he said, putting it inside his suit coat pocket.

While heading toward his car, he heard John call out, "Hey, Nick." He yelled out stopping his work of planting a rose bush, waving.

Nicolas thought about unleashing his fury on John for flirting with his wife, but John was a man and Tammy was very attractive, so he couldn't be mad at him for that. In a state of depression,

Nicolas got in his car, ignoring him and peeled out of the driveway. The car was driving, but no one was behind the wheel. Nicolas was crushed. He couldn't believe Tammy would play him the way she did.

Nicolas started putting everything together. Tammy had started to go the extra mile when it came to her appearance. Her shoes had to match her purse. She was going out her way to have her toes, nails, and hair done. She replaced her tomboyish ways for a more prissier one. Her paying more attention to her looks and giving detail to her hair and makeup, Nicolas took it as her trying to impress the neighbors, not a fuckin' cop.

He fought back the tears while his stomach knotted up. His whole world was shattered. He had to stay focused and try to think of a way to protect his freedom. Jail was certainly not an option. Stopping for gas on his way to work, Nicolas opened the back hatch of his SUV and wedged the diary under the edge of the carpeting in the back towards the right side for safekeeping, invisible to the naked eye.

CHAPTER FORTY-ONE

The Big Favor

Nicolas pulled out his cell phone and called out sick for work. He didn't want to hear Bill's voice, knowing Bill would have yelled through the phone as if Nicolas was deaf. So he left his secretary the message instead.

After disconnecting that conversation, he called Tony.

Tony answered with loud music blasting in the background.

"Hey Tony, it's Nick."

"Hey, what's up?"

"I need a big favor."

"Talk to me, buddy." Tony turned down the volume on his system.

"I need a place to stay for a few days to get my head together."

"No problem, I have a two-bedroom town house in Camden. I don't think it's a good spot for you and your wife though. It's in a pretty rough neighborhood."

"It's just for me," Nicolas said trying to keep himself together.

"Hah! Wife is gettin' on your last nerve, huh? That's what women do. Hey, you can stay there as long as you need to."

"Good lookin' out!"

"Not a problem, I just wanna let you know that Camden is very unsafe."

"I'll be a'ight. I'm from Brooklyn. So when can I come get it off you?"

"I'll give it to you at work."

"No can do. I'm not comin' to work. I called out sick."

"Daaaamn! You're doin' yours like that with less than a week in the buildin'?" Tony's voice was filled with excitement.

"I had to. Big problems at the home front. Gotta get my head right."

"Don't worry about it Nick, Saturdays don't count, it's a bonus day to catch up for us. Ah, you know I'm gonna be trainin' you since Gary Hanson got fired."

"Fired! For what?" Nicolas barked.

"Bill had to let him go for abusin' sick days."

Nicolas started to worry. He would need this job to pay a lawyer. He would never trust a court-appointed one when his life and freedom was on the line.

"Maybe I should call him back and tell him I'm comin' in."

"Don't worry about it. This day doesn't count. Gary's been abusin' sick days for the last three years. He's been callin' out over forty days a year mostly to fill in at his ice cream parlor business when one of his workers called out. Bill found out about it and let him go. I don't like to wish bad on people, but this guy was gettin' paid salary and workin' somewhere else while usin' his sick days. Not cool—Not cool at all. And now that you're callin' out sick, you're goin' to have to pay for my drinks tonight, since I gotta come in tomorrow on my only day off!"

Nicolas could barely make sense out of Tony's words. His mind felt like it was in a vortex. He had killed a cop, left his wife and would likely be facing murder charges before the day was over.

"No problem I got you man." He forced out a meaningless laugh.

"You can meet up with me after I get off of work at the Purple Parrot, the bar around the corner from the office, and I'll give you a spare set of keys. The place is furnished. I kept it as my *lay low* spot."

"Cool, I'll be there as soon as you get off of work. Drinks are on me." Nicolas disconnected the call and immediately dialed Mark's number.

"Nick, wassup, my nigga?" Mark immediately answered.

"Tammy cheated on me." The words tumbled painfully from his mouth.

"Whaaaat? Was it with that same guy you caught her with from her old job?"

"No, it was Pete."

"Pete! What Pete?"

"Pete Wright. The guy from high school."

"What, her ex-boyfriend Pete?" Mark's voice raised at a higher pitch.

"Yeah, that Pete."

"Are you sure?"

"I caught her in bed with him and I killed him."

"Yo...that's not funny, Nick. Stop with the bullshit."

"I'm serious dawg."

"Yo, that shit ain't funny at all, son."

"I'm real fuckin' serious about this shit, dawg. I came home early from work yesterday and found them in our bed." A fresh rush of pain stabbed his heart as his mouth formed the words.

Mark broke in with a quivering voice. "Yo—We shouldn't be havin' this conversation on the phone."

"It's cool. I...I thought he was the Merchantville rapist so I beat him to death with a baseball bat and then stabbed him in the chest with a stake knife tryna save her."

"Hold up! We watched that shit on the news last night, but they didn't release any names."

Nicolas told Mark everything that happened, starting with the first day he and Tammy moved to Merchantville. He told him about Wright and his partner harassing him and how he didn't recognize Pete because he never actually met him.

"You still got her diary?" Mark asked.

"Yeah. I got it and left the house before I killed her fuckin' ass," Nicolas emphasized.

"You better hang on to that! Where ya at now?"

"In my whip drivin' around on Route 130, tryna figure out on what to do." Nicolas ran a red light. Oncoming traffic slammed on brakes and beeped their horns. Nicolas was oblivious to them.

"I'm gonna meet up with one of my co-workers who's gonna let me hide out in one of his spot 'til I decide what to do next." Nicolas said, pulling into Cooper River Park before he ended up getting a traffic ticket for reckless driving or even worse, killing someone behind the wheel of his vehicle and add that to his murder rate.

Cooper River Park, just outside of Merchantville, is nearly three hundred fifty beautiful acres surrounding the river. A woman in white shorts and a halter top jogged past him and an elderly couple was walking an all black Pekingese. Several sail boats drifted along the cool river, their colorful sails rippling in the breeze. Despite the dark murky water, Cooper River Park was still a beautiful tourist attraction and a pleasant place to visit.

"So what's gonna happen now?"

"I dunno. But if this shit comes out to be true, then I'll spend the rest of my life behind bars."

"I think you better get a lawyer like a.s.a.p."

"Yeah, I will as soon as I get myself together." Nicolas watched geese waddling in front of the car, wishing he was as free as they were, no worries, no stress—no lousy cheating ass wife. You know the rest.

"Don't wait 'til it's too late. Once they slam those iron bars on you, you won't be able to make moves as easily."

"I got'cha. I'm callin' a lawyer as soon as we hang up."

"Hold on, Nick. Dave just walked in. He wants to tell you somethin'." Mark handed Dave the phone.

"Yo, wassup, fool?" Dave said with delight.

"Nuffin' much, just coolin'." Nicolas responded in a low tone, alternating between reality and denial.

"Did he tell you about that glow in the dark, light-skinned chicken headed bitch yet?"

"Naw."

"Well anyway, this bitch moved in to our hotel suite, tellin' Mark that she thinks she's pregnant."

"Pregnant! did he use a condom." Nicolas yelped, but what's the worse that could happen. As long as he pays child support he could still live his own life, but on a tighter budget. At least he'll have his freedom. There's no comparison to what Nicolas was about to face.

"Yeah! So he says. This fool claims that the condom bust when he was hittin' it. Yeah, right. We know how this dirty dick nigga rolls." Dave chuckled.

"Damn you hard on the nigga. Lighten up a little."

"Fuck all dat. This nigga is smarter then that with this bright ass bitch talkin' out the side of her face. But peep this shit. She was sayin' that shit after Mark fucked her the first night. Now ain't that a bitch?"

"Oh yeah," Nicolas dully responded. His mind was focused on what's going to be the outcome once they find out that Tammy wasn't raped. That would be so embarrassing; to lose everything he worked so hard for and be known as the guy who couldn't satisfy his own wife. He'll probably never see the light of day and live the rest of his life in shame and torment.

"Nick are you there? Man, wake the fuck up! What's the matter wit'cha, son? You sick or somethin'?" Dave yelled in the phone.

"Yeah, I musta caught a Jersey cold or somethin'," he lied.

"Well, you better tell Tammy to take care of that shit."

"I'll do just that."

"Yeah, have her make you some of that tuna with onions you had before you left for Jersey."

"Aw, you got jokes."

"I just tell it like it is, playa." Dave giggled.

"Well, just don't tell it like it is over here. My wife has no problem with takin' care of me and makin' me some tuna."

"Yeah, yeah, yeah. But, anyway, I'm ready to come home early, 'cause this bitch out here is stylin' on us hard."

"Well Mark should take her to get a pregnancy test and if she is pregnant, he'll need to get a DNA test done to make sure it's his."

"That's what I told him, but this girl got him shook. She's talkin' 'bout marriage and havin' more kids already."

"Oh yeah." Nicolas tried to act interested, his mind wandering. What had he done to deserve this? He believed she enjoyed being his wife. He's never heard her complain about their sex life. Did she get tired of him or bored with their relationship?

"Yo man, what the fuck you doin', jerkin' off or somethin'? You sound dead as hell right now. What's goin' on, nigga?" Dave asked, discerning the sadness in Nicolas' voice.

Nicolas wanted to tell him what was going on, but Dave was too immature for Nicolas to have a grown up conversation with him about this right now.

Dave would go to work in a business suit and use a Harvard educated voice and vocabulary, but once he left his job, he threw on his thug gear and acted like he was still in the hood.

"I'm listenin'—go head, nigga."

"Yo, she told him that she's gonna cut his dick off if she catches him cheatin' on her, like *Lorena Bobbitt* did her husband *John* on the night of March 13, 1989. This bitch remembered the date and time of day. But she said that she's not gonna throw it in the woods like Lorena did so they could find it and stitch it back on—oh no. She said that she'll put it in a blender and shred it up like hamburger meat. Now you know this bitch is crazy. I told that fool to just tell her that it's not gonna work and get the hell outta Dodge."

"Did he tell her that he wasn't ready to start a relationship?"

"Yeah, but she was talkin' 'bout he ain't gonna do her like this."

"Do her like what?"

"Hit and move type shit. Then she tells him to look where it got her first baby daddy. Yo, what the fuck does that shit suppose to mean?" Dave thundered.

"Did you ask her?"

"Fuck naw! Damn that," He sung, in a squeaky voice.

"So how are you gonna know shit?"

"That's Mark's problem not mine," Dave voiced out at Mark and Mark mumbled something in the background. "She need to start payin' rent around this muthafucka."

"Y'all shoulda told her that, too."

"Oh I will. Trust me." Dave chuckled like it wouldn't be a problem, but Nicolas knew better. "Why is it so hard for this fool to understand the obvious?"

"And what the fuck is that?" Nicolas asked, knowing he'll end up saying something stupid.

"That this glow in the dark bitch is crazy."

"Yeah."

"Yeah," Dave repeated. "She's crazy with a whole lot of issues, which makes a bad combination. As soon as she get's back, he'll have to tell her that she's either gonna start payin' some rent or leave."

"What ever dawg." Nicolas blew it off.

"What? You don't believe me, nigga?" Dave announced in a high pitch.

"Yeah, I believe you," Nicolas responded with mental rejection.

"Damn, dawg. You make it sound like this bitch got me shook."

"Both y'all muthafuckas sound like you're shook." Nicolas chuckled.

"Okay, okay. I'll step to her and holla back at you later, nigga."

"Cool, then on that note, I'll holla at y'all later."

Nicolas disconnected the call and stayed at the park for a couple of hours trying to clear his head and breathe normally before meeting up with Tony at the bar. Shit just started to spark off and Nicolas needed to stay cool. Nothing happened yet, and this shit may blow over. If he keeps acting nervous, then it may raise some flags.

CHAPTER FORTY-TWO

The Hook-Up

It was 5:03 p.m. when Nicolas entered The Purple Parrot located on 1406 Chapel Avenue in Cherry Hill. It was a nice-sized spot with eight large television screens on each wall, all set on sports channels. Six pool tables and at least a dozen pinball machines and arcade games were being played. Pop music came from a jukebox near the entrance. A large bar took up a majority of the place, with six bartenders serving customers. Tony was in the back of the bar shooting pool with a few guys, when he looked up and saw Nicolas.

"Hey, it's my main man Nick. Have a drink with us. These are my buddies—Steve, James, and Henry. And this big guy right here is my big brother Frankie. Fellas, meet Nick."

Everyone gave Nicolas a welcoming handshake.

"That's short for Nicolas, right?" Frankie asked with a strong New York Italian accent.

Nicolas nodded. "Yeah."

"Yo, did you know your name in Greek means power of the people," he exclaimed before taking a sip of beer.

"No, I didn't know that. I'll have to look that up when I get home," Nicolas responded, wondering if Tony's brother was trying to slip in some racial remarks.

In New York, the Italians don't use the word nigger anymore. They replaced the word nigger with Monday, because everyone hates Mondays.

"There you go with that fundamental philosophy bullshit!" Tony yelled out.

"What about it? It's food for thought, Tony," Frankie muttered.

Tony approached Nicolas, throwing his arm around him. "Don't pay him any mind, Nick. He's into that Greek mythology bullshit. I keep tellin' this stooge he ain't Greek, but he won't listen."

"Oh yeah? You wouldn't be sayin' that shit if I shoved this pool stick down your throat gladiator style," Frankie joked as his three goons laughed at his crude humor.

"Hey, Nick, you'll like it here. The hoes be comin' out the woodworks. Oh yeah, before I forget..." He reached in his front pants pocket. "...here's the keys to the apartment. If you're lucky enough, you may get to take one of these bitches home wit'cha."

Tony laughed hysterically, losing his balance and falling against his brother Frankie. Tony and Frankie somewhat looked alike, but Frankie was two inches shorter and had a stronger-looking chin with broad shoulders and a stocky build.

"Hey, watch it already!" Frankie said, breaking Tony's fall.

Tony reached over, putting his arm around Frankie. "You see, I love my brother 'cause he's always got my back." Tony reached for his beer with his free hand. "So what you say, Nick? Come have a few drinks wit' the fellas."

"What's da madda wit'cha? You too young to drink or somethin'? Frankie announced.

"Naw, I'm legit," Nicolas responded, chest out with his pride on the line.

"Then stop actin' like a big wuss and have a few beers wit' us," Frankie said.

What the hell, Nicolas thought. *Maybe a few beers will numb the pain enough to think logically about the situation and come up with a better solution.*

"I'll have a few drinks, and don't worry 'bout it. The drinks are on me."

Unlike Tony and his buddies, Nicolas had to show the bartender his I.D. because he didn't look of age with his baby face.

With his eye in a slit, Tony dangled his finger at Nicolas. "Yeah, that's right. You did promise to treat me. What happened? Why you late?"

"I had to clear my head a little. I really need to talk to you, Tony. Can we sit at the bar or in a booth for a minute?"

"Hey Nick, look at my brudder here, he pulls bitches wit' his cah. How you do it, cause Tony here tells me that cha scared of pussy. Is that true or what." Frankie commented in his ethnic accent.

The other three guys, who didn't say much, laughed. There was something eerie about them. They seemed more like Frankie's bodyguards than his friends. Their eyes continuously scanned the bar, and they only looked at Frankie when he wanted their attention. They only laughed when he laughed.

What's up with that shit? There's somethin' seriously strange with these guys! Nicolas thought.

"Don't pay my brother no mind. He's just bustin' your balls about Kim. He's been tryin' to get with her ever since she started."

"But I thought he wasn't tryna get wit' her?" Frankie squawked.

"He's not. I am, but she's not my girl," Tony said, wrapping his arm around Nicolas' neck and escorting him to the bar. "It's open season, Nick. So, that makes her fair game for anyone to lure her into their trap. All you need is the right bait."

"I wasn't thinkin' about it like that," Nicolas responded, taking another swig from his glass. The cold, smooth liquid began to soothe his nerves.

"Sorry about what happened to your wife yesterday. Are you okay, chief?" Tony asked, lightly punching him on the arm.

Nicolas looked at Tony with a surprised look. "How did you find out?"

"I watch the news, man. I recognized your house and that goofy-lookin' neighbor of yours. He tried to act like he was fetchin' the mail, but he kept lookin' at my cah in your driveway, tryna see if anyone was behind the wheel before he jumped in his cab and took off. He couldn't see through the tint. It's all good. I get that type of attention all the time." Tony winked at him.

"Does everyone at work know about this?" Nicolas inquired.

"Well, I did tell Bill." He paused. "And Kim. But, I wouldn't be surprised if everyone knows by now. The important thing is that you're both alive. Here, have another drink on me." Tony waved at the bartender. He made Nicolas' situation appear to be a small thing, like a command cold.

It's crazy how the words just flowed from Tony's mouth so easily without hesitation, somewhat like Tammy.

Nicolas took another tall drink from the bartender.

"Thanks," Nicolas said in response to her smile.

"You care to play pool wit' us?" Tony asked in a hardened voice, but his brown eyes were pleading for his company.

Nicolas took another long swallow. The alcohol started to taste so good passing over his taste buds. It was like a strong thirst his body had been yearning for…a thirst water couldn't quench.

"I can go a few rounds wit' y'all," he replied, refusing to put the beer down.

"Yeah, come over here and get some of this," Frankie said, as the other three guys chuckled and continued to look around the bar with stone faces.

Nicolas and Tony abandoned the bar and joined up with Frankie and his dry-ass crew at the pool table.

"So, Nick, enlighten us. How did you end up out here in Jersey?" Frankie asked with a crooked smile, while racking the balls up.

Nicolas shrugged as he applied chalk to the tip of his pool stick. "I was born and raised in the Bronx and ended up movin' to Brooklyn, where I met my wife Tammy. I put in a transfer to work out here and start a family. So, tell me a little about you," he said, knocking several balls in the side pocket.

Frankie frowned and nodded. He had an arrogance and cockiness that made him seem untouchable. "Well, I grew up in lower Manhattan centered on Mulberry Street, north of Canal Street where the cheap name-brand products are sold. It's off of West 114th Street near Morningside Park. My favorite spot was Fat Joe's Fatty Rolls on Amsterdam Avenue."

"That was the spot," Nicolas said, wide-eyed. This was the first time he had smiled since the incident. "I loved their chicken cheese steaks on a toasted roll. Whatever happened to that place?"

Frankie sighed. "They went outta business when the store got robbed three years ago. Joe got his head blown off by some lowlife meat stick for a measly fifty bucks. 'Til this day, I still can't find a place that makes sandwiches as good as Joe's."

Nicolas knocked the two-ball in the corner pocket. "So, Tony, what about you?"

Tony was sitting on a stool against the wall that had a big picture of Larry Bird for the Boston Celtics shooting a basketball against Magic Johnson of the LA Lakers.

"I was born in lower Manhattan and moved to Voorhees, New Jersey, when I was five years old," Tony told him.

"Voorhees is where the rich go," Frankie said, poking Tony with his pool stick.

"No, no, we were far from that. Believe me," Tony chuckled, trying to block the stick.

"Yeah, right. Dad made sure your sorry ass was alright," Frankie said, stabbing Tony even harder with the pool stick.

"Yo, Frankie, chill. I told you 'bout startin' yo' shit out in public," Tony barked.

Tony's happy-go-lucky expression was now threatening. Nicolas could see there was a lot more to their story than he wanted to know.

By the time the game of pool ended, the alcohol was kicking in good. This is what started his drinking problem in the first place. Nicolas looked at his watch again; his eyes could hardly focus enough to see the hands. It was definitely time to go.

"I've got to leave now!" he hollered over the loud music, handing Tony his pool stick.

"Come on, the party just started!" Tony said, dancing to the music.

Nicolas drained the glass and slammed it on the counter. "I really have to go while I still got enough sense to drive. Thanks for the room, Tony. I owe you one," Nicolas yelled, his hand fully extended.

"No problem, man," Tony said, gripping his hand for a firm handshake. His testosterone levels were working over-time. After saying their goodbyes, Nicolas took the address written on a piece of paper and bounced.

CHAPTER FORTY-THREE

The Unwanted Guest

It was 6:22 p.m. when Nicolas arrived in his car outside Tony's Camden rental property. He sat watching the drug dealers on the street corners in all black fading in and out of the darkness like shadows. The hookers walked the streets like it was a runway, trying to get their next fix, and crackheads crawled around like roaches looking for a hit. A man high on crack was running from a group of thugs chasing him.

"He got the stash," one thug yelled out as another gave chase.

What the hell is goin' on out here? Nicolas wondered.

The neighborhood looked like Iraq, with its abandoned buildings and huge potholes that resembled bomb craters.

How the hell did Tony find this place, much less use it as a lay-low spot? Maybe it's because he looks more Hispanic than Italian, so they don't mess with him out here. Maybe that's the reason he has a little soul in him after all.

There was barely enough daylight left for Nicolas to see his way up the steps to the townhouse. He hurried up the steps, unlocked the front door, and stepped inside. Locking the door behind him, he peered out the window to make sure no one had followed him. He did a walk through, checking the layout of the rooms. It was furnished just as Tony said, but there was no television or computer. In fact, there were no electronic devices except for a refrigerator and toaster in the kitchen. Sitting in a recliner, he powered his cell phone on and keyed into the television to watch the news. He had just started to relax a bit, when he heard a loud sound come from the bedroom upstairs. It sounded like someone had thrown something through the window.

Startled and scared, Nicolas bolted up the stairs and came face to face with the man who only minutes ago was being chased by the group of thugs. His clothes were covered with shards of glass, and he was bleeding from small cuts. He gave off an odor that smelled like *who the fuck did it and why*. The man looked as if he was knocking at death's door and begging for someone to answer. His lips were chalk white as if he had been kissing powdered donuts, and his skin was ashy as hell like he had been swimming in baby powder. He was so thin his skeletal frame could be seen beneath his skin. Fully alert, with more energy than that pink rabbit on that battery commercial, his eyes were wide open and super charged.

"You have to hide me before they kill me!" the doped-out man said, holding a brown paper bag that contained the dealer's stash.

"Look, man, I'm sorry for your troubles, but I can't get involved." The hairs on the back of Nicolas' neck stood at attention. "Now get the fuck outta here!" Nicolas thundered, hoping his voice carried weight.

"They saw me come in here, so you got to help me," he said, refusing to budge, his voice a deep, scratchy gargle.

"You have to go. The police are on their way," Nicolas lied, trying to bluff him.

"The cops! You called the cops? I can't go to jail, man."

The crack addict jumped up and down, exposing his rotten brown teeth. He had yellow-colored food stuck to his gums that looked liked cheese, and his breath smelled like he had just eaten a double-decker shit sandwich.

"Look here, man, I want you to get outta here right now." Nicolas picked up a two-by-four propped up against the wall near the doorway to scare the man off.

Suddenly, the group of thugs kicked in the front door and attacked the intruder and Nicolas, who tried to defend himself with the two by four. However, there was too many of them, and they overpowered him, taking the weapon out of Nicolas' hand. He tried fighting them off, but ended up falling down the stairs and landed on the living room floor. Nicolas attempted to run out the door, but more thugs rushed in the house, preventing his escape. He was then overwhelmed with a hailstorm of blows, inflicting pain and punishment. The last thing he saw before collapsing from his vicious beating were the thugs chasing the crack head out of the house and down the street.

He was a slippery muthafucka!

When Nicolas gained consciousness, one of the thugs was going through his pockets taking everything—cell phone, car keys, wallet, and even took the watch off his arm, the one his mother had given him for Christmas last year. Nicolas' body was too weak to respond. When the thugs had gotten everything of any value, they fled, leaving the empty wallet on the floor and the front door wide open.

Nicolas heard his car door slam and the car start. The roar of the engine and the squeal of the tires echoed in the air.

"I don't wanna die...not like this. Dear Lord, please save me," Nicolas cried out to God just before losing consciousness.

CHAPTER FORTY-FOUR

The Recovery Room

Nicolas slowly opened his eyes, dazed by the brightly lit room and the loud beeping of machines. Mind spinning, he turned his head to find Tammy standing by the bedside. Her eyes were swollen and red from crying.

"I was so worried about you. I didn't know what to do," she said, smiling.

"Where am I?" He was disorientated, only seeing his world in a haze of flashbacks.

"You're at Cooper University Medical Center in Camden."

"What happened?" Nicolas asked, not yet remembering all that happened in the last few hours.

"I got a phone call from the hospital telling me that you were attacked and robbed last night. You have a mild concussion, nothing serious and some mild bumps and bruises. The doctor said when the swelling goes down, you should be okay. They found my cell phone number on the phone bill you kept in your back pocket."

"What time is it?" Nicolas looked at his wrist to see his watch was gone.

"It's ten forty-two at night," Tammy told him.

Nicolas palmed his forehead with his left hand. It was slowly coming back to him. For some reason, he had stayed in one of Tony's rental properties in Camden.

"Do you remember what happened?" Tammy asked.

"Yeah. I got attacked by a bunch of thugs chasin' some crackhead who decided to break into the rental property looking for help."

Nicolas tried to sit up in the bed but couldn't, so he slid back down on his pillow. His head felt as though it was about to explode.

"They could have killed you." Tammy ran over to re-adjust his pillow.

"They were young kids just tryna get their stuff back from that crackhead and ended up robbin' me in the process."

"Yeah, but they took everything from you—your watch, credit cards, cell phone, and car."

"My car! Did you contact the police?"

"I did. They found it stripped to the framework in North Camden. The insurance company should take care of everything. I'll call them first thing in the morning. I think our policy says they'll send a loaner car to the house."

"Good, because I need somethin' to get me back and forth to work."

"I had your Visa and MasterCard cancelled, so you should be good. Thank God they left the house keys. Did you sign a lease for that apartment?" Tammy asked, wondering if he was leaving her.

"Nah, I wasn't plannin' on stayin' long."

Tammy gazed into his eyes with sincerity. "Look, Nick, there's no need for you to go back there."

She was trying to talk him into coming home, but Nicolas' anger resurfaced as his memory came back.

"I can't believe you cheated on me."

"Nicolas, I'm sorry."

He turned his head away.

"Don't shut me out. Can't you see what you're doing to me? Can't you see you're breaking my heart?" She dissolved into tears as the hurt flowed down her face.

"I can only speak with hurtful words after what you fuckin' did to me!" He gave her a somber expression as his anger simmered.

"Please forgive me," she begged.

"You said that same shit the last time I caught you fuckin' cheatin'," he said, reminding her of the time he caught her in the restaurant with her so-called male co-worker.

He held back the hot tears that were burning the back of his eyeballs. He wasn't going to let that happen.

Hell naw!

"I wasn't thinking straight then. I was stupid," was her excuse, tears added for good measure.

Usually the tears would soften him up a little, but not this time. He came back at her with more hurtful words.

"So you're a dumb fuckin' blonde now?"

"Yes. What I did was stupid," she agreed with no backtalk.

"I can't fuckin' look at your ass right now. Just get the fuck out my face!"

Nicolas turned his aching head away from her. Tammy's presence only fueled his anger.

"Nick, I know you're mad at me, and you have every right to be. But, now we have bigger problems. That detective came by last night looking for you. I told him that you said you were working late. He started asking me a lot of questions, but I refused to answer any of them. I told him that I wanted my attorney present. He gave me this hideous laugh and walked out." Tears started flowing once again. "Nick, I'm so scared. I never meant to hurt you. I love you so much. I don't know what I'd do without you."

Nicolas turned around and rolled his eyes at her with skepticism. "Why does everyone use those same lines when they know they fucked up?" He laughed sarcastically.

"I've never been so afraid in my life. Not only will I lose you, but that detective said he's going to put us both in prison and throw away the keys."

She laid her hand on his shoulder as the tears continued to flow from her eyes.

For reasons he didn't understand, her tears overrode his anger. The love he had for her was stronger than he thought. She looked so small and afraid, like a little girl.

"Well, apparently, he doesn't have enough evidence to do so or we'd be behind bars right now as we speak. So, as long as you don't say shit, we'll be a'ight until we find a good lawyer."

He could have stayed mad at her, but they were facing a bigger problem that needed immediate attention.

Tammy looked up with wet eyes. "I'm so sorry for what I've done. Tell me what I can do to make this thing better," she said, begging for his forgiveness.

Nicolas snarled. His eyebrows were arched with signs of anger evident on his face.

"You can start by tellin' me why. Why did you do it?"

"I don't know," was the first response that popped in her head as she looked dumbfounded.

"You don't know!" he snapped. "If you love me, what am I doin' wrong to deserve this?"

Tammy hesitated. Then in a low whisper, she said, "You didn't do anything wrong, Nick. I don't know why I did it."

"You don't know why you did it?" He yelled loud enough to catch the attention of the other nurses standing outside of the room. Realizing the disturbance he was making in the hospital setting, he adjusted his tone. "Listen, that's not a good enough answer. I've never cheated on you. I had plenty of chances to do so, which is irrelevant at this time, but I didn't!" he stated in a low whisper, remembering his desire and opportunity in the past.

"It's not your fault. It's me. I think I need professional help."

"Well, if we get outta this mess in one piece, we'll both get some counselin'," Nicolas said.

Feeling a bit stronger, he pulled himself to an upright position in the bed.

"Yeah, we did vow to stay together through thick and thin, and boy is this thick," Tammy said, smirking and rolling her eyes. "I just want to say I feel so bad for what I've done and promise to never do it again."

Nicolas stared at her. "I do love you, but it's gonna take a while to trust you again. Accordin' to the Bible, I gotta forgive you. This is a lot for me to swallow, though. I'll need some time to clear my head. I've been through hell and back."

"Did you say the Bible?" Tammy threw out, wide eyed, mouth agape. "What? Did you become religious all of a sudden after the bump on your head?" she jokingly said, smiling.

"Well, we went to church when we were in New York. These bad things happenin' to us must be a sign from God."

Nicolas could tell Tammy was absorbing his words.

"Tammy, when I thought I was gonna die last night, all I could think about was going back to church and gettin' my life right with God."

"If that's what it takes to get our life right, then you have my support." Her eyes filled with love and compassion.

"Good. Then we can go to church Sunday mornin'," Nicolas said, forgetting for the moment he had made a promise to Bill that he would be at work.

"That sounds good," Tammy said. "The doctor said you could go home today if you choose, but you would have to take it easy for a few days. He said the tests showed you didn't suffer any serious injuries."

Nicolas was uninterested in his condition. His major concern was securing the house.

"Did the alarm company install the home alarm system yet?"

"I never had a chance to reschedule after what happened the other day. But, I contacted your office call out number and told them what happened. Tony called back and left a message wanting details."

"His rental property is trashed," Nicolas replied. "I'll call him as soon as we get home. I refuse to spend another night in a hospital."

*****

Walking through the door of their home, the flashbacks of Tammy in bed with Wright churned Nicolas' stomach. He gave Tammy a cold, hard stare and headed upstairs to the bedroom, leaving her at the bottom of the stairs looking pitiful.

281

Entering the bedroom, Nicolas had visions of Tammy and Wright on their bed and then saw Wright lying on the floor dead. He wanted to pick up something and bust her upside the fuckin' head for the mess she had gotten them into. That brief moment of pleasure could have an everlasting effect on their marriage, but the big question is, was it worth it?

Going into the spare room, he laid down on the bed. His head was hurting again. Tammy entered the room and lay down beside him. When she moved a little closer to him for warmth and affection, he shrugged his shoulder and rolled over, turning his back toward her. He was hurt; what Tammy did was wrong—*dead wrong*. She was better off stabbing him in the back with the same steak knife he used on Peter Wright, and with his back towards her, it was the perfect opportunity for her to take advantage of the situation.

•

CHAPTER FORTY-FIVE

Trying to be Polite

Early Sunday morning, the brassy buzz of the alarm clock awakened Nicolas. He forced himself up, took a shower, and dressed for work.

"Good mornin'," Nicolas said, finding Tammy in the kitchen making breakfast.

Startled by his appearance, Tammy took a deep breath with her hand placed over her chest. This whole situation still had her spooked.

With a smile, she said, "Good morning to you. I made you some eggs, sausage, toast, milk, and even squeezed fresh orange juice." She pulled out a chair for him. "Have a seat."

"Thanks." Nicolas smiled. He couldn't remember when he had eaten last. "I see the rental out front. Who's it from?" Nicolas asked, looking at the silver Nissan Maxima parked outside.

"Enterprise Rental. Are we going to church today?" Tammy asked, while getting the toast out of the toaster oven.

"Nah. I looked at the lump on my head and it's not that noticeable. So, I called into work and said I'd be in today. I cancelled the call-out you made yesterday. I gotta go in and catch up on my paperwork."

"What about the doctor saying you need some rest?" Her tone was unsettled.

"I'll be a'ight. I gots to get back to work. The bills aren't gonna pay themselves."

"Especially if you're dead and gone. You're on salary plus commission. What does reporting to work have anything to do with it? I don't want you to kill yourself for this job, Nicolas!" Her troubled tone began to rise.

"Look, I don't have time for..."

Pounding on the front door stopped him mid-sentence.

"Yeah, who is it early in the damn mornin'?" Nicolas fussed.

"It's me Morris. We need to talk," he shouted from the other side.

Tammy looked through the living room window and saw a black, unmarked patrol car parked out front.

"It's that detective again. What do we do now?" she said, jumping up and down as she started to panic.

Nicolas grabbed her by the shoulders. "First of all, calm the fuck down. Then get upstairs and stay there. I'll handle this muthafucka."

Nicolas waited until Tammy was upstairs and out of sight before calling out through the door.

"Hold on a minute!" Nicolas put on his game face before opening the door. "Good morning, Detective. Come in."

"Nice ride out front. What is it, a rental?" Morris asked, wiping his feet on the doormat before entering.

"Yeah, until I get a new one." Nicolas tried to be friendly. "You care for something to eat or drink?"

Detective Morris held his hand up. "No, thank you. Sorry for coming so early in the morning. Where's your wife? I want to ask her some more questions."

Morris looked around the house, hoping to spot her. "S h e ' s upstairs in bed. I rather you talk to me, because she's been through a lot," Nicolas recited, trying to stay polite.

"Alright, I'll let her be for now and talk to you instead." His eyes widened with a sarcastic smirk. "I see you're alive and well after your attack last night."

Nicolas winced. "How did you know about that?"

"That's what I get paid to do." He stuck his chest out with a hard grin.

Displaying attitude, Nicolas crossed his arms. "Well, I know that's not why you're here, so what exactly do you want, Detective?" he asked with bitterness.

"You see..." The detective paused and looked around the room, as if he was watching his back or didn't want anyone to hear what he had to say. "I have a hard time swallowing your story about you coming home from work and catching your wife being raped."

"And why is that, *Detective*?" Nicolas gave utterance to emphasizing the word detective.

"For one thing, Wright was an outstanding officer. Two, he was a ladies' man. Why, out of all the women out there, would he choose your wife?" Morris questioned, his voice becoming bitter.

"Are you sayin' my wife is ugly or somethin'?" Nicolas said with fake laughter.

"No—not at all. All I want to know is why would one of *my* officers decide to force himself on *your* wife, when there's so many other willing women out there that would give it up to him for just a smile?"

Although Detective Morris tried to make it seem as if he was trying to make sense of the situation, Nicolas knew it was all an act.

"Because the muthafucka was sick and got his rocks off rapin' helpless women!" Nicolas argued with a sharp-tongue.

"Raping helpless women? Oh no, Nicolas. I don't think she was raped. If Peter Wright raped her, why didn't any of the neighbors hear her crying and screaming for help?"

Morris narrowed his eyes as if scanning Nicolas' inner thoughts.

"How would I know? Maybe he had his hand over her mouth. That's the question you oughta be askin' yourself, Detective."

"I don't think so. You see, in my line of duty, a rapist doesn't make his presence known. According to your neighbors, his vehicle was seen parked in front of your house for the last two days."

"If that's so, where was his partner Rodeski at the time?" Nicolas snapped back.

"According to Rodeski's statement, he partnered up with Officer Giordano at that time and the time of the incident."

Nicolas stood silent, thinking about Tammy letting another man in their house and ruining their marriage.

"Are you okay, Mr. Coles? You look lost and constipated at the same time."

The detective was breaking down his outer walls. Nicolas had to reinforce it with a stronger game face.

"So what are you tryna say?" Nicolas bellowed.

"I'm saying your wife had an affair with Officer Peter Wright *and* you knew about it. That's why you came down to the police station and fabricated that story about Officers Mark Rodeski and Peter Wright harassing you and your buddy Tony. You see, Nicolas, I find it very strange how you came to my office with that story. The story was so good that even I believed it. But, then, only two days later, you killed Wright in your own house for sleeping with your wife. Yet, you claim she was being raped. I tried talking to your wife, but she refuses to answer any of my questions. So, I thought since you're here, she'll probably talk now."

"I don't have time for this bullshit!" Nicolas hollered, gritting his teeth in frustrated anger.

"Oh, but we can make time for it at the police station. You see, I can run you both in with the evidence I do have and let you straighten it out with the judge—if you can. But, I think I'd rather let you sweat for a while. Eventually, you'll crack under pressure. Your conscience will get the best of you," Morris stated with a small grin of satisfaction. "Have you ever heard the expression 'Pressure bust pipes'?"

"I can see you gettin' a big kick outta this shit," Nicolas said, not quite sure if the detective had any real evidence and was only trying to trap him into a confession.

"That's why I love my job so much." Morris headed for the front door. "I'm not going to arrest you today, because I'm still collecting more evidence. But, listen, Mr. Coles, and listen good. The next time you and your lovely wife see me, I'll be carrying silver bracelets for the both of you to sport to the police station. And if you want to call the news, civil rights activists, or whomever you think is going to believe this fairytale story you got going on, it won't do you a damn bit of good. Go right ahead and call them. Hell, call President Barack Obama if you'd like. Even that won't help you." Morris smiled the smile of someone who knew he was sure to win. "Because I'm going to make sure they all get to see me send you to prison or the electric chair, if they ever reinstate the death penalty in Jersey, for the murder of a fine police officer."

When Nicolas didn't respond, the detective headed out the front door. Halfway down the steps, he turned before Nicolas closed the door.

Waving his finger at him, he said, "Oh yeah, did you ever get that alarm installed in your house yet?"

"No, I had to reschedule. It should be installed within the next few days."

"Now did the company tell you this or is that something your wife told you."

"My wife told me. Why?" Nicolas asked, seeing the detective was getting at something.

"Oh, too bad, because I bet even your wife knows that if you were to call the home alarm company, they can give you the date and time of when your wife entered and left the house. I thought you should know that in case you wanted to know the times of her activities. If I were you, I'd call the company myself, because your wife could have been lying to you about getting the alarm installed just so she could cover her tracks."

Nicolas knew the detective was trying to get on his last nerve, but he tried hard to restrain himself. However, Nicolas suddenly started to think he should have taken the initiative and called the company himself. If he had, would the outcome have been any different or would Tammy have been a little smoother at covering her tracks? Nicolas was a Temple graduate, but Morris made him feel more like a high school dropout.

Nicolas stood in the doorway until Detective Morris pulled out of the driveway. Just as he was about to close the door, John called out.

"Hey, is everything alright?" John stood in his yard holding a can of bug spray.

Nicolas was startled by his presence. "Were you standing over there listening all that time?" he snapped in a demanding voice that was elevated enough for the whole neighborhood to hear.

Nervous, John started to stutter. "No...ah, yes...well, maybe. I was checking my windows for wasp nests. Is that a crime?" he responded with an attitude.

"No, it's perfectly legal to check for wasp nests," Nicolas chuckled, after realizing he had snapped on his neighbor for no apparent reason at all except for being nosey. "Sorry. This whole thing has my wife and I upset, with the news media all over the place askin' you and the neighbors all types of personal questions about us, and that detective who keeps returnin' to ask us a hundred and one questions. This whole tappin' into our business is so embarrassin'."

John tried to offer some assistance. "Yeah, it's okay, Nick. You're right, and I'm sorry about your misfortune. Is there anything I can do?" he asked.

"Thanks, but no thanks. We'll be just fine," Nicolas said, hoping to hang on to what little privacy they still had.

"I hope I didn't say anything wrong when the police questioned me," John expressed with sincerity in his voice.

"As far as I know, you didn't. We just need some time and space to get over this."

"You should get that home alarm system installed," John suggested, giving Nicolas pause.

Great! Does the whole neighborhood know?

"Yeah, I already rescheduled an appointment with them. They'll be out here Wednesday. I gotta get inside and check on Tammy."

"Well, if you need anything, just let me know," John said as he continued to inspect the rest of the house for wasp nests.

John was aware that the best time to spray for wasps was at night, but Nicolas knew he was just prying in their business.

Yeah, right. Picture me askin' your nosey ass for anythin'. For all I know, you could be secretly tryna push up on my wife. Even worse, you could be tryna push up on me, fuckin' faggot. I'll have to keep an extra eye on yo' gay ass. For all I know, you may like dark meat. You're single, and I have not yet seen a nigga or a bitch enter your crib at all. What's up with that shit? Nicolas wondered.

"Thanks a lot," Nicolas said, then closed the door.

"I'm scared. What are we going to do?" Tammy said, standing at the top of the stairs.

"I dunno. I'll see if Tony can hook me up with a good lawyer."

Tammy ran down the steps to give Nicolas a hug, but he grabbed her shoulders to keep a distance between them.

"Don't worry. We're gonna make it through this," he told her, even though visions of Peter Wright kissing and holding her flooded his thoughts.

She reached out to him again, but he pulled back. Nicolas could see in her eyes that she got the picture.

"I understand." Heartbroken, Tammy lowered her eyes. "Please don't leave me here," she said, showing signs of guilt and regret.

Nicolas felt a rage building inside of him, one he could not control once released, a rage looking for a way out. But, the outcome would not be in his favor. So, it was best he had some distance away from her. The sight of Tammy put a nasty taste in his mouth, making him ill.

"I gotta go to work now." He couldn't stay home and rest like the doctor ordered. It would have made him crazy. He needed to keep busy. Maybe they could sort things out later, but not right then.

"I'm gonna get me a new cell phone from the AT&T store up the street. I called over there and they told me that they will be openin' early today for their grand-opening' sale on Hadden Field Road. So, I'm gonna pick one up before I get to work. I'll call and give you the new number, and you had better answer when I call." He gawked at her.

"I promise I will," she humbly answered without an ounce of fight left in her. This was totally unlike her.

CHAPTER FORTY-SIX

Phone Replacement

Nicolas called his mother on his upgraded Apple touch-screen phone as soon as he left the AT&T store, hoping she would cheer him up like she always did.

"Hey, Mom, what's goin' on?" He was happy to hear her voice.

"Hi, baby. Nothin' much. I called you yesterday and left a message on your cell phone, but you didn't call me back. Are you okay?"

Nicolas wasn't ready to tell her about the awful mess he was in. She would think she had to move in or try to convince them to move back to New York.

"Yeah, Mom, I'm good. I lost my cell phone and had to get a new one. They said I could keep my same number. They deactivated the other phone."

"Where did you lose it?"

"I left it in the bathroom at Burger King, and when I went back to get it, it was gone," he told her, lying by the minute.

There was no need in him getting her upset over it. Plus, no matter how big or small the situation was, Laura would use that as an excuse for her to come over and embarrass him even more.

"You see, Nicolas, I told you about goin' into those fast-food restaurants. You always end up losin' something—money, time, personal items—but you can't lose weight from goin' into those places." Laughing it off, she said, "So how's Tammy doin'?"

"She's fine. She's home bakin' a chicken," he told her, lying about that, too. "I'll probably call her this afternoon on my lunch break."

"Y'all find a good church yet?"

"No, but we're lookin'."

"Don't take too long. You may lose out on all your blessings. You know you always have a church home here."

"I know, but that's an awful long ride."

"No ride is too long for the Lord. Plus, you can come and eat Sunday dinner with yo' momma after church."

Laura's meals were definitely worth the ride. Home cooking was the sure way to get Nicolas to come over.

"Mom, I'm gonna visit you regardless. You just make sure you keep us in your prayers."

"I will. I've been praying that the Lord blesses me with some grand-babies."

"Aw, Mom, please don't start that again," he moaned.

"Okay, ya big baby. I gotta go so I won't be late for Sunday services."

"Okay. I love you. Bye."

"I love you, too, baby. Bye now."

Nicolas pressed the disconnect key and then called Dave.

"Hello," Dave answered.

"Hey, wassup, my nigga? What time are y'all heading back out this way?"

"Man, we're on the road now. We just dipped out on that crazy-ass bitch," Dave happily reported.

"What'cha mean?"

"She got hungry and wanted somethin' to eat, so Mark gave her some money and told her to bring us back some Chinese food. When she left, we grabbed all our shit and bounced," Dave said, laughing so hard he nearly choked.

"What about her pregnancy?" Nicolas asked.

He was concerned with the fatherless child that would enter the world. Who knows what the child would go through while growing up. That supercharged crackhead who jumped through the window of Tony's rental property could have been the result of a fatherless child.

"That shit ain't his. She's just lookin' for another dumb-ass baby daddy, and Mark was the prime candidate. If he was a super hero, he'd be *Captain Super Stupid*," Dave said, putting Nicolas on speakerphone.

"This fool can't never take shit serious," Mark commented, aggravation in his voice.

"So what are you gonna do if she has the baby?" Nicolas asked.

"I ain't gonna do shit. That ain't my baby. Plus, I ain't ready for any kids right now. I still got a lot of play in me."

"Yeah, but you got to know the game, so when usin' your dumb powers, you don't get played, Captain Super Stupid," Dave cracked.

"Yo, be easy on bruh, and holla at me when y'all get back," Nicolas said.

"We'll do better than that. We're headin' out your way first before headin' back to New York."

"Cool. I'll turn my ringer up so I don't miss your call. I just got the new iPhone," Nicolas boasted.

"How is it?" Mark asked.

"It's sweet as hell and does a whole lot more than the previous one. It has better features, more memory, and more megapixels. My favorite feature is the 3D navigation. The person that I'm talkin' with, their face appears on the screen, allowing me to see who I'm talkin' to."

"Good, then Mark can use it to find a girl that doesn't lick baby goat's ass to get high," Dave said, followed by a chorus of laughter.

CHAPTER FORTY-SEVEN

It's Hard to Say No

Nicolas walked past his co-workers, head hung low, hoping no one noticed the lump on his head. He could've called out, but he didn't want to have a bad reputation for abusing sick days. Plus, he couldn't stand being around Tammy. He needed an outlet, something to do to kill time, and making money was his favorite choice. He struggled to hold his emotions in. It was a lot to bear. Nicolas thought he would burst. Keeping his game face on and not letting anyone know what was wrong, he did his best to try to maintain his composure.

Nicolas went in his office and quickly closed the door behind him. He sat down at his desk and was starting to organize his thoughts, when Tony walked in.

"Hey, welcome back, buddy!" Tony sang, sounding excited to see him.

Startled, Nicolas knocked over a pencil holder, causing the pencils to roll across the floor. He was an emotional wreck.

"Stop actin' all nervous. Those guys back in Camden don't have you all shook, do they?" He frowned in disbelief.

"Nah, I'm good." Nicolas picked up the pencils.

"Good to hear that. Anyway, man, I missed you. I had no one to talk to that's on our level, since you and I are the youngest guys here. I get a bad vibe from the old heads that work here. They're all retired from some borin'-ass job, and all they talk about is their grandkids. Now how borin' is that shit? So what's good wit'cha, buddy?"

"Tony, I need a really big favor." Nicolas had no time to waste on trivialities.

"Talk to me, dude." Tony lightly punched Nicolas on the arm.

"I need a good lawyer. Do you know any?" His tone reeked with desperation.

"Ah...don't tell me that you and your wife are gettin' a divorce." Tony winced.

"No, at least not right now," Nicolas snarled. "I need one to get that Detective Morris off my ass."

"Is he still fuckin' wit'cha?" Tony slipped back into street colloquialism.

"Yeah," Nicolas responded.

"No problem. I got a good lawyer on deck." Tony took out his wallet. "Here's his business card. He works right outta his home office."

"I need him like yesterday and tomorrow may be too late. You think he'll see me today?"

Nicolas admired how Tony could get things done and make it look so easy at the same time, but this time, he needed him to make a power move. Nicolas didn't know anyone in Jersey, and Tony was the closest friend he had right now.

"It's Sunday, man. Everything's closed. But, I'll give him a call and ask him if he can see you this afternoon." Tony smiled.

"Yo, good lookin', Tone."

At last, Nicolas felt a glimmer of hope that he might not be growing old in a prison cell. "No problem. What are friends for?"

Tony threw his arm around Nicolas in one of those manly half hugs. "This guy is the best. He got me outta so many jams."

Nicolas read the card aloud. "Charles Hunt, Attorney At Law. Hunt...what a name for a lawyer." Nicolas laughed and then turned to Tony. "So, Tony, what did you ever do so bad that you needed this lawyer?"

Tony peeked out of Nicolas' office to make sure no one was ear hustlin'. He closed the door behind him and approached Nicolas.

"Have you ever heard of Frank DeBartello?" he whispered.

"Isn't he that big mob boss in Jersey? The one that's been gettin' his shit in the wringer over some hit-man that's been on a killin' spree?"

"Ssshhh! Keep it down," Tony said with his index finger over his lips. He stared intently at Nicolas before saying, "Well, that so-called mob boss is my father."

"Your father!" Nicolas blurted out, excited.

"Ssshhh!" Tony said again, this time placing his whole hand over Nicolas' mouth.

After he removed his hand from Nicolas' mouth, Nicolas whispered, "So how come you ain't workin' with him? He's filthy rich. You could run one of his pizza parlors or his collection agency or somethin'."

Nicolas looked at Tony as if he were the baby Don of the crime family.

Tony held both hands up, pushing downward with his palms, as if giving the invisible man a back rub. "It's a little more complicated than that."

"What does that mean?" Nicolas asked, oblivious to what Tony was talking about.

"Frank and my mother were engaged to be married, but my mother found out he was cheatin' on her and had a son by the other woman. You met his son at the bar last night."

"Oh yeah...your big brother Frankie," Nicolas muttered.

"Right, but things didn't work out right with him and my mother. So, he ended up gettin' married to Frankie's mother. A few months after that, my mother found out she was pregnant with me. She never told anyone about it, because it wouldn't look right for his image as a mob boss. Besides, I would be considered a bastard child. But, somehow, he found out I was his son. And believe it or not, he was excited to have another son, because his wife couldn't have any more kids after Frankie junior. He moved us to Voorhees for our own protection. He would come by every now and then to check up on me and make sure we were straight. I've been under investigation ever since the media found out I was his son. So, I found a good lawyer to protect me just in case they ever try to hang somethin' on me. I hired Charles Hunt to keep them off my back."

"So why would they bother you if you have no ties to his organization?" Nicolas grimaced.

Tony's eyes lit up, his eyebrow arched, and a sinister grin crept up the side of his lip. "Well, let's just say I'm a very bad boy, and workin' for this company is the only thing that keeps me outta trouble," he purred devilishly, with an added hiss in his tone.

Nicolas stared at Tony, his eyes squinted, trying to read between the lines.

"So Bill is your mother's brother?"

"Yep." Tony snapped his finger. "And he's on the straight and narrow."

"Okay, I got it," Nicolas said, hoping Tony didn't divulge any more information that may incriminate him.

Tony stared at Nicolas with a keen eye. "This conversation is just between you and me, capisce?"

"Don't worry. The last thing you need to be worried about is me snitchin'," he uttered with conviction.

"Good. If you need anythin' else, just let me know. And don't worry about the apartment. My homeowner's insurance will take good care of that mess, plus some, if you know what I mean. I'm just glad you weren't killed," he smirked.

Nicolas could tell by his sinister grin that insurance fraud was part of the equation.

"There is one more thing you can help me with," Nicolas muttered with a poker face. "I need some heat for the house."

Nicolas didn't know why he asked Tony for a thing like that. Maybe it was the way he made moves to get things done. Maybe it was the connects he had to get whatever he needed, or maybe it was the fact that his father was a big mob boss.

...Yeah, that's it.

The mafia, or what the rapper Nas would say Cosa Nostra— which in Sicilian means 'our thing' or 'this thing of ours'—referred to as a national crime syndicate...a criminal society with various criminal activities. Their organization got so much negative press that Nicolas didn't have a problem with asking.

"Are you registered to carry?" Tony asked with a raised eyebrow.

He said it so freely, like it was a part of an everyday conversation. Maybe his hunch was right. Maybe Tony did have some ties with his father's organization.

"No, but I need some protection until I get registered. The Merchantville rapist is still on the loose. Plus, those thugs in Camden stole all my information."

Nicolas didn't want Tony to know Tammy's infidelity led to an officer's demise. An innocent cop who got his gratification from sticking his dirty dick inside married men's wives.

"Well, accordin' to the Merchantville Police Department, there's another rapist on the loose, because his DNA didn't match."

"So there were *two* rapists?" Tony screeched with wide eyes.

"Apparently so, and I wanna make sure my wife doesn't go through another experience like that again. Havin' some heat would help her sleep better at night, and I can go to work knowin' she has some real protection."

Tony hesitated for a moment, beamed his eyes at Nicolas, and then said, "Okay, I'll do it, but don't tell anyone that I got it for you. Hear me?" He said with firmness.

"I swear on my unborn seed," Nicolas agreed, nodding his head.

"I mean it, Nick. My life depends on it. The cops would love to get somethin' on me, and I don't know what my dad would do if he found out. Even though he's in a lot of dirty shit dealin' with his business, he takes pride in my clean record, and I don't wanna disappoint him."

"I understand, Tony. I'll never tell a soul about it."

Why would he tell him such a thing and risk getting him a gun when they'd only known each other a few days? Nicolas wondered if everyone in Jersey was this trusting or just plain gullible. How did Tony know he wasn't an undercover agent or something? Maybe it was Nicolas' face or the way he interacted with people that made Tony trust him.

I could have been a head shrink or somethin', Nicolas thought, laughing to himself.

Tony leaned in toward Nicolas. "There's a guy in Camden by the name of Cat Daddy who has a drug spot on the corner of Broad and Van Hook. I'll take you there after you see Charles Hunt. Until then, you don't do or say shit about this to anyone," Tony said in a low voice, almost a whisper.

"Okay, I get it. Your secret is safe with me." Nicolas gave his word of honor.

"Good, I gotta go take care of somethin' and I already transferred my business calls to your extension. You're on your own, so make sure you answer your phone."

"No problem. I got you covered." Nicolas was alleviated and apprehensive at the same time. He didn't know what the hell Tony was into, but it was beneficial as far as he was concern.

"Good. I'll catch you later. And don't worry about those police reports. I got them from a contact of mine in the police department and put them on Bill's desk. So, if he comes lookin' for me, you don't know shit."

"Got'cha."

Nicolas realized Tony conducted personal business on the company's clock. But, as long as Tony's connects benefitted him, he had no problem going with the flow. That didn't mean for him to get involved, but to play dumb whenever he's questioned about Tony's activities. Yeah, Nicolas was very good at that.

"Here's my personal cell phone number in case you run into any problems. Only a few people have this number, and those people

I consider to be very close to me like family, Nick. So, don't leave this card lyin' around where somebody might get access to it."

Tony handed Nicolas a black business card with silver lettering.

"Don't worry, I got this," Nicolas responded, placing the card in his wallet.

Tony smiled and gave Nicolas a pat on the shoulder before heading out the door, but at the pace he was going, it looked more like a dogtrot. So, whatever his destination was, it had to be important.

CHAPTER FORTY-EIGHT

You're Talking to the Wrong Guy

Nicolas was in the office sorting out a few files, when the office phone started ringing.

"Thank you for calling Home Reality and Associates. How may I help you?"

"My name is Willy Mays," the raspy voice said. "I'm tryna buy a crib."

"You called the right place. Do you currently own a home?"

"Naw."

"Do you have a down payment and a secure source of income?" Nicolas pulled out a notepad.

"Yeah, I work as a cab driver."

"What is your annual income?" Nicolas asked, wondering if he would happen to know John, his nosey neighbor. Hopefully not.

"It fluctuates."

"So how did you do last year?"

"I only worked for three months...I mean, three weeks."

Nicolas shook his head. What he thought might be his first sale was beginning to look like a big waste of time.

"So what did you do before you became a cab driver?"

"I was locked up doin' a state bid."

"So how do you expect to buy real estate when you have nothing to bring to the table?" Nicolas asked, cutting to the chase.

"Maaan, I got over eighty stacks in my account," Willy said, laughing.

"Are you able to show the IRS where you got that money?" Nicolas asked, hoping the money was legit and he really might make his first sale. Thereby redeeming himself with Bill and get a chunk of money to pay Charles Hunt a retainer fee.

"Ah, no. That's what I wanna talk to you about. I got a few extra ones for you if you work wit' me." Willy tried to bribe Nicolas.

"What does that mean?" Nicolas wanted no parts of anything illegal.

"You know, like how you hooked my mans up," Willy explained.

"I don't know what you're talking about, Mr. Mays," Nicolas responded in a deep tone, trying to sound as professional as possible.

"Come on, Tony. Stop wit' the bullshit." Nicolas could hear the aggravation in the young man's voice.

"This isn't Tony," he responded in a challenging tone.

"Then who is the hell am I talkin' to? Willy roared with a deepened voice.

"This is Nicolas Coles. I'm taking calls for Tony until he gets back. I'll gladly take a message or number where Tony can reach you."

"Yeah, tell him that Cat Daddy needs him to hook me up wit' a spot," Willy stated.

His attitude was contagious and Nicolas was starting to catch it. Nicolas became alarmed. *Cat Daddy! What type of shit is this muthafucka into?* Nicolas thought. With everything else going on in his life, he sure didn't need this kind of shady shit added to it. For all he knew, it could be a setup or something. Plus, Nicolas sounded nothing like Tony, so why was this guy acting like he knew him when Nicolas answered the phone? And if Tony were waiting for this character to call him, surely he would have given him the heads-up. Nicolas tried to reason it out.

"Hello! Ya still there?" Willy said after Nicolas drifted off in thought.

"Yeah, I'm still here."

"Tony's got my number. Just have him call me as soon as you see him."

"No problem, Mr. Mays," Nicolas said, eager to end the conversation. "I'll have him call you back as soon as possible."

Nicolas pulled Tony's business card from his wallet, pressed the outside line, and dialed Tony's private cell phone number.

"Hello," Tony answered.

"Hey, Tony. It's Nicolas."

"What's up, Nick?" Tony sounded excited to hear from him.

"I just got a call from a Willy Mays. He says Cat Daddy told him that you were supposed to hook him up with somethin'."

"Did he have any money on him?"

"Uh, he claimed to have over eighty stacks in his savings account and a few extra ones to throw in."

"Damn, I can't make it. I'm all tied up. Listen Nick, I need you to take care of him for me."

Nicolas' face hit the floor. "Say what? Maaan, I don't want any parts of this," Nicolas sang, not wanting to listen to whatever Tony had to say.

"Hey, Nick, be easy. It's cool. All you have to do is show him a few properties so he can tell me which one he's interested in. That's all. Piece of cake."

"I know there's somethin' shady about this." Nicolas hoped to avoid any more police drama.

"You don't worry about that. I'll handle the shady shit. All you have to do is show him the properties."

"You're gonna make me lose my job." Nicolas' head began to hurt like someone had rammed a serrated knife through his right eye.

Tony started to work on Nicolas' conscience.

"Listen, when you asked me to do you this favor after work, did I give you a hard way to go about it?" Tony asked.

There was a calm in his voice, the kind of tone a father would use on his son when trying to explain something.

"No."

"When you needed help findin' your wife and filin' a complaint at the police station, who had your back?"

"I know, I know. You did," Nicolas sang.

"When Bill wanted those police reports, who went outta their way to get it?"

"You did," Nicolas answered, shrinking in his chair as if he were that little boy listening to his father probe at his manhood.

"When you needed a place to stay, who hooked it up?"

"You hooked it up."

"An when it got fucked up, who flipped the bill?"

"You did," Nicolas submitted, the weight of Tony's case sitting on top of his chest.

"So what the fuck, Nicolas?" Tony barked, abandoning his fatherly tone and raising it to that nagging wife voice.

"Okay, okay. I get the point. You don't have to rub it in."

Nicolas realized just how much Tony had gone out of his way for him.

"All I'm askin' is for you to return the favors. That's all." Tony flexed his con side.

Nicolas was on a guilt trip with no return pass. He felt played, and this time, Tony had him in his grasp and was squeezing harder by the moment. Nicolas wanted to kick his own ass. He had let himself be played, and now Tony had him in a headlock, refusing to loosen his grip.

"A'ight, I'll do it." Nicolas' conscious tapped out like a UFC fighter caught in a submission hold with no way out.

"Good. I knew I could depend on you, Nick. Just don't say a thing about this to anyone."

"Yeah, I got'cha," Nicolas said, knowing there was no turning back once he did him this favor.

"I mean that. Not anybody. Not your wife. Not your momma or your dearest most trusted friend. You got that, Nick?" His tone was commanding.

"The last thing you need to worry about is me running my mouth about any of this. I'll carry this one to the grave." Nicolas' bruised ego would not let him confess that some Italian muthafucka in Jersey played him.

Tony gave Nicolas the game plan before disconnecting their phone conversation.

"Now call him back and set somethin' up with him today. I'll be back before you clock out to take you past Charles Hunt's office and by my man's spot in Camden."

"I got'cha," Nicolas said, sounding more cooperative.

Nicolas picked up the phone and keyed in Willy's number.

Man, how could I have been so stupid? Nothin' in this world is free. This muthafucka was too quick to give me shit. What's Tony gettin' me into? I really don't know him. He could be settin' me up to take the fall for his dirty deeds...makin' me the fall guy, or even worse, blackmailin' me into workin' for the mob or somethin', Nicolas thought as he listened to the phone ringing. *Hold up. Do they even have blacks workin' for their organization or is it still just a family thing?'* he wondered, laughing at the thought of becoming a hit-man for the syndicate.

"Hello?" Willy answered in a voice that sounded as if he smoked a pack of Camels a day.

"Willy Mays, please."

"Who dis?" he responded with an attitude.

"This is Nicolas Coles. You spoke to me a short while ago about buying some property."

Willy suddenly had selective memory. "I dunno what you're talkin' 'bout."

"Listen, man, I spoke with my partner, and he told me to show you a few properties and that he'll contact you later to hook something up."

"I'm good, yo," Willy replied, being evasive.

"Look, I have a lot of work to do here and don't have time for games. Do you wanna do this or not?" Nicolas said, his voice forceful.

"A'ight, I'll do it," Willy said, laughing. "I'm jus' messin' wit'cha head."

"Well, I didn't find it funny at all, Mr. Mays. So where do you want me to meet you?"

"I was looking at this property on 32nd and Marlton in Merchantville. Meet me there in twenty minutes, Mr. Coles." His voice reeked with sarcasm, mocking Nicolas' professional voice.

"I'll do just that."

Nicolas slammed the phone down, shoved the paperwork in a file cabinet, and headed out of the office. The clown-ass joker was trying to buy a crib in his neck of the woods.

Hell naw! Nicolas wouldn't let this trash in his town, if he could help it.

"Hey, where you going?" Bill shouted from across the hall.

"I'm on my way out to show some properties to a client." Bill seemed to intimidate Nicolas to the point that it showed.

"Where's Tony? I thought he was training you." Bill's eyes danced up and down the hallway to see if Tony was around.

Nicolas felt tightness in his gut.

Make it sound good.

"He still is, but I don't need him for this one." Nicolas patted his chest with pride. "Bill, I got this," sounding like George Lopez from the comedy television show.

Nicolas tried to save both his and Tony's asses by putting up a front.

Bill looked around, sucked in his gut, and placed his arm around Nicolas. This was a form of intimidation he used to get the answers he needed.

"Let me guess, he left the office again and you don't know where he is."

Busted! No need in diggin' a deeper hole for myself. Nicolas thought.

"Well, yes. He stepped out, but he's gonna meet up with me in Merchantville to walk me through a showin'."

Bill smiled, tightening his stronghold. "Listen, Nick, you seem like a confident young man, and I like that. But, I don't want you running around here doing things just to impress me, because I will check your files to see if you're makin' any progress. And if you're not makin' progress, then I'm afraid I'll have to let you go. I can't afford a non-productive agent."

He patted Nicolas on the chest with his free hand before unleashing his hold that felt more like a headlock.

"I fully understand, and the work I did prior to comin' here speaks for itself," Nicolas threw in as an extra cushion for his evaluation.

"Gooood, I like to hear that. Oh and Nicolas, I'm sorry about what happened to your wife. If there's anything I can do to help, let me know."

"Thank you, sir. I appreciate that." Nicolas made a mental note of Bill's offer in case he had to use it.

"Well, don't let me hold you up. Get going. You don't want to leave potential buyers standing outside waiting. It puts them in a bad mood and we don't want them in a bad mood."

"I strongly agree, sir and thanks a lot."

"Oh, forget about it," he said with a wave of the hand, using his Italian accent.

Nicolas shook Bill's hand before rushing out of the building.

CHAPTER FORTY-NINE

It's Only a Tour

The white townhouse on 32nd and Marlton, with its black roof and closed-in porch, had not been well kept and looked even shabbier compared to the town-homes attached on either end.

Standing at six-feet even, weighing 180 pounds, and dressed in an oversized Eagles football jersey, baggy jeans, black boots, and a baseball cap was Willy. While talking on his cell phone, he leaned against his Chrysler 300 with limo-tinted windows and 22-inch chrome rims. Both Willy and his whip were too flashy and often attracted the attention of cops. According to Nicolas, first impressions are everything, and the impression he got from Willy was a thug—a product of his environment, which was a weak excuse used by those who accept and refuse to make a way out.

Not sure exactly how to approach Willy, Nicolas sat in his car for a few minutes and watched him parade around his whip in his thugged-out gear while talking and laughing on the phone. Willy reminded him of the guys who jumped him in Camden. That made Nicolas even more leery about him.

Could that be one of those niggaz?

Willy was an up and coming wannabe rapper. His skills were up, but chasing paper and getting high all the time did nothing more than slow his pursuit of making it big. Those two things were the main obstacles that got in the way of many talented artists who never had the chance to be heard. Becoming a rapper was the number one key for Willy to get out of the hood, but he couldn't use that key to open the door to success, because someone had changed the locks and that someone was the streets.

Nicolas finally got out of the car, paperwork in hand, and approached Willy cautiously.

"Hey, you must be Willy Mays, right?" Nicolas said, with his right hand extended to greet him.

"You already know. And you mus' be Nicolas," Willy replied, clipping his iphone to his hip.

Nicolas could see his whole attitude reeked with ignorance.

"True indeed." Nicolas shook his hand. "Are you ready to do this?" he asked still keeping it professional.

"Let's do dis before dat cop watchin' us decides to lock me up," Willy told him.

"What cop?" Nicolas asked, looking around, momentarily frozen with fear.

The last person he wanted to see was Rodeski. God knows what he had in store for Nicolas after killing his partner.

"There's dis cop that keeps circlin' the block and givin' me a hard look, like he wants some problems or somethin'."

"Then let's get this over with." Nicolas walked toward the front door of the townhouse.

The three-bedroom, one-bath townhouse with unfinished basement was empty and had no shades or curtains on its windows. Dirty blue carpet ran throughout, except for worn-out white vinyl flooring in the kitchen and bathroom. Its small backyard was surrounded with newly-installed chain-link fencing. The grass lacked attention and was covered with dry spots and weeds.

After the walkthrough with Willy, Nicolas checked his paperwork.

"This property is on the market for one hundred and thirty thousand dollars," he said, while looking out the window for the patrol car to make sure it wasn't Rodeski out to start trouble. Peter Wright had been Rodeski's partner and maybe his best friend. So, Nicolas feared that crooked-ass cop might be trying to set him up or look for a reason to put a few holes in him and make up some fictitious report to cover his ass. Only thing running through Rodeski's mind was revenge, and he probably had a lack of concern for the consequences.

"I'll get Tony to work somethin' out for me," Willy said, checking the kitchen sink to see if it worked, but the water was turned off.

"Are you and your family needing a bigger place to live?" Nicolas inquired, trying to figure out if Willy was really looking to move in and turn it into a crack house. But, why should he even care. A sell is a sell.

...Isn't it?

"My girl's pregnant, and I'm lookin' for a decent neighborhood to raise the kid," he responded as if the child was a thing, not a person.

"Oh yeah? That's great. How many months is she?" Nicolas asked, relieved that maybe Willy was clean.

"Only two months, but I wanna have a place ready by the time the baby comes."

"Well, this is a quiet neighborhood," Nicolas said, not really believing a word he said. "So where you from?"

"Camden," Willy howled proudly, head up and chest out, like he had done a good service to the community and was waiting for some type of retribution for his efforts.

"Camden," Nicolas repeated, thinking about the thugs who stole his whip and credit cards, and how disgusting Camden was with drug dealers and crack heads running the streets like they owned it.

"I ain't too comfortable with my girl livin' in that rough-ass neighborhood, even though she grew up out there. Naw Mean?" Willy professed.

"So what do you think of the house?" Nicolas asked, trying to end the conversation and be out.

"I like it." Willy nodded his head rhythmically and bounced on his toes like music was playing in his ears.

"Does that mean you want the property?" Nicolas stared, hoping he wasn't wasting his time.

"Most def." Willy nodded, shuffling his feet and rubbing his hands together with a thin smile. "I'll take this one. So, call your boy Tony and tell him to work his magic. I'll call Cat Daddy to set it up."

"I can do that," Nicolas said, befuddled. "Do you buy a lot of property from Tony?"

"I dunno the dude. We've never met."

The room got silent. Nicolas was momentarily at a loss for words. How could this guy make these illegal transactions with someone he didn't know, a total stranger?

"Oh yeah? Sorry to hear that. He's a cool guy," Nicolas threw out, not believing this joker could be stupid enough to risk his freedom. "So would you be able to put something down on it today?"

"Yo, stop askin' me a bunch of cop questions and call your manz up." Willy frowned with an attitude.

Cop questions? Who this fool think he's talkin' to? Don't you know I'm from New York, and we don't use that played-out slang? Jersey's always tryna fill our shoes, but end up gettin' throwbacks. Nicolas had confidence in his New York roots.

"Not a problem, man," Nicolas said, steering Willy toward the front door. The sooner he was out of this neighborhood and away from Willy and his pimpmobile the better.

"Okay then, nice doin' business wit'cha, Nicolas." Willy extended his hand.

"The pleasure was all mine." Nicolas shook his hand before entering his vehicle.

Nicolas sat in his car watching Willy in his rearview mirror. Willy crossed the street and stood in front of a small neighborhood corner store. Moments later, a patrol car pulled up and Officer Rodeski got out, his gun dangling from his side. Nicolas couldn't hear what was being said, but he could clearly see that Rodeski was up to no good.

Willy walked up, placing his hands on the hood of Rodeski's patrol car. Rodeski handcuffed Willy and put him in the back of his patrol car. Before entering his vehicle, he looked around as if making sure there were no witnesses and then drove off as Nicolas ducked down in the seat. When Nicolas was sure the patrol car had passed him, he threw his paperwork on the passenger seat and spun off.

CHAPTER FIFTY

I Got What You Need

Nicolas practically ran in the office building, carrying his lunch he picked up at Boston Market. He closed his office door, leaned up against it, and took a deep cleansing breath, exhaling like he was glad to make it past Bill. Now if he could just make it through the rest of the day without being bothered. He sat down and opened the Boston Market bag—chicken breast with a side of macaroni and cheese, corn, candied yams, and sweet bread—his favorites. He enjoyed every bite. It was the first moment of peace and enjoyment he'd had in nearly a week.

Clearing his desk of containers and crumbs, he reflected on the morning, which had been a total disaster. He had better get himself together before the rest of the day crumbled around him like stale cornbread. He decided not to say a word to anybody about the incident with Willy. If Bill asked how his walkthrough went, he would have to make something up. After a long and thankfully uneventful afternoon, Nicolas clocked out of work at 3:35 p.m. and headed out the door to meet with Tony. The cool air felt good on his skin.

"Hey, Nick," Kim called out as he walked to his rental car. "I see Bill's got you working on a Sunday. So how are you doing?" Kim asked with a smile, her teeth white and perfectly aligned.

Her body was impeccable and her eyes were enticing. She wore a gray, nicely-fitted, knee-high dress with sexy eight-inch

Gucci shoes with straps along the side. Tempted by her captivating physique, Nicolas struggled to keep eye contact.

"I'm doin' okay." Nicolas loosened his shirt collar that suddenly felt like it was choking the shit out of him.

"Where have you been hiding? I didn't see you all day." Her words were smooth as silk, slithering through his ears and massaging his eardrums.

Nicolas rubbed his hand across his forehead to wipe away the sweet that was forming. Nicolas tried to play cool, putting up a force field of protection, but Kim was too powerful for all his defenses. "I had to step out of the office and do a walkthrough."

"Okay. So how did it go?"

Damn, I love how her lips put words together, he thought, feeling his legs about to give out.

"Well, the buyer seemed very interested in the property, so I'm gonna talk to the seller tomorrow and see if they'll accept his offer," Nicolas lied. It was Tony's project Nicolas was trying to get all the credit for. Like Tammy did with her so called *home made soup.*

"Well, good luck on that. I hope it'll be your first sale in Jersey."

"Me too," he agreed.

Kim didn't know how bad he wanted to make a sell and needed all the luck he could get.

She looked vacantly into his eyes and whispered, "And, Nick, I'm sorry about what happened to your wife."

Nicolas felt like he had been punched hard in the gut. She either saw it on the news or Tony's big mouth told her, and Kim didn't seem like the type that kept up with the news media. She seemed more like the health and fitness type. Then Nicolas remembered Tony stating he told Bill and Kim about it and how Tony runs his mouth to them like a bitch. Not cool at all.

"If you need anything at all..." Kim said, moving closer, seduction in her eyes, "...anything."

Girl, stop frontin'. You know you want this, Nicolas thought, trying to encourage himself to make a move on her.

He couldn't keep his eyes off her pretty brown eyes. Her eyes didn't say she had a man. The way she smiled and looked at him, it told him something different.

You know you want me to stroke that thing nice and long with this magic stick.

Nicolas' imagination was already deciphering the positions he would put her body in. Her eyes were saying she wanted him bad. Nicolas' heart thudded through his chest. Kim was irresistible. She smelled so sweet and edible, like coconuts and strawberries.

"Thanks for offering." He slowly inched away from her toward his car door. Losing his balance, he accidentally fell forward and brushed up against her, which brought him back to reality.

"Don't worry. I don't bite," she moaned. Her hazel brown eyes were inviting and her soft tone was lustful.

She had penetrated his forcefield and destroyed all his defenses. Now in geek mode, he says, "I'm late for an appointment with a lawyer." Now that was a total cop out.

Nicolas' nervousness was quite obvious and he was losing cool points fast. He had played himself and had to get away. Losing this round, he needed time to prepare himself for a rematch.

Kim could clearly see that he'd had enough and was down for the ten count.

"Well, if you do happen to need anything at all," she handed him her business card, "here's my phone number. Call me." Kim slowly got in her champagne-colored Benz, nice and smooth like an exotic dancer.

Nicolas stood beside his rental car, mesmerized by her every move and numb to the world around him. When she drove off, he felt like an abandoned stepchild. Upset with himself for letting lustful thoughts torment him to the point where all his cool points went straight out the window, he shook his head to clear it. Kim's approach was strong, a little too strong for him to handle.

Nicolas looked at the business card with her phone number on it. Feeling like a kid who was eager to open his gifts the day before Christmas, he was compelled to call her. It was like a burning sensation flowing through his chest and throat. He yearned to unwrap Kim like a gift, tearing the fabric from her skin like it was Christmas wrapping paper. But, when he snapped back to reality, there were no gifts around, just him and his thoughts standing next to his vehicle in a vacant parking lot.

Suddenly, his cell phone rang, suppressing his thoughts.

"Yo, Nick, what's up?" Tony asked despite the bad cell phone connection.

"Tony, where ya at? I'm sittin' in the parkin' lot waitin' for you."

"I'm sorry, man. I got a little tied up in somethin'. But, don't worry. I already set everythin' up with Mr. Hunt. So, just head on over there. His office is located at 86 East Gate Lane right next to the Cooper Radiology Center on route 70 in Cherry Hill. He's waiting for you. When you're finished, meet me back at the office."

"Okay. You better be there. Don't leave me hangin' again."

"Don't worry. I won't, dude," Tony sang with laughter.

"Catch you later then." Nicolas disconnected the call and headed for Charles Hunt's office.

*****

Nicolas pulled up on 86 East Gate Lane. It was a busy street, and the office looked like a small corner house, part of which had been converted into office space. The well-kept lawn had a big sign out front that read *Charles Hunt, Attorney at Law.*

Entering the office, Nicolas approached a woman sitting at a desk and assumed that since it was a home office and it being a Sunday, the woman must be Hunt's wife.

"Good afternoon, and you must be Nicolas Coles," she said with a smile and a pleasant voice to match.

Her appearance was casual: a yellow polo shirt, blue jeans, and a pair of Anne Klein flat dress shoes. She seemed to be in her mid 40s with a black, layered hairstyle and Roundel colorful Montana Agate Beads dangling from her neck.

"Yes, ma'am. I have an appointment with Charles Hunt."

"I'll let Charles know you're here." She picked up the phone and pushed a button. "Charles, Mr. Coles is here to see you." She hung up the phone and handed Nicolas a clipboard with paperwork attached. "Please have a seat and fill out this form. Then sign it. When you're finished, Charles will see you."

Hunt's small, unassuming office made Nicolas uncomfortable. Over a dozen framed newspaper articles about Hunt's huge successful court battles hung on the walls like souvenirs. A built-in bookcase filled with hardcover law books took up the entire wall behind Hunt's massive oak desk.

"Come right on in." Hunt stood up to shake Nicolas' hand.

Hunt, an unimposing Caucasian in his early 50s, was casually dressed in a white polo shirt and khaki pants. He stood no more than five-feet six-inches tall with a medium build. His head was too large for his frame, and his eyebrows were black as coal, forming a narrow unibrow. It was quit obvious his wife wasn't attracted to him for his looks.

"Have a seat," Hunt said, motioning toward a small leather chair directly in front of his desk. "How can I help you today, Mr. Coles?"

"Well, I've got a big problem. Actually, I have several big problems. I don't know if you've watched the news lately, but I'm the guy who killed the cop that was raping my wife."

"Yes, I heard. Sorry about what happened to your wife." His motionless words seemed rehearsed.

"Thank you," Nicolas threw out.

"Continue." He rubbed his chin as if fully focused on what Nicolas was telling him.

"Well, there's this detective who keeps comin' to my house insistin' I knew the officer was havin' an affair with my wife and that I killed him in a jealous rage. Now he wants to throw me and my wife in jail for murder."

Nicolas inhaled a deep breath, as if he was alleviated from getting it off his chest. The back of his eyes were stinging from hot tears of hurt and fear trying to form behind them.

"That would be Detective Morris, right?"

Nicolas nodded. He knew Tony had already filled Hunt in with a majority of the story.

Hunt leaned forward across his desk. "Listen, Nicolas, if I'm going to represent you and save your ass from death row, you'd better not bullshit me. I need the absolute truth from you." He straightened up in his chair. "You never know when they might reinstate the death penalty in Jersey."

Nicolas sat there in deep thought, his head down and looking at the parquet oak floor.

Hunt opened a silver humidor, took out two Havana cigars, rolled one across the desk toward Nicolas, and lit the other with the humidor's matching silver lighter.

"So, Nicolas," Hunt said, exhaling smoke, "did you kill Wright in a jealous rage because your wife was having an affair with him, or were you trying to rescue her from what you thought was the Merchantville rapist that these Keystone cops couldn't catch?"

"I swear to you that I really believed she was bein' raped," Nicolas replied, slowly raising his head, exhaustion from the past few days catching up with him.

He was tempted to light the cigar, but remembered getting on Tammy about her smoking. So, he declined.

"Well, as long as you *claim* to be innocent, there's nothing to worry about. Even if the two were having an affair and you didn't know about it, the worse the police and D.A. can charge you with is manslaughter."

"Manslaughter!"

Nicolas hollered so loud that his voice echoed off the walls. That was not a plus in Nicolas' favor. Manslaughter alone was enough to get him ten to twenty years behind bars.

"I said the worse they can do is charge you with. It doesn't mean you'll get convicted of it. It's just a standard process they go through. My job is to get the best deal possible so you can go home a free man. I'll take care of Detective Morris for now. He won't bother you again once I'm done with him. That is, until he charges you with something. And be assured he will indeed charge you with something. We're dealing with a dead cop here, so they're not going to let you go that easily. You've killed one of their own, Nicolas, and they want restitution regardless of the circumstances," Hunt said, leaning further back in his expensive, black leather chair, taking another lung full of the prized and illegal Cuban cigar. "Now, Nicolas, I foresee a lot of work on this case. So, I'm going to have to ask for a ten-thousand-dollar retainer fee."

"No problem," Nicolas said, then pulled out his checkbook. Thank God he still had money left over after making a down payment on his new home.

He was relieved to have Hunt as a buffer between him and Morris. Ten thousand dollars was a lot of money, but the cost of freedom is priceless.

Hunt tapped the ashes that were building on the tip of his cigar into an ashtray "Now, start from the beginning and tell me about the events that led you to my office, and don't leave nothing out. I don't care if you took a long shit that day. I want to know what color it was, was it at the bottom of the bowl, or was it floating like a log. I want to know everything."

Nicolas explained everything from the day they moved to Merchantville, while Hunt sat there massaging his chin and silently listening with full attention. His gaze focused on the far right corner of the room, soaking everything in like a dry sponge on a wet surface.

*****

Tony was leaning on his whip when Nicolas pulled into the empty parking lot.

"Are you ready to do this?" Nicolas asked, feeling good that Tony kept his word and didn't back out on him.

"I've been waitin' here for at least a half hour now. What is it, seven o'clock already?" Tony raised his arm to check his GMT-Master II Gold Rolex Watch.

"Okay then, let's do this." Nicolas anxiously shook his tight fist.

"We're takin' my ride," Tony said, getting into the driver's side.

Tony's whip was unique and well known in the hood. So there was a less chance of him having any problems.

"No problem." Nicolas pressed the button on his keys, activating his car alarm on the Nissan rental.

CHAPTER FIFTY-ONE

Rough City

Tony had his iPhone connected to his car radio through a Bluetooth device; he used his iPhone as a wireless remote. The music blasted through the speakers as they headed toward Camden.

Turning the volume down, Tony asked, "What did Hunt have to say? Does he think he can help you?"

"He said he'd take care of everythin', includin' that smart-ass detective," Nicolas said, not telling him that Hunt said the police and D.A. would charge him someway, somehow for Wright's death.

"Good. I told you that he was a good lawyer," Tony bragged.

"Yeah, you were right." Nicolas gave Tony a pound for hooking him up with the lawyer. "Can you believe that muthafucka had the nerve to say we made the story up about those cops harassing us?"

"Who? Charles?" Tony woofed.

"No, Morris the detective," Nicolas announced.

"Nooo the hell he didn't!" Tony sang in a high pitch.

Nicolas waved an angry fist in the air. "And he's tryna get me for murder, because that dude I killed was a cop."

"A cop! Man, that's rough," Tony said, realizing the trouble Nicolas was in. "So what? You caught him rapin' yo wife, right?" Tony added, trying to find an out for Nicolas.

"Yeah!" he thundered, hoping the truth of Tammy's affair with Wright wouldn't be discovered.

Nicolas was scared to tell even Tony the truth. Maybe it wasn't the truth. Maybe what he read in Tammy's diary was just her lustful daydream. Maybe she really did get raped. Naw, she basically confessed to everything in the hospital or maybe his mind was playing tricks on him. He did suffer a concussion, right?

"So you're good then?" Tony asked, wanting to believe his friend would get out of this mess alive.

"Yeah." Nicolas nodded, not really convinced.

It was no use in pretending. It was no lustful daydream; Tammy had been having an affair with that cop, and he was too afraid to tell anyone. Besides, this was his ego on the line...his pride. Who would ever believe his side of the story anyway? A black man killing a white cop only proved the odds were not in his favor.

"Morris can't do shit to you. Don't worry about it, Nick. Hunt's good. Expensive, but good. He'll get you outta this mess in one piece."

"I hope you're right." Nicolas couldn't control the look of concern that showed on his face.

"If anybody can help you, it's Hunt. They don't come better than him," Tony said, while passing a Ford Explorer that had been riding too slow. "Plus, he's on the company's payroll, and to be on our payroll, you have to be good."

"Yeah, you're right." Nicolas felt a little bit at ease knowing Hunt was good enough to make the job's payroll. That said a lot, especially with it being a big firm.

"So what happened with Willy today? Did he check the house out or what?" Tony rode the bumper of a Dodge Charger like an aggressive driver trying to intimidate other drivers to let him pass.

Nicolas hesitantly responded. "Uuuhh...yeah...he did, and he wants it."

"Good. A big, fat commission check is comin' my way." A grin graced his face. "I'll give you a cut for showin' it today."

Nicolas winced, ducking his head in shame. That was nice of Tony to share his cut of the profit, but he couldn't leave Tony hanging like that.

"Well, I think that's gonna be a problem."

"Problem? What problem?" Tony asked, visualizing dollar bills flying away.

"Well, after we checked the house out, I got into my car to straighten out the paperwork. When I looked up, Willy was headin' to a store across the street. But, that crooked-ass cop Rodeski pulled up on him in his patrol car. The next thing I knew, Rodeski jumped out with his weapon drawn, like he did us. He then put his ass in handcuffs, and threw him in the back of his patrol car," Nicolas reported, staring out the window and nervously biting his bottom lip.

"Did he say why he was takin' him in?"

Nicolas could see Tony getting ticked off.

"With the shit I got goin' on, I wasn't gonna get outta my car and start askin' questions. I ducked in my seat until they drove off," Nicolas said, embarrassed he didn't do anything to help Willy out. But, hey, he didn't even know the dude. For all he knew, it could have been drug related.

"Yeah, but now I gotta find out what Cat Daddy's gonna do about it." Tony picked up his cell phone and started to dial Cat Daddy, but changing his mind, he put the phone back down. "I better talk to him in person."

"I'm positive that crooked-ass cop Rodeski is a racist," Nicolas said, bile rising in his throat. "How could one person waste so much time and energy discriminatin' on people from a different race?"

"I agree one hundred percent. That crooked-ass cop is a straight-up redneck. Somethin' needs to be done about him. Just don't say shit to Cat Daddy about this."

Tony gripped the steering wheel so tight that the veins on his hands and forearms protruded through the skin and his knuckles turned white.

"I won't," Nicolas assured Tony, leaning over toward him. "Hey, Tony, can you keep a secret?"

Nicolas needed to think of something besides trouble. He could see Tony's tight grip on the steering wheel loosen up.

"Sure. What's up?" Tony quickly looked at Nicolas a few times, trying to read his facial expression and keep an eye on the road at the same damn time.

Nicolas kept taunting Tony with a long grin, waiting to see if he would lose his patience.

"Yo, stop fuckin' around and tell me already!" Tony barked, revealing he was very impatient.

"Kim is pushin' up." Nicolas smiled, as if he just received extra brownie points.

"Yeah, right! Stop fuckin' around. That's my future wife you're talkin' 'bout," Tony said, punching Nicolas playfully on his left shoulder.

"Real talk, man." Nicolas laughed. "She stepped to me in the hall the other day and made a pass at me."

"No way," Tony said, pronouncing his words like a straight-up geeky white boy.

"Yes way!" Nicolas replied, mocking his white-boy inflections. "And she pushed up on me again today in the parking lot. Even gave me her phone number," Nicolas added, pulling out her business card to show him.

Tony snatched it out of his hand and quickly glanced over it, flipping it from front to back. "Get the hell outta here. I always took her teasin' as a mind game she likes to play. Nobody's been able to get with that, and here you come along—a married man no less—and she's all over you. Man! I never took her seriously. I was startin' to think she was a lesbo, which woulda been a major plus if I was to hit that."

He gave Nicolas a devilish grin to say if the opportunity present itself then he's all over it.

"So are you goin' to hit that or what, man?" Tony asked with excitement, vicariously thinking of the prospect.

"I can't. I'm married, man," Nicolas responded, acting modest.

"That's why she wants you. Ah, the forbidden fruit and no strings attached. Plus, I told her about the incident you had in Camden." Tony re-adjusted his body in the seat.

"What did you say to her?" Nicolas asked as his spirit of inquiry started to build.

Tony made up a fictitious story. "I said you got attacked by five thugs in Camden, and you knocked three of them out before the cops came. But, when they got there, the other two ran off and you were sent to the hospital for some treatment," Tony said, as the lies flowed naturally.

"No, the fuck you didn't." Nicolas giggled, imagining himself as a superhero and eager to hear more. "Well, what did she say?"

"She asked if you were okay, and I said yeah. She smiled and walked away. Yeah, she really wants you, man. Now be honest. Would you if you had the opportunity?" Tony bumped him with his elbow.

Nicolas thought about how good it would feel to have her body up against his, to feel her smooth skin and kiss her soft lips.

"No," was his first response, but his tone didn't sound convincing to Tony.

Tony detected the lie in Nicolas' voice. "Come on, man. Stop lyin' on your dick."

"I dunno. She does look good," he told him.

Nicolas thought about Kim's beautiful dark chocolate skin, her toned physique, and seductive brown eyes. He sat quietly, lost in a fantasy, imagining Kim in a white camisole, thigh-high black fishnet stockings and six-inch heels dancing slowly to soft music. He would have her slowly remove the camisole as he scanned every body part for marks or blemishes. Nicolas would be the detective searching for clues in her secret parts. The mere thought of it excited him, as his body started calling for her.

"Yeah," Nicolas admitted in a low voice, "I would. But don't tell her or anyone else that I said that shit or I'll kill you," he added in a grave tone.

Tony held his right hand up, as if in court under oath. "Nicolas Coles, I swear on my life not to tell anyone about this, not even myself." He laughed. "Don't worry about it. Just give me details when you hit it and the truth, the whole truth and nothin' but the truth, so help you God."

"I told you that I'm a happily married man!" Nicolas recited, both of them laughing as they entered Camden City limits.

CHAPTER FIFTY-TWO

Just Merely a Whisper

They drove up Broadway, made a left on Ferry Avenue and another quick left up an alleyway that lacked a street sign, which was common in Camden. Crackheads, if given the opportunity would scrap it at the junk yard for a quick fix. The street was narrow and dark, littered with trash, and had graffiti-covered buildings tagged with elementary school artwork.

"They never clean these filthy-ass streets," Tony voiced. "And this alley is so small that if you were to grab the window ledge of one house and fully extend yourself with your arm up, you could touch the row homes across the street with the tips of your toes," he said.

Nicolas sat silently, full of trepidation.

Camden was no more than a deserted, urban island. No one gave two shits about it or the people who lived there. It was more like a dumping ground for the unwanted and less fortunate. The streets were filthy and poorly lit. There was a mixture of rap, hip-hop and R&B lingering in the air. Unattended children ran up and down the street with no supervision. It looked like a scene from *The Living Dead*. Everyone, including the drug dealers, walked around like lifeless zombies.

"Do you know they don't even plow the streets here when it snows? How fucked up is that? How can the people of Camden just sit back and allow the government to treat them this way? The sad part about it is that every city has a poor section that's just as bad or even worse with no voice. It's heard through the city, but outside these streets it's merely a whisper, like someone hit the mute button," Tony said.

He became angry as he started to remember when he and his mother lived in a housing project for a while before his father found out about him and started giving them money to live a decent life outside the projects.

"Well, this is it. Let's get what we came for and get the fuck outta here," Tony said, slowly cruising up the alley. "Let me do all the talkin' and don't say shit about Willy gettin' locked the fuck up, even if he asks you about it. You don't know shit!"

"Got it." Nicolas looked around, trying to get his bearings.

Twilight was fading fast and Nicolas wanted to get out of there before dark arrived.

They drove up to a stocky black man dressed in dark baggy clothes sitting on the steps of an abandoned building.

"What!" he said, biting off his words with icy disapproval. His tone gave Nicolas the shakes.

"I need some heat," Tony said, looking in the distance to see if there were any cops around.

The man leaned toward Nicolas, giving him a hard, menacing stare. His hair was extremely nappy and he was overdue for a shave and haircut, like his barber was on strike. His eyes were bloodshot red, his lips a deathly shade of purple from smoking too much weed and his body smelled like a dumpster. There was no doubt he was on the run and hiding, keeping a low profile.

"Wait a minute. Who the fuck is dis muthafucka right here?" he asked, pointing at Nicolas.

A cold chill ran through Nicolas. It was a scary feeling not knowing what to expect.

"Chill, man. This is my main man Nick," Tony said, motioning toward Nicolas.

"I dunno dis nigga, so bounce," the man said, raising himself to his full height—six-foot-seven of massive bulk bulging through his black material. From his height and size, he could've been a pro football player or pro boxer, but now he was just a pitiful excuse of a hulking meat stick prepped for prison life.

"Be easy, dawg. He's cool," Tony tried to explain.

"How the fuck am I supposed to know he ain't Five-O?" the man said, his voice rising as two other guys appeared out of nowhere, approaching the vehicle with cold stares. Their hands were tucked under their dark, hooded sweatshirts like they were packing heat and ready to pull out at any moment and start shooting up Tony's pride and glory.

We're sitting ducks, Nicolas thought to himself.

"Hold on a minute, man. Chill...chill. He works with me, and you know I wouldn't do anythin' to jeopardize our relationship," Tony stated, trying to calm the man before anything sparked off.

"Look, first get rid of this muthafucka and meet me back here later, 'cause I'm gonna lose patience out this muthafucka and start poppin' off out this muthafucka. And I don't give a fuck who yo' fuckin' daddy is," he roared, his words ricocheting off the tight walls.

"Okay. No problem, Cat Daddy. I got it," Tony said, feeling threatened with the thugs in their hoodies surrounding them.

"And stop sayin' my muthafuckin' name, bitch." The man grabbed Tony by the shirt to get his point across—and yes, it was working.

"Sorry about that, cousin," Tony said, holding his hands up in submission.

The man moved in closer, getting in Tony's face. "I ain't your muthafuckin' cousin, pussy. You better bounce before I change my mind up in this muthafuckah," he said, his breath smelling like barbecued horse shit. "Now!" he said, shoving Tony into his seat and then letting go of his shirt.

Tony placed his vehicle in gear and peeled off.

"You see how they are? I told you that they don't play around. I'm goin' to drop you off at the Asian store up the road and go back for the gun," Tony said, accelerating at a high rate of speed.

"No problem. Just slow down before you attract some unwanted attention or crash yo shit up."

CHAPTER FIFTY-THREE

Packin' Heat

Nicolas approached a skinny Chinese man standing behind a thick bulletproof glass that had a rotating glass door for taking money and exchanging goods. The Asian had short, straight, black hair and the look on his face emanated an unfocused hatred.

A young Spanish couple stood in a corner of the store by the dairy case, hugging and kissing, not a care in the world about the stares they drew. A group of young black and Hispanic males all dressed in dark-color clothes alarmed Nicolas, reminding him of the attack at Tony's townhouse. Maybe they belonged to a gang and were just waiting for a new face to kick in.

Nicolas ordered a small bag of Lay's potato chips and a Coke. While waiting for the Asian proprietor to ring it up, one of the young Hispanic males approached him.

"You need somethin'? I got that shit." The Hispanic guy showed Nicolas the edge of a brown paper bag stashed in his pants pocket. He slid two fingers into the bag and pulled out a handful of small clear plastic bags filled with crushed green leaves, which was marijuana of course.

Say what! How the hell is this stupid muhfucka gonna come up in my face and disrespect me like that? I oughta beat his ass right in front of his boyz!' Nicolas thought.

Instead, he said, "Nah. I'm good," hoping that would end the sales pitch and they would leave him alone.

Nicolas chose to enjoy his soda and chips outside in case the cops decided to raid the place. He didn't want any parts of it. His freedom was too important to him.

He waited under a bus sign for Tony. That way, the cops wouldn't snatch him up, if they decided to raid the area.

Traffic was light and slow, nothing like New York traffic, which made the neighborhood seem even more foreboding. Cars coming down the streets on either side of the intersection were few and far between. Every time someone walked around the corner, Nicolas' heart would jump, bracing for a mugging or worse. By the time Tony pulled up, the chips he had just eaten were making his stomach sour.

"What took you so long?" Nicolas asked, throwing his soda and bag of chips in the nearby wastebasket before getting into the vehicle, but from the way the street looked it didn't matter if he threw the trash in the can or on the ground. "Did you get it?"

"Listen, we're both lucky to get outta here with our heads still connected to our necks." Tony tensed up from having to deal with Cat Daddy and his thugged out buddies. Now he was anxious to get out of the neighborhood and head back to civilization.

"You'd better never tell anyone where you got this piece from or I'll kill you myself."

"I swore to you that I wouldn't. You looked out for me, and I can't thank you enough. So, me playin' you out is the least of your concern."

Tony reached under the seat for the gun and gave it to Nicolas.

"This thing is nice," Nicolas said, looking at the nine-millimeter.

"Keep that thing low. These young boyz out here might mistake you as a stick-up boy or a cop, and blow both our damn heads off!" Tony told him, pressing the handgun down in Nicolas' lap.

Nicolas gazed at it as if it were a souvenir. "After I get me a carryin' permit, I'll get rid of it and purchase a legal one."

"Don't get rid of it. Give it back to me and I'll take care of it...understand?"

Nicolas gave him a stiff nod, seeing how Tony was looking nervous about the weapon being in his possession. "Sure, not a problem. How much do I owe you?"

"Five hundred."

"Say what!" Nicolas thundered.

"Hey, these things don't come cheap. That's an all-black nine milly with a hairpin trigger. It'll do some serious damage."

"Got'cha. Just take me to an ATM so I can get yo money," Nicolas said, playing with the gun like a kid, pretending to be a cowboy.

"Hey, what the fuck!" Tony rolled his eyes. "Seriously, Nick, are you tryin' to get us both killed or sent to prison?" He pushed Nicolas' arm down again.

"Sorry," Nicolas responded, realizing the kid in him got the best of him.

"Then put that shit up or give it to me. Never mind, I got a place to put it." Tony electronically opened a secret storage compartment in the dashboard.

"Ah, that's some James Bond 007 shit." Nicolas laughed, tucking the gun securely inside, next to Tony's personnel handgun. Both of them watching it slowly close.

"And yeah, that's a secret, too," Tony said, turning to give Nicolas a threatening look that meant business.

"I got you, dawg. Calm the fuck down," Nicolas sang, pumping his hands back and forth.

As soon as the anger in Tony's expression evaporated, Nicolas' curiosity kicked in.

"So, Tony, tell me how you do it. I wanna be down."

Tony frowned and replied, "I dunno what you're talkin' 'bout."

"I know you got a master plan of makin' money, and I wanna be down," Nicolas said as his lust for cash coated his expression.

Tony exhaled as if pressure had been building inside of him and he couldn't wait to confess his sins to Nicolas.

"Alright, since I laid out all my dirty laundry. You know if you spend ten thousand dollars or more on a car or house, the IRS wants to know your source of income."

"Yeah," Nicolas agreed.

"Well, I got these drug boys investin' all their blood money in me. They give me whatever they have on a house, and I do the paperwork."

"What, you buy the houses in your name?" Nicolas asked with open ears.

"Exactly. You see, Nick, you're a very smart man." Tony chuckled.

"Okay and then what?" Nicolas' eagerness was getting the best of him.

"Calm down now, fella." Tony slapped him on the chest a few times. "I make it seem as though they're rentin' the property off me until I'm able to borrow from the escrow."

"To make up the difference," Nicolas chimed in. "That's a good way of doin' it without gettin' caught."

"I knew you were an intelligent individual." Tony playfully punched Nicolas on the left shoulder.

"So what happens if you can't get any money from the property or they refuse to pay up?"

"Well, that's when I go campin'. There's nothin' better than an old campfire to warm the spirit and let the insurance company take care of the rest. Either way, I still get paid." Tony smiled.

"I understand," Nicolas said, putting his questions on pause. That was sharing too much information on Tony's part.

"Before you start to act like a pussy, let me tell you this. If you work with me, you don't have to worry about the big shit. All I would need from you is the paperwork done right. You'll get paid well and not have to worry about gettin' your hands dirty."

"I know there are risks involved when dealin' with fast money, but I don't wanna end up doin' time in prison for it."

"Don't worry about it. I told you that Hunt is on our payroll, and with all the connects he has, you don't even have to worry about bein' selected for jury duty."

"I feel you on that." Nicolas nodded.

"So what you say?" The motivation in Tony's voice sounded as if he was ready to get Nicolas started right away.

"I'll have to sleep on that thought and weigh the pros and cons," Nicolas responded, thinking about his youthful years in New York when he would hustle on the street corner selling weed.

The fast money was addictive, but Nicolas promised his grandmother that he would not sell any more drugs before she passed, and he stuck to it. However, the urge to make fast money gave him a boost of adrenaline. If he decided to do this, he wouldn't be breaking his promise with his grandmother...or would he? There was so much he could do with the money, including paying his house off early. But, he didn't want Tony to see the desperation in his eyes.

"Listen, Nick, I need you to make the right decision to be down with me on this. I can't afford to have you walkin' around the street with that much information."

"Don't worry about it, Tone," Nicolas said, using his phrase in an Italian accent. "Your secret is safe with me. Once I see this plan is foolproof, I have no problem with being down wit'cha on this."

"Good, I like that. You and me can go far with this. You'll see."

They pulled up near the ATM on Broadway and Market Street, which was almost deserted. The few businesses were closed except for Poppa Mario's Pizza, but no crowd was waiting to get in like during lunchtime. Tony parked on the practically empty street and waited for Nicolas.

The night was quiet. A light misty rain began falling, and mixed with the aroma of pizza, it gave a scent of wet bricks and pasta. A homeless man leaned against the side of the bank near the ATM machine. Nicolas reached in his pocket and gave him a five-dollar bill and loose change. The man thanked him and went on his merry way. Reaching the ATM, Nicolas looked left and then right for possible problems before keying in his PIN number. He quickly made the transaction from his account and headed back to the whip.

"Did you give that old man my five hundred?" Tony asked, laughing as Nicolas slid in the vehicle and buckled his seatbelt.

"I gave him a five piece to get a pizza or a bottle of cheap wine," Nicolas said, while handing the money to Tony.

Tony smiled and put the money in the inside pocket of his Armani suit coat. "Yo, let's go hang out for a few at the pool hall. Drinks on me."

Nicolas considered going home or at least calling to check on Tammy.

"Come on, man. What, the wife got you shook or somethin'?" Tony cracked.

A vision of Tammy and Pete sneaking around behind his back formed just behind his eyes, and he felt like he was going to be sick in Tony's immaculate ride. He swallowed hard.

"What the hell? As long as you're payin', I'm stayin'," he said with a *fuck it* attitude.

"That's my manz!" Tony yelled, stepping on the gas and turning the volume on blast with DMX's "Slippin'" pumping through the speakers.

CHAPTER FIFTY-FOUR

The Boys' Hangout

Nicolas and Tony entered the Purple Parrot at 1406 Chapel Avenue. The heavy drinkers hadn't arrived yet and the bar looked empty, but a good crowd of pool players and sports fanatics were watching an airing of *Sports Center* on the big screen TVs while throwing back cold ones.

"Hey, the offer still stands whenever you feel like you wanna burn some extra calories," Tony said to Candy, the long-haired brunette mixing drinks, her large breasts peeping out the top of her blouse.

"What about my husband?" she asked, holding up her left hand, flashing a three-karat Princess-cut diamond on her ring finger. Her bright smile revealed teeth so white she could do commercials for Crest White Strips. Candy was petite and well proportioned with a small ass that was round and sweet as a nectarine.

"It's okay. He can watch. I might teach him a thing or two," Tony cracked, releasing some post-project-buying-a-gun tension.

"I don't think so." Candy turned to wait on two men in expensive business suits at the other end of the bar.

"Ya see that, Nick? She wants me bad," Tony told him as they took a seat at the bar.

After handing the two men their drinks, the bartender strolled back over to where Nicolas and Tony were seated. "So what do you and your lover boyfriend here want to drink?" she asked, giggling softly.

"He's married, but I could throw him in for free," Tony cracked.

"Only if you let me watch." Her baby blue eyes sparkled like stars.

Tony waved his hand. "Nah, I think I'll pass."

Candy placed her hand on her hip. "Let's see here. Last week you were saying how it's okay for me to be with another woman, though, right?"

"Alright, alright, Candy. You win. Now take me home and punish me good," Tony said, trying to avoid the conversation they had last week about how he would love to see two women having sex with each other.

Candy laughed and playfully hit Tony with the bar towel hanging from her shoulder. "I gotta get back to work. So what you want? The usual?"

"Yeah. Looks like that's all I'm gonna get," Tony said in a saddened voice, hoping to get more out of her.

Candy turned to Nicolas. "And what would you like, handsome?"

"Whatever he's havin' since he's treatin'."

"No problem, but first, I need to see some form of I.D.," Candy said, looking at Nicolas' baby face.

Nicolas handed over his old New York driver's license and she looked it over. The due date on the license was expired. Nicolas explained to the bartender that the newer license was stolen and that's all the information he had. The bartender studied the photo for a moment before accepting it.

"A New Yorker, uh. Okay, big spenders, two beers comin' up." She handed back Nicolas' driver's license and reached for two frosty mugs.

"Candy doesn't know it, but she's goin' to give it up to me one day," Tony stated in a loud whisper.

"And what make you believe that?" Nicolas asked, trying to talk over the loud music and chatter.

"You ever heard the expression, 'If you believe in somethin' strong enough, it'll come true?'"

"Yeah, I've heard that shit." Nicolas said as the bartender delivered their bars.

"Well, it works the same way with women." Tony said tilting his glass mug back in big gulps.

Nicolas shook his head and pressed his hand on Tony's shoulder. "You see, Tony, with that mentality, you'll never get ass."

"Oh, I get ass," Tony howled.

"But was any of it free?" Nicolas threw out.

Tony paused, caught off guard by the question. Before he had a chance to answer, Nicolas' cell phone rang. Nicolas checked the caller I.D. before answering it.

"Yo, wassup, son?" Nicolas answered, raising his hand for Tony to wait while he took the call.

"Yo, we're just enterin' Jersey from Delaware. Where ya at?" Mark asked.

"I'm in Cherry Hill at the bar."

"That's even better. We'll meet you there. We could use a few drinks."

Nicolas gave them the address so they could program it into their GPS system.

CHAPTER FIFTY-FIVE

Who's Drunker than Who?

When Dave and Mark finally arrived, they were introduced to Tony and had a few drinks at the bar. Nicolas showed off his new cell phone. "How did y'all get here so fast?" he asked, after everyone had a chance to checkout his iPhone.

"Man, I had the pedal to the floor doin' a hunit at times," Mark boasted.

He bragged about the phone numbers that he got from the women in North Carolina and how good the food was there. Dave just continued to make wisecracks and tease Mark the entire time.

"Yo, let's shoot some pool," Nicolas said, trying to maintain his balance after getting up from the barstool.

"I got winners," Mark yelled, slurring his words.

*****

"Yo, Mark here is cool as hell. I love this guy," Tony yelled, throwing an arm around his shoulder and kissing him on the top of his bald head.

"You better watch it, Tony. Mark's girl will have you spendin' time in jail with her babies' daddies for tryna take her man," Dave laughed, stumbling around the pool table, struggling to line up a shot.

Nicolas laughed and joked most of the night and for a brief moment, he was able to forget the deep pit of trouble that awaited him.

"Yo, it's gettin' late, Tony. You gotta sober up so we can get outta here."

"No problem. I got'cha, Nicolas." Tony stumbled toward the nearest table and plopped down in a chair.

"You guys can't handle your liquor 'cause ya soft!" Dave said, finishing the game of pool by himself.

"Good, then yo' ass can drive us back home then," Mark retorted, as he and Nicolas stumbled toward the bathroom.

"Yo, Mark, you didn't tell Dave what I told you about Tammy over the phone, did you?" Nicolas asked, pulling down his zipper to use the urinal.

"Naw, dawg," Mark said, standing at the urinal next to him. "You asked me not to, so I didn't."

"Thanks, man." Nicolas stared down into the urinal. He wanted to tell Mark about the thugs that attacked him in Camden, but felt that he'll save that conversation for later. He wasn't ready to deal with the multiple questions and just wanted to relax and get his head together.

"No problem, dawg. So what's goin' on with that anyway?" Mark asked while keeping his focus on the wall in front of him.

"Tony hooked me up with an attorney out here."

"Yo, that's what's up. Tony's good peoples," Mark stated with excitement in his voice.

"Yeah, and the attorney said he's gonna make sure those cops don't harass me again."

"Good. I don't wanna see you in jail for some dumb shit," Mark uttered, sounding like a big brother trying to school his little brother.

"Yeah, I agree, 'cause this muthafuckin' detective just keeps poppin' by my crib every mornin' with more bullshit. I ain't gonna lie, this fool got me shook."

"I hope this attorney can get him off your back."

"Yeah, I hope so, too, 'cause I was thinkin' 'bout..."

Just then, Dave walked in, stopping Nicolas in mid-sentence.

"What the fuck y'all doin' in here, dick watchin'?" Dave pushed his way into one of the empty stalls.

"Yo, dawg, don't disrespect me like that," Mark barked. "You know better than that shit."

"Yeah, if I had waited ten more minutes, you two woulda probably been sword fightin' right about now."

"You jealous 'cause we didn't invite you over?" Mark cracked.

"Fuck y'all, niggas. I gotta take a shit. Aaaahh!" Dave said, unleashing his bowels.

"Damn, it sounds like your asshole is doin' the beat box. If you had a little rhythm, you'd be the baddest shit talker around," Mark said as they both laughed hysterically.

"Yeah, that's the shit!" Nicolas blurted out as the two laughed even harder.

"Fuck y'all, muhfuckas." Dave unleashed a ton of fury. "Aaaahh!" he grunted.

"Yo', dawg, you didn't even put any toilet tissue down. You gonna get a red rash around yo' yellow ass," Nicolas cracked.

"Fuck you, country, corn-ass havin' muhfucka."

A stink cloud quickly permeated the room. Mark and Nicolas threw their hands over their faces trying to block the smell.

"Daaamn! Dis muthafucka's lettin' loose up in here. What the fuck did you eat, pickled shit with soy sauce and onions?" Mark cracked.

"Fuck y'all! Aaahh!" Dave yelled and groaned simultaneously.

"Yo, I'm outta here. That shit sounded wet," Nicolas said, bouncing up and down to pull up his zipper.

"It is wet," Mark chimed in. "Hurry up. I'm gettin' light headed," he said.

They quickly washed their hands and ran out of the bathroom laughing.

"Fuck y'all!" Dave yelled loud enough for all the people at the bar to hear him.

Nicolas found Tony asleep, his head on the table.

"Yo, Tone! Wake the fuck up. Someone could've robbed you while you were sleepin'," Mark yelled in his ear, shaking him.

Tony sat up and rubbed his eyes. "What time is it?" He squinted his eyes trying to focus on his five hundred thousand dollar Rolax watch.

"Time for you to sober up," Nicolas said.

"I'll be good in a few." Tony looked around the bar. "Where's Dave?"

"He's in the bathroom committin' an act of terrorism," Nicolas answered.

"What, he's blowin' it up?" Tony asked.

"Hey, you catch on fast, dawg," Mark noted, ordering juice and coffee so they could sober up faster.

Nicolas sat across from Tony and Mark, watching them sip hot coffee as they talked about the New York Mets. But what did he care? His life wasn't worth two cents now. Tammy didn't love him and probably never had. If push came to shove, she would sell him out to Detective Morris in less than a heartbeat. She'd lie and say he knew she was having an affair with the officer and had premeditated his death. Oh, she would alright. Anything to save her cheating ass. And Nicolas? Oh, how he would take the fall. No one would believe the truth. They'd be too willing to believe a white woman and a white dead cop over any black man on Earth. Well, he might just cheat them out of their circus. End it all on his terms. Better to be dead than spend the rest of his sorry life in prison on death row waiting for some new governor to initiate the moratorium on executions. It was hard knowing his wife lied to him. It was hard knowing the cop that was harassing him was messing around with his wife, but what hurt the most was coming home after a hard day at work to see another man ramming his dirty dick all up in his wife! He was pounding it as if on a mission to stretch out her pussy and the worse part of it all is that she voluntarily allowed this muthafucka to run all up in it raw. There's no telling what type of STD this pussy gave her.

"Fuck dat shit," he mumbled.

That was the straw that broke the camel's back.

Dave returned to the table, interrupting Nicolas' contemplation.

"Yo, Dave, what took you so long?" Tony asked, smirking.

"He had to shit his insides out." Mark laughed, his head clearing of the alcohol.

"Fuck y'all," Dave howled, pulling out a chair.

The walls seemed to be closing in on Nicolas; he had to get out of there. Get some fresh air that wasn't filled with cigarette smoke, Jack Daniels, and stale shit.

"I gotta go," he told them, rising from his chair.

"Bye. I love you!" Tony called out to the bartender as all four guys left.

"Yeah, I love you, too, Tony!" She smirked while drying off a glass mug.

CHAPTER FIFTY-SIX

Look What the Cat Drug In

It was after 2:00 a.m. when Nicolas finally got home. Hoping Tammy was asleep, he opened the door softly and took off his shoes. He felt his way to the lamp on the end table and switched it on to see Tammy sitting in the corner of the love-seat waiting patiently for him.

"Where have you been? Smelling like alcohol and cigarette. So now you're back to drinking again, huh?"

"I was out..." Nicolas responded, before cutting the rest of his sentence short. There was more to fire back at her, but he held it in, as if he knew she wasn't ready to hear what followed.

"Out?" she barked. "Now you want to just throw our whole marriage out the window?"

"What, like you did with your commitment to bein' faithful?" he threw back.

The look on Tammy's face was priceless. Hurt, she couldn't take the impact of his words. Nicolas realized he was harsh and couldn't accept hurting her feelings. He loved her too much to hurt her physically or emotionally.

So, he broke down and told her, "I've been talkin' to a lawyer about Morris. Then Tony and I stopped for a few drinks with Dave and Mark."

"What did the lawyer say?" she asked, jumping to that topic first, absorbing everything with a keen eye.

"He said he's gonna take care of it and he'll make sure Morris leaves us alone."

"And then what did you do?" she asked as if she knew there was more to the story.

"I took care of some business," he replied.

But, his response was too general. She wanted specifics.

"What business?" she inquired, eyes widened with curiosity.

"I had to make sure you were alright while I was at work."

"What do you mean?" she impatiently cried out. "Stop beating around the bush and get to the point, Nicolas!"

Nicolas huffed before saying, "I got some protection for the house."

He handed Tammy the brown paper bag that contained the handgun. Tammy pulled the gun out of the bag and dropped it on the floor, as if it was an infectious disease.

"Be careful! It's loaded," Nicolas said, picking the gun up.

"Loaded!" Her voice shrieked with revelation. "What the hell are you doing bringing a loaded gun into my house? How you know that thing ain't hotter than a New York stripper?" She used one of Nicolas' phrases to get her point across. "Get it out of this house right now, Nicolas!"

"No, it stays here. Comin' home from work and seein' that goon all on top of you, it made me feel helpless. I made a promise to myself that I would never be stuck in a situation like that ever."

Their eyes made contact and stayed locked in a stare down. Nicolas refused to back down or take back what he said.

"I want nothing to do with it," she murmured in a defeated tone. "And if you needed protection, why didn't you buy me mace or something that's legal?"

Nicolas chuckled with sarcasm. "That shit don't work."

"How would you know? You ran like a little girl when your mother pulled hers out."

"Now you wanna bring that shit up. She only wanted to show me that it still worked after I told her it didn't!" Nicolas roared, defensive and embarrassed that he reacted the way he did when his mother tried to test it out on him. Now Tammy was hanging the shit over his head.

"Then why were you running and screaming like a little bitch?"

Now she was trying to use hurtful words to piss him off, but that wasn't going to work.

"I had to go to work the next day and I didn't wanna do anythin' that may ruin my image on my first day at work."

Tammy gazed at Nicolas as if she couldn't believe the words coming out of his mouth. She winced and said, "You always have some type of lame excuse to justify all your actions."

"Whatever you say, Tammy," Nicolas sang, brushing her off.

Tammy pointed her index finger at the brown bag Nicolas was holding, which contained the handgun. "Is that thing registered at all?"

"No." Nicolas frowned.

"Where did you get that thing?" Her voice quivered.

"I bought it off the street from some drug dealer in Camden."

Tammy placed her hand over her gapping mouth. "Are you crazy? Don't you know it probably has a body on it?"

"Yes, I do know that, Mrs. Detective," he said sarcastically. "I wanted to buy a legal one, but with all that's goin' on right now, I don't think that would be possible."

Tammy rolled her eyes and stormed upstairs, slamming the bedroom door behind her. She was pissed off and didn't like the way Nicolas was talking to her.

Nicolas placed the brown bag containing the gun in the bottom drawer of the China cabinet, then grabbed a blanket from the linen closet and laid down on the sofa. He lay in the dark replaying the events of the past few days in his head like a bad movie.

She's the one who fucked up, not me, he thought. *And now she's tryna reverse all this shit on me. I don't think so. So why am I bendin' over backwards for her ass after comin' home and findin' her takin' care of another man's needs? Fuck dat bitch!*

Nicolas couldn't sleep that night, waking up in cold sweats. Tammy's infidelity haunted his dreams, converting them into nightmares. He buried his face in the throw pillow and wept. He cried for lost trust, lost dreams, and lost love.

"Why am I here? What is there left to live for?" he asked himself, as selfish thoughts plagued his mind.

His marriage was over and his career would never survive the storm that was to come.

CHAPTER FIFTY-SEVEN

The Silent Treatment

Nicolas awoke the next morning to the aroma of bacon frying and homemade pancakes being prepared for breakfast. It was Monday, May 30th. The hurt and depression of the previous night had not dissolved completely. Feeling a little better, he got up from the couch and went into the kitchen to give Tammy a kiss on top of her head. Tammy moved her head away and silently flipped the bacon.

"Another day of silence, huh?" Nicolas said. "Fine then."

With his hunger overriding his anger, he grabbed some bacon, put it on a cold slice of toast, folded it over, and got a glass of orange juice. He ate quickly and headed upstairs to get ready for work.

*****

Leaving the house without saying another word to Tammy, he pulled out of the driveway, passing John who was outside washing his cab. Nicolas was still bent out of shape over what Tammy had written in her diary about John flirting with her, but realized he shouldn't have been mad at John. He hadn't done anything but catch Tammy's attention. On second thought, that was a good enough reason for him to be mad at John.

Fuck'um! his thoughts interjected.

Nicolas noticed another "For Sale" sign in another neighbor's yard. Lately, there had been signs popping up everywhere. Seemed like everyone was trying to get out of the neighborhood, but no one was interested in buying in the area, because of the rapes broadcasted on the news.

Nicolas arrived at the office and clocked in, noticing Kim at the end of the hallway talking to Bill. He headed for his office and closed the door, not wanting to talk to either of them. He sat at his desk trying to relax a little, but his head kept spinning out of control, causing it to ache. He went through all the files and started shredding some papers from a few folders, including one containing Willy's information, so as to cover his ass just in case the cops tried to involve him in something else that would cause him more trouble than he was already in.

His cell phone rang. He answered it without even looking at the caller ID.

"Yo, dawg, you won't believe this shit!" Dave yelled. "You got a minute, son?"

Nicolas could hear the intensity in Dave's voice. So, he knew it had to be some good shit. He stopped shredding and poked his head out the door to make sure Bill wasn't around.

The coast was clear.

"Go 'head. I'm listenin'."

"This crazy-ass, glow-in-the-dark, light skin-did bitch came all the way out here tryna kick Mark's front door in this mornin'."

Nicolas quickly grabbed a seat behind his desk, giving Dave his full attention.

"No, she didn't. How?" he bellowed, all ears.

"This girl went to the hotel manager posing as an undercover detective with some crazy-ass story and ended up gettin' Mark's full name. She found out his name wasn't Mike Williams but Mark Wilson. Then she Googled him and got his address and phone number. Mark Wilson is a common name. Do you know how many Mark Wilson's she had to call and knock on doors to find the right one?"

"I couldn't even imagine that, but she did know y'all were from New York and that narrowed the field."

"You're right, but there's still a lot of Mark Wilson's in New York. So, it shoulda taken her longer than that to find him."

"Maybe she got your information somehow."

"No, that's unlikely. I kept my info stashed away in the ride where no one could find it except me."

"And she told you how she was able to find Mark?" Nicolas asked, elbows on the desk.

"Yeah, she broke down spillin' all the beans when I got there. She was cryin' and screamin' like a maniac. I tried to calm her crazy ass down, but it didn't work. She was yellin' so loud that the whole neighborhood heard her say she was pregnant with his baby and how he ran off on her, leavin' her to raise it and her other three kids!"

"Did anyone call the cops?"

"Yeah. They're here now with her in the back of the cop car."

"For what?" Nicolas called out.

"For what...?" Dave repeated in a high pitch. "Nigga, this crazy ass bitch snapped and swung on the police."

"So what are her charges?"

"The cop said he's not gonna charge her with assault or resistin' arrest, but he has to charge her with breakin' and enterin'."

"Breakin' and enterin'?" Nicolas uttered.

"Yeah, through the back window, and stop repeatin' everythin' I say like a damn parrot. It's startin' to become annoyin'," Dave said, getting irritated.

"My bad, dawg. Continue with the story."

"Mark said he heard someone bangin' on his front door like the police. When he peeked through the window, he saw Rolisha standin' there yellin' and bangin' with her three kids. So, he called me on the phone for back up and the next thing I heard was him yellin' that she was climbin' through his back window. I flew out here just in time to see her swing on the cops. I was able to talk to her while she was in the back of the car, because the cops couldn't calm her crazy ass down and needed one of us to talk to her. That's when she broke down and started spillin' the beans. Mark wouldn't say shit. He just stood there lookin' dumbfounded. The cops asked if he wanted to press charges and this fool said no. He just stood there lookin' like a dead bird."

"A what?" Nicolas asked for better clarification.

"You heard me, a *dead bird*. Mark just stood there with his eyes big as hell and his mouth wide open like one of Jerry's kids."

"So what about her kids?"

"Child protective services got them. Her family's gonna have to drive all the way out here to get 'em."

CHAPTER FIFTY-EIGHT

The Web of Seduction

Ignoring the time and work that had to be done, Nicolas stayed on the phone. Kim walked into his office, locking the door behind her.

"Uh...Dave...I'm gonna have to call you back later," Nicolas said, disconnecting their conversation. "Good mornin', Kim. What can I do for you?"

"We need to talk. Call the receptionist desk and tell them to hold your calls."

Nicolas picked up the office phone and did what Kim asked.

"So what's the problem?" he asked.

"I heard what happened in Camden and I was worried about you. I wanted to say something in the parking lot yesterday, but figured it could wait. Well, last night in bed, I couldn't sleep thinking about you. So, I just wanted to tell you before anything else happens to you."

She took a deep breath and paused a moment before continuing.

"You seem like such a decent guy. I can't stop thinking about you. Since the first day we met, I've wanted you so bad. But, you keep playing hard to get and I just can't take it anymore. The suspense is killing me. Do you have any feelings at all for me?"

"I'm a happily married man," Nicolas said, laughing inwardly at the absurdity of his words.

"That makes me want you even more. I'm not really looking for a relationship. I just want you to take care of my physical needs."

Her words softly kissed his eardrums as they started to penetrate through all his defenses. Nicolas couldn't help but gaze at her beauty under the fluorescent light.

Now let's weigh the pros and cons. I could fuck her, two maybe three times a week without Tammy knowin' shit. This would be good for those days that she wants to put the pussy on lock-down when she gets upset with me for whatever throws her chemical imbalance off track. Now the con to this is I could end up fallin' for the chick and leavin' Tammy for her. The sneakin' in and outta different hotels and motels could end up being costly. I could lose my job, lose my wife and end up payin' alimony. That shit ain't worth it. Then there are Tammy's big brothers. I'll have to carry some protection in case I gotta use it on those two big albino lookin' gorillas.

Nicolas felt himself slipping into her black widow's web. S h e slowly approached him. Her hair smelled like pear blossoms in April, and her skin and make-up was flawless.

"I can't," Nicolas stuttered as Kim moved even closer.

It was like his breath was being taken. He sucked in some air and tried not to let his nervousness show.

"Kim, what are you doin'?" he quietly muttered, voice sounding hoarse.

"Nicolas, I know you want me. It shows in everything you do. Even when I walked in, I could see desire in your eyes. I gave you all the signs, so stop toying with my emotions. Give in to this, Nicolas, here and now," she whispered in his ear.

Her words were enticing and he couldn't help but to be intrigued by her.

"I can't take no for an answer," she whispered in his ear.

Alone in his office, her approach was strong and aggressive. She was the hunter, and he was the prey.

Suddenly, all of Nicolas' problems receded into a mist. He stood up, knocking a penholder off his desk. Kim grabbed him by the wrist before he had a chance to bend over to pick it up.

"Don't worry about that. Just let it flow."

Kim drew him into that powerful vortex of seduction. She pulled Nicolas toward her and passionately kissed him.

For the first time in weeks, Nicolas felt something more than pain, fear, and disappointment. Her lips were soft and sweet, tasting like cotton candy. She pressed her body against his, closing the space between them completely. Pheromones filled the air and intensified her passion and his arousal. Kim knew exactly where to touch him, how to hold and caress him. Her touch was so different from Tammy's, but the strangeness of it felt wonderful. Nicolas looked into her eyes and saw pure eroticism. The room blurred as the rest of the universe ceased to exist. Only the two of them existed now.

Nicolas had passed the point of no return. He was Superman and she was breathing kryptonite. His body melted, becoming liquid fire.

Kim unbuckled his belt, unzipped his pants, and dropped them to his ankles. Nicolas was lost in his fantasy, in a world where everything was the way it should be and only joy was to be found. He placed her on top of his desk, pushed her skirt up around her waist, and took off her red silk, laced Victoria's Secret g-string. Her long, tawny legs were perfect and the V between her legs looked as lush as a rain forest in Africa. The sweet fragrance of her skin was intoxicating and heightened the length of his passion. Overwhelmed by the intensity of her touch, Nicolas' dick got so hard it ached. She teased his ear with her tongue and slid her warm hands down the front of his underwear and began massaging his rock-hard shaft.

"You like that?" she whispered, the words spilling from her mouth like warm cream. She wasn't talking in her professional voice this time; her tone was gentle and provocative.

Nicolas slowly penetrated her vaginal walls without the foreplay. It was too much excitement for him to withstand as they both moaned in ecstasy. A chilled surge of energy raced through his spine with each stroke. Kim started to hum in his ear. She sounded so good...so sexy. It was getting him even more excited. He humped her hard as she arched to meet him, forgetting they were at their workplace.

Kim pulled him close and whispered in hot breaths, "Ooh yes, fuck me...aaahh... yes...oh, fuck me...that feels sooo gooood...I'm gonna cum...I'm gonna cum...I'm cumming! Uuummm...aaaahhh!"

With each stroke, Kim's moans grew louder. Nicolas covered her mouth with his hand as she began to scream with each orgasm. He then removed his tie and wrapped it around her mouth, tightening it at the back of her head. At the peak of her fifth orgasm, Nicolas began to cum with her, his body eager to pump his seed deeper into her throbbing secret parts. He opened his eyes, kissing her sweet wet lips over his tie, ready to force all of his milk inside her. Her lips were parted, anticipating the reverberations of pleasure when she came, revealing perfect teeth like white snowflakes. It felt so good, so right, like they were meant to be.

Is this what I've been missin'? Why does it feel so good? Why am I enjoyin' this so much? Am I wrong for feelin' the way I do? Got damn it, I love it so much. You are so fine.

Nicolas couldn't take it anymore. It was too much for him to handle.

"Uh...uh...aaaahh!"

Nicolas' body exploded in climax with great force. As the last of the repercussions began to fade, they slid off the desk and lay on the floor, exhausted and weak.

"Are you okay?" she asked, her body still trembling in pleasure.

"Yeah. My legs feel weak, though."

Kim smiled with contentment. "I have to go. Maybe we can continue this tonight at my place." She got up slowly, adjusting her skirt and slipping into her g-string.

Nicolas got up and began dressing, wishing they were far from this place, maybe in a beach house where no one could find them.

"You may have to give me a rain check as I sort this one out." He straightened his pants and slipped into his dress shirt. He stumbled to his desk, his leg muscles trying to recover.

She smiled at his weakened condition. "See, that right there turns me on."

Kim handed him his tie before walking out of his office, swaying her hips with satisfaction. She grabbed the doorknob and turned with a smile on her face before opening the door. She was startled to see Tony standing in the doorway, his hand in the air about to knock on the door. With guilt written all over her face, Kim walked out, ducking her head under Tony's raised arm. With a quick hi, Tony watched her walk down the hall for a brief moment. He then turned his gaze to Nicolas.

"Tell me you didn't, you sly muthafucka!" Tony sniffed the air. "Yeah, you did! I can smell it."

"Close the door." Nicolas waved his hands for Tony to keep it down.

Tony closed the door, turned around and rubbed his hands together as if trying to start a fire. "Tell me what happened. I want details, man and don't leave nothin' out."

"I dunno what you're talkin' 'bout, Tony." Nicolas laughed.

Tony started pouting. "Come on, I shared with you one of my darkest secrets that could ruin my life and you can't tell me that you fucked Kim? What kind of friend are you? You knew how bad I wanted it and you act as if you don't trust me. Nick, don't hold back on me now," he whimpered.

Nicolas saw the desperation on Tony's face.

Surrendering the secret that would end his entire career, Nicolas said, "Okay, okay, just calm down." He placed both hands on the edge of his desk to hold himself up. "Yes, I hit it and you better not say shit."

He gave Tony a hard stare, but Tony could see he was too weak to do anything.

"Trust me, I won't. So how was it?" He stood there eagerly waiting with a Kool-Aid smile.

Nicolas smiled and rolled his eyes. "It was all that, like a balloon explodin' inside me. I think I'm in love," grabbing the left side of his chest with both hands, one on top of the other.

"But what about your wife, man? I thought you were a happily married man, Nicolas," Tony joked.

"She mustn't know. This is the first time I've ever cheated on her."

Despite all Tammy had put him through, Nicolas started to feel bad. He thought revenge would be sweet, but it wasn't. Someone forgot to add the sugar to it, leaving him feeling humiliated with a bitter taste in his mouth. "How can I face her once I get home?" The look of fear was now present on his facial expression.

"Just don't say shit when you get home. It always works for me," Tony said, wishing he hadn't added his two cents.

"I won't be able to look her in the eyes. Her female intuition's gonna kick in," Nicolas cried, as anxiety started to build.

"Just play it cool, man. You'll be all right. Just get it together." Tony grabbed Nicolas by the shoulders, shaking him. "Don't crack up on me now, man. What the fuck!"

Beads of sweat started forming on Nicolas' forehead. "I need to go home, Tony. I need to go home right now," he demanded, unable to take the heat starting to rise.

"Why? To tell her that you were with another woman? I was only jokin' when I said all that *happily married* bullshit. I didn't expect you to lose your mind over it. Plus, the office rules prohibit us from havin' any sexual relations with other co-workers and you fuckin' her at the workplace can lead to automatic dismissal. So, calm the fuck down and just think about this for a second."

"I am thinkin' and what I did was wrong." His eyes drifted in space and his lower jaw hung.

Tony quickly covered Nicolas' mouth with his hand when he heard a knock at the door.

Both men stood up straighter than a telephone pole, facing the door apprehensively.

"Come in," Nicolas called out after clearing his voice.

The door opened and Bill walked into the room.

"Great. Now what," Nicolas mumbled.

"Hey, what's goin' on?" Bill announced in his amplified voice, as if he wanted the whole world in his conversation.

"Oh, nothin'," Nicolas said, laughing nervously.

Bill stood still and sniffed the air. "What's that smell?"

Nicolas had to think fast on his feet. "Oh, I just got finished eatin' a hoagie I brought yesterday."

Bill lowered his nose from out of the air and directed his focus at Nicolas with a look of dismay. "For breakfast?"

"I was cravin' it and couldn't wait for lunch."

Bill lifted his head back up, sniffing all the oxygen out of the air in one deep breath. "That sure smells good." He exhaled heavily. "You should have saved me a piece."

Tony and Nicolas exchanged glares, holding in their laughter.

"And by the way, I heard what happened."

Nicolas' body went numb and his heart went into tachycardia mode. Did Bill know he and Kim just had sex in the office? Were there hidden cameras in his office? Did he come to tell him face to face that he was fired? How would he explain that to Tammy? Preparing for the worse, Nicolas collected himself and looked Bill in the eyes.

"Heard what, sir?"

"About you getting attacked and robbed by some gang bangers in Camden."

"Oh that," Nicolas said, relief flooding his mind.

"Yes, that," Bill winced. "Unless there's something else I need to know that you two are hiding from me."

"Oh no, everything's okay, sir." Nicolas struggled to maintain his composure.

"And for the twentieth time, stop calling me sir!" Bill barked.

"Sorry about that," Nicolas replied, his voice deepened.

"That's okay, Nick. But, anyway, I'm sorry about that attack you suffered the other night. If there's anything I can do, just let me know."

"Thank you, Bill. I appreciate that," Nicolas nodded, feeling like he might really pass out. His legs were still shaky from the sex and the scare Bill just caused didn't help.

How much can a man take in one mornin'? Nicolas' mind shouted.

"Are you okay, son?" Bill asked, with a look of concern on his face. "You don't look so good."

"Well, I'm not feelin' so well this mornin'. Maybe it was that hoagie." Nicolas looked at Bill like an abandoned child. "Could I please have an emergency comp day to get myself together?"

Concern wrinkled his forehead. "No problem, son. Go on home and get some rest." Bill patted Nicolas on the back. "Tony will take care of everything while you're gone."

Realizing he would be stuck with the rest of Nicolas' paperwork, Tony stood in disbelief. Hoping he, too, might con Bill, Tony asked in his most humble voice, "Hey Unk, can I leave early, too?"

"No. Get back to work!" Bill yelled.

"What! That's not fair." Tony pouted like a spoiled brat, then stormed out of the office. He swung the door open with so much force that it banged off the wall and closed automatically without any assistance.

"Don't mind him." Bill waved his hand. "He's spoiled and always looking for an excuse to get out of the office early. Now go home for the day and enjoy your lovely wife. Just make sure you're here tomorrow to catch-up on your work."

"No problem, Bill, and thank you very much. I won't disappoint you."

Nicolas shook Bill's hand and practically ran out of the building.

CHAPTER FIFTY-NINE

Don't Break the Man Code

Tony tracked Nicolas down in the lobby right before he walked out of the building.

"Nicolas, wait up!"

"What's up, man?" Nicolas said as Tony approached him.

Other co-workers were passing them like they were in a rush to reach their destination. "You're not really gonna tell your wife about you and Kim, are you?" Tony said, sounding like a sad puppy.

"I have to," Nicolas insisted, looking as if he was about to lose it.

Tony grabbed Nicolas by the shoulders again. "What the fuck, Nick! Now you're thinkin' like a lady and actin' like a bitch. What, you been readin' that Steve Harvey book or somethin'? You never confess to somethin' like that, even if you're caught with your pants down and dick all up in it. You better think about this before you ruin your marriage."

Nicolas thought about all the trouble he was in and the cause of it all...Tammy. Ruining their marriage? What a joke. Their marriage was already on life support and the plug could be pulled at any moment. He wanted to make things right, go back to the way things were like before they moved from New York. *Before* he caught Tammy in bed with that cop. *Before* he bashed in the cop's head beyond recognition. *Before* Morris knew his name. Nicolas rubbed his face, which felt like it was on fire.

"If I don't tell her, it's gonna eat me alive."

"And if you do tell her, she's gonna eat you alive...literally. Wait and see. That pretty wife of yours will soon be in charge. They all are when you cross them. She might get revengeful and cheat on you," Tony stated in exasperation.

If only you knew, Nicolas thought to himself. He didn't know whether to laugh or scream. Images of Peter Wright on top of Tammy in their marital bed reignited his anger. Feeling closer to a complete mental breakdown, he shook his head, walked through the huge glass doors and headed for the parking lot, with Tony on his heels.

"She might try to hurt you or worse—kill you. She may decide to divorce you and take it all," Tony warned, still following Nicolas to his car.

"No, she won't. She'll understand," Nicolas said as if he was trying to convince himself as well as Tony.

"Nick, that's a bunch of bullshit and you know it. That's like snitchin' on yourself. It's more like breakin' the man code."

Tony tried to prevent Nicolas from getting to his vehicle. Nicolas stopped in his tracks and frowned at Tony.

"The man code. What the hell is a man code?" he blurted out.

"You know, the code we live by. Never tell on yourself or put our secret out there like Steve Harvey did with his book *Act Like A Lady, Think Like a Man*. I can't be mad at him for it, because he made millions off it." Tony chuckled at the thought of it.

"I don't know what you're talkin' about and I ain't snitchin' on myself. I'm just tryna build a trust between us," Nicolas told him, knowing damn well what Tony was talking about, because Tammy stood in line at Borders Book Store waiting to get a signed copy of the book to use to her advantage on him.

Tony jumped in front of Nicolas, blocking his path when Nicolas tried to go around him. "You got it all twisted. You think telling her the truth about you cheatin' is goin' to build trust?" he asked in a squeaky voice.

"Yes, it will. She cheated on me and told me the truth and I forgave her."

"Before or after she got caught?" Tony smirked, as if trying to degrade Nicolas.

Nicolas pushed Tony out of his way. "It doesn't matter. I gotta go. I'll call you later."

Nicolas got in his car and drove off, leaving a stunned Tony standing in the parking lot with both arms in the air like a scarecrow in a business suit.

Cruising down Route 38, Nicolas tried calling Tammy, but got no answer.

The city of Merchantville was shaken by these gruesome murders. The city subsequently became a ghost town. More and more "For Sale" signs were being placed in neighboring yards. However, with the economy being so bad, none of the homes were selling. Some neighbors got so desperate that they put their homes on the market for as low as thirty to fifty percent lower than the property value, but were still unable to get a single buyer. All the buyers must have been watching the news.

Nicolas planned on sitting Tammy down and discussing their current situation. He decided on putting in a transfer at work and moving from their present location. Since they'd been here, their lives were in shambles. They both cheated on each other, which caused him to commit murder of a police officer. The entire police department would love to have his head on a silver platter. There was a rapist still on the loose who had a fetish for white women. With all the neighbors moving out of town, it made Tammy more of a prime target. Nicolas would be a fool for trying to stay and work things out.

CHAPTER SIXTY

Special Delivery

"Hi. How are you doing?" Tammy asked politely as the mail carrier handed her a package.

"Just sign right here." He handed her the electronic tablet and pen.

"Thank you." She took the package from him.

"My name's Carl," he said flirtatiously.

"Hi, Carl. My name's Tammy. Pleased to meet you." She extended her hand.

Carl accepted with a soft handshake. "So now that I know the Coles live here, you have nothing to worry about. I've been working this route for over seventeen years, and I always made sure the mail was delivered to the right address," he proudly stated.

"That's a pretty long time, Carl." She smiled, finger combing her hair away from her eyes.

"Yep, but knowing who you're dealing with makes the job a whole lot easier."

"I understand what you're talkin' about," Tammy replied, still smiling at the mail carrier.

"Yep, and the only protection I have is this small bottle of mace. I thank God that I never had to use it in my seventeen years working this route. Knowing my luck, it might not even work."

"Yeah, my husband said the same thing to me last night," she said, laughing at the mere thought of him running from a dog that wasn't affected by his hot juice.

The mail carrier stood silently, wide eyed as if he didn't catch on. "I'm talking about the mace." Tammy giggled, thinking about how Nicolas said his mother's mace didn't work, but ran away from her like a little girl.

He tried to laugh it off, but it was a weak attempt. "Well, I hope it never comes down to that."

"I hope not either."

Tammy signed for the delivery and handed him the tablet and pen.

"Hey, I got to get going and finish my deliveries. Nice meeting you, Mrs. Coles."

"Thanks a lot, Carl," Tammy said, going back in the house.

She looked for the sender's name on the package to see if it was the Gucci bag she'd ordered online. Eagerly opening her package, Tammy didn't notice the red light, which indicated a recorded message from Nicolas, blinking on the answering machine. She pulled the black leather Gucci bag with the big silver clasp from the tissue-filled box and hung it over her shoulder to see how it felt and looked through the bedroom mirror, when someone knocked on the front door. Tammy ran downstairs. Looking out the window, she saw no cars parked out front. So, it couldn't be the detective. *Who could it be?* She looked through the peephole, but could only see the back of a man's head.

"Yes? Who is it?" she called out in a timid voice through the solid oak door.

"It's John from next door. I need to use your phone." He turned so she could see his face.

"For what?" she asked with uncertainty.

"My drainpipe burst. I tried turning the water off, but I couldn't. Now there's water everywhere. I need to call an emergency plumber and my phone's not working."

Tammy hesitantly opened the front door. "Come right on in. Nicolas doesn't like me letting anyone in the house when he's not home, but I'll make an exception this time."

She smiled.

"Thanks, and I promise to keep my lips sealed," John said, pinching his lips together like he was sealing them with glue.

"Oh, what the hell. He's working late anyway. The phone is on the end table next to the sofa."

John picked up the receiver and keyed in some numbers, but couldn't seem to find his party. "Hello! Hello! I can't seem to get through to anyone." He pouted, looking hot and bothered.

"Why? Is my phone not working as well?" she asked incredulously.

"No, it's not that. I'm trying to get through to my nephew who's a licensed plumber, 'cause I figure why pay someone four hundred dollars when I can get it done for free."

As John tried more numbers, Tammy looked him up and down. He was wearing gray sweat pants and a gray sweatshirt. Yet, his clothes were bone dry. Not a drop of sweat or water on his hair and there was no mud on his dry boots.

"I bet it was no fun wading through a house full of water," Tammy said, adding a fake laugh.

"Yeah, I needed a rescue boat to get me out." He chuckled.

Tammy squinted her eyes like a detective trying to solve a case. "How were you able to avoid getting wet?"

"Uh, I was out for a while trying to find a pay-phone that worked. Then I remembered you were home, so I turned around and came here instead. So, I guess I had time to dry out a little."

"Were you walking or driving?"

"I drove," he said, smiling.

"So where is the nearest pay-phone, 'cause I've never seen any in this neighborhood."

"The nearest pay-phone is at the Stop and Go market down the road."

Tammy gave him a dirty look that told him that she was not falling for that one.

"Why would you drive all the way there when you could have just walked next door first and asked me?" she asked with skepticism.

"I didn't want to bother you," John responded, but his tone was not persuasive.

There was a brief pause, a moment of silence. Tension in the room became so thick it could be cut into squares. A chill formed around Tammy's hairline as she started thinking about all the weird things John did, such as watering the grass for hours until it was about to rot and watching their house all the time, knowing their every move. No matter what time of the day, John was always outside whenever they stepped out the front door.

"Oh, okay," she responded in a whisper. Her eyeballs cut the corners of her eyes as if she was looking for the quickest way out of this conversation. John stood there holding the phone as Tammy watched his "used car dealer" smile turn into a hard stare. Becoming more uncomfortable, she started toward the kitchen, planning to escape out the sliding glass doors with John blocking the front entrance, but John stepped in front of her and blocked her path...the same way the priest had done when he was a little boy roaming the cathedral halls at night.

John was an innocent little boy being taken advantage of by a man he looked up to. A man he trusted. A man overpowered by his lustful thoughts. A man who was a representative of God. How could they do that to such a little boy? It wasn't lust that did it; it was a sickness. A sickness that was highly contagious and John caught it at a very young age. No one should have gone through what he went through and now that sickness was implanted in him as a child, which grew and matured into a madness of evil proportion.

"What are you doing?" Tammy demanded, extremely scared now.

"What, you don't believe me?" His tone was sharp.

He tried reaching out to her, but Tammy pulled back. An ice-cold fear ran through her body when she saw evil in his dark eyes.

"John, stop this! You're scaring me." Tammy told him, shaking uncontrollably.

"I'm sorry," John said, trying to hug her, but little did Tammy know that her fear was arousing him.

Tammy shoved him, causing him to drop the phone.

"No! Stop it, John. What the hell are you doing? Get the hell out of here! Now!" she said sternly, hoping the authority in her voice would offset him enough to make him leave like she'd learned in a verbal defense class she took at her previous job as a requirement.

It didn't work, though. Instead, John grabbed Tammy's arms from behind, holding them so tightly they burned.

"Please don't hurt me." Her eyes danced around the room, looking as if she was trying to decide whether to run or talk her way out of the situation.

John pulled out a switchblade, grabbed her hair with his free hand and started dragging her up the stairs. Tammy kicked and screamed, knocking a chair over and grabbing the stair rail. John struck both her hands with the heavy knife handle, causing her to release her hold. Then he locked her in a bear hug, restricting her movement. Tammy tried using her feet to kick at John's legs, but it had no effect.

John half carried–half dragged her to the bedroom and threw her on the bed. She tried to crawl backward, but John leaped on top of her like the pro wrestler Jimmy Fly Snuka and placed the knife to her neck. With all of his weight now on her, she could do no more than squirm. Everything she was taught in defense class was useless against John. It was a waste of six months training, because her fear caused her to forget everything she learned.

The expression on her face told him everything she was thinking and he loved it...every bit of it. With a chilling smile on his face, he began rubbing the sharp side of the blade down the left side of her face until he came to a stop against her cheek. When he began licking the right side of her face like an ice cream cone, she realized he was the Merchantville rapist and she was his next victim. But, the thing about John is he didn't get pleasure out of raping these women. Oh no. Even he knew it was wrong. His thrills came with the power he had over these women to control them and make them do whatever he wanted against their own free will. They were his puppets...his playthings. John understood what the priest was after when he was only a little boy. Now he was after the same thing…and it felt so good…too good!

How could this be so wrong? John's psychopathic brain echoed.

Petrified, she asked in a low voice, "Why, John?"

Panting from all the physical activity and his warped desire, he stopped licking her and looked deep into her eyes.

Her only hope was to try to talk her way out of being murdered. She had learned how to handle deviant behavior and how it was helpful if the victim could get their assailant to identify with them—to try to talk them down.

"John, you need some professional help. Please don't do this. It's not too late for you to get some help. Let me help you do that."

John pressed the blade harder against her cheek.

"Shut the fuck up!" Condescension dripped from his voice.

He placed his hand over her mouth and moved the blade of the knife to her throat.

Tammy breathed hard through her nose in short, shallow breaths. Tears rolled down her face as John began pushing up her blouse.

She kept asking herself where was Nicolas. This was when she badly needed him to bust in the room like a cape crusader, but he wasn't there to rescue her. She finally gave up the struggle. There was no more fight left in her. Tammy was beaten and she knew it. All she could do was close her eyes and let her mind run free, taking her somewhere far away to a place of happy thoughts.

CHAPTER SIXTY-ONE

Not Again

It was 11:53 a.m. when Nicolas approached the house. He thought about taking Tammy to McCormick & Schmick's, a very expensive, but classy restaurant in Cherry Hill, New Jersey. He wanted to start all over—make things right—and the best way to do it was to impress her by taking her to a five-star restaurant. Nicolas loved Tammy with all his heart and couldn't imagine what life would be like without her. What they did was wrong and in order to make their marriage work, they would need to open up and be honest with each other starting today. Nicolas was surprised to find the door unlocked. While removing his suit coat, he walked into the house and just as he was about to call out to Tammy, he noticed the chair lying on the floor. He quickly scanned the room and when he saw the landline was off the hook, he realized something was terribly wrong or Tammy was fucking cheating again. Either way, the shit didn't look good.

He walked softly and as quietly as a house cat to the china closet, opened the drawer slowly, and took the gun out of the same brown paper bag it was in when Tony got it off of Cat Daddy. Nicolas checked to make sure it was loaded.

Yeah, it's loaded.

He then disengaged the safety and headed up the stairs toward the master bedroom fearing the worse. He was no stranger to guns.

Back in his hustling days, guns were a requirement and Nicolas wouldn't hesitate to use it if he had to.

This can't be happenin' again! I know that muthafucka Pete is dead. I saw his lifeless body lyin' there in front of me after I killed him with my own two hands. Or is there someone else in my bed fuckin' the shit outta her? Nicolas didn't know what to think.

As he neared the bedroom door, he could hear his heart beating through his ears. Anger began to build as he visualized Tammy having rodeo sex with that crooked-ass cop, Peter Wright. He could still hear Wright encouraging her orgasm, while Nicolas was out working, trying to provide for her. Now right outside the bedroom door, Nicolas heard heavy breathing and believed Tammy was having sex in their bed again. Nicolas' hands gripped the gun tightly as he slowly cocked the hammer back. Someone was going pay for this shit. He looked into the bedroom.

What the fuck is this? No the fuck she ain't! Nicolas felt like he was going to snap.

He saw Tammy having sex with John, their neighbor. The scene was no different than last time. Only difference was his ass was pale and hairy as hell. Blood rushed to his head so fast that it felt like his brain might explode before he could get a shot off. In a rage with his hand shaking, he stepped into the room and pointed the gun at John.

"You muthafucka!" Nicolas thundered, his voice deep with fury.

John quickly turned his head, startled by Nicolas' sudden appearance. Nicolas had the weapon pointed at John's unshaved miserable excuse of a face and pulled the trigger.

BOOM!

The sound of the shot reverberated throughout the room as the bullet hit John in the left eye. Bits of bone, blood and the grey matter of John's brain shot out his face like soda from a shaken bottle, dispersing throughout the room and sticking to the walls, ceiling and floor. John dropped like a stone, pummeling to the floor and ended with a loud thud.

Nicolas stood over his body and fired two more rounds of anger into John's midsection, his body jerking from the impact of each bullet. An odoriferous mix of gunpowder and the coppery smell of blood filled the room as Nicolas stood gazing at John's dying body. He stood there and watched the life slowly escape John's nasty ass. Once satisfied that John was dead, Nicolas looked up at Tammy, who was sitting on the bed and turned the gun on her.

Unable to speak and explain what had transpired before Nicolas arrived, Tammy could only let out a barely audible cry.

"What do you have to say for yourself now, bitch?" Nicolas wailed like a wounded lion.

He had come home early to talk to Tammy, to try to save their marriage after everything that transpired over the last few days, only to catch her in bed with another man, who was their neighbor at that. Nicolas started thinking about all the nice things she said about John in her diary and how John would flirt with her every time he saw her.

Is she really that desperate to sleep with John's old ass? Who's next, the mailman? We'll be the laughin' stock of town.

Nicolas had had enough! He was a broken man in mind and spirit. Seeing the scratches on her neck, he felt the tears stinging his eyes, but he refused to let them fall. His hands started shaking like a crazed maniac, the gun still pointed at her beautiful face.

"Let me guess, a cat got your fuckin' tongue again. How could you? Why would..."

BOOM!

The unexpected blast caused Nicolas' hand to jerk back with the barrel pointed towards the ceiling now. He had accidentally pulled the trigger. The gunshot startled him and he looked at the smoking gun in his hand.

He became aware of a low wheezing sound coming from Tammy and looked up to see her holding the right side of her neck, blood flowing through her fingers, down her arm and onto her breasts. Her eyes rolled back, as she collapsed and fell off the bed on top of John's corpse with blood spurting from her carotid artery.

His anger was now replaced with loneliness. Tammy was the only connection he had to the real world. Nothing else mattered. Tears of pain fell from his eyes. There was no controlling the hurt. At this point, it was impossible. Tammy was his everything. The air he breathed was secondary. She was the small flame that lit the darkness in his cold chest, adding warmth. It felt like a sharp object had penetrated his rib cage, breaking bones.

In a panic, Nicolas ran over to her, picked her up off the floor and sat her on the bed. He tried to stop the bleeding by pressing the bed sheet against the wound. Blood soaked the sheet as Tammy gasped for air, blood gurgling and bubbling from her mouth. As Nicolas reached for the bed comforter to press against the neck wound. That's when he spotted the knife on the bed, which explained the cuts on her neck that looked like scratches. He then realized John had been raping her and from all his weird behavior, it was a good indication that John was nothing more than a sick pervert.

"Don't die on me, baby. Please don't die. I'm so sorry," Nicolas cried out. Tears began to shed as he wrapped her in his arms.

Tammy's eyes rolled toward the back of her head while she continued to struggle for her last shallow, dying breaths. Nicolas held her and rocked her like a baby until she died in his arms.

"Nooooo! I'm so sorry. Please don't die on me. I don't want you to leave me here all alone. Why didn't you say somethin'? I love you so much."

But, it was too late. His words fell on death ears. Tammy was gone forever in a deep sleep that she would never wake up from again.

*****

"9-1-1 emergency, what's your emergency?"

His ears still ringing from the gunshots, Nicolas could barely hear the operator.

"I just found my wife in bed with my neighbor rapin' her! I've shot both of them," he cried out.

"Sir, are they still alive?"

"What? Talk louder. I can't hear you!"

"Are they still alive?" the woman shouted.

"No! No, they're not. I'm holding my dead wife!" he said, now crying uncontrollably.

"Just calm down, sir. I have units on their way to your location right now," the operator said, trying to calm him. "Sir, are you there? Sir, can you hear me?"

"Please help me bring her back!" Nicolas cried, dropping the phone. "Please don't let her die on me!"

*****

Sirens wailed through the neighborhood as they approached the house. Three units, blue and red lights flashing, pulled up in front with police pouring out of them. Several circled the house and four went through the front door. All had their weapons drawn. Two entered the bedroom where Nicolas sat soaked in blood and holding Tammy's lifeless body. Blood was everywhere. One went to the left corner where John lay in a pool of blood from his wounds to the head and chest.

"Let go of the woman and put your hands in the air!" the burly policeman demanded. "Now!"

Nicolas, reluctant to let go of Tammy, gently lay her body on the bed and softly kissed her on the forehead. He was in shock and deprived of all sensation.

"Where's the weapon?" the officer shouted.

Nicolas pointed to the floor behind a stack of Tammy's paperback books.

"Place your hands behind your head! Get up and walk slowly toward me. Now!"

Nicolas put his bloody hands behind his head and slowly stood up, his legs wobbly. A third cop wearing rubber gloves slammed him against the wall and cuffed him, while two EMT units pulled in the driveway, their sirens signaling the cry of trouble.

CHAPTER SIXTY-TWO

Mamma's Raising Hell

"May I help you, ma'am?" asked an officer in his early 20s with straight brown hair and thick glasses.

"I wanna see my son...Nicolas Coles!" Laura said with conviction.

"You're not allowed back here ma'am and what is your relationship to Mr. Coles?" the desk officer asked.

"I'm Laura Coles, his mutha," she answered impatiently, taking an immediate dislike to the young, white officer. The lenses of his glasses were as thick as the bottom of a Coke bottle.

"I'm sorry, ma'am. Mr. Coles is not allowed to have visitors at this station. He still has to be processed first and transported to the county jail."

"What do you mean transported? I'm his mutha," she said, using an agitated tone. "What's his bail?"

"Sorry, but at this time, he has no bail. He's in processing and booking. We don't have visiting hours here. You'll have to set that up with the county jail on Federal Street."

An old black sergeant, his head almost completely bald, walked up behind the desk officer. "What's going on in here?" he said in an authoritative voice.

"This is Coles' mother. I told her that he has no bail and it was impossible for her to see him today."

"How did she get back here?" he asked with a stern voice and a militant stance.

"I guess the door wasn't secured, sir," the officer answered in a mousy tone.

"Uh, she'll have to leave right now," the bald sergeant ordered.

"I'm trying, sir," he responded with nervousness.

"I demand to see my son!" Mrs. Coles said, trying to force open a second locked door that led to the booking and processing area.

The bald sergeant called for back-up to the front desk, and in less than a minute, two officers took each of Mrs. Coles' arms, escorted her through the door to the main lobby and secured the door behind them.

Mrs. Coles went to the small window of the officer's desk and continued her argument.

"I demand to see my son Nicolas Coles today!" she said loudly. "And I ain't leavin' until I do! I wanna speak to your sergeant."

Pressing the intercom button on his desk, the officer called for another sergeant.

"Sergeant Keen to the front lobby. Sergeant Keen to the front lobby."

Immediately, two officers, one of them female, along with Sergeant Keen, a gray- haired white male, came through a side door.

"What's the problem here, ma'am?" Sergeant Keen asked.

"I wanna see my son and these fools won't let me back there."

"Her son is Coles," the desk officer informed them through his small window.

"Ma'am, there is no way you are going to get to see Coles here. Now you can leave peaceably, or we can charge you with disorderly conduct," the gray-haired sergeant told her. "It would be better for you to go now. You can call the county jail later and they'll tell you the first available time you can see him."

Frustrated, crying, and trembling with sorrow and rage, Mrs. Coles allowed the female officer to escort her out of the building. But, before she had a chance to walk through the double doors, Martha walked in with her two bulking sons. They looked like her bodyguards and both of them were yelling and screaming. Martha and Laura confronted each other by the doorway.

"That son of yours is a killer and I want his head on a platter!" Martha yelled with fury.

The two officers held them back, trying to separate the two.

"You never did like him," Laura said to her, while trying to work her way past the officers.

"Yeah, because I knew he was no good for her the first time I laid eyes on him." Martha tried to break through the officers' barrier, while her two sons stood neutral.

"When you laid eyes on him, all you saw was a nigga!" Laura howled. Her eyes were filled with resentment.

"Yeah, and a thug, too," Martha threw out.

More officers finally arrived, escorting everyone out of the building and to their vehicles as they continued to yell and scream.

*****

Three officers escorted a handcuffed Nicolas to a small well-lit room with an enormous mirrored glass wall for interrogation. The room was empty and dark except for a small light above a small square table in the center and two straight back chairs positioned across from each other. The chair's legs scraped across the concrete floor, echoing off the wall as one of the officers pulled it out and motioned for Nicolas to take a seat.

Nicolas' head felt as if it might explode and he wished he had blown his own brains out before calling 9-1-1.

Too late now, he thought.

All that had happened to him within the span of a week was unimaginable. At one moment, none of it seemed real to him. The next moment, the reality of it overwhelmed him like a tsunami.

Detective Stewart, standing at five-feet, nine-inches, was a potbelly white male dressed in a cheap black suit and cheap haircut to match. He was clean-shaven with a cigarette in his ear...a desperate way of persuading people to talk. He was an experienced interrogation detective walking into the room. Closing the door behind him, he sat down across from Nicolas.

"Now, Mr. Coles, what happened in that bedroom today?"

Nicolas looked at the detective, but refused to speak.

Stewart leaned forward and looked at Nicolas, eye-to-eye. "Look, I'm tryin' to help you here. I know you're hungry. I know you're tired. So, let's not waste each other's time. It's real simple. Just tell me what happened in that bedroom and we'll order you somethin' good to eat and I can go home."

Home, Nicolas thought. *I don't have a home to go to. I just killed my wife. I'll never go home again. Not this time, you selfish son of a bitch ass nigga.*

"Listen here, Mr. Coles. Your ass is on the line and this is the last chance you're gonna have to help yourself. Now, New Jersey lawmakers abolished the death penalty in 2007, but don't let that comfort you. You've killed three people, one of them being one of Merchantville's finest. So, if you don't cooperate, the only way you'll be leavin' prison is toes up…dead from old age…and that's only if one of the gang members there decide not to kill you after they wear your sweet ass out every night. Now, let's get down to business. Tell me what the hell happened this mornin' that resulted in two dead bodies in your home?"

Nicolas remained silent. Maybe this was all a bad dream. He waited for his alarm clock to sound and wake him up, but nothing happened. Maybe Tammy and Dave were playing a big joke and would soon be busting through the door hollering surprise, you just got punk'd. But, Dave and Tammy didn't get along nor would they agree to do anything together. Besides, how could Tammy fake that scene back home in the bedroom? It was just too real. Stephen King couldn't pull a crazy scene like that. Maybe all this really did happen and if so, Nicolas was facing some serious charges.

"Fine. You can sit here and rot for all I care!" Stewart said, walking toward the door.

Nicolas dropped his head on the table and wept. His life was over and there was no magical lamp or shooting star that could make things right again. He wished he could go back in time—be back in New York—back to the day he and Tammy were in high school, standing outside on their lunch break when she admitted that she still had feelings for that muthafucka Peter Wright. If he could go back to that day, he would have left her where she stood and never looked back. How different his life would have been today if he had done that.

*****

Detective Stewart stood beside Detective Morris watching Nicolas through the one-way glass.

"This guy would give me nothin'," Stewart stated, taking a swallow of stale coffee from a Styrofoam cup.

"He's either a good actor or he's dumb as hell," Detective Morris said, his arms crossed as he watched Nicolas.

"I got a phone call from forensics a few minutes ago. His neighbor's DNA matched the DNA of the Merchantville rapist. We searched his house and found the black Mercury Grand Marquis LS with the dent in the rear bumper in his garage. DNA from all his other victims was still in the car. He left us a whole trail of bread crumbs. Plus, we found out that this sick wacko collected all the house keys from his victims and carried them around like a high school janitor. My guess is that Coles was in such a rage seeing his wife in their bedroom with yet another man that he either thought she was having an affair with him and killed them both or he thought the man *was* the rapist, but accidentally shot her in the neck while trying to shoot the guy."

"The same rage he was in when he killed Peter Wright?" Stewart threw in, his tone dripping with sarcasm.

"I don't know," Morris huffed, shaking his head. "But, I have some evidence that may prove he knew about his wife's affair with Wright. I'm hoping to prove intent to kill and motive, so I can charge him on murder one."

"You think you can break him?" Stewart asked.

"I don't know, but I'm goin' to try like hell," Morris said, shrugging his shoulders.

CHAPTER SIXTY-THREE

Let's Try This Again

"Well, well, Mr. Coles, you seem to be a very busy man." Morris said entering the room. "Every time something happens in my quiet little town you seem to be in the middle of it. It's amazing how one man can bring so much excitement and attention to a small town. Let me guess, you caught your cheating-ass wife in bed with your neighbor and blew them both away. That about right?" he said with an expressionless glare he kept on Nicolas as he took a seat across from him.

Nicolas gave Morris a hard stare, wanting to lunge at him and choke the living shit out him, but Nicolas wasn't stupid. He knew what Morris was trying to do. If he couldn't get this case to stick, then he'd have him locked up for assault on an officer and that would carry enough weight for him to get a good five-year prison sentence.

Morris leaned back, hands in the air in submission. "Did I touch a nerve? Do you want to kill me, too? Come on, Mr. Coles, we both know you're not a cold-blooded killer. Now tell me what really happened today, because I know your wife and that man didn't just kill each other. So, did you kill them?"

There was a long pause before Nicolas decided to break the silence.

"Yes," he said just to relieve some of the pressure in his chest.

Containing his excitement like the professional cop he was, Morris put his hands down. "Okay, now we're getting somewhere. So tell me, Nicolas, what really happened?"

He switched to a calm, soothing voice to urge Nicolas on.

"I came home from work to talk to my wife about tryin' to make our marriage work, but when I got home I found her in bed with the neighbor John. I guess I blacked out, because the next thing I remember was seein' her covered in blood," Nicolas said, unable to hold the truth inside him any longer.

"Well, I got some good news for you. You caught a break on this one, buddy. Your neighbor was the Merchantville rapist."

Nicolas' head snapped back. "He was?" he said in a low whisper.

"Yeah. It'll take a few weeks to get the full DNA test results, but preliminary forensics indicates it's him."

"Thank you, Lord Jesus!" Nicolas murmured, believing all he had to do now was prove that killing Tammy was an accident. Maybe his life wasn't over. Maybe he would have another chance to live and to love, to have children and build a successful career. Now he could give Kim a shot at building a relationship with him.

Morris raised his hand. "Hold on there, speedy. You might not be charged with the murder of the rapist and you may even *possibly* get away with killing your wife. But, there's no way in hell you're going to get a pass on the murder of Officer Peter Wright. You see, Nick, searching your car. The one your wife reported stolen. It was found stripped in North Camden. We took your car apart looking for evidence and found your wife's diary."

Morris reached in his suit coat pocket and pulled out a plastic evidence bag holding Tammy's pink diary that was stashed in the back of his whip.

"Reading through her diary, I discovered that your wife and Peter Wright dated in high school. You took her away from him and married her. When you moved out here, she mysteriously runs into Wright at a grocery store and they continued their affair. Your fingerprints are all over this pink book—even on the pages where your wife writes details about her relationship with Wright," Morris stated with great professional and personal satisfaction. "Why did you move from New York City to this hamlet?"

"She told me that Merchantville would be a good place to raise a family." Nicolas wanted to kick himself for being in this predicament.

"Interesting...well, according to Peter Wright's mother, your wife kept in touch with her, asking her about Peter. She told her that her son was a cop out here. So, that leads me to believe your wife had this whole thing planned from the beginning."

"That fuckin' bitch played me!" Nicolas said bitterly, his voice low and vehement.

"Wow! Calm down now, killa." Morris smirked. Nicolas sat with his face reflecting the hurt and anger he felt. "Is that the same anger you had when you killed Officer Peter Wright?"

"No. I swear I thought my wife was bein' raped, so I was tryna protect her."

"Look, I read the diary," Morris said, tapping a finger on the evidence bag. "The only people who knew what happened are the three of you and you're the only one left standing. When you entered that room and saw your wife having a good time letting another man run all up in her bareback, did you know about their affair?"

"Fuck no!" Nicolas roared, as Morris continued to fuel the fire, hoping to get a full confession out of him.

Nicolas held his ground and continued to let his anger simmer.

"Come on Nick, it's hard for me to believe you didn't know it was her ex-boyfriend, the football jock that broke that pussy in during high school, all up in your bed fuckin' the dog shit out of her wet ass. According to her diary, he made her cum multiple times while you were at work. She also wrote in her diary that he was her first love." Morris grinned.

In a rage, he barked, "Fuck you, Morris! That shit ain't true!"

"Where did you get the handgun Nicolas? It has to belong to you and not the rapist, because your fingerprints and Tammy's were all over it, but not the rapist's."

Nicolas stared at the diary. *Damn, why didn't I get rid of it when I had the chance? Now it came back to bite me hard enough to take a big chunk outta my ass,* he thought to himself, seeing his whole world being sucked out of him all because of that little pink book.

"Come on! Fuckin' work with me here! Maybe I can help you. Did you get it off the street for protection or to pump fear into her? Because the first time I questioned you at your house, you said you would kill her ass if you found out she was cheatin' on you."

Nicolas sulked. He saw how this detective could use those words against him and get him with premeditated murder. But, then, he remembered the oath he made to Tony and how he would never tell anyone where he got the gun. He would not betray Tony. He was the only person who'd been honest with him and tried to help him—the closest friend he had in this rotten State.

"Have it your way then. I tried to work with you, but I see you're not going to cooperate."

Detective Morris picked up the diary, stood up and started walking toward the door. Before signaling the officer to let him out, he turned around and looked at Nicolas.

"Oh, and by the way, that gun you used—the one with your fingerprints on it? It had a body on it. Some young kid in Camden got shot up the other day in the projects and ballistics matched the gun that we found on you. I hope you have a good lawyer, because you're going to do time for murdering Peter Wright, that's for sure and maybe for the murder of your wife. Your refusal to cooperate may even lead to you doing time for the murder of that kid in Camden. His name was Raymond Johnson, seventeen years old."

Morris turned toward the huge mirror. "Alright, get his stupid ass out of here before I get sick." Two officers entered the room and escorted Nicolas to his holding cell. Later that evening, Nicolas was transported to the county jail.

CHAPTER SIXTY-FOUR

You've Got a Visitor

It was 7:45pm when Tony approached the front entrance of The County of Camden Correctional Facility.

"Good morning, sir. How may I help you?" asked the tall, thin officer behind the glass, unusually cordial for a place like this, but this officer welcomed everyone with a smile and hearty hello.

"I'm here to see Nicolas Coles," Tony said.

"All right, just sign in and have a seat in the waitin' room while I get him."

The officer handed Tony a clipboard with a blue ink pen attached to it with a white shoestring.

"When was he arrested?" the officer asked.

"Today around noontime."

The officer looked at Tony. "Do you have any identification on you?"

"Yeah, right here."

Tony handed the officer his driver's license. The officer looked it over.

"Okay, sir. Have a seat in the visitor's room. They have to get him out of his cell, but it shouldn't take too long." He returned Tony's driver's license and pointed toward a door to Tony's left with an officer posted between the door and metal detector. "I'll buzz you in once you go through the metal detector."

Tony made it through the metal detector undetected and took a seat in one of the hard plastic chairs bolted to the concrete floor. While waiting, he thought about how much fun he and Nicolas had with Dave and Mark at the Purple Parrot in Cherry Hill. He thought about all the jokes Dave had busting everyone's balls. It was good to have someone that he worked with on his level. Nicolas was in a tight situation, and once he got out of this one, that would make him a single man, which meant he could hang out late nights. All he had to do was stay cool and get his story right.

Then he thought of how much information Nicolas had on him. If Nicolas were to cop-out, he could blow his whole operation sky high. Nicolas couldn't be that stupid to snitch him out. Tony would deny giving him some heat. Nicolas had no proof that he gave him the gun and Tony knew he had Mr. Hunt on his side to help him out of sticky situations. If Nicolas decided to rat him out about his illegal rental properties, he would need proof for that, too. Everything Tony said to Nicolas was hearsay and that shit couldn't hold water. As for his secret compartment in his dash, Tony took care of that too. But, before he got ahead of himself, he had to talk to Nicolas and see if he could find a way to bail his ass out so he could get Hunt to work his case. All he needed was for Nicolas to keep his head on straight and his mouth shut.

CHAPTER SIXTY-FIVE

Back To The Present

"And that's how I ended up here in this small-ass cell havin' this conversation with you. Hunt better show up soon. I've already given him a retainer. I'll go back home to New York and deal with the polluted air, congested traffic and that old-ass bitch with that loud-ass dog. Just get me the fuck outta here!" Nicolas said as Willy leaned against a wall.

The little distraction was all Nicolas needed to get his mind off of the situation he was in. Of course, he couldn't get the look of Tammy's face and her contorted features as the bullet he fired shredded her lovely neck out of his mind.

"Man, that whole story does sound fucked up." Willy shook his head. "It's hard to believe all this shit happened in less than a week, even though I lived every minute of it. Shit, a movie writer couldn't make this shit up."

Nicolas wondered if he was giving Willy too much information. What did he know about Willy? He might find a way to use something he said against him if it cut a day off his jail sentence, but it would be his word against Nicolas'.

"So, Willy, what happened with that property? Did you end up buyin' it?" He tried to change the topic to get the attention off himself.

"What? The one you showed me?" Willy's eye lit up with excitement.

"Yeah," Nicolas murmured. "Tony said he was gonna take care of it, but I wasn't sure if he did or not."

"Maaaan!" Willy couldn't contain his coolness. It showed how bad he wanted to tell his side of the story and Nicolas was all the audience he needed. "That redneck, crooked-ass cop kept me away from it."

Willy waved his hand like he was swatting at a flying insect.

"Say what?" Nicolas barked, failing to correctly understand what he was trying to say.

"He said he didn't want me movin' in his neighborhood 'cause of my criminal background. I told him this is America and I can live wherever I wanna live and he got mad as hell, talkin' 'bout, '*Good, then you can live at the county jail for all I care,*' and locked my ass up on an old bench warrant. I ain't worried 'bout it, though. I'll jus' ride this shit out for a few more weeks. My girl's gonna do the paperwork on another crib we looked at in Pennsauken, with Tony.

"Isn't that right outside of Camden?" Nicolas inquired.

"Yeah, so is Merchantville, but anythin' outside of Camden is better than bein' in Camden. So when I get outta here, she should have everythin' moved in dat crib. Then after dat, I'm tryna touch miles. I'm tired liven poe. I got my peoples Dj Cooley workin' on my album. No one's touchin' his beats. He's the baddest DJ wit' the hypest beats. You ever heard of him?" he asked with enthusiasm.

"Yeah, I heard one of his tracks on the radio," Nicolas said, casting his mind back to the time when he and Tammy were enjoying the music when they first moved to Jersey.

Nicolas couldn't get her beautiful smile out of his head. He missed her so much and wished she were still here with her playfulness. He thought about how she loved to smack his ass hard to get his attention, no matter how much it angered him. His anger never lasted long, because her smile would douse it. Tammy was his life and the only person that he had seen himself building a future with, but that was all gone now. Nicolas was on his own.

The sound of Willy's voice quickly brought Nicolas back to reality.

"But, for now, I gotta work on survivin' in here, and you outta be doin' the same."

Willy walked out of the cell and headed down the hallway. Loneliness filled the room. It was like someone had shoved him in a small box and sealed it shut. Breathing felt more like a challenge. All he could do was stare at the walls. It was like everyone had abandoned him. His life ended before it got started. No seeds to carry his name. By the time he got out—and that's if he got out alive—his shriveled up dick would be useless for reproduction.

*****

Willy approached a tall, white male with shifty eyes and tattoos all over his body. He had a bald head and a cold stare. He had a laid-back attitude and a mean streak a mile long. Larry 'The Hit-Man' Payne was a very dangerous man. The inmates knew him as the grim reaper, because he was responsible for a majority of the deaths in the jail. Somehow, he always made the murders look like accidents or suicides. He was the only white guy in the prison who got respect from both black and Hispanic inmates, although some of the Haitians believed he could steal a man's soul and send them straight to hell. He was pure evil—the devil's sidekick. They wanted no parts of him and kept their distance. Willy strongly admired Larry for being the only man who was able to get so much respect from the hardest criminals through shear intimidation.

"Yo, what's up, my dude?" Willy said as he approached Larry.

"Hey, what's that guy's problem?" Larry asked, leaning on the rail while smoking a Camel. He kept his eyes on the inmates in the tier.

"Who, Nick?" Willy pointed his thumb in Nicolas' direction.

"Yeah—Nick," repeated Larry sarcastically.

"He's that guy we caught last night on TV who killed that Merchantville cop, the Merchantville rapist and his own wife," Willy said, bouncing on his toes, excited to get to tell the story to Larry.

Larry took a long drag on his cigarette, held it and blew it out the side of his mouth before saying, "Yeah, I heard the story." He then took another long drag and let it out slowly before continuing his sentence. "That's the guy we need on our team."

"He ain't about that life. He's jus' an emotional wreck, that's all. A stupid realtor who fucked up. Plus, he was the guy who I told you 'bout, the one who showed me that crib out in Merchantville before I got locked the fuck up by that crooked-ass cop."

With a turn of the head, Larry looked at Willy with a cold stare. "Then we need to school him and put him down with us. It would look good for the squad and since he's your peoples, introduce him to me," Larry said, tossing his cigarette butt over the rail.

With Nicolas having three possibly four murders on his jacket, he would be a huge source of speculation with the other inmates. But, if Larry got Nicolas on his crew, it would make them look good and elevate Larry's status as the guy not to be fucked with.

"No problem."

They walked toward Nicolas' cell.

*****

Willy stuck his head around the side of Nicolas' cell. "Yo, my manz wants to holla at'cha. Hold on." Willy stepped back and let Larry go in the cell. "This is my manz, Larry. I know you heard about him."

"Naw," Nicolas mumbled, sitting on the end of his bunk, staring at the floor.

"Well, anyway, he wants to put a little somethin' in yo ear," Willy said, ignoring his lack of enthusiasm.

"This is my peoples, Larry 'The Hit-Man' Payne."

"Why do they call you The Hit-Man? Because you be knockin' niggas out?" Nicolas asked, not bothering to look up.

Larry broke out in a deep laugh, as if that was the funniest thing he had heard all day. He turned his back to Nicolas and faced Willy.

"Hey, Willy, you didn't tell me that this guy was a comedian."

Willy laughed along with him, but his fake laughter sounded more like a cough.

Larry turned his attention back to Nicolas. "Well, let me put it to you this way. I do a better job than the grim reaper. There is no comin' back once I put you out. Understand?" He leaned in Nicolas' face to get his attention.

Nicolas looked up. Their eyes connected.

"I watch the news. I know who you are. You work for that mob boss Frank DeBrillo," Nicolas said, having trouble pronouncing the last name.

"That's Frank DeBartello, but we don't discuss that behind these walls. Have you ever been locked up before?"

"No." He looked pensively at Larry.

"Well, I'm here to let you know that in this place, a man alone can't make it. He's gotta have protection. Nothing to be ashamed of. Everyone needs protection one way or another. We have a membership here, which—if you decide to join—gives you all-around full protection. If you choose not to be down with us, then you'll need to get your own protection. But, no one here can protect you from us but us. Comprehend?"

Nicolas shook his head in disbelief. "So what you're tellin' me is that you guys run this place?"

"You can say that." Larry glanced back at Willy. They both shared a cold grin. "There are a few other gangs in this facility, but ours is the biggest and most respected. If you do decide to be with us, no one will lay a hand on you without our permission." He stared hard at Nicolas.

Maybe they're tryna scar me into joinin' because their gang is small and needs help, or maybe they're just lookin' for a new butt buddy and I'm the fresh meat on the block.

Nicolas started to have second thoughts about having even spoken to that fucking Willy!

"I'll have to think about it," Nicolas responded in an undertone.

"You'll have to think about it?" Willy chimed in. "Man, this ain't the Home Shoppin' Network. I told you that he was jus' a waste of time, lame ass nigga."

"Shut the fuck up, Willy," Larry ordered, raising a hand in the air for him to calm down.

The cell got silent as the noisy chatter from the tier flooded the room.

"Nicolas, it doesn't work like that. You don't just walk around this facility window-shopping for the best alternative route. Plus, our numbers are too large to give out second invitations. You're in or you're not; it's your decision. Only you have to make it and this is your last and final chance."

Nicolas believed if he gave in too fast, they'd use him like a tackle dummy and make him start fights to prove his worth. Who knows, these guys might start all kinds of gang wars, getting him involved. If the courts saw that on his paperwork, it would kill his already badly-dented credibility and ensure them of giving him the maximum sentence. And how would he know if this gang was the biggest baddest one or not? He couldn't trust that weasel Willy to vouch for anything or anybody. He didn't want to be fighting for the rest of his life. No, he'd rather end it now on his own terms and in his own way.

"I ain't sayin' I'm with you or against you. I just need time to straighten my head out. This is all new to me. I need time to think, to adjust," Nicolas tried to explain to him.

"Welcome to the real world, Nicolas Coles. A world where there is no time for adjustments—only reactions. I gave you a chance and you've made your decision. So, watch your back."

Larry's eyes were hard and icy. The seriousness of his tone caught Nicolas' attention.

What had he done? Start some crazy war with no protection? He needed protective custody. He needed Hunt to get him the hell out of there or set bond. His mother's mortgage on her house was paid off. She would put it up as collateral to give to the bails bondsman or he could use his own house.

"I can't deal with this right now." Nicolas tried to defuse the situation and get this prison ape off his ass. "I need time." The tension in the room was so high that it caused Nicolas' throat to dry out. He turned to get a swallow of water from his sink.

"Pussy, don't you turn your back to me!" Larry said, wanting to teach this rebel a lesson.

"Don't do it, dawg," Willy said, coaxing Larry out of the cell.

*****

Willy and Larry were heading to their cell to discuss the matter. Still irate, Larry's face was ugly and his head as red as Rudolph the Red-Nosed Reindeer's nose.

"Hold up, Willy. I forgot somethin'. I need to talk to that Nick again for a minute. Keep an eye out and watch my back," Larry ordered.

"Go on. I'll make sure no one goes over there." Willy leaned against the rail as Larry's lookout.

*****

Nicolas lay on his bed, the ceiling becoming a movie screen on which he watched the past week of his life replay and his future unfold.

He'd lost it all. Love, marriage, his career—maybe even his soul for killing three people, regardless of the reasons. Memories of his childhood appeared on the ceiling; Sunday afternoon picnics with his mother and Grandmother Coles. He could almost taste the fried chicken and fresh tomatoes from their small garden.

The sudden end of the life he knew stunned him. Last week, he was living the American dream. Married to a beautiful woman, had just bought a house in the suburbs and was advancing in his career. How did he let these things slip away from him? How did he let it happen? Had he not played by the rules? Kept away from the really bad guys? Stayed in school and even gone to college? He'd paid his taxes, prayed, been good to his mother, never robbed a bank or a liquor store or even shoplifted a pack of Spearmint gum. Yeah, he sold a little weed in the past, but that was the past. And Tammy? What reason did she have to cheat on him? He'd been a good husband and provider. She didn't even have to work unless she wanted to. He'd worked hard all his life and tried to do the right things. And for what? To end up in a cage like an animal on display at the Philadelphia Zoo?

What hope did he have that life would ever be good again? Even if he didn't get the maximum sentence of life without the possibility of parole, he'd be a very old, impotent man unable to appreciate or enjoy the finer things of life–the soft firmness of a woman, a tender T-bone steak, or the salty mist of the ocean. He'd be a dried shell of a man if and when the system let him breathe free air again.

I know this shit with those fuckin' thugs ain't over yet. They will be back to fuck me up. Hopefully that shit would get me in the hole or protective custody. This is my freedom on the line here. Sorry Tony, but I'll have to use the info you gave me on your illegal business to make some type of deal to get out. I'll have to go into witness protection, because his dad would send his goons after me. Fuck it. My freedom is priceless.

The small cell became even smaller, its air devoid of oxygen. Nicolas felt like he was breathing through a bale of cotton. When a sea of the darkest horror appeared before him, he realized there were worse things than death and that life in prison was one of them. He sat in his empty space deflating all the built-up emotion inside him. Then suddenly, Nicolas felt the presence of someone standing over him. He looked up to see Larry staring at him with a devious grin.

Okay, lets get this over with.

Nicolas stood to his feet, eagerly ready to fight. Larry was going to earn this ass whoopin'.

CHAPTER SIXTY-SIX

Inmates Do Lie

"Nicolas Coles, you have a visitor. Nicolas Coles, you have a visitor," the young recruit called out over the intercom. When Nicolas didn't appear at the visitor's room, the recruit repeated the announcement over the intercom. "Nicolas Coles, you have a visitor. Please report to the visitor's area."

A veteran sergeant approached the recruit. "How's everything going here?"

"Well, sir, I've called Nicolas Coles four times to report to the visitor's center and he still hasn't shown up."

"Oh yeah, the realtor guy who killed Wright and the Merchantville rapist—and I think his wife, too. Have you made sure Olsen's been makin' his security checks?" the sergeant asked the recruit as they entered the housing unit.

"Yes, sir," he said with a proud tone.

"Let's go see where the hell he is. Now there's no need to ask the other inmates any questions, because they'll never give you a straight answer unless they get somethin' in return. And nine times outta ten, whatever they tell you is a lie. Watch this." The sergeant cupped his hands around his mouth like a bullhorn. "Does anyone here know where Nicolas Coles is?" he yelled, his voice echoing off the walls.

There was a quick silence.

"Nah," the inmates responded simultaneously and then continued doing whatever they were doing.

"See what I mean?" the sergeant said.

"Yes, sir," the recruit responded as they climbed the stairwell leading to Nicolas' cell.

"He's in the corner cell." The recruit said as they advanced toward it.

*****

Larry and Willy were entering their cell when they spotted the two officers approaching from the other side of the walkway.

"Coles, you have a visitor," the sergeant called out while approaching Nicolas' cell. Suddenly they looked inside with horror.

"Code Blue, A-Block!" was announced over the radio by the sergeant. "Code Blue, A-Block! Lock down! Lock down!" he ordered.

An officer keyed in a computerized code, activating the system-wide lockdown. The simultaneous slamming and locking of cell doors echoed loudly as the inmates were secured in their cells without further incident. Then the prison medical team arrived to assist.

CHAPTER SIXTY-SEVEN

The Bearer of Bad News

Down in the waiting room.

Tony sits in the waiting room thinking about Nicolas and wondering if he might fold under pressure. Three officers enter the room. The one in a blue suit was in charge. They approached Tony with stone expressions. Tony stood to his feet.

"Can I help you." Tony said with weary eyes.

"Are you Antonio Satario?"

"Yes, why you ask?" Tony said trying to maintain his cool.

"Sir, are you here to see Nicolas Coles?" the officer asked Tony.

"Yes. I was told I could see him today. Is there a problem, officer?" Tony looked around for Nicolas to come through one of the doors.

The officers gave each other a knowingly gaze before turning there attention back at Tony.

"What is your relationship to Coles? Are you a family member?"

"I'm his brother," Tony lied, desperate to see Nicolas and see what he could do for him. He knew this place was a hellhole, and he didn't trust prisoners or guards.

The officer looked at Tony in disbelief.

"Look," Tony said, irritated with the questions and the look on the racist jackal's face. "We have the same father, different mother. Need I say more?"

"No, sir, you don't have to," the officer said with a long delay. "Well...there's something we need to tell you and you won't like what we have to say. So we need you to come with us."

Tony wondered if all the information he said about his illegal side business was going to come back and bite him in the ass. *They ain't got shit on me.*

It was his word against Tony's. Tony was then escorted by the three officers into a back room. He was in deep thought, wishing he'd never got Nicolas involved as the heavy medal door slams behind him.

If you enjoyed the reading of this book
HOLLOW DREAMS
Please continue on for a quick sneak peek of part 2

PROLOGUE
Part Two

The cold night was bone chilling, enough to make Willy's teeth rattle. The temperature had to be in the low 50's, but with the added wind factor made it feel like it was in the low 40's. Winter was right around the corner. Where the trees are stripped of their thick green leaves, only baring the skeletal structure of it's wooden branches. It gave them an eerie scene of darkness where all evil things dwelled and flourished. The fragile moonlight was shattered into glowing glass shards through the winter bare branches of the ancient oak trees. The wind was blowing extremely hard as if there was a huge leaf blower hovering over the city. Willy couldn't get upset about the weather condition, because this was the only time the streets got cleaned. The city was too cheap to have a street sweeper cruise by now and then like they do in the uppity neighborhoods. The wind howled as it glided across the car, seeping through the cracks and crevices. It was constant—more like a strong gust of air, as if the blower needed to inhale a big gulp of oxygen before unleashing it's power like a raging bull trying to flip the car. The cold air seemed thin as hell, making it hard for anyone to breath through their noses.

The bluish colored numbers on the digital screen read 3:15 in the morning and Willy looked as if he was in a wrestling championship tournament and lost. His body was behind the wheel of a Chrysler 300, but his mind was in oblivion. He fucked up and didn't know how he was going to explain this one to his girl, Melody.

Slowly he pulled up in front of the apartment projects on 9th and Ferry Avenue better known as Centerville. One of the worse places to be in Camden. This is where majority of the killings in Camden took place. The heat on low at 80 degrees. The cars Michelin tires crackled as it drove across the small rocks and pebbles along the curb. He sat in his whip, while the engine was idling, staring at the row of red brick buildings defaced with graffiti and shattered glass covered walkways sparkling under the night lights like glitter. Compliments to the liquor stores on every corner. Willy sat there listening to the wind howling in the dark with a hollow cry. It's sound was so in tuned with the lack of attention the neighborhood received. It was the cry of death which filled the air. A theme song for those who were gone, but not forgotten. He gazed at the bright neon lights flashing over the front entrance of the liquor store on the corner.

Melody peered through the window blinds. She must have heard his ride pull up only to see Willy sitting there in a deep gaze. He was not himself tonight and Melody could tell. No matter how hard he tried to hide it, Melody always could sense when something's wrong and now her senses was working over-time.

Willy was worried and didn't know what to do about it at this point. Melody opened the front door and stood by the doorway with a blank stare, waiting for him to come in. He looked up and noticed Melody standing there, her hand on her hip. The light from the living room lamp spilled onto the walkway with her shapely silhouette extending to the car. It traced her physic perfectly, giving him a full view of her drop dead gorgeous framework.

Melody was looking so good right now in her tight purple t-shirt and black spandex bottom, but his head was too fucked up to appreciate her beauty. Cutting the engine off, he slowly got out of the vehicle like an 80-year-old man. The blistering wind howled with a loud hollowing sound as if death was in the air. Each one of his steps seemed thought out in advance as he strolled across the cold pavement. *How is she gonna take this shit?* His eyes filled with fear. He looked at Melody as if his eyes were begging for help....and they were.

"Willy what's wrong." She winced. His facial expression must have been quite obvious and the love that she had for him showed in her beautiful brown eyes, but what could he say.

I was tryna make this a better life for us, but desperation kicked in and took full control of what little sense I had left. She's not going to accept that. There was other ways to get the money up and he chose the fast lane.

He kissed her on the cheek and headed for the kitchen, totally ignoring the question.

She ain't even give me a chance to come in the fuckin' door yet. What ever happened to hello Boo. How was yo day? But that's how she rolled. Always tryna get to the meat of the shit. Nuffin' watered down.

Melody followed him into the kitchen as he grabbed a can of soda and started chugging it down. "I know you heard me the first time." She stood there with her arms crossed demanding an answer. The look on her face said she meant business.

Wooow...she looked like she was gonna beat the shit out my ass. My girl Mel can be very persistent to the point that it's scary. Willy thought to himself.

Willy raised his hand for her to yield. "Give me a moment to gather myself," he said taking another sip to cover his facial expression. He had to think of a way to tell her the softer side of the story, so that she doesn't go off on him. Mel didn't play around once she's in her detective mode.

"I'll do just that." She raised her voice. "Whenever you're ready, I'll be in the livin' room," rolling her eyes, as she marching out of the kitchen. Willy couldn't keep his eyes off her stretchy polyurethane fabric that gave him a good view of them juice ass cheeks. That ass could easily calm Willy's nerves enough to approach her in a relax fashion, but he couldn't tell if that was her aggressiveness or if she had an attitude with him.

...*So what else was new?*

Ever since she found those Email letters from Crystal on her computer, getting upset with him became a daily ritual. Willy was glad that she kept it in the family and didn't snitch him out to Cat Daddy. If he were to find out, Willy wouldn't be here telling this story. This whole thing was his fault, so he'll have to man it up and carry the weight for that.

Cat Daddy is the biggest drug dealers in Camden. He's well organized with a strong team. Willy was one of his workers. Willy's job was making sure that all the vehicles were running right. Willy was good with painting and fixing rides, after taking up a few classes at Lincoln tech institute. He never finished, but the schooling he got was good enough to make Cat's whips run right. All his vehicles came with secret compartments that he used to stash his shit. Each one had a special way of opening.

Cat Daddy was one individual that you didn't fuck with. He was cold as ice. A killer if need be. He was know for his gun play ever since he was a young gunner. He wouldn't hesitate to pop a muhfucka in the melon. He got the name Cat Daddy for being so smooth with it. He would pop a nigga in his dome and walk away like a pimp. Those with less fear or lack of respect were easier targets. They would walk around with their heads so high that they don't see it coming. There was no rules to the game. He'll even walk into your house and off you and your family. Cat Daddy just didn't give a fuck.

Willy lend against the sink shaking his head with the empty can in hand. Mel's been with him through thick and thin. He couldn't leave her hanging like that. If anyone should know what's going on, it should be her. She had his seed and held him down while he was up state. He had to keep it real with her and not hold anything back. Tossing the empty can in the trash he re-adjusted his appearance the best he could with his own two hands.

Now here goes nuffin'. Willy said to himself, taking a deep breath before entering the living room.

Made in the USA
Charleston, SC
15 July 2013